THE EDGE OF DARKNESS

THE EDGE OF DARKNESS

A NOVEL BY
AVRAHAM TZURI

P·U·B·L·I·S·H·E·R·S
New York · London · Jerusalem

For Galila

Copyright © 1990

All rights reserved.
This book or any part thereof,
may not be reproduced in any
form whatsoever without the express
written permission of the copyright holder.

Published and distributed
in the U.S., Canada and overseas by
C.I.S. Publishers and Distributors
180 Park Avenue, Lakewood, New Jersey 08701
(201) 905-3000 Fax: (201) 367-6666

Distributed in Israel by
C.I.S. International (Israel)
Rechov Mishkalov 18
Har Nof, Jerusalem
Tel:02-538-935

Distributed in the U.K. and Europe by
C.I.S. International (U.K.)
1 Palm Court, Queen Elizabeth Walk
London, England N16
Tel: 01-809-3723

Book and cover design: Deenee Cohen
Typography: Shami Reinman and Nechamie Miller
Cover illustration: Greg Hinlickey

ISBN 1-56062-037-4 hardcover

PRINTED IN THE UNITED STATES OF AMERICA

Table of Contents

EDITOR'S NOTE • 9

CHAPTER ONE • 21
Plunged into Night

CHAPTER TWO • 41
The Sorcerer's Revenge

CHAPTER THREE • 66
Behind Closed Doors

CHAPTER FOUR • 80
Brother against Brother

CHAPTER FIVE • 99
On the Edge of Accord

CHAPTER SIX • 114
The Cluniac Threat

CHAPTER SEVEN • 127
The Royal Audience

CHAPTER EIGHT • 140
Journey into the Unknown

CHAPTER NINE • 156
Skirmish at Dawn

CHAPTER TEN • 187
The Black Monks

CHAPTER ELEVEN • 210
Tempest at Sea

CHAPTER TWELVE • 226
Intruders in the Palace

CHAPTER THIRTEEN • 247
The Sands of Fury

CHAPTER FOURTEEN • 265
The Way of the Desesrt

CHAPTER FIFTEEN • 282
Treachery Revealed

CHAPTER SIXTEEN • 301
Darkness over Castile

CHAPTER SEVENTEEN • 321
The Hidden Lights

Editor's Note

HISTORICAL FICTION INVOLVES A NUMBER OF FASCINATING questions. What might have happened if certain important people of an era had interacted? What immense changes might have been achieved in the progress of world civilization? *The Edge of Darkness* provides absorbing avenues into plausibility, while incorporating a wealth of well-researched information on life in Spain during the twelfth century. Complex motives guided the key figures in the politics of that age. The novel is true to their historical identities while exploring, through fiction, what might have been. The Sephardic forms of transliterated Hebrew words have been used to maintain the authenticity of the Sephardic setting.

The period in which this novel takes place was rich in Jewish scholarship and culture. *Rishonim* such as Rabbeinu Bachaye, Rav Shlomo Ibn Gabirol, Rav Shmuel Hanaggid and

Rav Yitzchak Alfasi (the Rif) had deeply influenced the thinking of scholars less than a hundred years before. The disciplines of Talmudic research, grammar, poetry and mathematics meshed to create heights of scholarship thought by many to be unsurpassed.

Yet the flourishing Jewish life in Spain in the twelfth century was often flecked with difficulty and persecution. Christians and Muslims fought for dominance in Andalusia (southern Spain), often impacting on the Jewish communities as well. Under Muslim rule, Jews became powerful in the courts and major cities. Often sent on diplomatic missions, the Jews were highly respected as physicians and astronomers as well.

The advancing armies of the fanatical Almohad sect ended this glorious era. Determined to stamp out all remnants of non-Muslim belief, the Almohads fiercely persecuted Jews who would not convert to Islam. The migration northward to Christian territory had begun as early as 1066 and increased significantly as the Almohads conquered more and more of Andalusia.

In Christian Spain, treatment of the Jews varied from one province to another. It must be remembered that Spain was not a united country at this point and Spanish nobles alternately extended kindnesses or issued harsh decrees, depending on whether or not they needed Jewish help.

In Castile, the principal kingdom of Christian Spain, Jews had been granted considerable privileges and freedom. They engaged in commerce, industry and the administration of nobles' property. They often developed a Jewish aristocracy which mirrored the aristocracies which employed them. As Jews, they could not hold political power, but they performed a critical service to kings and caliphs as advisors and financial experts. Indeed it did not take long before even petty nobles employed Jews as advisors in imitation of their superiors.

Internally, the Jewish community tended to its own affairs. Other than their duty to pay taxes to the king, they enjoyed relative autonomy. Their legal status was defined as "Jews of the Realm." As such, they owed their loyalty to the king and were entirely under his domain and protection. This privilege held true even if they occupied lands owned by the Church or the nobility. At the time of this story, the Jews were subject to the enlightened rule of Alfonso VII.

King Alfonso VII of Castile was crowned Emperor of Spain in 1135 and later expanded the influence of his kingdom into a true empire. Yet his idealistic motives of returning Spain to a national unity, lost since the days of the Visigoths, could not be attained. He was a Christian king, yet he was a dedicated patron and protector of Muslims and Jews in his realm. His goals of accommodation between the powerful Catholic Church and the aggressive Almohad Muslims could only delay, not deter, the Christian reconquest of Spain, which the Church encouraged. At the time of this story, Alfonso is a young monarch, still grappling with problems of his sovereignty acquired only four years before. He depends heavily on his chief advisor Don Garcia. Though a fictitious character, Don Garcia is modelled after the powerful nobles who often guided royal princes until they were of sufficient age and experience to govern on their own.

Joseph Hanasi Ferrizuel ("Alkabri") is a character modelled after a Jew who held a position of great influence as Secretary (*Katib*) in the Spanish Court. He was also known by the Latin name Cidellus. Heretical Karaite Jews established a strong presence in Castile, but Alkabri managed to have them expelled from the cities and towns of the kingdom.

While the Christian king sought accommodation, he had the ill luck to fight a new wave of fanatical Muslims of the Almoravid dynasty. From the year 1053, the Almoravids had been spreading the faith of Islam throughout North Africa under the leadership of their greatest caliph, Yusef Ibn Tashpin.

Tashpin, King of Tunis, is modelled after a subsequent Almoravid chieftain, Ibrahim Ibn Tashpin. Ibn Tashpin was courageous and firm in his own religious beliefs, but a new dynasty, the Almohad, was gaining ground in North Africa, having sprung from a rival Berber tribe in the Atlas Mountains of Morocco. Ibn Tashpin fought the Almohads in the desert of Tunisia, but his treacherous "allies" left him to a certain death just before a dawn battle. In the king's desperate attempt to reach his ships, his horse lost its footing on a cliff overlooking the sea, and the King of Tunis plunged to his death. For the purposes of this novel, Tashpin is portrayed in a moment of truce with the Almohad Caliph Al-Kumi before his tragic end.

Caliph Al-Kumi was named successor to the Almohad dynasty in 1130. At the point of action in this book, Al-Kumi had not completely bent Tunisia to his control. It would take another two decades before he would defeat the Almoravid Tashpin in battle. A fierce opponent on the battlefields of Andalusia, in southern Spain, Al-Kumi threatens the peace and scientific progress of Alfonso VII's empire.

Hostility between great political leaders naturally raises the expectation of a great mediator.

Rabban Avraham Ibn Amram, modelled after the historical Rabban Avraham Ibn Ezra, is that man of peace. Born in Tudela in 1092 and raised in Saragossa, Rabban Ibn Ezra travelled far beyond his native Spain in his quest for knowledge. He passed away at the age of seventy-five. Some historians presume that he died on the frontier of Navarre. Others place his death in Rome.

Between his birth and his death, many blanks meet us in the biography of this great man. Facts are instructive in their very omission. Rabban Ibn Ezra made few attempts to clarify the many confusing details about his busy life. An authoritative biography is lacking, but the body of his work more than compensates with volumes of Biblical commentary, grammatical lessons, astronomy, mathematics, poetry and philosophy. His traveller's eye even advanced the study of geography, as shown by the keen geographical insights included in his commentary on the *Book of Daniel*. He must have had a voracious appetite for knowledge and mastered it all.

In spite of his prodigious mind, Rabban Avraham Ibn Ezra never succumbed to the arrogance of intellectual superiority. He kept his feet planted firmly on the ground and readily admitted his own failings with sardonic wit. Time and again, he poked fun at his own inability to make money. In one poem, roughly paraphrased as follows, he reveals an inner strength that mocks misfortune:

> I simply cannot make money, the fates are against me
> If I sold funeral shrouds, no man would ever die
> My birth was guided by the wrong star, the planets
>   have short-changed me
> If I sold candles, the sun would never set!

In his commentary on *Bereishith*, Rabban Ibn Ezra wrote that blind-hearted men think riches are a sign of excellence, yet he was convinced that the example of Eliyahu the Prophet proved the contrary. Poverty was a conscious decision for the wandering sage. This attitude pervades his writing, guarding him against the disappointments of life with a constant heart that found humor wherever he went. Ibn Ezra travelled far and wide, writing his Biblical commentaries in various towns on his travels.

It is not known clearly why Rabban Ibn Ezra felt impelled to wander from one community to the next. One legend relates that his father, Rav Meir Ibn Ezra, appeared to him in a dream, committing his son to a life of travel, spreading Torah to Jews in distant lands.

Times were troubled for a Jewish traveller in the twelfth century. In the Holy Land, Rabban Ibn Ezra did not venture far from Tiberias in the Galilee, since Jerusalem was held by a hostile Christian king. Later, he would visit England and Persia. At one point in his life, he was shipped to India as a captive.

The man of action was also a man of letters. Rabban Ibn

Ezra's literary career began in earnest when he translated the grammar lessons of Yehudah Chayug from Arabic into Hebrew. He discovered that many rabbis in the Diaspora had only a rudimentary grasp of Hebrew grammar. His lessons and treatises on the subject filled a special need. By the fifth decade of the twelfth century, Rabban Ibn Ezra was prepared to begin a new facet of his career, turning his talents to Biblical commentary. The first two works which held his attention were *Koheleth* and *Iyov*.

By 1145, he undertook his first draft of an ambitious commentary on the *Chumash*. Thereafter, speed became characteristic of his work. He set himself the task of developing shorter, more manageable treatises, which meshed with the time constraints of his travels. It has been estimated that he tackled well over one hundred such works, although considerably fewer have survived into the present age.

After a sojourn in Rome and Lucca, many other towns in Italy welcomed him, including Salerno and Mantua. By 1147, the attraction of Italy was waning and Rabban Ibn Ezra turned to the duchies of France. Rabban Ibn Ezra was a man of reason and a man of feeling, exemplified by his authority as a Biblical commentator and his success as a poet. It was inevitable that he should garner the friendship of like-minded rabbis on his travels.

A lasting comradeship developed between him and Rabbeinu Yaakov Tam, the leading Tosafist of Champagne, who is represented in the novel by the character Rabbeinu Vitale. Rabbeinu Tam was the grandson of Rashi, one of the most illustrious scholars of the age. From the village of Ramerupt in northern France, Rabbeinu Tam held court over a *beit medrash* which attracted the brightest minds from as far away as England, Bohemia and Russia.

Rabban Ibn Ezra contributed his own intellectual stimulation to the gifted Rabbeinu Tam. Some of his questions to the Tosafist have been recorded in the *Tosafoth*, which form a running commentary on all standardized texts of *Gemara* to this day. In addition, Rabban Ibn Ezra introduced the French Jews to the rhymed poetry of the Mediterranean lands.

It must be clearly understood by the reader, however, that the fictional character of Avraham Ibn Amram is not meant to be a direct representation of the holy Rabban Ibn Ezra, nor is this work meant as a historical telling of Rabban Ibn Ezra's life. Though based strongly on the interests and characteristics of the *tzaddik*, it would be presumptuous to ascribe temperament and dialogue to the true historical figure.

Yerucham Halevi is patterned after Yehuda Halevi, master poet and leader of his generation, who was undoubtedly a close friend and, quite possibly, both relative and father-in-law of Ibn Ezra. In our story, he is depicted as Ibn Amram's father-in-law who impacts strongly on his character, Torah study and leadership qualities.

Avraham Ibn Daud (Ravad I) of Toledo was the author of *Sefer Hakabbalah* in which he listed all important people and events of Jewish history from the time of Adam. A leader in the forefront battling the spread of Karaism, he used his study to support the authenticity of the *Mesorah* from the time of Moshe Rabbeinu to his own day. He is known to have authored other works refuting the Karaites as well as treatises ranging from astronomy to philosophy. His life was taken at the age of seventy by the King of Toledo for his refusal to convert from Judaism. We meet him in this novel as a vibrant young scholar, intent on turning back the tide of Karaite heresy through logic and persuasion.

The personality of Rabban Ibn Ezra and his involvement in the life of Spain when both Christians and Muslims disputed each other's authority over the lands of southern Spain is compelling. In his day, the power of the Church had to be taken into account regarding all political matters. A number of churchmen in this novel are historically accurate.

Peter the Venerable, Abbot of Cluny, was the head of the order of black monks which had originated in Cluny, in the

French province of Burgundy. By the eleventh century, the Cluniac Abbey had extended its influence over Castile, practically reducing it to a vassal state. For much of his time as the Abbot of Cluny, Peter the Venerable focused his attention on southern France, where Cathars were spreading a Gnostic heresy that undermined established Catholic doctrines. As his denunciations of the Cathars slowed the advance of that heresy, Peter the Venerable chose to visit Spain to combat the creeping acceptance of Islamic culture amongst Christian Spaniards. It is also true that he travelled to Spain to negotiate payment of lucrative taxes owed the Abbey.

The black monks lived a life of luxury, with little interest in manual labor. As Abbot of Cluny, Peter the Venerable made some sincere efforts to reform his order. His efforts were too little, too late. The Cluniac Order was in decline, eclipsed by the reforming popularity of the Cistercian Order and other orders of mendicant monks. Maintaining great abbeys in foreign lands, subject to a French superior, was a daunting task, and the Cluniac monks simply failed to meet the challenges of their changing society. At this time in the twelfth century, they were still a powerful order, aware of their own liabilities and all the more likely to lash out fiercely at their opponents.

When Peter the Venerable makes his appearance in this novel in the year 1140, he is rabid in his attacks on both Muslims and Jews. Ironically, it would be three more years before his translator, Robert of Ketton, would complete a Latin version of the Koran so that the abbot could better grasp just what it was he opposed. Likewise, his opposition to Jews was based on shaky information. Just before his trip to Spain, he began a work against the Jews which showed Karaite influence: he refuted aspects of the Talmud, criticizing the Jews for adding books to the accepted canon. Thus his voice was added to the confusion surrounding the Karaite heresy.

It is interesting to note that at this point in history, upsurges of heresy were common and created significant

EDITOR'S NOTE

threats. Jews met the challenge of Karaism with solid affirmation of the truth of the Oral Law and unswerving allegiance to its practices. At the same time, *lehavdil*, the Catholic Church ruthlessly persecuted the Cathars, while the Almoravid and Almohad dynasties fought out their differences on the battlefield.

But the fight was not entirely over men's souls. The forces of Christianity and Islam met time and again, each trying to wrest control of the rich resources of Spain. In 1140, great battles were imminent, but a peaceful mediation was still possible. What if the decisive Battle of Calatrava between Christians and Muslims had never taken place in 1147? How might the fate of Spanish Jewry have changed had peace emerged and the ferocious power of the monks been subdued?

The Edge of Darkness explores an intriguing alternative in which Christians and Moors might have forged a peaceful accommodation in the disputed lands of Andalusia. To that end, a man of linguistic skill and profound moral integrity would be the focal point of a bold plan for peace. Such is the premise of this novel.

Moral and celestial darkness are a constant backdrop to the tension of the story. In the end, a resolution emerges, true to the actual eclipse of 1140 and equally true to the superstitions of the age. Levels of meaning unfold as fast action and courage are destined to save the day.

C.F.

THE EDGE OF DARKNESS

CHAPTER ONE

Plunged into Night

TUDELLA, NAVARRE
SPRING, 1139

ANTICIPATION OF THE HOLY SABBATH RIPPLED THROUGH THE Jewish quarter of Tudela. Across the many patios encircled by high-walled homes, the sounds of last-minute cooking blended with the jesting of boys sent to the well to draw a little more water for the Sabbath.

For many months, Tudela had been gripped by a bristling tension between the Jewish community and the group they considered intruders. Settled on the outskirts of the quarter, the newcomers were Karaites, dressed like Jews, yet flaunting their ignorance of the most basic principles of Judaism as a brazen badge of honor; they delighted in entering the shop of the butcher and asking for cuts of meat forbidden by the dietary laws of *kashrut*. Fists were shaken in anger, but the intruders persisted in their taunts.

On this *Erev Shabbat*, the Jews of Tudela sensed that their uneasy accommodation of the strangers would be changed forever. All afternoon, wagonloads of the intruders had poured ominously across the bridge which traversed the Ebro River. They swelled the ranks of the few strangers already living at the edge of the Jewish quarter. In groups of six or eight, they wandered up and down the streets and alleyways of the *Juderia*, the Jewish quarter, pacing out the dimensions of the town as a tailor would measure a bolt of cloth.

Many strangers sauntered through the streets as the congregants approached the synagogues in the late afternoon, seeking to prepare for the tranquility of the Sabbath within the cool confines of the *beit midrash* but feeling fear and foreboding instead.

"Look at how many there are!" old Shlomo whispered to his cousin from the open window of Beit Aaron Hatzaddik.

The cousin nodded, gazed at the increasing number of strangers who strode haughtily past him, then sighed in frustration. The strangers ignored the open door of Beit Aaron Hatzaddik, continuing down the street, with old Shlomo craning his neck out the window to see where they were going.

More men of the community entered the synagogue and took their seats in silence. It had become an established tradition in Tudela that either Rabban Avraham Ibn Amram or his father-in-law, the great poet Yerucham Halevi, would usher in the Sabbath in prayer and song. But neither had yet arrived. A group of strangers had begun to loiter outside.

Suddenly, the intruders briskly entered the *beit midrash* and took seats within the congregation, staring down the elders of the community with withering glances. They chose aisle seats, obliging each Jew who entered the *beit midrash* to request permission to squeeze past them.

The apparent leader of the intruders, a hawk-eyed and very heavy man, took up a position in the doorway of the *beit midrash*, his eyes riveted on the corner of the street. His hands, well scrubbed for the Sabbath, were callused like those of a laborer. As each Jew entered, he grudgingly drew aside from the doorway, and as they brushed past, he squared his shoulders and scowled fiercely without taking his eyes off the distant corner. His companions had taken their positions on either side of the stairway which led up to the *aron kodesh* and the *bimah*, their arms crossed belligerently on their chests, waiting for a sign from their hawk-eyed leader.

The reader's *siddur* remained unopened on the table. The shadows on the east wall were lengthening. Still, Rabban Ibn Amram had not arrived to begin the service.

A sound carried from the third alley. The hawk-eyed stranger turned from the doorway with satisfaction.

"Sit!" he shouted at old Shlomo at his window post, his tone as menacing as his bulk.

He heard a new sound and turned back sharply towards the doorway. Boots echoed on the cobblestones of the alley. Someone was running frantically towards the synagogue. A lad burst through the doorway, his Sabbath coat dishevelled by his haste.

"*Rabbotai!*" the boy shouted. "Gentlemen!"

"Get away!" the hawk-eyed stranger shouted, dashing suddenly to the door to cut off further conversation. He raised both beefy hands to push the young Jew back into the street.

"Let me go!" the boy screamed, darting under his hands. "I must tell the elders. They have extinguished all our lamps. Darkness! You must do something. Darkness!"

Then sighting the mighty fist of the hawk-eyed stranger, the boy fled. More footsteps echoed on the cobblestones, this time from the direction of another synagogue. The new messengers were also turned away by the angry stranger, while the elders of the congregation leaped from their benches and shouted their protest. Old Shlomo rose on arthritic legs and tottered over to the stairway. He waved his cane at the strangers who commanded the ascent to the *bimah*.

"Sit!" the hawk-eyed man commanded with an even harsher edge to his voice.

His thumb and forefinger reached out to snuff the flame of the lamp nearest him. His signal sent the other strangers through the synagogue, snuffing lamps and pushing away the Jews who dared oppose them.

The air filled with a blue haze as each wick sent a puff of smoke into the heavy air. For a moment, many Jews in the assembly had the horrible notion that the strangers were attempting to burn down their synagogue.

"Save the *Sifrei Torah*!" they cried in anguish.

A young man burst forward and clambered up the stairway, practically over the shoulders of the astonished strangers. He leaped in three paces to the *aron kodesh*, withdrawing two silver-encrusted scrolls from the interior.

"Idolaters!" he roared. "Would you extinguish the light of the *ner tamid* as well?"

He planted his feet squarely in front of the *aron kodesh*, his arms clutching the scrolls, a pinpoint of light from the eternal flame just behind his head. A stranger reached out in frenzy and tried to shove him aside. The young man almost stumbled.

Shlomo's eyes glared in fury as he attempted a handhold on the balustrade to climb the stairway. The hawk-eyed man rushed promptly forward, kicking Shlomo's cane from out of his hands, sending the old Jew toppling to the bottom of the stairs.

Coughing in the smoky haze of the sanctuary, more Jews were roused to action.

"We have endured enough," one of the men shouted, leading a wave of rebellion against the rude takeover. Others cringed in the deepening shadows, wondering what had become of their peaceful synagogue and the peace of the Sabbath.

Rabban Avraham Ibn Amram and his student Joseph Vitale had been walking leisurely down the hillside toward the synagogue. As they drew closer they could hear the echoes of discord reverberating across the narrow alleyways. Ibn Amram tapped his student on the shoulder and broke into a run. His long black coat flapped in the wind as he hurried to Beit Aaron Hatzaddik.

A roar of pain and anger billowed from depths of his *beit midrash*. Ibn Amram's jaw dropped in astonishment as he pushed open the door. It was not easy to gain entrance. A cumbersome weight was pressed against the door. Rabban Ibn Amram discovered a young man squeezed in fright against the side door, holding his hands in horror to his mouth.

"Joseph, tend to this fellow," he called to his student without a second thought. "Don't let the intruders threaten this traveller."

He hurried past the darkened galleries into the open area of the *beit midrash*. In the melee, benches had been knocked over and *siddurim* had been sent skittering across the floor, their pages open. Rabban Ibn Amram bent and picked up the nearest *siddur*. Clutching it with indignation, his eyes fastened upon the hawk-eyed stranger at the center of the commotion.

"You!" he bellowed. "How dare you enter our house of worship to cause this scene? Answer me!"

A hush fell over the synagogue as Jews and strangers alike lowered their fists to gaze on the commanding presence of the sage. Taking their cue from Ibn Amram, the elders of the community bent to pick up the *siddurim* from the floor.

The hawk-eyed man seemed cowed by Ibn Amram. He lowered his eyes, taking comfort in the sight of the cold wick of the oil lamp at his elbow.

"We have succeeded in our purpose," the stranger declared, glancing up at the waning light of the sun. "I know you Rabbanite Jews. You will not dare light your candles now. That would be a desecration of the Sabbath, even though you are so blind that you cannot see how a burning flame on the Sabbath is a far greater desecration."

"You have entered our beloved Navarre with plans to make it a shambles of broken *mitzvot*," Ibn Amram replied in a strangely soft and detached voice. "You are wasting your time here."

A deeper hush fell over the synagogue and over the two conflicting groups within. The stranger clenched his fists.

"Your words mean nothing, Rabbanite Jew!" He stepped down from the stairway, glancing scornfully at the young man who still clutched the *Sifrei Torah*. "Our cause is true. Do not try to stop us, Rabbanite, or Tudela will be the worse for your efforts!"

"*Am ha'aretz*!" old Shlomo tossed back, pleased to be protected by the unflinching courage of the leader in their midst. "Ignorant boor!"

More words of rebuke, retort and hatred were tossed back and forth, but Ibn Amram remained aloof. He stood silently beside the open door and beckoned the strangers to leave. As the last of the intruders passed through the open door, Yerucham Halevi entered the *beit midrash* and surveyed the scene.

Rabban Ibn Amram shook his head. "The darkness is spreading," he said sadly. With full deliberation, he straightened his Sabbath coat. "Let us prepare our thoughts for prayer. We will have to forego the joy of the Sabbath lights, but tomorrow will bring the sun and an ample afternoon to increase our Torah study in the face of this adversity. Let us begin."

Yerucham Halevi nodded and stepped forward from the shadows to ascend the stairway. His rendition of *Kabbalat Shabbat* was all the more compelling as he beseeched the mystical Sabbath Queen to visit them from the distant reaches of the setting sun.

The *bimah* was a haze of shadow by the time he began *Maariv*. Normally, he would read word for word from the *siddur*, but on this night, reading was impossible. He immersed himself, heart and soul, in the words and melodies which he knew so well. As his voice groped through the eerie shadows, Yerucham Halevi turned his skills of the poet to exceptional measure, suffusing the darkened synagogue with his own inner light. At the end, barely discernible in the weak light of the moon, he strode to the balustrade and gazed down upon his fellow Jews.

"Go home, my friends, in peace. *Shabbat shalom*."

The Sabbath greeting was returned to him with fervor.

Joseph Vitale, still ashen-faced from the altercation with the strangers, stepped out from under the obscurity of the galleries.

"I never saw anything like this back home in Laon," he muttered. "And so it would seem, neither has this traveller. Can you imagine, Rabban Ibn Amram? The poor fellow was tongue-tied with fright. But I think he is coming around now. He told me his name is Yissaschar Rikuv. But that is all he said to me."

He pulled the shivering youth out of the shadows and gave him an encouraging thump on the back.

"Yissaschar, do not think that this fracas is typical of Navarrese hospitality," Ibn Amram said jovially. "Where are you from?"

The boy made no reply.

"But that question can wait for the moment," Ibn Amram continued. "You will come with us tonight. The *eiruv* is intact, so you need not leave your belongings here. A hot meal after your travels on the roads of Navarre will put the color back into your cheeks."

He motioned to Joseph Vitale who plucked up the few belongings of the young traveller, tied in a simple satchel. Yissaschar clutched a tattered *Chumash* tightly to his chest. The Jews of Tudela had dispersed, returning home quickly to begin their evening meal.

The cool night air of Tudela was slowly bringing the traveller back to his senses. "What horrors!" he said. "If I had been a Jew of Tudela, I would surely have complied with the wishes of the strangers, even if it would have meant a night of darkness."

"Ah, you do not know the mentality of our community," Ibn Amram answered. "We do not allow helpless resignation in the face of injustice. We know our rights as Jews of the Realm, and we exercise them fully."

"Why does the King of Navarre permit these intruders to act this way?" Joseph asked, trotting along at the right hand of his teacher. "The Count of Champagne would never allow this kind of outrage in my home town!"

"It is a serious problem," said Ibn Amram with a sigh, pausing for a moment before he continued. "What shall we do with these Karaites who accept only the *Torah Shebichtav*, the Written Law, as their source of religious law? The Talmud means nothing to them. They pervert our holy Torah."

"It is such nonsense not to have an Oral Law," Joseph mused in perplexity. "How do they transmit their teachings to their children? How is it possible to reach a *psak* on a legal question without the clarifications of *Mishnah* and *Gemara*? Their confusion must be endless!"

Ibn Amram smiled at his student. It was not for nothing that the youth was the son of Rabbeinu Vitale, the great scholar of Laon. The traveller at his left side said nothing to join in this conversation.

"You have seized upon their true dilemma, Joseph," Ibn Amram agreed. "I can assure you that this sect has not yet come to terms with it. Meanwhile, they reject the Talmud and cause us no end of discomfort. Their extinguishing of our oil lamps tonight shows how far apart our thinking is. The Torah forbids us to kindle a fire in our homes on the Sabbath, which the Karaites view as an injunction to sit in darkness, when in fact the Almighty has not forbidden the existence of a flame on the Sabbath, only the kindling of a flame."

They paused at the end of the wall and gazed at the panorama of roofs of the Jewish quarter ranged below them. The serried rows of stone houses thrust thatched roofs against the darkening hillside. Beside them, flowering vines clung obstinately to the low stone wall, casting a rose-like fragrance into the twilight. Ibn Amram's breath was labored by the time they reached the iron gate between the patio and his home.

"Come along, Joseph, and you, too, Yissaschar," he said. "My wife has prepared a wonderful meal for *Shabbat*."

The *sala grande* was a blaze of candles. In one corner was Ibn Amram's study table, piled high with his manuscripts. The beds were hidden away behind the tapestry on the facing wall. And at the other end, a large trestle table was crowned with glittering pewter and more candles.

"I will be just a moment, my husband," Naomi Ibn Amram called out from the kitchen. "Then you may begin *Kiddush*."

Naomi Ibn Amram entered from the kitchen with two large loaves of *challah* and placed them in a position of prominence on the festive table.

"You can tell our guests that there is more for them to enjoy," she said. "I have a big bowl of beans and stuffed grape leaves as well."

She stood expectantly behind her chair. Ibn Amram rose, steadied his *Kiddush* cup and prepared to recite the blessing in a melodious voice.

"Oh, I have forgotten to wash," Rikuv blurted out, stepping back in near panic from the table. "Do not wait for me!"

"But none of us has washed," Ibn Amram remarked in some astonishment. "We will all do that next."

He pointed to the small washstand in the corner where a laver of brass was ready. The agitation of the youth was increasing.

"I will wash in the kitchen, if you please," he mumbled. "I have not yet washed from my trip. My hands are very dirty."

He rose abruptly from the chair. Rabban Ibn Amram put down his *Kiddush* cup and nodded at his guest.

"I will show our guest to the kitchen," Naomi said pleasantly. "We will be back shortly."

The visitor almost fled into the corridor which led to the kitchen. Joseph shrugged at this strange behavior. He leaned his elbows on the window sill. The scent of myrtle and mimosa drifted through the wide window from the garden. For Joseph, the perfumed air seemed to mingle sweetly with the strains of a *zemer* coming from the home of Rabban Ibn Amram's father-in-law. A cricket chirped rhythmically in the darkness.

"How melodic are the night creatures of Navarre," Joseph said, peering out. "Rabban Ibn Amram, did I ever tell you about my friend Amatzia in Laon? He could compose *zemirot* from the inspiration of a babbling brook. I am sure he could make a hymn from the melody of this single cricket. You know, one day, I hope to be a singer just like Amatzia."

Ibn Amram chortled and raised his head at the sound of footsteps from the kitchen. Suddenly, a thump was followed by a hollow clatter of dishes. Then a scream shattered the air. Ibn Amram leaped to his feet, noting the sudden darkness in the corridor which previously had been lit by the candles of the kitchen.

"Naomi!" he shouted. "Don't move about in the darkness! I'm coming!"

The twists and turns of the corridor did not permit the light from the *sala grande* to penetrate into the kitchen. Ibn Amram raced blindly along the passage, scraping the palms of his hands on the rough stuccoed walls and sending a heavy barrel rolling from wall to wall.

Young Luisa, the kitchen girl, stood in the archway, sobbing like an infant. "A man, a stranger . . ." She could say no more.

Naomi came up behind her and spoke in soft tones. The sobs of the trembling girl subsided. The dark room became at once peaceful and quiet.

"I was walking with the platter balanced in my arms," Naomi whispered. "I could not move my head quickly for fear of tripping, but I saw someone. Someone snuffed out all the candles. Then I tripped over the salt box!"

"Praised be Hashem that no harm has come to you," Ibn Amram answered. "Joseph! Are you there, Joseph? And where is my Sabbath guest? Heaven forbid that something has happened to him in this accident. Where is Yissaschar?"

Catlike, Ibn Amram's eyes had become accustomed to the dim light. He saw a shadow moving along the narrow corridor toward the stable. A finger to his lips cautioned Naomi to remain silent. The shadow paused for a brief moment. Ibn Amram paused as well, pressed against the stucco wall. The shadow veered sharply into the doorway that led back to the far side of the *sala grande*.

A figure reached out for the candle on Ibn Amram's study table. The light was extinguished. The shadowy hand darted to the trestle table. More candles guttered between the intruder's thumb and forefinger. The air became heavy with puffs of waxy smoke.

Plucking up his robes to his knees, Ibn Amram dashed forward. His footsteps were heavy now, echoing dully off the floor and rebounding from the bare walls.

The furtive shadow sensed the danger and raced toward the final pinpoint of light on the mantlepiece. Ibn Amram leaped across the storage box, grabbing the raised hand roughly.

"You are hurting my hands," Yissaschar Rikuv hissed through his pursed lips.

At the discovery that his guest was the perpetrator of this evil, Ibn Amram's face contorted into disbelief. His left hand clutched at his heart. With his right hand, he pulled the intruder's clenched fingers away from the flickering flame.

Their violent motions had almost snuffed out the candle. Now the pulsating light soothed into a steady glow. Flushed with anger, Ibn Amram's strength was immense. He could have broken the boy's wrist as one wrings the neck of a chicken. Struggling to control his fury, he slowly breathed his anger from his body, pausing for a moment to look away from the youth's flashing eyes before inhaling and exhaling deeply again. His right hand clenched and unclenched spasmodically. Then placing himself between Yissaschar and the remaining candle, he folded his arms across his chest.

For the briefest instant, he thought he saw a sudden sign of shame in the eyes of the young man. Then a blank look settled across his face, deadening the lively features with the dull obstinacy of a simpleton.

"How dare you burn this candle on the holy Sabbath?" the youth jeered. "The Torah teaches us that it is forbidden. You have committed a terrible sin."

Ibn Amram pulled the lad away from the mantlepiece and pushed him onto a bench.

"Do not speak to me of sin," he said at last. "I trusted you, young man. I gave you shelter in my home. Now I discover that you masked your true identity to gain entrance to my house. You are no better than those other misguided intruders."

"I am proud to be Yissaschar Rikuv the Karaite," the youth said smugly, tossing his head with self-righteous pride. "Know that name well, Rabbanite! Yissaschar Rikuv has committed his life and his future to the only true Torah, the *Torah Shebichtav*. There is no need to add to the Word of the Almighty. It is all in these Five Books."

Ibn Amram wearily took his seat at the head of the table, scratching his temple with his palm.

"Where have I heard that family name of yours?" he mused. "It sounded familiar when I first heard it. Rikuv. Rikuv. Rabbi Avraham Ibn Daud once mentioned a rabble rouser. Did you say your family is from Toledo?"

"Not from Toledo," the youth sniffed. "My family is from Burgos, the capital of Castile."

"All the same, that name Rikuv sounds familiar. Who is your leader, Yissaschar Rikuv? I don't think the mastermind of your obstinacy is that hawk-eyed man we met tonight."

The rabbi looked down at the slight young man and sensed the depth of his conviction, however wrong it might be.

"You cannot pry that information from me," the youth answered hotly. "I have taken an oath to act for the good of my people. Our leader is a wise man who cannot be brought low by your tricks."

Again, Rabban Ibn Amram's broad palm rubbed his temple.

"I regret my sudden anger, Yissaschar Rikuv," he whispered. "On the holy *Shabbat*, we are given an additional soul, a *neshamah yeteirah*. Do you know what that means, young man?"

His question was gentle yet direct. Yissaschar Rikuv, still stiff and unbending, shook his head almost imperceptibly.

"I did not think you would understand the idea," Ibn Amram sighed. "We are taught of this mystery in the Talmud. Your teachers have refused to show you the delights of the wisdom of the Oral Law. It is a shame, because they have deprived you of a special joy and great insight into the meaning of the Sabbath, as well as many other aspects of our faith."

He twisted around on the bench and raised an eyebrow in looking at Joseph.

"Who was Resh Lakish?" he queried.

"Oh, he is one of the great personalities of the Talmud, my teacher," Joseph answered. "He reached great prominence in the Academy of Tiberias about nine hundred years ago."

"Exactly," Ibn Amram agreed. "Someday, I might have a chance to tell you more about Resh Lakish, Yissaschar Rikuv. But for the moment, I will simply say that he has explained to us the *neshamah yeteirah*. The Master of the Universe gives every one of us an additional soul on *Erev Shabbat*. It came to all of us this very evening. But it will be taken from us as we smell the spices and inspect our fingernails by the flames of the *Havdalah* candle tomorrow night."

"It means nothing to me," Yissaschar Rikuv said flatly. "I have never read of this *neshamah yeteirah* in the *Chamishah Chumshei Torah*. It does not concern me."

"Then tomorrow night, after the *zemirot* of *melaveh malkah*, I will have to raise questions for our elders which do concern you," Ibn Amram said sharply. "Who is your leader?"

The young intruder sat in obstinate silence.

Naomi stepped forward, her small hands clasped tightly in entreaty. It was as if her own son Yitzchak stood before her, so wrapped up in his poetry and heady with the power of his wealthy patron in Baghdad. She had begged her son not to go to that strange land. She had pleaded with him not to immerse himself in that strange culture. But he had put his poetry above all else, even his own faith. Now another man sat before her, inflexible and haughty, just as Yitzchak had been.

"For just one day out of seven, we have this special gift from Hashem," she said. "He gives us special holiness for the Sabbath. Did you really think you could take it from us, young man? Even if you have never experienced the wisdom of the great Resh Lakish?"

She looked down at him, then let her gaze wander across the signs of recent pandemonium in her home. She sighed reproachfully, but Yissaschar Rikuv turned his gaze from her.

"I do not need your lessons," he warned. "And do not pry into the business of the Karaites. Everyone in Castile will one day follow our teachings. Soon the power of our great leader will reach from Burgos to the heart of Navarre. So don't tell me fairy tales about this ancient Rabbanite named Resh Lakish. No one will be permitted to stray from the truth of Torah."

"You are imbued with only part of the truth," Ibn Amram said peremptorily. "But enough said of your opinions. I must go now to speak briefly with Yerucham Halevi, my father-in-law, about organizing a meeting tomorrow evening. If you please, Joseph, do not let our guest extinguish that last candle. When I come back, we will make *Kiddush,* wash and enjoy our meal."

With that, he walked through the door and crossed the *patio* to his father-in-law's house.

Joseph stood stiffly. His head cast a shadow directly onto the face of the supercilious young stranger.

"Do you think I would wrestle you for the privilege of snuffing out that last candle?" the Rikuv youth scoffed. "It will gutter of its own accord and the true light of Torah will shine through the Sabbaths of Navarre. For now, I am going. I cannot stay in a house with such a blatant sign of *avodah zarah*. Don't look so surprised, my foolish friend. That candle is nothing more than idol worship!"

He rose to this fullest height, which was not quite to the tip of Joseph's nose. Then he gathered up his satchel, his *Chumash* and his walking stick and plunged up the incline toward Yerucham Halevi's home.

Yerucham Halevi was waiting in the doorway.

"Do you have plans for my candles as well?" he asked, his arm blocking the entrance, his face unsmiling.

Yissaschar Rikuv stopped on the path and crouched down to peer under the arm. Inside the well-lit sitting room, he could see Ibn Amram pacing back and forth.

"Like a moth to an open flame, he has fluttered back to his prohibited candle," the youth mocked. "With the help of the Almighty, your wings will soon be burnt! *Avodah zarah*! *Avodah zarah*!"

Yerucham Halevi's booming baritone burst into laughter. "I did not think that a Karaite could dabble in poetry, young man."

"Good Master Poet," Yissaschar chided, throwing his cloak over his shoulder before retreating into the darkness of the cool night air. "There is a poetry in the literal truth. We know it as Torah. It is the sublime Word of the Creator. My father and my father's father have taught me to love the words of Moshe. I do not need any commentary to grasp the meaning of Torah. I will be honest, Master Poet. I prefer the company of these simple insects in the dark to the presumptuous idolatry of a Rabbanite Jew fluttering around his forbidden candle."

With that, the young man turned on his heel and flounced angrily back down the path. The insects fell into silence at his passing.

"The Karaite does have a way with words," mused Rabban

Ibn Amram, who had come up behind his father-in-law. "Tomorrow night, we must decide on a course of action. The Karaites must be halted before they can imbed themselves in Castile and Navarre. We must find a way to rout them from our communities."

No further talk ensued on the topic of the Karaites during the late *seudah*, but the topic was still bubbling in the back of Ibn Amram's mind. That night, he went to bed with uneasy thoughts that sent grim nightmares flashing across the vision of his mind.

Early the next morning, he rose and, after just a few sips of water, returned to the synagogue for morning service. By midday, he should have been happy and hungry. Instead, a nagging pain throbbed at his temples. He could only pick at the meal Naomi set for them.

A mood of grim expectation was building throughout the day. When the congregation immersed itself in an afternoon study group, everyone's gaze flickered from time to time to the doorway, half expecting and half fearing that the Karaites might return.

The lack of lamplight that evening was again a painful reminder of the activity of the intruders. The *Maariv* service was intoned by the sallow light of the moon. It was not until the many wicks of the *Havdalah* candle burst into flame that the Jews of the community could breathe a collective sigh of relief. The flames were distributed to the oil lamps on all the tables. Even now, the songs in praise of the departing Sabbath Queen were subdued, tempering the mystic joy with a grim reality of the conflict with heretical brethren.

After the *Havdalah*, Ibn Amram cleared his throat and invited the opinions of the congregants.

"It is a stupid and bothersome thing when strangers come into my shop and dream up their own theories of *kashrut*!" the butcher exploded in disgust. "Why, these fools do not even grasp the fundamentals of our dietary laws and what it takes to make meat kosher. If they lived their own life in peace on the outskirts of our communities, it would be one thing. But when they try to impose their dark ignorance on us it is quite another."

"That's right!" old Shlomo agreed. "I feared for my life when that big ruffian told me to sit. It was on the tip of my tongue to ask him how he dared tell me what to do in my own *beit midrash*. Then I looked into his hawk eyes. Demented! I'm lucky to be alive."

"If they make inroads into our trading routes, they might claim to be the proper Jews of the Realm," a surgeon reasoned, looking glumly around the group of men who nodded approval at his insight. "Suppose they promise to give Garcia Ramirez more taxes than we do? That could mean that the Karaites would entirely supplant us in King Alfonso's favor."

"But we are the Jews of the Realm, not the Karaites," old Shlomo piped in. "We have influence!"

"The king is influenced by the flow of money into his royal coffers. There is no doubt that money talks," Yerucham Halevi sighed. "What happened in Burgos when the Karaites made that generous offer to King Alfonso? You were in Burgos at the time, Avraham."

Ibn Amram turned in his place, drumming his fingers lightly on the tabletop.

"I am not sure," he replied. "The king's advisor clamped total secrecy on the proceedings of their meetings. The Karaites are powerful in Toledo, and they have a strong vocal presence in Burgos. I do not think they have yet convinced the king to put them under his protection. But one thing I do know, they are too wily to give up after one defeat."

"What kind of a man is the King of Castile?" the surgeon asked.

"A Christian, to be sure," Ibn Amram responded. "But this Alfonso is not so bloodthirsty as some of the kings who came before him. He is young and energetic. They say he has reigned wisely these past four years, as he still follows the sound advice of Don Garcia, his Chief Minister. The Chief

Minister has been his mentor since childhood."

"That stepfather of his was a real battler," Yerucham Halevi added. "Wars for the sake of war. Many of us thought young Alfonso would be as bad. Thank Heaven, we were wrong. He has ruled with wisdom and strength. Even Garcia Ramirez, the lord of Navarre, is his vassal. A strong king must be influenced by strong voices from our community, and to that end, we have the Ferrizuel family, including Alkabri who single-handedly saved the Jews of Guadalajara."

"It's all very well that Alkabri saved the Jews of Guadalajara, but what can he do for us here in Navarre?" the butcher asked bluntly. "In Navarre, they listen to those fanatical monks from Cluny. How those Latin-speaking Frenchmen ever came to such power in Spain, I'll never understand."

"They root out heresy even where there is none," the surgeon added mournfully. "And they will next turn their attention on us poor Jews!"

"I warrant there will be a reform of the Spanish Church if the monks have their way," a merchant declared. "And the first to feel the heavy hand of that reform will be the Jewish merchants. I shudder at the thought! These unlettered Cluniacs don't even know Hebrew from Arabic. How can they possibly read our contracts?"

The meeting deteriorated into a wrangle over the monks of Cluny, the elders feeling suddenly more threatened by the Frankish monks than by the Karaites of Tudela. Yerucham Halevi brought the meeting back to order.

"*Rabbotai*, let us not forget about the Karaites," he chided. "What will we do if the Karaites in the capital find a glib spokesman who can turn King Alfonso against us? We cannot be sure what might happen. With one stroke of the pen from his palace in Burgos, the king could raise the Karaites to favor as Jews of the Realm in all the cities and towns of Castile."

The meeting became very serious.

"You have heard of Rabbi Avraham Ibn Daud in Toledo, the Rabad, who has learned much of the Karaite dogma in order to better refute it," said Ibn Amram. "Perhaps we should consult with him about the weak points of the Karaites. Armed with that knowledge, we could approach the king from a position of strength. I would be most interested to seek his counsel on this matter."

The assembly murmured its eager approval of Ibn Amram's plan when the door to the synagogue eased open, revealing a single young man.

"Yissaschar Rikuv!" Ibn Amram exclaimed incredulously. "What has brought you again into our midst?"

Old Shlomo raised a cane and shook it silently at the Karaite. The others sat in frozen attention.

"I have come to tell you that I tidied up the mess I made in your *sala grande*, rabbi," the youth said contritely. He hung his head in shame. "I could not erase the sorrowful image of your wife from my mind. I saw the overturned table and the dishes scattered across the floor. I could not bear to think I had done that to the mistress of the house when she had worked so hard to make the *Shabbat* a success."

"And what have you done?" Ibn Amram asked, perplexed by this new facet of the youth's character and almost doubting his own ears.

"I put everything right, rabbi," the Rikuv youth answered. "I have swept all your rooms, not just the *sala grande*. I have put everything in place. And I have apologized to your wife. Now, with the help of the Almighty, I wish to apologize to you and hope you and I might make amends."

"Be watchful," the merchant whispered. "He is as subtle and as persuasive as Satan!"

Ibn Amram waved the warning aside and motioned the youth to join them. The merchant grudgingly shifted to make room.

"Sit, young man. It took great courage to return to us," Ibn Amram said. "I see a core in you that I admire. Now I must mention that my anger has not entirely abated. Yet I will overlook the past in hopes of a better future. Perhaps you can return to Burgos with a happier reflection upon your brethren. We are not your enemies, Yissaschar. We want to help you see the light. May it be the Will of Hashem that our paths cross again."

The young Karaite colored at the compliment and the attention, then dropped his gaze again to the floor.

"Tomorrow's dawn will soon be here, Rabban Ibn Amram," the surgeon declared. "And Toledo is many leagues away."

He almost bit his tongue at the gaffe of revealing the destination of their envoy, but the young Karaite still stared at his boots, apparently oblivious to their plans.

They parted company at the steps of the synagogue, but the last image of the impressionable lad in the moonlight remained with Ibn Amram for the rest of the night. He dragged his feet with reluctance back home, not relishing the chore of revealing yet another mission which would take him from his wife.

The door squeaked on its hinges. Naomi glanced up from the book work in her lap.

"Shall I make tea for us, my husband?" she asked.

"Yes," Ibn Amram answered. He watched her steady, reassuring movements as she stirred the embers of the fire. "I am sorry that I must leave you again. I am off to Toledo to enlist the aid of the Rabad against the Karaites."

"It must be done." Her smile was wistful. "I counted the days of your absence on your last trip to Africa. I counted the very sunsets and daybreaks of each day while you tarried in Guadalajara. And now, I am prepared to count again."

CHAPTER TWO

The Sorcerer's Revenge

TUDELLA, NAVARRE
SPRING, 1139

AS THE GRAY LIGHT OF DAWN SPREAD THROUGH THE STABLE doors, Joseph Vitale, with the unbounded energy of youth, was ready to mount up and ride out into his first bold adventure in Spain.

"I can hardly wait to see the Tajo River," he whooped.

Ibn Amram's enthusiasm was less pronounced. He knew his student had not the slightest inkling of the dangers of the road. He had studied Torah far into the night, fortifying his rational motivation for journeying to Toledo on behalf of his brethren.

"Come, my master," Joseph called, already in the saddle. "The day is opening before our eyes. To pass the time, I will harmonize with the sounds of the mountains that I see in the distance. Just as my friend Amatzia taught me."

It was a pleasant picture which the young man brought to

mind, an image of soaring birds, whispering brooks and mountain insects. Ibn Amram looked with muted apprehension at those same mountains. He knew they could harbor highwaymen or Muslim raiders who would slit their throats for a bag of *dinarim*.

Joseph paid little attention to the occasional backward glances which Ibn Amram cast along the road as they travelled. Few travellers ventured forth on the Christian day of rest.

By mid-afternoon, Ibn Amram reined in his pony to survey the vast azure of the firmament. The sight was both peaceful and reassuring, as well as exciting. His thoughts were caught up with his great good fortune in combining this mission with his ongoing study of the sun and the stars. He relished the opportunity to share the mathematics of his notations with the sage of Toledo.

There was some urgency to his thoughts as well. The notations that spread along the page in his notebook tracked the changing positions of important stars as well as the sun and the moon. He suspected a convergence of immense magnitude. If it occurred soon, he knew that the sunny countryside would be plunged into an unnatural darkness, an eclipse. He shuddered as he thought of how such an event could spread superstition and calamity throughout the realm.

Ibn Amram's gestures were methodical as he combined his movements with unspoken thoughts. He dismounted, feeling under his robes for an instrument which swung by a cord from his waist. His mind raced with the premonition of celestial darkness, and the darkness he himself had witnessed just six years earlier. Taken by itself, the eerie phenomenon of eclipse was unnerving. But when it was played in Ibn Amram's mind against the havoc caused by the benighted Karaite heretics, his mood was far from tranquil. His right hand continued to fumble under his cloak.

"*Mori,*" Joseph called out. "If I can hold your reins, you can reach what you need with both hands."

Joseph quickly slid from his saddle and ran over to hold the halter of Ibn Amram's pony, an animal that answered to the name of Constancia.

Ibn Amram's right hand drew forth a circular bronze instrument, ornately inscribed with Arabic letters.

"It is advantageous to have a ring on the astrolabe, like so," he said in his absent-minded manner.

Joseph leaned forward to get a better view of what was undeniably the finest example of the oldest scientific instrument known to man. Devised by the ancient Greeks, the astrolabe provided calculations for the altitude of heavenly bodies as well as the time and latitudes for celestial events. The sight rule bobbed with each movement of Ibn Amram's hand, swinging its edge along the graduated rim of the instrument.

Schooled from childhood, Ibn Amram was an expert in the study of the sun and the stars. With the algebra taught him by Moorish mathematicians of Saragossa, he was able to deduce what the stars would do in the heavens. Not everyone, even in the liberal culture of Spain, could countenance this daring science. For that reason, Ibn Amram was usually cautious in displaying the instrument to the probing Churchmen back in Tudela.

For the moment, he was more involved in the prosaic need of unhooking the astrolabe from his belt. The mysteries of the universe could come later.

"Some suggest that it is better to have a ring within a ring," he told his student, straightening the double rings which hung from the top.

"Why is that?" Joseph turned his eyes from the instrument just long enough to reach down and hobble the shanks of Ibn Amram's pony. He then released his own pony to join Constancia in grazing on the plain.

Ibn Amram laughed at the sustained quizzical look on Joseph's face.

"Here at the top you see a ring," he explained. "This is important because on the ring is attached a chain and from the chain you hang the astrolabe on your belt when it is not in use. A single ring works like so. But a double ring permits you to hang the instrument higher."

Joseph relaxed his frown and smiled at his teacher's sardonic wit. "But truly, *Mori*, your marvelous astrolabe has many parts."

The rabbi raised the mysterious instrument and sighted on the afternoon sun.

"You must master the parts to master the whole," he answered. His fingers flashed as he reverently pointed out each part of the astrolabe in turn. "On the bottom of this special astrolabe, Achmed Ibn Muhammad has fashioned a very useful latch. It acts like the brake on a wagon. When I am counting degrees as I do at this moment, and I come to the end of my counting, I simply press the latch forward to retain the count. Achmed was the master astrolabist of Saragossa and a great admirer of my father's skill."

Joseph squinted at the sun high overhead where Ibn Amram had just sighted.

A cloud of dust from under the scrub trees on the distant edge of the plain heralded the approach of a group of herdsmen, languidly followed by their scrawny long-horned cattle. A grizzled herder slowed his mount, eyeing Ibn Amram carefully. He took full note of the distinguished black gown of the sage, and he showed great curiosity about the astrolabe.

"Good afternoon, learned doctor," he said with a smile. "I saw the reflection of your instrument in the sun. What are you finding in the heavens, learned doctor?"

"It is an immense tale, which a mere mortal can scarcely hope to see, let alone understand," Ibn Amram answered with jovial evasiveness.

The herdsman drew back. His eyes turned to slits of suspicion.

"Do you mock me, doctor?" he asked in a hoarse whisper.

He leaned forward, balancing his weight on his hands that gripped the pommel.

"I saw you look at the sun," he persisted with a note of anxiety in his voice. "He rises in the morning to start my day, and he signals the time for my campfire at night. I could not enjoy life without him. You will not take away his light from me, will you, learned doctor?"

The other herdsmen had dismounted and stood scrutinizing Ibn Amram's instrument from a safe distance. Ibn Amram felt a growing sense of unease at this topic of celestial darkness.

"I cannot take the light from the sun," he answered brusquely. "The Master of the Universe has decreed that the sun will shine, and so it shall. I merely watch it trace its path in the heavens. A man can do nothing more than watch."

A cloud from a single horse spread across the plain behind the herdsmen. The lone rider approached, reining in his mount with a fine flourish.

"Stay away from that magician," the newcomer warned the herdsmen. "He will play games of sorcery on that devilish instrument of his. He will take away the light, and next, he will take away your life. Return to my protection!"

Some of the herdsmen groaned in fear and retreated from Ibn Amram's presence. The stranger, who appeared to be a soothsayer, sat tall in his saddle, proud of his influence on the simple men of the plain. Ibn Amram turned his back in disgust on the soothsayer. He lifted his hand again to take a final sighting for the day. The chief herdsman moved closer.

"I have heard a rumor of coming darkness," he said in a confidential tone to Ibn Amram. "By the love of my life, I fear it would be cold in a world of darkness. My cattle would flee. What would I do? Would the dark heavens fall down onto this plain and crush me? You can tell me honestly, learned doctor! I am man enough to know."

Ibn Amram dropped his arm holding the astrolabe. He felt pity for the guileless man, cowed by the fantastic stories the soothsayer must have fed him.

"Someone has been telling you nonsense," he said grimly.

"The heavens will never crush us."

"Lies!" the soothsayer screamed. "All lies! You would deceive these poor men."

He grabbed at the cloak of the chief herdsman and tried to pull him away. The herdsman shrugged off his grasp.

"Let the man go," Ibn Amram said sternly. He tucked his astrolabe back under his coat to free both of his hands.

"These men belong to me," the soothsayer bellowed. He pushed back the sleeves of his ill-fitting garment and flung his arms up to the heavens. "The sun is moving more and more slowly. I have proved it with my sightings. When the path of the sun is slow enough, the darkness will be ushered in both to the east and to the west. The sun will careen to the topmost rung of the heavens. It will teeter there for a long instant, then it will topple to earth. After the final fire, there will be unending darkness."

The younger herdsmen began to sob in fear.

"Stop this nonsense this very instant!" Ibn Amram demanded.

The soothsayer would not let go of the young herdsman.

"They are mine, I tell you. I laid claim to these men and their cattle before you were born."

Ibn Amram called for the ponies and quickly retrieved his reins while Joseph loosened the ropes. He rose into his saddle with a speed that expressed, as no words could, his total disgust with the soothsayer.

The soothsayer, caught up in his own fury, raced to Constancia and grabbed her reins.

"Give me the instrument!" he demanded. "You have no right to deceive my men. The instrument is mine!"

His eyes rolled deliriously in his head. Ibn Amram kicked him away and turned to the herdsmen.

"Be mindful of my words, cattlemen," he cautioned. "The only darkness is the darkness of men's minds. If the sun ever darkens, it will be for a fleeting moment, as decreed by the Master of the Universe, not by this babbler. Remember who is the Master and who is the fool!"

He motioned a gesture of disgust at the furious soothsayer sprawled in the dust, then flicked his reins across the flank of his pony.

"I will divine the future," the soothsayer shouted after him. "And it will be with that instrument! Your skills are no better than mine. But you have the magic of that instrument!"

Ibn Amram would not look back. The thought of a crafty soothsayer preying on the fears of gullible peasants outraged him. He rode in silence for a long time.

At dusk, when the sun seared its yellow heat into a ruddy orb before sinking below the horizon, Ibn Amram decided to make one more calculation on the path of the fiery star.

For a moment, his hand shook as he thought about the momentous calculations. The readings again and again pointed to a coming darkness in the heavens. How great this darkness would be was a matter of finer calculations. He now carried his astrolabe wherever he went and continued to make notations from various latitudes, copying the results in his copious notebooks.

His agitation gave way to anger as he caught sight of the soothsayer, once again riding near them. He pretended not to notice, taking his accustomed stance and facing the west with the astrolabe.

In a resentful voice, the soothsayer bid Ibn Amram good afternoon. He whistled for his cow and her two calves, which approached with the perfect trust of all young creatures. Again, Ibn Amram tried to ignore the soothsayer who had dismounted.

At the instant that Ibn Amram raised the astrolabe to sight on the setting sun, the grotesque man threw one of the calves to the ground and promptly disembowelled her with a sturdy knife. The bellowing soon subsided, leaving the cow to pace in abstraction around the lifeless form of her calf. With his bare hands, the soothsayer reached into the abdominal cavity of the calf to examine the entrails.

"Here! You can't do that! Pagan!" Ibn Amram rushed forward, waving his arms as if he were frightening away a vulture of the arid countryside.

The soothsayer, bloodied to the elbows, drew back indignantly, still clutching the pale organs.

"I will perfect my magic through your magic," he declared. His stare was baleful. "Do not think that the stars are the only source of truth, learned doctor. My father knew the secrets of the Romans from an unbroken line of augurers. I trace my family directly to the Emperor Trajan's seer. Can you do that, doctor?"

"You come from an unbroken line of fools!" Ibn Amram retorted, stamping his foot. "Get out of my sight, miserable man. The mystery of the stars is not replicated in that poor creature's stomach."

He bent down, as if to pick up a rock to throw at the diviner. The descendant of Trajan's seer chose safety over vainglory and beat a hasty retreat.

With the dead calf slung across his saddle, the soothsayer hurled one final warning at Ibn Amram.

"Do not think you have seen the last of me, learned doctor. I have sighted what you have sighted, and in my own way, I will discover the magic of this alignment of sun and earth."

Joseph likewise bent, as if to look for a stone, and the soothsayer kneed his pony into a quick trot.

"I think that we have seen the last of him," Joseph said with relief. "His superstition has fueled the fears of those poor herders."

"There is much superstition in the kingdom," Ibn Amram said sadly. "Witches! Warlocks! If only the peasants would laugh at the antics of these practitioners of false wisdom, the charlatans would slink off in shame. But the people do not laugh, and tales of black magic darken men's minds."

"I am glad that you keep your astrolabe out of sight," Joseph noted. "Foolish people should not mistake you for a wizard."

Ibn Amram did not respond to Joseph's words. His mind was far away. His thoughts raced to the superstitious views of the monks of Cluny who were trying to dominate the Spanish Church. He remembered the unfortunate leader of the Jewish community in Toledo who had dared criticize the actions of the monks in brown. The monks had tried to imprison the old man as a messenger of Satan. It was no secret that they condemned "star-gazing" as the devil's work, too. Ibn Amram wondered if they would consider him a wizard if they knew of his astrolabe.

Their ponies labored up the steep trails of the Celtiberian Mountains. Once, Ibn Amram heard a stone in the distance and wondered if a bear were hunting during daylight hours. No signs of recent travellers greeted their eyes, only the burnt embers of cold campfires. The embers had been dead for weeks.

Joseph wrapped his overblouse more tightly around his neck on the long ascents through chilly pines. When the sun blazed forth at the crests of craggy hills, he had to loosen the overblouse again as he perspired in the sudden heat.

Ibn Amram squinted, reckoning the distance they had travelled and scouring the panorama of parched plain ahead of them for any sign of dust clouds in the distance.

"Tudela will be far behind us when we cross that pass," he said, pointing up toward a crag in the mountains. "From there, our trail is a precipitous descent until we reach the plateau north of the Tajo River."

He did not wish to worry his young charge with the dangers of that arid plateau. Looking back again at the trail they had just ascended, Ibn Amram noted the faintest wisp of dust blown across a copse of pine. His sharp eyes could not be deceived; they were being followed.

He thought back nervously at the earlier sound of a stone. Apparently, it had not been a bear prowling for honey. Someone was deliberately in pursuit. Ibn Abram considered all the possibilities. The astrolabe would be a handsome prize, worth many *dinarim* in the shops of Cordoba. Or perhaps it was a fierce bandit who did not know how slim their money pouches were. Ibn Amram decided not to mention his apprehensions to his student.

As the shadows of early evening lengthened, Ibn Amram pointed to a small mountain stream that had cut a jagged path through a shallow gorge. Their snorting ponies had disturbed a mountain goat which bleated her displeasure. On the far side of the gorge, two kids, scarcely more than newborn, nimbly bounded from rock to rock.

"A fine place to stop for the evening," Ibn Amram declared. "We shall have fresh water to replenish our waterskins and a soft bed of pine needles on which to spread our blankets."

Joseph busied himself collecting firewood while Ibn Amram rummaged in his saddle bag for winter peas and a twist of rusk for *Hamotzi*. A sudden sound, like a snorting animal, reached his ears on the gushing mountain wind. He whirled around to check the two ponies. They were silent. He glanced sharply up at the ewe and her two kids, but they stood motionless and sleepy on the ridge of shale, soaking up the last rays of the sun.

Not even half the trip is passed, Ibn Amram thought with mounting worry. With the stealth of a hunter, he rose to his feet, slipping the saddle bags silently to the ground. He walked on tiptoe to the ridge that separated their campsite from the trail, his hand pressed the astrolabe against his side to silence any jangling. No sound came from the deepening shadows of the trail. But a bird which had squawked noisily at their approach was flustered again.

Perhaps another traveller has come on our path, disturbing the bird's roosting grounds, Ibn Amram surmised. He swallowed twice to clear his ears in the mountain altitude and waited patiently.

"*Chacham Mori*," Joseph called out from the campsite. "The wood is ready to light. Do you have the flint?"

Ibn Amram turned away from his vigil. He clambered down the path to search in the saddle bag.

"The flint is here. You may try your hand with some shavings, Joseph. I'll select some peas to roast."

"Was there an animal on the path?" Joseph asked. "I saw you standing."

"An animal or another traveller," Ibn Amram said. "I have felt the presence of someone all day. Perhaps my senses are too acute in this thin mountain air. They may be very distant travellers. They might catch up with us tomorrow."

Ibn Amram was by now an experienced traveller who had mastered journeys throughout the peninsula and as far away as Tunisia. He arranged stones with great artfulness to roast the peas in their shells.

They ate quickly to save enough daylight for a *shiur* beside the fire. Poetry, grammar, astronomy and medicine were all intense interests of Ibn Amram, but it was above all his genius as a Torah scholar which endeared him to Rabbeinu Vitale. The leading Tosafist of Champagne had often said he would someday entrust his impressionable son to no one but the holy sage of Tudela. Now that Joseph had reached the proper age, Rabbeinu Vitale had kept his vow. With the well-worn copy of his *Gemara* open to where they had left off the previous night, Ibn Amram commenced with a *shiur* and invited Joseph to suggest a summation of what they had learned. Joseph labored to explain in detail.

"Yes, that is it," Ibn Amram said slowly, with a lingering note of reservation in his voice. "But could you express the thought more succinctly? Brevity is the soul of truth, and when we shape the grammar to its barest form, we come face to face with the truth of Torah."

He smiled in encouragement, knowing with deep satisfaction that this rigorous discipline would benefit Joseph on his return to Laon. His skills of clarity and precision would serve to make him an invaluable aid to his erudite father as a finely tailored glove fits a hand.

The boy tackled the challenge again, and Ibn Amram applauded his efforts. In the waning light, they moved forward to new ideas, whetting their anticipation for the thread of logic that would be resumed on the next evening. There was just enough time to conclude with *Maariv*. The soft sounds of their whispers ceased, and the campsite was enveloped in peace.

It felt like but a few moments later when a twittering bird brought Joseph back to consciousness. He blinked at the azure sky through the latticework of pine boughs above his head and groaned at the stiffness of his back.

His pony had wandered into a nearby thicket where mountain flowers proved a tasty appetizer. But Ibn Amram's pony was nowhere to be seen. Joseph felt his heart pounding at the thought of such a predicament.

"Oh, I must be dreaming," he whispered. "I should pinch myself to wake up."

"Constancia," he called out. "Where are you, Constancia?"

"What is wrong, Joseph?" Ibn Amram asked, immediately wakeful.

"Constancia has wandered off. I can't even see any signs of her hooves on this crumbling shale."

Worried and distracted, Joseph ran first a few steps in one direction and then a few steps back the other way.

A weight like a millstone around his neck instantly burdened Ibn Amram. Remote and alone in the mountains, they could easily be killed by bandits. So many more miles of mountain trail had yet to be crossed. Ibn Amram wondered for the first time if he was strong enough to meet the coming challenges.

"Then we shall have to follow both possibilities of her escape," he said at last. "Either she has retraced our steps or she has gone ahead. I shall go back and you will go forward. I doubt that she will be far away. Her stomach rules her senses."

He tried to sound jocular, but he feared that an intruder in the dark had stolen the pony and retraced his steps. Rather than put Joseph at risk of an ambush, he chose the more dangerous of the two paths for himself.

Ibn Amram called for the pony, but only an echo returned his calls. The disappearance was too coincidental. Signs of a traveller on this barren trail and now the vanishing pony only added up to a sinister picture that Ibn Amram tried to shake from his thoughts.

A faint call carried across the trail from a distant point. Raising his eyes to scan the horizon, Ibn Amram caught sight of Joseph coming toward him, happily stroking Constancia's nose.

"She is artful." The boy laughed. "But I lured her from a bed of mountain asters with a piece of turnip. I would have thought that the asters were tastier than an old turnip, but Constancia has her own way of looking at things."

Ibn Amram felt like weeping with relief.

"Our progress would have slowed to a snail's pace if we had lost her! How did she get away?"

"I guess she broke the rope during the night."

Ibn Amram bent down to examine the strands of the rope.

"No, that's the wrong conclusion," he said, pointing to the end. "Joseph, think! If you tried to pull a rope until it broke, what would happen to the strands?"

"They would snap, of course." Joseph bent down to look over his master's shoulder.

"They would break in a tangle of strands. Hemp never breaks cleanly, does it?" said Ibn Amram.

"Of course not," Joseph answered, mystified by his master's persistence.

"Then how do you explain this clean cut on every strand? Each strand is cut as if a knife had been drawn across the tight rope. You see?"

Joseph gasped in surprise. The signs of treachery were hard to refute.

"From now on, our suspicions will guide us to take every precaution on this trip," Ibn Amram whispered gravely. "At first I had just a hunch, but now I am more and more certain that the vengeful soothsayer has chosen to dog our steps with his tricks."

He fell silent, avoiding the next step in his thoughts for fear of terrifying his student. The trickery was more than an inconvenience. The soothsayer could have crept up on them in their sleep and slit their throats with the same knife he had used to slaughter the calf. His eyes twitched at the ugly thought, but he said nothing.

A light drizzle further dampened their spirits. Few birds rustled in the sodden trees. The absence of their songs left Joseph silent and songless, too. As the trail dropped step by step into foggy mountain gorges, both Ibn Amram and Joseph had to lean back more often to balance themselves.

At a particularly steep and treacherous corner of their trail, Joseph's pony dislodged a shard of limestone, and he fell heavily against a fallen log. His hooves clattered desperately to regain footing while the log tumbled silently into the deep gorge where mists hid its plunge. A hollow crash returned to their ears. Joseph scrambled to his feet shaken but apparently unhurt and climbed back into the saddle.

"It is as I remember it," Ibn Amram observed, pointing through the wet gloom to a strange outcropping of limestone that reared its fantastical head like an icon of black magic. "At the foot of this trail, we will cross a mountain torrent. Icy cold but none too deep. The ponies must be alert and nimble to cross every stone on the path."

"Should we walk them down?" Joseph asked.

"There is no need," Ibn Amram answered, polishing a small apple on his sleeve before tossing it to his companion. "They know how to follow the path. Just give the pony sufficient free rein to let him know that he is in charge."

As they descended into the mountain gorge, the light became dimmer and dimmer, filtered through the scraggly pines overhead and diffused by the steep limestone walls that hemmed them in. High above them, the gray sky was a jagged rip through the edges of pines and stone. A blackbird shrieked from a treetop with raucous disdain.

A few drops of rain fell unimpeded onto Joseph's forehead. In spite of the rain and the mist, he noticed the vultures which circled in silence. Vultures and blackbirds were too much like evil omens for his liking. He averted his gaze.

The sound of rushing water became louder, amplified by the bare walls of the gorge. Ibn Amram forged ahead with a certainty of purpose which reassured Joseph. Occasionally, his words to Constancia rose above the sound of rushing water. The last few steps lay ahead, waiting for the careful footwork of the pony. A startled whinny reached Joseph's ears, and he watched in horror.

Constancia suddenly writhed in pain and fright, lifting her neck to an impossible angle before balancing on her hind hooves. Ibn Amram struggled to balance himself.

"Whoa, Constancia! Back!"

The words were torn by the sound of gushing water. The reeling pony slipped, sending a small landslide of man, horse and rocks to the bottom.

"*Mori!*" Joseph screamed, leaping from his saddle and struggling to reach the fallen rider.

Ibn Amram looked up with a dazed expression and waved his arm in reassurance. A streak of blood dribbled from his wrist to his elbow.

"No, no! Stay there!" he commanded. "One fall is enough for today, Joseph. I hope the pony has not broken a leg."

The animal breathed heavily but struggled to regain her footing. Ibn Amram gently ran his hands along the withers and then down each leg to the fetlocks. The pony jerked spontaneously as he touched the left leg.

"Thanks be given to the Merciful One!" Ibn Amram sighed. "The leg is not broken. But I suspect that it is badly bruised. How did that happen to you, old friend? I always believed you were as sure-footed as a gazelle."

Constancia flared her nostrils in recognition of the gentle

voice. Joseph had stood up and examined the scene of the accident where a chance misstep had almost brought tragic results.

"*Chacham Mori*, look!" he gasped.

A thin black line above his head had caught his attention. He reached up and touched it. The rawhide thong twanged sonorously, sending a cascade of raindrops onto his face.

"We could have been killed!" he exclaimed.

Ashen-faced at the discovery, Ibn Amram worked his way up the trail to examine the treacherous snare. Stretched from tree to tree across the path, it was positioned to knock a rider from his mount, sending him tumbling to his death.

"At the last second, Constancia must have seen it and raised her head," Ibn Amram exclaimed. "Simple creatures often notice things that escape our senses. The soothsayer is no longer an inconvenience, Joseph. He is a dangerous enemy!"

That night, Ibn Amram tethered both ponies to a tree that commanded a strategic view of both directions of the trail. The fire was blazing, sending shadows against the rocks.

"Tonight we must separate the vigil into shared hours of wakefulness," he told Joseph. "Now, if you sit there beneath this bough, you will have a clear view of the moon. When it follows its circuit of the heavens to reach over there, where your eyes, the bough and the moon will be in one line, then you will wake me for the second watch."

"And what if I hear something in the stillness of the night?" Joseph asked nervously.

Ibn Amram smiled his encouragement.

"Then I am sure your cries of alarm will wake me at once and make the soothsayer think better of his evil ways. Remember, Joseph, Hashem protects us always. Review this evening's *shiur* and calm yourself."

He eased himself with a groan onto the damp blanket, cradling his right arm across his chest. Soon, he closed his eyes, leaving Joseph to ponder their evening's discussion.

Yet, somehow, images of the soothsayer slithered repeatedly in and out of his thoughts, like a serpent about to strike its prey.

A silent rustle of wings and the mournful hooting of an owl startled Joseph. He thought he had heard the terrified shriek of a mouse caught in the talons of the owl, but he wasn't sure. He wasn't sure if he had been dreaming. He wasn't sure if the last time he had looked, the moonlight had been so penetrating in a starless sky. He gazed across at the ponies, but they ignored his stare. One of them stamped a foot in reflex, sending a ripple through the muscle of his hindquarters. A night insect had probably bothered him.

Joseph sat straight and leaned forward to listen. The concentration tired him. He positioned himself as Ibn Amram had shown him to judge the placement of the moon and the consequent passage of time. There was still time left in his vigil. The mountain air was cold. He rubbed his hands together to stir the circulation. He did not dare stamp his feet. Something was snuffling on the far side of the thicket, digging and then snorting in the moist earth. Joseph could not imagine what it was, but he listened intently to hear if it caught any prey.

The pauses between the snuffling seemed to lengthen interminably. He felt his head nodding forward until his chin almost touched his chest. Then he was jerked abruptly into wakefulness again. The snuffling creature was gone. The moon was almost aligned with the branch.

"*Chacham Mori*, it is time to begin your watch," Joseph whispered sleepily.

Ibn Amram blinked and smiled in the moonlight. Joseph fell into a troubled sleep for the rest of the night. The snuffling creature returned to his dreams. He tossed and turned in his sleep to escape the inquisitive nose that pressed forward in the dark. Again, the nose pressed into his worst secrets, snuffling for his frailties. He sat bolt upright, bathed in a cold sweat and breathing heavily.

"It is soon dawn, Joseph," Ibn Amram said. His hand had been gently prodding Joseph's shoulder. "Did I startle you? We shall say *Shacharit* and continue on our way before the heat is too oppressive. It will take a while to walk out Constancia's lameness, I am afraid."

In spite of their slow pace, the mountains receded behind them, giving way to flat open countryside, where hares dashed from rock to rock. The expansive vista was a relief from the constrictive environment of the gorges. But it was not a welcome relief, since this marked the beginning of the most difficult part of their journey. Ibn Amram looked up at the early morning sky, hoping that some clouds might appear to ease the heat on the uplands.

"We will have to travel quickly," he warned. "The sun can do its worst when we do not expect it. It can leave us raving in a painful delirium if we fall prey to thirst. Let us take a bold step, Joseph, and put this upland desert behind us."

Their pace was slow but measured.

Familiar with this rocky stretch of lifeless terrain, Ibn Amram had wisely chosen to ration their limited water supplies. At last, when his mouth was beginning to burn from the dry heat, he turned around to lift up one of the waterskins draped over the saddle bags.

"Why did you not fill this waterskin, Joseph?" he asked sharply. "I distinctly remember asking you to look after the water." His arm held up a limp skin that obviously held nothing.

"But I did, *Mori*," Joseph responded with puzzlement. "I went down to the stream at the beginning of my watch with all four waterskins and filled each of them to the top. Then I carefully placed the bung in the mouth of each."

Ibn Amram grimaced, raising the second waterskin that was as limp as the first.

"The bung is in place, but the water is not."

He dropped the reins for a moment while he pried one of the bungs loose. With the mouth of the waterskin pressed tightly against his mouth, Ibn Amram blew vigorously into the skin. It whistled and gurgled at a small puncture at the bottom.

"The soothsayer has played his worst trick on us! Evil man!" Ibn Amram declared and threw the waterskin to the ground in frustration.

"What will we do?" Joseph cried, kneading his own limp waterskins with a growing realization of their extreme danger.

"I know now that this trouble is of my own making. I tried hard not to fall asleep last night. But the snuffling sound in the bushes was so soft and subtle that it lulled me into this grievous error."

Ibn Amram retrieved the reins of his limping pony and pulled his hat a little more tightly onto his forehead.

"Don't blame yourself," he cautioned. "The mind's eye is not always willing to remain open, no matter how much we prod ourselves to keep our inner vision alert. But the situation is not lost, although it means many hours of painful walking. Are you prepared to suffer some thirst, Joseph?"

Ashamed of his own failure, yet heartened by Ibn Amram's words, Joseph assured him that he was. Ibn Amram realized that the young man had been a *bar mitzvah* for fully three years but his secluded activities in the *beit midrash* had not yet prepared him for the worst challenges of life. The time had now come. Paradoxically, this growth to greater self-reliance would occur in sun-baked inaction. But Ibn Amram knew that an inner discovery was just as important as the actual trip they must now take to the grasslands of the river.

"It's a hardship," he said to his young charge. "But you will be the better for it."

For a full day, the searing heat bore down on them, yet no sign of relief appeared in the shadowless jumble of rocks on that grim plateau. They stumbled in pain, often losing sight of the trail. Ibn Amram wrapped their sleeping blankets across the heads of their suffering ponies to give them a little relief.

Bent over from the pain and dizziness of thirst, Joseph at

first did not catch sight of the image on the horizon. When at last his eyes could make out the outline of tall, shady trees, he wept for joy.

"We are saved, *Chacham Mori*," he whispered through dry lips. "There is our relief, to the east."

Ibn Amram rubbed a dusty hand through his beard in indecision.

"It is not the right direction," he noted. "The Tajo River should be directly south of this plain. But I will trust your senses."

They turned the unwilling ponies in the new direction and continued with rising hopes. A rocky outcropping of limestone obscured the copse of trees, and Joseph anxiously clambered up a face of burning stones to relocate the welcome sight. Ibn Amram stood at the foot of the boulder, shielding his eyes with a hand to watch Joseph's ascent.

"No, it cannot be! I have lost it!" Joseph cried out.

Joseph desperately struggled to climb down the far side of the boulder, but Ibn Amram sternly called him back. Maddened by the desire to retrace his steps and find the precious trees, Joseph lumbered across a dry river bed and scaled yet another boulder. His cries of anguish stated more clearly than words that the trees had disappeared.

"Come, young son," Ibn Amram called gently, beckoning the boy with a wave of his hand. "It must surely have been a mirage. These strange sights will occur in a desert, and now we know that they can also deceive us in these badlands." He glanced at the sun to retrace their steps to the south. "We have not lost too much time. And when the sun sets, the worst of our ordeal will be over."

Many times on that shimmering plateau, Joseph felt compelled to lie down and give up. No enemy appeared on the horizon to test his courage. Rather, the enemy lay within, mocking his strength and his will to live. Ibn Amram roused him each time he gave up.

"Think of the ponies, Joseph," he suggested. "They suffer

as we do in this desolate corner of Castile. We must help them."

The sage adjusted the blankets again to shield the ponies' heads. Joseph looked up at him, bleary-eyed from the heat.

"Is this a plan to test me?" he asked in disbelief. "I have never felt any strong sympathy for a beast of burden in my life. And now you would have me rise to my feet in this horrible heat to comfort Constancia?"

Ibn Amram nodded. He hoped fervently that he could get the young man to forget for the moment his own suffering by thinking about the affliction of others.

"It is a matter of being sensitive to *tzaar baalei chayim,* the pain of a living creature, Joseph. Just as Hashem takes pity on us in our times of need, so we must try to save these poor animals."

Ibn Amram chose not to dwell on his own dry tongue and his throbbing head. He did not wish to reveal to Joseph how much he was suffering.

As Joseph struggled to his feet, a brilliant flash of green darted from between the stones. As it flicked its tail, the lizard dazzled them with an iridescent array of blue spots along the length of its body. Distracted from his discomfort, Joseph blinked to see it better and leaned forward. Ibn Amram studied the lizard with mounting excitement.

"Can the gold and silver of a king sparkle with more beauty than this little lizard?" he asked suddenly. "Can any of us hope to lay claim to the precious bounty of Creation?"

Joseph peered up at his master and wondered vaguely if Ibn Amram was delirious.

"Again, you are testing me, Rabban Ibn Amram," he blurted.

"You do not understand, Joseph," Ibn Amram answered. "The lizard has come to us, don't you see? The lizard does not care at all whether we are rich or poor, healthy or dying. The joy I feel right now is much like that strange emotion I felt when my son Yitzchak smiled for the first time. It is a gift of beauty, like this gift from the lizard."

Joseph stared again at the lizard. "Perhaps I missed something," he muttered.

"I think I have found a missing piece in my analysis of *Koheleth*," Ibn Amram continued enthusiastically, "right here on a sun-baked plain! Could Shlomo Hamelech have enjoyed his sparkling gold any more than I have enjoyed the sight of this sparkling lizard?"

He paused because his sudden movements had brought the dizziness back to his eyes.

At last, Joseph smiled in recognition of the subtle thought.

"The Master of the Universe has not given us a ready supply of water on this *mesa*, but the beauty of His Creation is here to sustain us. Is that what you wanted to say?"

He extended his hand, and the lizard dashed back to the rocks.

Ibn Amram seemed lost in thought, as he closed his eyes and murmured passages of *Koheleth*.

Joseph surveyed the scene, his eyes falling once again on the empty waterskins. He was suddenly roused to anger at the memory of the smug soothsayer.

"When we survive this trip, I hope that we return to that evil man and repay him for this misery!" he declared.

Ibn Amram noticed that Joseph was walking with greater steadiness, now that his thoughts had turned to future matters instead of current troubles.

"It is as *Koheleth* has taught us," Ibn Amram said, hastening his pace so that Joseph would not slow down. "If I concentrated on the wrongs which someone has done to me, I would be so absorbed in planning my revenge that I would probably turn away from the joys of Torah. That is why one handful of tranquillity in the study of our Law is much better than two handfuls of toil."

The sun was soon to set, giving both men and beasts a welcome relief from the intense heat. Ibn Amram took time to make another calculation with his astrolabe. He had trouble adjusting the instrument, but when at last the count was verified and recorded in his notebook, he turned to Joseph to make a simple statement.

"Here we are, baking in the heat of the sun, yet my calculation tells me that soon there will be darkness in the heavens as the sun and the moon align."

Joseph was startled, in spite of his thirst.

"You mean it is the darkness the cattlemen feared?"

Ibn Amram nodded. "My calculations are not yet complete, but the evidence is mounting."

He attached the astrolabe to his belt and drew out his *siddur* so that they might say *Minchah* together.

Ibn Amram paused while he calmed his thoughts for prayer. A worrisome memory raced through his mind, disturbing his concentration. Just six years earlier in Languedoc, he had seen an eclipse, with fearsome results. Men had been trampled to death in wild, superstitious crowds that foolishly sought to flee a Christian apocalypse. Might the peasants of Castile react to the coming eclipse with the same blind frenzy? Would they blame the Jews for the darkness and rampage through the Jewish quarters of every city and town? He shook his head to chase those thoughts of death and agony.

For long minutes, a static tableau remained on that *mesa*. The ponies hun their heads in resignation while the two men wavered in fatigue and in prayer, the final rays of the sun scorching their backs.

Nightfall was sudden, and as is common in arid lands, the shimmering glare of heat was swallowed up by the cool night air. Ibn Amram felt the leg of his pony again and made a fateful decision.

"Blessed be Hashem, her lameness has been walked out," he said. " We will ride all night if we have to."

Their pace was slow and unsteady, but neither man hurried his mount. After the moon came out and blotted the myriad stars from view, Joseph's pony perked up his ears. He made little sounds of excitement and tugged at the reins. Even

Constancia, still limping a little from her fall, whinnied with new hope and managed to break into a slow trot.

"Oh, if only I had a drink of water," Joseph cried, rocking in his saddle. "What is it that this animal smells?"

Ibn Amram smiled and settled back into his saddle.

"You will see," he said. "A beast of burden is attuned to delights that we can scarcely sense."

The half-smile on Ibn Amram's lips remained inscrutable. With each step his pony took, Joseph felt the pace increase until the trot turned into a gallop. The gallop became more violent, and Joseph hunched painfully over his saddle, clinging to the pommel. By slow degrees, the barren rocks gave ground to broad expanses of spring grassland. The pony whinnied in delight, heading straight for a long line of willows. A different fragrance was in the air. There before them was a broad expanse of water, shimmering like a jewel in the moonlight.

"The Tajo!" Ibn Amram called out exultantly. "For miles, I suspected that the ponies smelled a breath of water in the air. But they could not tell us of their discovery."

His pony broke through the rugged undergrowth at the river bank and waded into the shallows of the smooth flowing water. Joseph, whispering thanks to the Almighty, slipped from the saddle to wallow in the clear water.

"Joseph, not so fast," Ibn Amram warned. "We must control the urge to drink and drink, even though it is difficult. It is wise to drink in moderation after a day of extreme thirst. We can drink again in a little while. Do you hear me? Not until our stomachs are ready for more!"

He pulled Joseph from the water and shook him.

"You are right, of course," Joseph said, coughing and sputtering after his impetuous behavior. "You are always right!"

He clambered up the river bank to sit on a stump. A large shrub with lance-like leaves caught his attention. He turned and saw more of the shrubs ranged along the river bank.

"In a week or so, the oleander will transform the greens and browns of this river bank into a sea of white and pink," he mused. "The world is beautiful again."

They pitched camp for the remainder of the night under a large willow. There was no need for a blazing campfire. Now they had met the enemy and vanquished him.

If the soothsayer lingered on the edge of the plain to relish their pain, he was disappointed with what he saw. The two men had confronted death and fear and had won. Toledo was less than a day's ride away.

CHAPTER THREE

Behind Closed Doors

TOLEDO, CASTILE
SPRING, 1139

IBN AMRAM MOTIONED TO HIS STUDENT TO COME ALONGSIDE. His hand gestured with pride as they beheld the arrogant walls of Toledo rising above the gorges of the Tajo River.

"The weeks you have spent with us in Tudela have not yet given you a sense of the real Spain," he said. "There, in the distance, is a true expression of Castile. Not the meek little town of Tudela in a minor principality of the peninsula but a bold city that is part of Imperial Castile. And each city with its walls and ramparts expresses in its own way the essence of Castile."

"Castile is truly the land of castles," Joseph breathed in amazement. "And Toledo is entirely a fortress."

He stared at the majestic spectacle of the cathedral towers which dwarfed the remains of the old Roman fort in the foreground.

"I would not wish to be a general trying to take this city," Ibn Amram noted. "The promontory is entirely of granite and totally impervious to any catapult devised by man. The Tajo River protects every flank except the north in its watery embrace. There is no way across the river gorge except the bridges, and both are fortified."

"Which bridge shall we take?" Joseph asked, motioning to a fork in the road.

Ibn Amram guided his pony to the west.

"We will take the one that leads directly to the Jewish quarter," he replied thoughtfully.

Thursday had been a busy market day in Toledo. Now the streets were emptied of the noisy vendors, leaving a tired calm in place of the previous day's frantic activity. They picked their way through sparse crowds across the bridge and made their way through a maze of dark and winding alleys to the Jewish quarter. At last, they had arrived.

"Hold the reins, Joseph," Ibn Amram advised, "and I will see if Rabbi Ibn Daud is able to greet his unexpected guests."

He climbed unsteadily up the steep staircase of white-washed stone until he reached a somber oak door studded with iron. The massive ring clanged with a hollow yet imperative note, and Ibn Amram disappeared from view.

Very few minutes passed before a stable boy scurried past Joseph from the side entrance and grasped the reins of both ponies.

"Please, sir," he said meekly. "My master asks if you will join him in the house."

He pointed up the flight of stairs and then ran back down the narrow lane with both of the animals.

The master of the house appeared in the doorway, welcoming Joseph with open arms. Considering his growing fame as a scholar of history, Ibn Daud was surprisingly young. Joseph observed him keenly, from the poise of his athletic frame to the black hair under the broad brim of his hat. Avraham Ibn Daud appeared to be a man of strength and courage. Joseph judged the rabbi to be little more than thirty years of age.

"You seem surprised!" Rabbi Ibn Daud said, hands on hips. "Is it the travail of this startling trip that your master has just recounted or the untidiness of my humble residence?"

His hand swept an arc across a staggering scope of shelving in the study. Each shelf was crammed with manuscripts. And truth be told, the immense library was by no means tidy.

Joseph looked down at his shoes in embarrassment.

"Excuse my stare, Rabbi Ibn Daud," he answered. "The trip has left me tired." He did not wish to remark on the man's youthfulness.

"Then my wife will restore your flagging spirits with a fine meal," Ibn Daud promised. He glanced out the window of the study which overlooked a neighboring roof. Spying a kitchen boy at the doorway, he called down. "Luis! Will you set three places for lunch, please? Yes, on the *patio* over there by the geraniums. I'm sure my guests will appreciate their color."

He turned from the window and ushered Ibn Amram and his student into the corridor, carefully closing the door of his study behind him.

In the afternoon sun, the stuccoed walls that enclosed the *patio* were a blaze of painful white which made the rows of scarlet geraniums dance like fire in their eyes. Ibn Daud rubbed his hands in delight as his servant brought bowls of soup.

"Has Avraham introduced you to the tasty treats of Spain?" he asked Joseph pleasantly.

"So many dishes are different from those in France," Joseph answered. "I particularly enjoy the salad of eggplant, although I must admit it did not please me at first."

He watched with great concentration as Ibn Daud poured a red soup from the pitcher into each bowl.

"Yes, I assure you that you will enjoy *gazpacho*," Ibn Daud said with enthusiasm. "Icy cold and flavored with olive oil and crushed almonds."

He pushed the bowl toward Joseph. A second servant had appeared with perfect timing, carrying a platter of saffron rice flavored with pimento.

"This meal reminds me of my childhood days in Cordoba," Ibn Daud continued heartily. "My preference for food will always be Andalusian."

"Rabbi Avraham has a soft spot in his heart for the south of Spain," Ibn Amram explained to Joseph. "You might think his memories are all rosy, but that is not the case."

Ibn Daud's cheery countenance turned thoughtful at the memory.

"I would have been happy in Cordoba, but the Caliph's Muslim fanaticism was sweeping the countryside like a scimitar. I still miss many of my boyhood friends. We learned together in the *beit midrash* before my uncle and I moved here. Those were good times."

His fingers toyed with the bread, while his mind searched sad images of the past.

"Cordoba's loss is Toledo's gain," Rabban Ibn Amram declared loudly, shaking his friend from his reveries. "Many of the Jews who were dispersed by the vicious bloodshed have made their way to this Jewish quarter. You have stood as a beacon for them."

Ibn Daud raised an eyebrow without thanking Ibn Amram for the compliment. The gracious and slow pace of the meal continued. Later, Ibn Daud led his two guests into the main sitting room of his home. The boyish enthusiasm had returned, but again it was muted to stern-faced anger when Ibn Amram recounted his misadventures with the Karaite youth.

"It is always the same with these heretics!" Ibn Daud exclaimed, striking his knee in frustration. "They are desecrators of the faith, yet they do so with a perfect piety that unnerves many of the faithful. That is the effect of perfect piety motivated by perfect ignorance. But I have found the weak link in their view of the world. As you know, I immerse myself in history, not from idle fascination but to survey the unbroken chain of inheritance from the first of the Chosen People right down to the present."

His hand waved with new significance to the closed door of the study to his right.

"On those shelves in there are the compilations of all my thoughts on our *Mesorah*, an unending chain of law and observance based on the *entire* Torah given to Moshe Rabbeinu at Mount Sinai. I suppose I could have launched a heated refutation of the Karaites, but I prefer to take the more arduous path of reason and evidence."

"I have heard of your work and look forward to the day you will provide us all with copies," Ibn Amram said. "But can we wait until your treatise is ready? The threat is here and now."

"History is not the only refutation of the pious but misguided heretic," Ibn Daud said firmly. "In fact, I am sure this self-centered piety of theirs will be their downfall. They are less and less observant as they hold to a narrow grasp of literal truth. Did you know that in the time of the *Geonim* these heretics still accepted Rabbinic decree? But step by step, they have moved into a world of their own curious practices."

"Rabban Ibn Amram tells me that their calendar is in error," Joseph interjected. "That means that they perform many kinds of forbidden work on days which we know are *Yamim Tovim*, even *Yom Kippur*!"

"Quite right," Ibn Daud replied with a nod. "And have you ever seen their prayer book? It is not worthy of the name *siddur*. Imagine a *siddur* without the *Shemoneh Esray*."

"I am beginning to see now why Yissaschar Rikuv was so strange that night," returned Joseph.

"Rikuv, you say?" Ibn Daud asked, leaning forward and raising an eyebrow at the fateful name. "I have heard of the activities of that family in the capital. They hold firm to the most extreme form of this bizarre heresy. I have all the evidence in my manuscripts.

"Many of the current leaders of the Karaites have had the good sense to modify the twisted ideas of their founder Anan ben David. But there will always be simple-minded fanatics who won't give an inch, even when their own leaders concede ground to Rabbanite wisdom."

"My heart grieves when I think of that misguided youth," Ibn Amram said, rising from the chair to pace back and forth in thought.

As he neared the door of the study, he paused and stared quizzically at the space between the door and the floor, half expecting a mouse to show its nose. He took another step back towards Ibn Daud, then paused again to listen.

"Yerucham Halevi returned from a trip to Burgos this past winter," Ibn Abram said. "He says that the Karaites who live in the capital fawn on the young king and plot to win his favor. They could easily be used as a tool by the monks to drive a wedge between us and the King of Castile."

Again his pacing had brought him back to the door. Again, he paused to listen for a fragment of sound that eluded his ears.

"Then it is good that you have come to me," Ibn Daud concluded, leaning forward to share the confidence of his inner thoughts.

Tentatively at first, both rabbis voiced their fears that the Karaites were the unwitting tool of the French monks who were trying to subvert Alfonso's power by siding with Karaite heretics.

"This support puts a heavy burden on the young king," Ibn Daud whispered, daring to express his worst fears. "He is obliged to justify his role as the defender of all religions while acquiescing to the monks' demands about the Jewish problem. I have few doubts that, in a sudden crisis, their ardent support of the Karaites would challenge his protection of the Jews in the realm."

"It would be a delicate dilemma for any king, even one rich in wisdom and experience," Ibn Amram mused. "How long can he maintain a balance, thrust as he is amongst so many conflicting influences?"

"He shall keep that balance, old friend, if we are united in our response to the heretics."

A faint rasping sound from inside the study, like a chair leg scraping across terra cotta tiles was unmistakable. It made the hairs on the nape of Joseph's neck stand on end. Rabbi Ibn Daud jerked his head abruptly towards the closed door, but he modulated his resonant voice with extreme caution.

"Yes, we must examine our options in Burgos, Avraham," he rambled on, neither changing the tempo nor the pitch of his voice. "Indeed, we must do all that is necessary. That is a good idea, Rabban Ibn Amram. A very good idea, indeed."

Ibn Amram took the cue, stepping on tiptoe towards the door. "I myself was just thinking that we must examine our options," he said. "Our options in Burgos, I mean."

Another sound came from beneath the door of the study. This time, it was loud and distinct, like the sound of a leather boot scuffing on a window sill. Ibn Daud did not delay to ponder the possibilities. Flinging open the door with all his weight, he burst through like a projectile from a siege machine.

"Halt, thief!" he shouted, waving his arms.

"Aiee!" screamed a youth in fright, slipping off the topmost shelf. Buckling beneath his weight, the shelf toppled onto the heads of two older men standing beneath him. They cursed the bookshelf roundly and heaped curses on the rabbi as well.

"Avraham, quick! The window!" Ibn Daud exclaimed, gesturing to Ibn Amram to stop one of the men about to escape with an armload of manuscripts.

Ibn Amram raced to the open window, dragging the man back into the room by the nape of the neck. Scowling like a criminal, the man nevertheless was cowed by Ibn Amram's great strength. The other man was not yet about to surrender.

"Rabbanite!" he shouted.

He flung a massive manuscript at Ibn Daud which grazed the rabbi's head. Pages leaped into the air like snow.

Joseph squirmed under the table and grabbed the man's leg. A vicious kick caught him on the temple, but he would not let go. He could hear Ibn Daud wrestling the intruder into submission. His vision was blurred, but his handhold on the leg was unshaken.

Ibn Amram stared with unparalleled disgust at the youth hiding behind the shelving.

"I see we meet again, Yissaschar Rikuv," he said with undisguised loathing. "And who is this that you have brought with you?"

The older man with scruffy white hair tried to shake free from the grim grip that Ibn Daud maintained on his shoulder.

"Pah! Don't touch me, Rabbanite," he shouted. "The name is Rikuv, if that means anything to you!"

"Indeed, it does," Ibn Daud answered darkly. "It is a name that has already brought ignominy to your sect. And now you have dared to bring violence into the home of your brethren. At one time, we had all hoped for a peaceful dialogue with your leaders, but your kind has squelched that hope."

For a brief moment, Joseph felt he could detect a fleeting look of shame cross the younger Rikuv's face. Avraham Ibn Daud had likewise noticed the look.

"What are you doing here, young man?" he asked gently. "You could be an upstanding member of your community, if you tried. You might even be a leader, if you dared. Could you not have come to the front door to seek whatever you wanted with my permission?"

Tears welled up in the eyes of the youth.

"You would never have given what I need," he answered in broken phrases. "Of that I am sure."

"What is it that you wanted?" Ibn Daud persisted in his rich, gentle voice.

"Shut your mouth!" the elder Rikuv snapped.

Rabban Ibn Amram restrained him with a firm hand on the shoulder. His eyes flashed animosity towards everyone, including his own son.

Torn between loyalty to his father and the persuasive tact of the sage of Toledo, Yissaschar Rikuv began to blurt out their abortive plan.

"Silence!" the elder Rikuv exploded.

Rabban Ibn Amram, taller and more powerful than the fanatic, pressed him onto the overturned bench, holding him by the collar.

"I wanted to come here to locate your manuscript," Yissaschar Rikuv continued. "You know which manuscript! We have heard rumors of your golden tongue and how it will damage our cause in Spain. Everyone in our community is talking about your manuscript. They know you will use it to attack our people and our beliefs. I knew it had to be somewhere here in your study. If I could have found it and taken it back to my master, he would have known how to prepare for your charges and refute them."

"Sniveling child," the elder Rikuv taunted. "Do you really think we intended to steal only a single manuscript? If I had my way, I would torch this entire library. Vile scribblings!"

The youth shrank back further into the toppled shelving. His shoulders shook in silent sobs.

"I think that you have destroyed enough already, Rikuv," Ibn Daud intoned, surveying the torn manuscripts, then glancing with compassion at the sorrowful young man. "I will thank you to leave before I report you to the *beit din*. Your kind works in shadows, I can see. You wouldn't want the notoriety of a public debate, would you?"

The elder Rikuv cursed Ibn Daud and raised a manuscript to throw at his head. Ibn Amram quickly wrested it away.

"You're a sly one," the elder Rikuv snarled at the unsmiling Ibn Amram. "Always full of tricks. Always dodging me. I thought I had you when I strung up that strip of rawhide across your path. But you somehow got past me."

"You!" Ibn Amram exclaimed in shock. "You mean it was you who dogged our steps on the trail from Tudela? Surely not!"

Rikuv folded his arms across his chest in satisfaction. "I thought I could humble you, but no, you kept on finding ways to avoid the hard lesson. But at least you couldn't escape the reality of an empty waterskin, could you? Your evil magic couldn't make the water return to the skin after I punctured it."

Ibn Amram sat down heavily, holding a hand to his heart.

"This is too much," he whispered. "I could live with the soothsayer as an enemy. But to think that a Jew has tried to kill me and the boy? That is too much for me."

Rikuv drove home his message of hatred, leaving Rabban Ibn Amram no choice but to accept the man's enmity in all its horrid breadth.

"You haven't defeated me yet, liar," he scolded. "When I return to Burgos, I will turn the king on the pack of you. He'll see you for what you are. A pack of liars! And he'll spit in your face. Yes, I will have my way. He will send you from Castile, and you will wander in shame across the face of this world. You will wander for the sin of your idolatry!"

"I have had enough, Rikuv," Ibn Daud said sharply, stepping away from the open door. "You will now leave."

The elder Rikuv left, and the third Karaite followed close on his heels.

Yissaschar brushed away a tear and looked up at Ibn Daud.

"I had hoped to help my master win," he said. "He is an expert at logic. The two of you could have debated our argument. It should never have come to this!"

Ibn Daud reached forward to touch the boy on the shoulder, but Yissaschar squirmed away and left.

"Shocking," Ibn Amram muttered to himself as he slowly regained his voice. "I had never thought a Karaite would try to kill us. I thought it was the soothsayer. How wrong I was."

"I don't intend to take the words of that madman lightly," Ibn Daud said, looking out the window at the three men slinking away in the street. He fell silent in thought as he kneeled to retrieve the jumble of papers on the floor. He kissed each in turn. "If he has the influence he thinks he has in the capital, he might be successful in his lies against us. You know that the monks are only too anxious to hear the worst that slanderers of our faith can tell them."

"What should we do now?" Ibn Amram asked, drumming his fingers on the table. "Events are moving so quickly, I fear we will have to run to catch up, my friend."

Ibn Daud tidied the papers on the table and looked up at last. "There is one powerful remedy left to us which would stifle the growth of the Karaite communities in Burgos or in any other city of Castile. What do you think, Avraham, of a *cherem hayishuv*?"

Rabban Ibn Amram carefully considered the suggestion. "A ban on settlement could stop them in their tracks. With no opportunity to bring more people into their existing communities, the popularity of the heresy would wither and die."

"Then we must act quickly," Rabbi Ibn Daud said. "Joseph Hanasi, a fellow Jew, is a favorite of the king. He is known to King Alfonso and the court by his Arabic name of Alkabri. If you undertook a trip to Burgos, you could make him our mouthpiece. What do you think, Avraham?"

Ibn Amram looked across at Joseph.

"I had hoped to rest my weary bones after that ordeal on the *mesa*," he said. "But perhaps leisure just wasn't meant to be. What do you say, Joseph? Are you ready to accompany me to Burgos?"

"I will go wherever you lead me," Joseph answered promptly. "But who is this Alkabri? Can we trust him?"

Ibn Daud raised his hands to explain the situation.

"Joseph Hanasi is probably the most influential man in the capital. Thank Heaven, he is a loyal Jew and fully prepared to act for the best interests of our community. You must understand how the court of Castile works. Alkabri is more than advisor to King Alfonso. He is in all matters the Royal Secretary. If anyone can forestall Karaite slander, it is Alkabri."

Ibn Amram had been pacing back and forth while Ibn

Daud explained matters to Joseph. Now, he slumped onto the broad window sill.

"Suddenly, I feel very tired," he admitted. "It is as if I threw a stone into a pond and the ripples continue to reach out from the first splash. That was my mistake in inviting a Karaite for a *Shabbat* meal. Now the throw of that stone into the pond has been made and the circles are becoming wider and wider. That arrogant young man plunged our home into darkness, and his father will not be happy until all of Castile is plunged into darkness. Just think, my friend, how this bigotry coincides with the coming solar darkness. Observe how superstitions and ignorance rise up together and run rampant in the land!"

"A darkening of the sun, Avraham?" Ibn Daud asked. "I didn't know you were anticipating such an event."

Ibn Amram felt underneath his coat and withdrew the papers on which he made his notations of the solar count.

"It is all here for you to inspect," he answered, knowing that Ibn Daud's keen knowledge of the rules of the stars could make sense of his numbers.

"Before the cycle is complete, I anticipate a solar darkness. I am not ready to tell of my findings just yet, but I strongly feel that the people should be prepared for this natural event before it comes. We must prevent the panic and bloodshed of past eclipses."

Ibn Daud paused in deep concentration while he considered the neat columns of figures and the algebra.

"Be strong, Avraham," he encouraged. "These are difficult times, but we must continue to pursue truth. If the Cluniac monks had their way, your calculations would be destroyed today. Too much enlightenment would get in their way and impede their mission. I see the growing domination of the Spanish Church by the Cluniac fanatics from Burgundy."

"Why should I care how the Churchmen fight amongst themselves? " yawned Joseph with a wave of his hand. "What difference would it make who wins?"

"You must consider the effects of this battle on the Jews of Castile, Joseph," Ibn Amram explained. "The more fanatical the Church becomes, the more it tries to destroy us. With enough influence in the king's court, these French monks could persuade the king to banish us from his kingdom, may Heaven forbid such a thought!"

"In my opinion, the worst offender is the Archbishop of Toledo," ventured Ibn Daud. "We must never let that man turn our knowledge of the stars against us. He would take these very papers, Joseph, and use them to prove that the Jews are stargazers, in league with the Devil. He would take all science and turn it into superstition."

He handed back the papers.

"Life would be so much easier if I could retire to a life of Torah unhindered by the problems of the outside world," Ibn Amram sighed. "I could make my daily sightings on the sun and the nightly sightings on the stars with no vexation."

"It is a perfect world you are imagining," Ibn Daud suggested, rummaging in a dusty corner of his shelves. "It is either the Garden of Eden which occurred long ago or the age of *Mashiach* which has not yet arrived. We wait between the intervals, and in the meantime, our wisdom must be kept from the prying eyes of our enemies."

His hands retrieved a slim volume which had slipped behind a number of other manuscripts.

"Ah, here it is! I believe this gift should help you to regain some of your accustomed strength. You have heard of Al-Magriti?"

"And who has not?" Ibn Amram responded, rising from the sill to come closer to the shelf. "On his deathbed, Achmed Ibn Muhammad promised to give me a copy of that great astronomer's work, but it never reached my hands."

"Until now," Ibn Daud replied proudly, extending his hand with the treatise.

"How is it possible?" Ibn Amram asked. His delight was boundless.

"Let's just say that I have my contacts within the Church and saved this work from the fires of their censorship. It is now yours. It might help you to determine more accurately the coming darkness."

"This is truly an excellent gift," Ibn Amram declared. His fingers flicked through the pages, resting here and there at various drawings and charts before continuing an excited search for the hidden wisdom. "I will have to take time to digest the thoughts of Al-Magriti. Let the Cluniacs drown in their ignorance! I feel my spirit renewed for the next challenge!"

"All the same, good friend," Ibn Daud advised, pointing to Ibn Amram's cloak. "Carry your astrolabe well hidden. It is enough that we must battle the heretics of our faith. There is no need to excite the wrath of those who hate our science."

Ibn Amram nodded grimly and returned the double ring of the astrolabe to its position, high up under his long black coat.

CHAPTER FOUR

Brother Against Brother

BURGOS, CASTILE
SUMMER, 1139

THE LONG ROAD FROM THE DOURO RIVER PIERCED UNENDING stretches of tall beech trees that broke the early sun into stark patterns of light and shadow. Ibn Amram and Joseph Vitale rode through those rhythmic slashes of light, nodding to the occasional traveller heading to market. But once they approached the teeming capital city, Ibn Amram noticed a distinct change in the people.

"That's strange," he called over his shoulder to Joseph. "Now the majority of travellers are leaving Burgos."

Not only that, the numbers were greater and greater as Ibn Amram and Joseph reached the crest of each successive hill. Many were carrying bundles on their backs. Some even had carts and donkeys to aid their exodus.

"Isn't it rather early to leave the town on a market day?" Joseph questioned.

Ibn Amram nodded and managed to catch the eye of an old man grumbling to himself as he trudged along the dusty narrow trail. He waved and called out as the traveller passed by.

"Good morning, old man," he called out. "Is everything sold already? Surely, the vendors have not finished this early."

The man scarcely raised his head. He jerked a rigid thumb at the hazy outline of the town in the distance and spat on the road.

"Not sold! Canceled!" He tramped away angrily before Ibn Amram could question him further.

"I really do not understand at all," Ibn Amram admitted, reining in his pony. they passed a cluster of monks who were also making their way towards the city, carrying gaudy banners and intoning a warning in Latin to the indifferent travellers, "Remember, you are dust and to dust will you return." Ibn Amram flicked the reins across his pony's flank to sidestep the nearest monk.

"Is that the bridge we must cross?" Joseph asked in dismay.

Unlike the stoneworks of the bridges approaching Toledo, this old wooden bridge was nothing to warrant confidence. The construction was flimsy and in bad repair. Its center span shook visibly in frightening ripples of vibration as the multitude of people poured out of Burgos and crossed the river.

"Follow me closely," Ibn Amram called.

As they pushed through the crowd, the throng of people swirled and closed again on their progress like a river of humanity. In the middle of the bridge, a small cart lodged a wheel in the loose boards, and the driver lashed his mule mercilessly.

The *plaza mayor* was down the street and to the left, but it would be impossible to reach it on horseback. In the noise and confusion of the numberless people, Ibn Amram rose up in his stirrups and motioned Joseph to the nearest stable. The stalls were almost empty, an unheard of event on a normal market day.

"Good fellow, can you tend our ponies?" Ibn Amram called out to the stable boy who lounged in the shadows of the last stall.

The boy reluctantly stepped forward to take the reins. "It will cost you one *mancuso*, father," he responded in gruff Castilian. "I haven't much else to do today, thanks to these cursed Karaites!"

Ibn Amram reached into his purse, found it empty and motioned to Joseph to locate the needed coin in his purse.

"Karaites?" he asked sharply. "What have they done?"

"What haven't they done, the fools?" the stable boy retorted. "They have spoiled our market day is what they have done, what with their fool expulsion!"

"Expulsion?" Ibn Amram shouted in complete disbelief. "They are expelled from Burgos? But how is it possible?"

The stable boy glanced back resentfully. "You are a one for questions, aren't you, father?" he muttered. "The *mancuso* is for fodder, not for folly. You'll find your answers in the streets!" He bent over a pail of malt, ignoring his customers entirely.

Ibn Amram hastily tightened his belt, drawing the empty money purse and the astrolabe further from sight.

"Come, Joseph," he said. "Something very grave is happening, and it is not necessarily for the good of the Jewish people."

He retraced his steps to the surging streets and elbowed his way across the seething mass of Karaites in the *plaza* to Las Huelgas, the summer palace of the King of Castile. With his footsteps echoing dully on the stone steps that led to the portico of the Moorish castle, Ibn Amram tried to assume the authoritative manners of a courtier.

"*Tengo prisa!*" he called out to the surprised guard. "I'm in a hurry!"

The guard was not flustered by the false bravado.

"Halt!" he commanded. "No one enters the king's palace."

His lance struck the floor tiles with a menacing thud.

"I have urgent business with His Highness," Ibn Amram declared. "It cannot wait."

The guard scoffed and spat on the stairs at the feet of the rabbi, much to the amusement of his fellows.

"*No tengo prisa*," he muttered. "I'm in no hurry."

Ibn Amram turned sharply on his heel.

"Come, Joseph," he said, drawing his student by the arm. "If we cannot enter the palace, we shall enter the king's court." They raced back down the marble steps. "If the guards will not let me see King Alfonso, I will see Alkabri instead. He is an old student of mine, and he will be able to explain the cause of this expulsion."

Like the doors to the palace, the doors to the court were likewise barred, but the guard did not refuse the rabbi who demanded an audience with the minister. The oak door swung open heavily on well-oiled hinges. Ibn Amram and Joseph entered the cool confines of a balustraded room. Sumptuous tapestries from Almeria hung from the walls, balancing the bold colors of the tiles.

"I told that guard outside to let no one enter," an irritated voice called out from behind a virtual mountain of court documents. "Throw them out at once!"

The bodyguard stepped forward, withdrawing his sword from its scabbard.

"Joseph!" Ibn Amram called out with mounting alarm. "You wouldn't evict your old friend, would you? It's Avraham of Tudela."

The guard paused in indecision while Joseph Hanasi delayed his next move. A stillness hung like a fog from the tapestries themselves. At last, the courtier deigned to rise from behind his heavy responsibilities.

"*Shalom aleichem*," the *Nasi* said in stiff formality to his unexpected guests. The words of welcome were not accompanied by a smile. "Why have you come to the capital at such a troubled time, Rabban Ibn Amram?"

The sage took a seat on the nearest cushion, and then he

motioned Joseph to sit beside him.

"These are troubled times, indeed," he agreed. "I meant to discuss with you the problems of the Karaites and enlist your aid in suggesting a *cherem* through the *beit din* of Burgos. Now the problem seems to have exploded in our faces with this tragic expulsion. What is happening, Joseph? What is the meaning of this?"

Joseph Hanasi retreated to the far side of his table, relying on his many documents as a bulwark against the insistence of his old teacher. As the secretary of the king, he wielded extraordinary power, and it would be futile to deny he was somehow involved in the expulsion.

"I will not be badgered," he muttered, his fingers drumming on the table in ill-disguised exasperation. "What do you mean by terming this expulsion tragic, Rabban Ibn Amram? Can you not see with your own two eyes that the Karaite problem had reached impossible proportions? There is only one answer now to their challenge of our authority. Expulsion!"

"I know, Joseph," Ibn Amram said in a placating voice. "I too have had my patience tried to the utmost. But why would the king resort to such an extreme solution? I intended to propose to you a *cherem hayishuv*. We would have left Karaite families where they were established but forbidden new families from entering our cities and towns. That would have been the path of tolerance, and I always thought King Alfonso was a model of tolerance. He safeguards all of our freedoms in Castile."

"The king has ears," Alkabri hissed, waving his hand to the narrow windows which carried frantic noises of unrest and upheaval from the street below. "When the king bends his ear, he is prepared to listen."

Ibn Amram caught his nuance immediately and rose to his feet.

"To whose mouth does he bend his ear, Joseph?" he asked. A pained look crossed his eyes. "Have you reverted to your hot-headed ways? I always had to curb your impetuous conclusions when you were a student in my *shiur*. Was it you who incited this tragic expulsion, Joseph Hanasi? Speak truthfully."

Alkabri drew himself up to his full height and stared back indignantly at his former teacher. He wouldn't give an inch.

"You do not hold the exclusive right to truth, Rabban Ibn Amram," he retorted. "If you cannot see the enemy within our midst, then happily I can."

Ibn Amram averted his gaze from the steely eyes of his sudden adversary and listened to the hubbub from the street.

"You are still the same, I can see," he said, casting a sidelong glace at the resolute chin of his former student.

"You wrong me, Rabban Ibn Amram!" Alkabri exclaimed, closing his manuscripts with a snap. "You wrong a scion of the House of David!"

"We cannot all aspire to be kings and princes of the land," Ibn Amram answered sharply. "I think it is time we all thought of the common man and tried to feel what he feels. Yes, these Karaites can be foolish madmen when they impose their ideas on us. But does that warrant an expulsion of all of them? Did the children I saw trudging in the street deserve that hardship?"

"What do you know from your peaceful *patio* in Tudela?" Alkabri exploded. "You might have experienced one or two isolated incidents of Karaite intolerance, but it is nothing to compare with the problem in Burgos and other cities of Castile. These heretics proselytize amongst our faithful. They disrupt our services. They mock our rabbis. They scuffle outside the *beit knesset* on *Shabbat*.

"I did not invite these blasphemers to persist in their evil ways. My men have warned them repeatedly. I have had numberless protestations from the *av beit din*. When the head of the Jewish Court cannot control them, I must step in! And now the latest rumor from the archbishop's palace indicated that some of these hotheads have even slandered us to the French monks. They hoped to see *us* expelled from Castile. Well, the trick has been turned on them!"

Ibn Amram nodded thoughtfully. "I did not realize events had reached such a serious turn here. I see more clearly that such violence could push you to the limits of endurance. But why would King Alfonso agree to such a drastic plan? It just doesn't make sense to me." He continued to stroke his beard in thought.

"The Karaites must take the bitter consequence of their own actions. They willingly chose to disregard my warnings," Alkabri fumed. "I act in accordance with royal policy which, in turn, is in agreement with Church mandates." His hand reached out to point to a document written in a crabbed hand before him. "As you can see, the Catholic Church has, with notable generosity, accepted our motives for the expulsion of our heretics."

He waved the document lightly, like a handkerchief, before the eyes of his visitors.

"You would go to our worst enemy to sort out a problem that exists within our faith?" Ibn Amram stormed. "That is incredible! I felt ill at ease contemplating the aid of King Alfonso. I weighed the merits of seeking help from a non-Jew to resolve our difficulties. At least, he sees himself as the Guardian of the Religions, all religions. But to ask the Church!"

"Do not act out your role of astonished surprise, Rabban Ibn Amram," Alkabri said softly, stepping down to the wash basin and the tray of sweetmeats. "I have seen your abilities at mock outrage in the past."

He daintily selected a sugared candy and offered the tray to his old master. Ibn Amram declined. The silent pause was painful, and Alkabri chose to break the somber still with more arguments in his favor.

"Besides, what right have you to call the Catholic Church our worst enemy? Have you forgotten my dear brother? He had the courage to travel to Africa on a mission of peace. But the caliph mocked his intentions and slew him. Would you deny that Almohad Islam is our worst enemy? Would you, Rabban Ibn Amram?"

"I do not underestimate the fierceness of the Almohad Berbers," Ibn Amram agreed. "But you are sidestepping the point. We should seek the help of neither Christianity nor Islam. The problem of the Karaites is a Jewish matter, and it should be solved by Jews."

He stepped away from the deep shadows under the balustrade and walked to the far side. Turning, he surveyed the impassive face of his old student in the clear sunlight that streamed through the eastern window.

"Who in the Church would agree to your plan, Joseph?" he asked. "And what did you have to give up to get this concession? Have you weighed the possible repercussions for our own people?"

"I have not survived the intrigue of the Court of Castile all these years without becoming a master of political subterfuge," Alkabri noted pridefully. As he noticed the look of wonderment cross the face of his visitor from Champagne, his smile became more sardonic. "The Bishop of Burgos has concurred with my decision. The two of us explained to the king that the Church simply could not endure heresy in any guise, or in any religion."

"And the concessions? Tell me what concession you made. You know in your heart that the Church has no interest in solving our problems. Why should the Church wish to see Judaism united against her? It is much better for the Christians to keep us weak and divided. If a dispute has simmered all these years between Rabbanite Jews who hold firm to the Talmud and Karaite heretics, then it can simmer for a few years more, in my opinion. We must fight them with words. With words, not with expulsion!"

He slumped back onto a cushion.

"Do not raise your voice to me," Alkabri responded coldly. "Feverish words are unbecoming to an old master. The politics of Castile are best handled by the young. Go back to your *patio* in Tudela. You must trust my authority and youthfulness and, above all, my intentions to serve the people better than anyone else."

"It is not your intentions I question but your methods," Ibn Amram answered slowly. "It is too simple to suggest that King Alfonso would passively fall into line with your wishes at the behest of the Church. There must be a better reason." He paused while he scrutinized the haughty brow of the Prince. "Could it be that the duties of Yaakov Ferrizuel have something to do with this hasty expulsion?"

"What do you mean?" Alkabri shot back, dropping a sweetmeat back onto the tray.

"I hear your brother Yaakov is very adept as Collector of Revenues for the king, and that he is very persuasive," Ibn Amram continued, discerning a chink in Alkabri's prideful armor. "I know he cannot be matched by any other tax collector in the realm."

Alkabri nodded defensively. "Thank you. Many appreciate my brother's skill."

Ibn Amram was now enjoying his line of reasoning. He stepped back to the tray and took the sweetmeat which he had previously refused.

"It is fortunate for King Alfonso that he has such a diligent tax collector in these troubled times. The Almohad caliph threatens to take over much of southern Spain, costing the king untold losses of tax revenue. A talented and diplomatic person such as Yaakov could prove invaluable in quelling the revolt against the king and keeping the taxes intact." He turned to Joseph Vitale and offered his young student a sweetmeat. "A man like Yaakov Ferrizuel could even strengthen the allegiance of Arab nobles to King Alfonso. They are men of letters, cultured and highly civilized. Like Alfonso, they encourage the study of science while they fear the caliph's primitive fanaticism."

"But they are Muslims all the same," Joseph Vitale ventured to say. "And Muslims all have the same goal."

"Not so, young man," Alkabri interjected, warming to the topic. "These Moorish kings have two conflicting loyalties. For one, they want the protection and the tolerance shown to them by King Alfonso, even though he is Christian. But a conflicting loyalty cannot be ignored. Because they are Muslims, they hear the call of Islam and that primitive urge to join arms with the caliph. He wants to conquer the entire peninsula with his bloody scimitar. If he could, he would kill King Alfonso tomorrow and seize all of Castile."

"Then what is stopping him?" Joseph Vitale asked. "Wouldn't the Moorish overlords ultimately betray Alfonso and side with the caliph?"

"Ah, that is where Yaakov Ferrizuel comes into the picture," Ibn Amram interjected. "If the Arab emirs ever did revolt against Alfonso, the Moorish conquest would begin in earnest. When Yaakov meets them, he tries to accommodate them. By pleasing them, he ensures their loyalty and a steady flow of gold *mancusos* from Andalusia to Castile."

"Yaakov is a sophisticated man and he deals with these kings on their level," Alkabri said with family pride. "He has no affinity for the unwashed bands of nomads in North Africa who only know the fierce message of the Koran."

"Yet the caliph is not as unwashed as we might think," observed Ibn Amram. "He has been successful in sowing the seeds of revolt in two of the principalities. They have agreed to back the caliph and stop sending their tribute money to the Christian King of Castile. If more of the emirs of Andalusia make that same fateful decision, King Alfonso could find his royal coffers empty. Then the caliph would prepare for his final crushing blow."

"Then that is why the caliph's troops are massed on the shore of Tunisia!" Joseph Vitale exclaimed. "Will the war come soon?"

"The decisive battle could be delayed for years, or it could happen tomorrow, depending on whether King Alfonso shows further signs of weakness," responded Ibn Amram.

"That brings our discussion to the curious role of Yaakov Ferrizuel in this delicate situation. Doesn't it, Alkabri?"

Alkabri stepped back to his documents.

"I am too busy for this idle speculation," he muttered, opening the first manuscript at his fingertips and trying to look deep in thought.

"You know, as I know, that Yaakov Ferrizuel is vitally important for the finances and security of Castile," said Ibn Amram. "King Alfonso could not afford to offend him. Nor could he afford to offend his powerful brother, knowing that both brothers are so active in supporting Jewish goals in Castile. Perhaps he would agree to one favor in return for another. Perhaps Yaakov assured King Alfonso that he would continue to collect tribute money from the southern emirates with all the persuasion and arm-twisting he can muster; and the king agreed to expel the Karaites!"

Alkabri buried his face in his hands. "You make it sound so sordid, Rabban Ibn Amram," he answered, crestfallen at his master's persistence and insight. "My brother Yaakov serves the king well. And what is good for Castile is good for our people. Surely, you will agree?"

"Yaakov serves King Alfonso all too well," Ibn Amram noted drily. "These are not easy times for the king. If I were in his place, perhaps I too would bend to a shameful act of intolerance to sustain the royal treasury."

"Why must you call the decision shameful?" Alkabri cried, humbled at last by the moral weight of Rabban Ibn Amram's words. "Neither Yaakov nor I thought the decision was shameful when we made it."

"The *cherem* could have been a better solution," Ibn Amram declared. "It would have taken longer, but it would not have heaped punishment on the innocent shoulders of the women and children of these heretics. I have already seen first-hand that one of the leading Karaite families is torn by conflicting dogmas. The son does not think as the father thinks. With time, we could have convinced them."

"We don't have the time," Alkabri groaned. "This is not a situation of black and white. There are infinite shades of gray. I would have thought that you of all people could see that complexity and come to my aid. It is not easy to be both a loyal and observant Jew and the secretary of a king."

"I do not fault you," Ibn Amram said gently, touching his old student on the shoulder. "I agree the responsibilities of the King's secretary are onerous. For that reason, you must not hasten to act on your own in times of trouble. You and Yaakov are not alone in this problem. There is an established *beit din* in this capital which is well qualified to judge these matters and make sound decisions. Politics without justice is a sorry business, indeed."

A light rapping sounded against the stout oak door. Voices could be heard arguing on the other side, as the guard apparently tried to turn away an unwelcome visitor.

"You must grant me an audience!" The high-pitched woman's voice was thin but very insistent. "Alkabri!" The rapping resumed with firmer resolve. "I know that you are in there, Alkabri!"

Upon hearing the woman address him in Arabic, Joseph Hanasi sprang to his feet and shrank back against the wall with a combination of fear and loathing.

"It is Al-Muellima," he whispered, "the widow of Al-Taras, that Karaite."

He began to silently gather up his documents to retreat into a more distant room. A few pages slipped from his fingers onto the floor, but he did not bend to retrieve them.

Further screams and bangs from the far side of the door distracted Ibn Amram. When he looked back, Alkabri was gone. The guard on their side of the doorway stood in the center of the floor unsure whether he should accost the woman or retreat with Alkabri to the next room. Ibn Amram shook his head in disbelief. He turned to the perplexed Joseph Vitale.

"This Karaite, Al-Taras, was remarkably successful in recruiting proselytes to the heresy throughout Toledo and the towns of the plain," he explained. "When he died, many of us thought his death would end his influence. How wrong we were! Yerucham Halevi has told me that Al-Taras' widow travels the byways of Castile, lecturing the Jewish communities. She has become as articulate a speaker as Al-Taras himself had been, according to Yerucham."

"She must be a fierce opponent," Joseph noted, listening to her gibes and dares from the far side of the door. With only the guard to accompany them, neither Joseph nor Ibn Amram was entirely sure of what to do.

"Such men the Rabbanites have!" Al-Muellima screamed in a mortal fury. Even the thick oak door could not block her voice. "I have seen mice with more courage to meet me! Are you afraid of my poor teeth, you Rabbanite mice?"

Her words tumbled out in a curious mixture of Arabic and Castilian that only served to heighten the mystery of the woman called The Teacher.

"Shall we fall into the clutches of the cat?" Ibn Amram asked his student, stepping towards the door. The guard took the hint and unlatched the door just wide enough to let the two men exit. He just as quickly slammed it shut again.

"Where is he?" Al-Muellima screamed in frenzy. "Where is Alkabri?"

"*Senora*, he is not disposed to see you now," Ibn Amram said softly. "I am sorry that today is a black day for the Karaites. It is not an event I would have initiated."

She stepped back, gathered up her veil more tightly across her face and surveyed her opponent.

"You are a Rabbanite like the rest," she declared. "It is enough that you will eat a warm meal tonight and sleep in a comfortable bed while I and my people roam the desolate roads of Castile in search of a homeland."

"Again, I must say that I grieve for your misfortune. No one should be homeless. If I had the power, I would resolve this matter in an entirely different way."

She paused to size him up more closely. Evidently, his sincere words had gone far to mollify her.

"You are a man of experience, I can see. For those who have never known suffering, it is easy to inflict suffering on others. But a man who has felt the keen edge of poverty can sense what others feel. Nevertheless, if my heart bleeds, can you feel the pain?"

"Madam, each heart bleeds alone, but we are one people," Ibn Amram answered. "I pray to the Master of the Universe that He may resolve this bitter dispute and reunite our disenchanted brethren with ourselves."

"You speak well," she commented, turning to go. "But it is mere words. I want you to feel what we feel today. If that princely Alkabri does not have the courage to see and feel what he has done, perhaps you might serve in his place."

"We will do our best," Ibn Amram answered, following her down the steps.

"Then proceed to the South Gate," she commanded. "Survey the misery which you Rabbanites have caused. Watch our exodus from our homeland and speculate on your own future as we pursue our wandering."

With a toss of her head, Al-Muellima disappeared into the crowd. A stiff wind from the north sent cirrus clouds scudding over the tops of the distant mountains. Pained by the discomfort around him on the south road, Ibn Amram continually shifted his gaze to the heavens, seeking a moment's solace in the eternal certainties of the sky.

"How long must we wait here?" Joseph asked timidly. "Dozens of Karaites pass by us in silence. They seem to know that we are Rabbanite Jews, and their eyes speak volumes."

"I am trying to seek an answer," Ibn Amram answered, gazing with compassion at a fatherless boy who guided his mother's rickety carriage. Most of the Karaites seemed ill-equipped for a long march. He wondered if they really knew how distant the sea was. Few people in that procession carried anything of lasting value. Their meager household effects were of the most basic variety.

Suddenly, in the midst of this sea of impoverished humanity, there rose a carriage of great ostentation.

"Such a carriage," Joseph breathed, pointing to the remarkable sight.

On the south road was a vehicle unlike any they had seen driven by the Karaite refugees. The lacquered wheels shone with a brilliance that held the dusty road in contempt. The golden tracery of the carriage would have made the wealthiest nobleman envious. And the horses, though tired, were well-fed and well-groomed. A postilion rode on the left horse guiding the team with an authoritative pull on the traces.

"It is surely the carriage of a prince," Ibn Amram declared. He stepped forward to get a clearer view of its trappings and its occupant.

Slowing to avoid a deep rut in the road, the carriage brought a wan face to Ibn Amram's eye level. The occupant reached forward briskly with a walking stick and tapped his coachman smartly to stop.

"Do I not know you, rabbi?" the pale-faced man asked.

"I am Avraham of Tudela, and this is Joseph the son of Rabbeinu Vitale of Laon," Ibn Amram answered. On an impulse, he extended his hand.

The pale-face man blinked momentarily at the unexpected gesture of friendliness, but he instantly extended his own hand in a formal handshake.

"I have heard of your fame from your many travels, Avraham," he said. "And I have heard of this boy's father."

He paused while more Karaites streamed by the carriage. They all nodded deferentially to the occupant.

"Yes," he said, returning his gaze to Ibn Amram. "As you can see, I am Joshua ben Judah. And these are my people." His gaze focused on Joseph. "If you gawk at this carriage, young man, I must insist that its princely trappings do not reflect my own simplicity. I suffer just as my people do. But they enjoy elevating my status in our dealing with the court. They take pride in this symbol of substance. I cannot fault them, even if I must wear the hat of a pampered prince. You understand, young man?"

"I think I do," Joseph responded. "And I am sorry that you are forced onto the road like this."

"It is a tragedy that it has come to this," Ibn Amram agreed. "I said that to Al-Muellima this morning."

"You have spoken to Al-Muellima?" Joshua ben Judah said, warming more to his counterpart on the road. "I would not have thought that a Rabbanite leader would wish to speak with her at this time."

"At this time, or at any time," Ibn Amram countered. "We must never close off our dialogue, Joshua. The rift is never so serious that we cannot keep speaking to one another."

The old man smiled back in return.

"Your wisdom belies your years, Avraham," he answered. "I wish times were different. There have been mistakes on both sides. I regret that some of my followers have been very bellicose. Their arguments have disaffected many of the Jews we wished to reach."

Ibn Amram's nod was knowing.

"I have experienced the brunt of that zeal myself!"

"Then I wish you well and I apologize for our mistakes."

Joshua ben Judah withdrew his hand and tapped his driver again to continue.

"Wait!" Ibn Amram shouted, and stepped forward to catch up with the carriage. It slowed again while the horses snorted with impatience. "My decision is sudden and we both might regret it, but I would like to invite you to my home, Joshua. Yes, it is improbable at this last minute. But I want you to know that it is never too late to begin a dialogue. Tudela is on your way to the sea, if that is where your expulsion must take you."

"It is indeed the sea that will take us to safety," Joshua ben Judah agreed. "I anticipate three weeks in the port of Tarragona to arrange passage for all of my followers to Jerusalem."

"You may stay with me on the way. Take the road east and follow the river. It is your most direct route to Tarragona and a stopover in Tudela is no inconvenience to you."

"But your wife?" Joshua ben Judah asked politely.

"My wife will be honored as I am honored to have you as a guest," Ibn Amram said firmly. "I will ride ahead and prepare our house for you and your family. Is it agreed, Joshua?"

A long pause followed while the Karaite leader pondered the kindness of this stranger. Like his namesake, Avraham went out of his way to sit by his tent and invite strangers for a meal. It was an uncomplicated act of piety in a time of great complexity. Joshua ben Judah saw the simplicity of the gesture and agreed.

"But before you leave, Avraham, you must tell me one thing. You are well versed in the rules of the stars?"

Ibn Amram nodded hesitantly. He could almost anticipate what was to follow.

"Then I have come to wonder if this hard-heartedness which has come to our Castile, in which brother fights brother, and the stronger evicts the weaker, is not symptomatic of that rumor."

"Rumor? Which rumor?" asked Ibn Amram.

Joshua ben Judah leaned further out of the carriage so that his voice would not carry to unlearned people.

"The rumor of a coming darkness. They say that the light of the sun will be blotted from the sky. Darkness will bring a cold wind that will sweep all life from Castile. They say that nothing will matter any more. There will be no right and no wrong, no good and no bad. Only death and destruction. It is a frightening rumor at which we try to laugh, but still it is whispered by the poor people of the land. If the darkness is coming, I am glad that I have rescued my people in time. Will we be safe in Jerusalem? Will the darkness reach that far?"

"This is a rumor I soon will have to combat," Ibn Amram admitted. "The time is not yet right, but I can assure you that I will not sit by idly while unprincipled rogues make a heavenly darkness into a justification for moral blindness."

"Bravo, Avraham," Joshua ben Judah applauded. "Your words have cheered me already, although I have no guess as to how you could uproot such a firmly held belief. Perhaps we can pursue this line of thought when we meet in Tudela. Until then!"

His walking stick tapped the driver's shoulder, and the horses bolted forward in pursuit of the open road.

The clouds from the north had reached them while the conversation occurred. Now a large shadow passed across the landscape as the clouds raced further south. Ibn Amram glanced up at the feeble sunlight which attempted to pierce the darkening clouds. The last vision of Joshua ben Judah troubled him. The man was so optimistic, even in the darkest moment of expulsion. He wondered if this leader were not merely a good actor, putting on a show of false bravado. Or perhaps, the Karaite had plumbed the mysteries of Torah and come face to face with tranquil wisdom? He wondered if this enlightened scholar truly thought that any mortal could outrun a solar darkness. He turned back to Joseph, but his heart was heavy. A pain pinched his side like a knife.

"Let's return to the stable, my boy," he said. "We can outpace a band of weary travellers by almost two days on the trip to Tudela. That will give us time to prepare the house for a final meal with these wanderers."

"I never would have thought your mission to Toledo would lead us to such a strange conclusion of the Karaite affair," Joseph admitted. "*Gam zu letovah*. This too, is for the good."

Ibn Amram nodded. "It strains our happiness to the utmost to see our own brethren treated so harshly. Still, even in the worst moments, we must repeat that this, too, is for the good."

Though aware that all things in the world are controlled by the Will of the Almighty, Ibn Amram returned to the ponies with a very heavy heart. Many of the certainties he had taken for granted for years were severely challenged by his fellow Jews' insensitive treatment of the Karaites.

Heat and a heavy heart were painful afflictions on that dog day of summer in Burgos. Ibn Amram returned to the court of Joseph Hanasi to mention his finding and bid his former student farewell. Alkabri tried his utmost to make Ibn Amram and Joseph stay at his home for supper, but Ibn Amram, with sober-faced civility, declined. It was too difficult for him to think of enjoying the luxury of Alkabri's home while his dispossessed brethren jammed the streets.

They returned to the stable and remained there in the relative coolness until evening. They planned a more comfortable journey at night, once the hot sun of summer had set. Ibn Amram's mind was sorely troubled.

CHAPTER FIVE

On the Edge of Accord

TUDELLA, NAVARRE
SUMMER, 1139

THE SAGE AND HIS STUDENT RODE IN SILENCE FOR LONG stretches, listening to the occasional cries of the night birds and watching the fluttering silent shadows of bats in the night. Ibn Amram's eyes searched the skies for the reassuring, twinkling lights which he had come to recognize as easily as the landmarks of his many roads. Joseph was sorry to see his master struggling with a difficult problem, but he personally could not feel the pain which Ibn Amram felt. That was the blessing of youth.

The only sound to break the silence was a restless water bird on the Ebro River. The pony snorted as the road dipped, but the sage did not notice. Joseph caught sight of him on occasion striking his chest with his fist and sighing aloud. The young man decided not to speak. Ibn Amram glanced up again at the night sky and took note of the position of the moon.

"Soon it will be the second vigil of the night," he told Joseph. "Even when the sun is absent from the sky, we proceed in a world controlled by time. The mouth cannot speak and the ears cannot hear and the toiler cannot seek wisdom until he has clarified his soul. I think I have pierced one of *Koheleth's* mysteries tonight, Joseph! In all this blackness, I have found the flicker of light. Do you remember when we came across the passage, 'All his life he eats in darkness'?"

"Certainly. You were much troubled by it. Have you come to an understanding now?"

"Everything is under the dominion of the sun, except the soul of man. I believe that 'all his life he eats in darkness' means that man toils because the sun controls time and all things of this world. All things except for the timeless soul."

A weight seemed to fall from Ibn Amram's shoulders. He threw back his head and breathed deeply of the cool night air.

"Yes, we have made excellent progress tonight," he sighed with satisfaction. "Let's leave the road and make camp by that copse of trees. At last, I have calmed my mind. Now we can rest our weary bodies."

The next two days of the trip back to Tudela passed much like the first, with Ibn Amram taking a more optimistic perspective on his challenging *Koheleth* commentary. He compared his progress to a watershed in the uplands. From that point, the rivers would now flow in a different direction, gaining volume as they flowed. By the time they reached Tudela, he was fortified with many new ideas on *Koheleth* which he wished to explore with his father-in-law.

Little time was spent in providing Yerucham Halevi with a briefing on his trips to Toledo and Burgos. Ibn Amram was simply too engrossed in his new avenues of speculation to turn his thoughts to political matters. He and Yerucham Halevi sat down practically as soon as greetings had been exchanged. Their copies of *Koheleth* were opened to the relevant chapter, and soon they were immersed in their analysis.

"I see I won't have a second to bend my husband's ear until he rouses himself from his studies for *Minchah*," Naomi said with an indulgent laugh.

She busied herself with the preparations for her guests. The cook had already sent her strongest kitchen boys to the marketplace for extra provisions. Luisa was assigned to the *sala grande* to polish the brass trays and dust the fading cushions.

On Friday morning, Ibn Amram rose early to ride out and greet his guests. As he and Joseph prepared to leave, he was grateful to see his father-in-law coming toward him.

"Will all his followers be staying within the town walls?" Yerucham Halevi asked, somewhat apprehensively.

"No, Joshua ben Judah mentioned to me that most will encamp on the river bank just north of the main gate. His assistant will proceed alone on the road to Tarragona to requisition a ship. Only Joshua ben Judah's immediate family will stay with us."

"Perhaps it is just as well. I heard some words of rebuke directed towards you at the *beit medrash* yesterday morning for this charitable gesture. I couldn't altogether blame old Shlomo for expressing his abhorrence of the Karaites. But some of the younger men were too hot-headed for my liking. They rallied to the outraged cries of the old man and made some bloodthirsty threats."

"Let them," Ibn Amram responded gently. "Our Sages have taught us not to rejoice when our enemy falls or to let our heart be glad when he stumbles."

"I agree, Avraham. But tongues will still wag. Your motive is pure, and I will not have your name sullied. When Joshua ben Judah comes to Tudela, he will be my guest as well as yours. Old Shlomo and his sons will not dare whisper about me!"

A wordless interchange passed between the two men as they stood in the *sala grande*. Ibn Amram stepped forward and threw his arms around his father-in-law.

"Come, Joseph," Ibn Amram said briskly, wiping his sleeve across his eyes. "Let's mount and ride to the hill. We can greet Joshua there."

They did not have long to wait. Already signs of a vast sea of people stretched across the flat plain south of the river. The shepherds, in ill-concealed irritation, were driving their flocks out of the way towards the uplands. But a single freeman on the banks of the river was content to lean on his sheep crook beside his ramshackle cabin and survey the busy tide of people.

The sumptuous carriage was easily visible beneath the trees. Ibn Amram raised his arm and waved. A veiled woman retreated from sight within its darkness, but Joshua ben Judah stepped down from the carriage and waved back.

"I hope your trip so far has been uneventful," Ibn Amram said. "Your people have enough water here. Do they have enough food?"

"Thank you, yes, good friend," Joshua ben Judah answered. "There is no problem at present with money. The king in his wisdom has chosen not to confiscate all our properties as some of his advisors had apparently instructed. I understand he had decided to turn much of our property over to the ecclesiastical domain. It is a pious gesture of a pious king. And if we did not quite get fair market value for our possessions, at least the few coins we received were better than nothing."

"You are irrepressible, Joshua ben Judah," Ibn Amram commented, noting the man's twinkling eyes. "A lesser man would see the hand of fate in this misfortune."

The freeman had ventured nearer to the magnificent carriage. He stood open-mouthed in astonishment. Behind him, a barefoot child peeked from behind his legs at the unexpected sight.

"I am afraid we will be the sensation of this valley soon," Joshua said with a knowing nod. "Shall we follow the road to Tudela and escape their stares?"

"Yes, that is why we are here," Ibn Amram answered.

He dismounted and handed the reins to Joseph to tie behind the carriage. Joshua ben Judah stepped up on the wooden rail lightly and turned around to offer Ibn Amram a helping hand into the carriage. The same coachman as he had seen at the start of the trip stared stoically ahead. Joshua touched the driver's sleeve with his hand, and the horses pressed forward.

Joshua ben Judah reached into a capacious sack at his feet and withdrew a handful of ripe figs for Ibn Amram and Joseph.

"Take it, please! I insist!" he entreated, selecting the choicest to put in the hands of his hosts.

The carriage raced along the rutted road, jostling them into a lengthy silence. Joseph looked across the carriage to Joshua's wife and daughter, sitting in the far corner. The two women hid behind their veils, only whispering between themselves. Joshua ben Judah's father ignored them, preferring instead to chant a melody to himself. Joseph thought he recognized some of the words and asked him if the phrases were from *Tehillim*. The old man looked up flustered, smiled at Joseph while he retraced his steps through the words, then proceeded again in a low voice. He clutched a Torah scroll tightly to his chest during the entire trip.

They listened to the coachman's shrill commands as the horses slowed to ford a muddy creek. A jumble of stones plunged the carriage into shadow as the road dipped down to the creek. The boulders were the bleak remnants of the siege of Tudela two decades earlier and a mute reminder that the Moors had released their hold on this outpost with great reluctance.

As the wheels ground into the mud, shifting the balance of the carriage to a precarious angle, none of the occupants noticed three figures rise from behind the rubble. A sharp cry of pain and the thudding rattle of a stone at his feet brought Ibn Amram immediately to his fullest attention.

Joshua ben Judah toppled from his cushion, clutching his

ear. Blood trickled from between his fingers. The coachman, sensing the extreme danger, whipped his horses into a wild gallop, but more stones struck the carriage, bringing it to an abrupt halt.

The women fell upon Joshua with screams of alarm, shielding his body from further blows.

"Ruffians! Murderers!" Joshua's father cried hoarsely and staggered out the door on the far side, his Torah scroll still pressed tightly to his body.

Ibn Amram stared up in amazement at the source of their attack.

"Why, they're only children!" he exclaimed. "I can't believe it."

He clambered out of the carriage and shook his fist at them.

"How dare you do this?" he shouted.

The eldest boy stood frozen, his hand raised with another missile. With his hood thrown back on his shoulders, Ibn Amram's familiar face was unmistakable.

"Please get out of the way," the boy warned. "I have good aim, and I can finish off the hateful Karaite with this stone!"

"You will do nothing of the kind to my guest!" Ibn Amram stamped his foot in anger.

The other two boys immediately dropped their stones and slid down the far side of the boulder to run for safety. Their leader stared at his dwindling forces but would not give ground.

"Do not tempt me, rabbi," he shouted back, swinging his arm with a menacing skill. "I haven't yet finished what I set out to do."

At that moment, the youth caught sight of the old man with the scroll and took deliberate aim. The stone struck Joshua's father on the shin, sending him sprawling in the sand by the side of the creek. His fall was all the heavier because he did not drop the Torah scroll to save himself.

Eyes blazing, Ibn Amram marched quickly across the

stone rubble. The youth, now without the comfort of a heavy rock in his hand, watched in wild-eyed wonder as the rabbi approached.

"Do you think it is a *mitzvah* to hurt an unprotected old man?" Ibn Amram thundered. "Do you think I will deal with you now? You are wrong! When you approach the Almighty with your *viduy*, He alone will weigh your sin. It is too late for me to deal with you. *Yom Kippur* is fast approaching!"

The boy cowered at Ibn Amram's feet, but the rabbi would offer him no solace. He turned and hastened back to the creek where the old man was struggling to regain his footing without dropping the scroll.

"Joseph, if you please," he called out to his student.

Joseph Vitale gripped the man with a steady hand and raised him gently to his feet. Again, the recitation of *Tehillim* caught Joseph's ear.

"I am ashamed of this ugly welcome," Ibn Amram said to Joshua ben Judah when he reached the carriage.

"Let it be so," Joshua ben Judah quipped. "My opponents have always accused me of being hard-headed, and now that hard head seems to have saved me."

His wife glanced up anxiously at Ibn Amram while she adjusted a strip torn from her robe around her husband's head.

"I admire your courage, Joshua," Ibn Amram said. "When we get home, I will apply a poultice to your cuts. It will help ease the swelling."

He reached forward and checked to see that the bandage was tight enough to staunch the flow of blood. Joshua ben Judah settled back onto the cushions and closed his eyes. Slowly, the carriage began its final leg of the dismal journey.

"It is more and more as the rumor suggests," Joshua ben Judah said sadly. "Brother fights brother in our land. I never anticipated that a boy in your community would be so moved to hatred. And I have seen the same hatred demonstrated in some of my young followers."

The two opposing leaders fell into silence as the carriage entered the winding streets of the Jewish quarter and traced the labyrinthine twists and turns which led to the courtyard of Ibn Amram and Yerucham Halevi. Naomi greeted them at the gate.

Shabbat was fast approaching. So many last minute details had to be looked after, but secretly, Ibn Amram wondered if his hospitality towards a Karaite would again result in extinguished candles. The horses were stabled, and the grand carriage sat proudly in the shady courtyard. No voices whispered from the iron tracery of the gates. But Ibn Amram was sure that neighbors clucked their disapproval from the darkness of the windows overlooking the patio.

Ibn Amram led his guest to Beit Aaron Hatzaddik for *Kabbalat Shabbat* with dignity and pride. Seated between Yerucham Halevi and Ibn Amram, the Karaite leader watched the service with fascination. The scornful sneers forming on the faces of his fellow congregants withered with the merest glance from Ibn Amram.

When they returned home, Naomi joined them in the sitting room. Ibn Amram's gaze lingered on the many candles which Naomi had placed throughout the room, as was her custom for the holy Sabbath.

"I must not mince my words with you, Joshua," he said simply. "A bitter taste was left recently when a misguided youth from your followers entered our home. Within a few moments, nearly all the candles had lost their light to his nimble fingers."

Joshua sat down and glanced across at the candles with undisguised joy.

"I know that boy. He is encamped with my followers even now by the river. He has on more than one occasion confessed this type of activity to me. You know, I believe he acted in what he thought was good faith."

"And you, Joshua?" Ibn Amram asked. His hand was poised near the *Kiddush* cup, delaying the formal entry of the

Sabbath into his home until he had determined what his guests would do. "Are you unhappy with the *Shabbat* lights?"

Joshua ben Judah laughed merrily, and his aged father joined in the good humor. Ibn Amram stared back quizzically.

"Put your mind at ease, Avraham," Joshua ben Judah said. "I will not race through your home snuffing out the candles. In fact, my followers know my position, and it is not at all like the benighted position of Anan ben David. Candles are part of the joy of *Shabbat*. I teach my people that we must have them."

"That is a relief," Ibn Amram sighed, and he raised the cup.

The meal was begun, and as they lingered over the many delicacies which Naomi had prepared, the Rabbanite Jews at that table were able to see that Joshua ben Judah represented a far different authority from the rigid fundamentalism of Anan ben David.

It seemed as though he differed with strict Karaite policy on almost everything. When the subject turned to marriage, he became especially animated.

"You mean that you do *not* uphold the Karaite rulings on forbidden marriages?" Yerucham Halevi asked in utter surprise. "I thought it was a cornerstone of Anan's teachings."

"It *is* a cornerstone of Anan's teachings," Joshua ben Judah agreed with a nod. "But it has proven an impossible idea. Our communities have never been huge. If I we accept Anan's principle that all people related by marriage are to be considered blood relatives, you can imagine how difficult it would be to find a legal marriage in our small community! You can see the foolish results of such a ban. Even now I am drafting my next treatise on the subject. I think I will settle for a set of six regulations."

"It is so much work, with doubtful reward, to create these special regulations," Ibn Amram mused. "How much easier it would be if you would accept the Talmud and the regulations on marriage which are specified in it."

"But then I would not be a Karaite," Joshua countered,

"and there would be no further need for our opposition. Oh, you are a worthy opponent, Avraham! How I wish you would reconsider and make your way with me to Jerusalem! You'll think about it again, eh?"

Their discussion was suddenly cut short by an imperious pounding on the outer door. The noise echoed through the room, scarcely subdued by the few tapestries on the walls. Yerucham Halevi leaped to his feet.

"Who has come at this time to disturb our *Shabbat?*" he cried. "Surely your followers would not venture into the town."

Ibn Amram strode to the door and opened it a crack, but the man on the other side pushed it wide open.

"In the name of the king, all rise," he barked.

Three guards from his contingent stepped into the room.

"What is the meaning of this, commander?" Ibn Amram asked, stepping back to make room for the soldiers. "Do you not know that this is our holy Sabbath?"

"The king's command will be done," the commander answered stiffly. "Who amongst you arrived in that carriage?"

"Commander, you have no right to interrogate my guests," said Ibn Amram. He stepped forward, but the guards shouldered him aside.

"Your business is not with this gentleman, commander," Joshua ben Judah said in a clear voice. "If you have business here, it is with me."

He rose to his feet and stepped clear of the table. The commander stepped closer to note his height and features.

"Then you must be the Al-Furaj Furgan who leads this group of Karaites. My men stopped your lieutenant on the road, and he has named you as their leader."

"The identification is correct," Joshua ben Judah answered in Arabic. "Or by my Hebrew name, you may know me as Joshua ben Judah. The man is one and the same."

"By orders of the king, Alfonso of Castile, and his trusted liege, Garcia Ramirez of Navarre, you are ordered to stop forthwith the pillage and plunder of the realm," the commander intoned.

For a brief moment, the customary smile on Joshua ben Judah's face disappeared, and a nervous tic twitched his left eyelid.

"There must be some mistake, commander," Joshua objected.

"Yes, this surely is mistaken identity, commander," Yerucham Halevi agreed, rising as well from the table. "Our guests have been with us all evening. There could not possibly be any chance that they could take anything from the realm."

The commander turned slightly to gesture to his men waiting outside.

"More to the point, there has been a plundering of the gardens of Tudela. The king will not permit this abuse."

Three soldiers entered, dragging two hapless young men and a small child into the room. They threw them at the feet of Ibn Amram.

"These are your guests?" the commander asked vindictively.

Two strangers looked up at the rabbi with stark fear in their eyes. Spilling from the folds of their garments were a few overripe fruits and vegetables left from the harvest.

"Please, it was just a few apples!" the little boy begged, raising his hands to Ibn Amram. He cringed and moved back quickly when one of the soldiers aimed a kick at him.

Ibn Amram was momentarily distracted by the soldier. He opened his mouth to stop him, but he was diverted by the sight of the youth in the corner. It was no stranger. For an instant, his mind raced like the wind. Ibn Amram wanted to shout out Yissaschar Rikuv's name in surprise and aggravation. He wanted to ask the boy what trouble he had now managed to find. He wanted to turn to the Karaite leader and point to this living proof that the Rikuv family had gone too far.

Instead, Ibn Amram swallowed his anger and managed to regain his voice.

"I will thank you not to kick anyone in my home, soldier! Yes, these are my guests. You certainly came to the right door. If their actions have offended you, I will take full responsibility."

The Commander of the Guard was unnerved by Ibn Amram's involvement in the affair and scratched his ear in thought.

"These boys are thieves, learned doctor," he said harshly. "And if they are thieves and you are responsible, then it seems to me that you are a thief, too!"

He looked back at his lieutenant for encouragement in this startling conclusion. The lieutenant nodded grimly. Ibn Amram shook his head placidly, motioning to Joshua to remain silent.

"If you have a moment, commander, I can explain to you why there has been no crime," said Ibn Amram.

He turned to the youngest Karaite who had edged back to the wall.

"Where did you find your apples, my child?" he asked. "Were they under a tree?"

The boy needed no time to remember.

"No, sir. If you please, they were at the top of the hill, where the path leads down to the house."

Ibn Amram turned to the youth who had hidden a cabbage in his robe.

"And you, young man. Was the cabbage in a furrow?"

The boy hung his head in shame.

"It was, sir. But it was such a tiny cabbage down at the end of the furrow, and no one seemed to care about it."

"Just as I suspected," Ibn Amram declared, turning back to the querulous commander. "The fruit and vegetables are ownerless property. We Jews consider such produce as *hefker*, perfectly free to anyone who finds it. As they found these items in Jewish gardens of our quarter, they were committing no crime in taking them. There is no thievery when the owner disclaims ownership."

"Do not mock my judgment," the commander warned.

Incensed at this turn of events, he whirled around to stare down at the three youngsters. For a moment, he was at a loss for words.

"In the name of the king, it must be thievery," he snapped. "Even if it was found in the corner of a Jew's garden."

"No, it is simply *hefker*," Ibn Amram reiterated placidly. "We are Jews of the Realm, and this law of Judaism cannot be subrogated by any other law of the land. We do not reap the corners of our fields, and we do not gather fallen fruit. We leave them for the poor and the stranger. Even in the diaspora, by rabbinic enactment. King Alfonso understands this full well. That is why he is Guardian of the Religions. May his years be blessed!"

"May his years be blessed!" the commander instantly responded, snapping to attention. He sensed that the matter was slipping out of his control, but he was not prepared to lose face in the presence of his men.

"The king's will is done. But I will thank you, learned doctor, to keep your *hefker* out of my sight while these Karaites pass through our realm. And the sooner they leave, the better!"

With that vague thrust of his authority, he turned on his heel and left. With a jangle of lances, the soldiers followed him into the darkness. As the sound of their footsteps died out in the cobblestone street, Joshua ben Judah breathed a sigh.

"By my soul, I must thank you for your intercession, Avraham," he said fervently. "I do not know what I would have said if that soldier had questioned me."

A sense of irony crossed Ibn Amram's mind at this convergence of doctrine and practicality.

"I have only touched on the matter of *peah* in this brief conversation with the soldiers," he answered. "But it is a matter of great significance. In fact, the second tract of the *Mishnah* is entirely dedicated to it."

Joshua ben Judah fell silent at this news, and Ibn Amram turned to the boys.

"What are we to do with you, Yissaschar?" he asked.

"I am sorry, rabbi," the youth answered. "We were hungry, and we thought no one would notice. I did not think to answer the angry soldier with an explanation from the Torah. But then, I did not think that there was much to explain."

Ibn Amram smiled again. "Oh, there are pages and pages in the *Gemara* with which a true student of Torah can learn to explain more and more. It is wise to know such important facts. But then, no one has permitted you to learn this wisdom."

"Perhaps one day, Avraham," Joshua ben Judah interjected, realizing how neatly the lesson turned on the validity of the Oral Law. "Perhaps one day my followers will learn what you learn."

"I hope it will be in our days," Ibn Amram answered, returning to the table of pastries. "Perhaps one day you will explain to me why Karaites do accept certain points of the Oral Law while rejecting the rest."

He paused, and with the same wily grasp of political realities which Alkabri had shown, he extended the plate of sweetmeats to his opponent.

"It is not the right time to answer this question, Avraham," Joshua ben Judah answered, glancing meaningfully at his three young followers. "I must have time to frame my thoughts concisely."

"This dreadful expulsion has left no one with enough time!" Naomi interjected, much to the surprise of everyone, especially Joshua ben Judah's reticent wife. "Tonight, the king's soldiers have thrown Karaite children at our feet and unjustly accused them of thievery. Who knows what tomorrow will bring? If they turn on the Karaites now, they may next turn on our community."

"That is true," Yerucham Halevi said, nodding in agreement with his daughter. "The fanatical monks in the realm will not be happy until they are rid of us."

"And while the world acts out its insolence, the children

are always the first to suffer," Naomi continued. She gestured to Yissaschar with open arms. "You said you were hungry, Yissaschar, and you once were our guest. Our table was adequate then, and it is adequate now. You are welcome to remain. I have a spare room that would suit your needs."

She dropped her arms while her thoughts returned to her son. She wondered if he had a comfortable room like the one she now was offering Yissaschar. She wondered if people in Baghdad treated him well and made sure he was well fed. So many questions flooded her mind, but no answers were possible.

Yissaschar turned away and returned to the side of his two young companions.

"No, I must go with my people. I love the holy Torah, and I must be true to my faith."

As he left the room, a pall of embarrassment settled on the remaining guests.

CHAPTER SIX

The Cluniac Threat

BURGOS, CASTILE
AUTUMN, 1139

A BRISTLING STILLNESS HUNG IN THE AIR ON THAT HARSH AUTUMN day. In spite of the commanding location of the royal palace at the top of the highest hill, not a breath of wind shifted the deadening heat of the chamber where the king held session with his court.

Don Garcia rose to his feet. Tall and masterful, the king's most trusted advisor sighed pointedly and walked away from the massive table. The hand of Alkabri, the King's Secretary, paused in mid-sentence.

Don Garcia gazed out past the delicate columns of the portico to survey the blazing blue sky. In spite of his apparent nonchalance, he knew that the eyes of Archbishop Bernard were rivetted to his back. But more importantly, he knew that the eyes of King Alfonso, his life-long student, were following his movements, waiting for a sign to resume the discussion.

The advisor needed this precious moment to marshall his thoughts. More and more French monks had taken positions within the Spanish Church, achieving the inevitable cross-appointments to King Alfonso's council. The young king was learning the hard lesson that a royal council crafted by monks from Cluny put a distinctly French accent to the agenda. Brushing away a speck of dust from the black sleeves of his gown, Don Garcia surveyed his opponents on the opposite side of the table.

On this hot morning, King Alfonso was perspiring profusely, from both the weather and the aggravation of dealing with his stubborn French advisors. His nerves were clearly frayed.

"I have had enough of Church matters, Bernard," King Alfonso said resolutely. "This is *my* Palatine Council!"

Archbishop Bernard rose heavily to his feet. The broad table groaned under his weight as he leaned forward. His stern gaze sent his countryman, the notary Matthew, into a frenzy of nervous chewing on the end of his scribe's quill.

"None of us can turn back the march of time, Alfonsus Augustus," the archbishop declared solemnly.

His voice lingered with a sonorous caress on the imperial title which had been granted to Alfonso just four years before. He expected that the grand title in Latin would be an emollient for the king's frustration.

"Your grandfather began the change many years ago when he invited the first monk of Cluny to bring a breath of fresh air to the dead chambers of the Spanish Church," the archbishop continued. "I needn't remind you that he was a pious admirer of Abbot Hugh of Cluny, and he asked my master to establish the first of many Cluniac monasteries in this realm. Every monastery has flourished under his and your continuing support, Alfonsus Augustus!"

"There is more to this meeting than Church affairs," Alfonso muttered with quiet intensity. His eyes motioned to his advisor.

"You have been insisting on Church matters while the most urgent matters of state hang in the balance," Don Garcia said flatly. "His Majesty has a call for the defense of a beleaguered fortress. Look! The Commander of the Guard must wait here while you dabble in Church matters!"

Even the Legate Paul blanched at the intensity of this outburst. The commander, Don Umar, stood stoically, revealing no emotion.

"Calatrava is under siege, Bernard," King Alfonso interjected. "Do you know what that means? Commander Don Umar has no time to waste. If you waste his time and mine, you cannot save a single Christian soul in that fortress. They will all be killed by Arab raiders!"

Archbishop Bernard sat back in his cushioned chair, ignoring the call for speed. He motioned to the Legate Paul. A paper passed wordlessly between them. The notary stopped scribbling as Bernard read the message. It disappeared into the capacious folds of his garments. He leaned forward to address the king again.

With haughty disdain, King Alfonso ignored the archbishop and fingered the astrolabe which lay on the table in front of him. On several occasions, the archbishop had glowered at the offending instrument, but he had refrained from commenting on it. The astrolabe was a visible sign of the worldly influence of Don Garcia on King Alfonso's enlightened court. Peter the Venerable, Abbot of Cluny, had recognized this threat of science and reason and had recently preached angry sermons against the false doctrine of the Moorish and Jewish stargazers.

The king's astrolabe sat as mute testimony to the fact that the Cluniac monks did not as yet fully control his court. The young king pushed it away from him, to a position of greater prominence at the center of the table.

For a moment, it seemed that the anger of the king had subsided. Then the papal legate rose to his feet.

"If it please Your Majesty," Paul said, clearing his throat for the coming invective. "I took a personal vow from the Pope to expunge the many faces of sin in all the lands that I visit. Truly, there are not enough waking hours in the day to serve that divine and monumental task. I saw most clearly the heresy of the cursed Karaite Jews, who cling to their testament of Torah while denying our testament. When you signed the decree for their expulsion, I believed that a momentum was finally building to start the holy work of Our Father in Rome.

"Now the Karaites are gone, banished across the Mediterranean where they can contemplate their piteous future in the company of Arab infidels. But their departure has still left a major problem unanswered in Castile."

Bernard grimaced, fearing that this intemperate envoy from Rome would ruin what little control he exerted over the king. As for Alfonso, the effect of Paul's words was like throwing oil on the fire of his anger. Bernard's sharp eyes noted the darkening crimson at the king's temples, contrasting the deathly pallor of his cheeks. These were signs the newcomer Paul could not read.

Bernard tugged insistently at the legate's sleeve to stop his talk. But Paul ignored him, casting a disdainful look at Alkabri, expressing with one glance his utter abhorrence of the cursed Jew. In response, the Secretary merely glanced away, busying himself with his royal documents.

"It is time to take the next step, Alfonsus Augustus," Paul intoned, trying to mimic the archbishop's smooth tones. "The Karaites are gone, but the Jews of Castile remain! They, too, have their testament of Torah and an Oral Law which daily teaches them to mock us. Is that not so?"

His eyes fastened again on the Secretary, but Alkabri refused to look up. Archbishop Bernard, seeing that too much was being attempted in a single day, pulled at Paul's sleeve with greater vigor. Again, the legate ignored him, shaking his arm free of the restraint.

"Take the next step, King Alfonso," he urged. "Dictate and

sign the decree banishing the hateful Jews from your realm." He pointed to Matthew, who sat with his quill poised for writing. "Get ready to write, Matthew!"

"Another Frenchman to infuriate me," the king shot back angrily.

Don Garcia caught Paul's attention. "Do not press too hard, Paul," he said. "His Majesty is sick to death of the way Cluniac monks have tried to reshape his Council and dictate his decisions."

"It is the influence of the Jewish secretary," Paul answered in taunting insolence. "I have heard of this Alkabri. A cultured Jew of the south, who has rubbed shoulders with the decadent emirs of Andalusia. He can curry favors with his charm and his money. Small wonder you balk at signing the decree when your own Secretary attends the Synagogue of Satan!"

Alkabri, a master at weathering the rivalries of the Castilian court, sat in stony-faced silence. Don Umar sat transfixed at his side. His eyes widened as he saw the king suddenly raise his sword in fury.

Don Garcia stood up suddenly and faced Alfonso. A deadly calm pervaded the Royal Advisor's entire being, spilling over to his young master. The tip of the sword had risen high over the legate's head and remained there, trembling.

Now it stopped. Don Garcia calmly extended his right hand, neither motioning to continue nor gesturing for an end. The dark cloud seemed to pass from Alfonso's face with difficulty. The dire moment passed, and Alfonso released his steely grip on the sword hilt.

"You speak to the Guardian of All Religions," Don Garcia warned darkly. "Your words have offended His Majesty."

The legate fell to his knees and crossed himself abjectly.

"My words are words of love for Your Majesty," Paul answered humbly, crossing himself again for good measure. "Please put away your sword, Alfonsus Augustus. I love you as my Christian king, perfect in judgment and piety."

The king turned his back on the kneeling legate. He

blinked once, as if mentally dismissing Paul as a gnat not worthy of a warrior's response. With a tired wave of his hand, he dismissed Paul from the room.

At first, the legate was simply too imbued with his own importance to realize he had been dismissed from the meeting. He stood open-mouthed while Don Garcia and the king busied themselves with papers that Alkabri extended across the table.

Archbishop Bernard, shrewder in matters of the royal court, rose pompously.

"If it please Your Highness," he said, "we will now conclude our participation in this meeting so that you may attend to the matter of Don Umar. That and nothing more, for the present. I bid you good day."

He started toward the door, pulling Paul firmly by the sleeve. The notary, seeing his patron leave, hastily gathered up his parchments and followed.

As the chamberlain closed the door behind the churchmen, Alfonso feigned a silent sword thrust against the closed door. A weight seemed to be lifted from his shoulders.

"At least that is over for the moment," the king said, reverting to the comfortable vernacular of Arabic.

He turned his attention to Commander Don Umar in a cheerful yet business-like manner. Their discussion quickly centered on the number of horsemen and foot soldiers needed to break the siege of Calatrava. Alkabri's fingers rifled through the complex lists of men and materiel pledged by the king's many vassals. It was a question of determining the strategic locations of foot soldiers in the region.

Don Garcia's finger paused at the midpoint of the list.

"If it please His Majesty, Zafadola is the most trusted vassal in the area," he said. "Draw up a letter, Alkabri. Address it to Zafadola. Begin with the usual compliments, well wishes for his family, long life to the Emir Zafadola. That sort of thing. Then introduce our trusted Don Umar. Make known our needs concisely, Alkabri."

He pushed back the document, written in Alkabri's neat hand, listing Zafadola's armies and their deployment.

"There is no need to hedge words with Zafadola," Alfonso added. "Promise him that if he is successful in a thrust south of the Guadiana River, he may keep the fifth of the booty customarily reserved for me. Tell him I place my entire share in his hands alone."

"A munificent gesture, Your Majesty," Alkabri murmured. His quill was already busy. He did not look up.

After the black storm of anger, the nobler instincts of the king shone through. He was calm and reflective, interested again in proving himself an enlightened ruler.

"There is no reason to skimp on my gifts to my vassals," he noted amiably.

Don Garcia's eyes crinkled into a smile. He reached across the broad table to the astrolabe and placed it in the king's waiting hands. Now that the churchmen had left the Palatine Council, Alfonso felt no compunction in checking the sky. He took the astrolabe and walked to the narrow window. With dexterous fingers, he readied the instrument for a new sighting.

"If the Cluniac monks had their way, I would have no more dealings with my Moorish vassals, above all, Zafadola of Saragossa," King Alfonso reflected, pleased with his sighting. He turned his back on his advisors and looked downhill towards the tower. "I feel I am overrun by Frenchmen."

"They would have you sever your contact with your loyal Jewish subjects as well," added Alkabri. "Peter the Venerable blames the Jews for the evils of what he calls pernicious stargazing."

"I would wager that if the Legate Paul could have his way, he would personally requisition wagons that would take the Jews from Castile," remarked Don Garcia. "He is frantic to please the Pope."

"Never mind the legate," Alfonso cut in abruptly. "I can handle him."

Alfonso returned to the table as Alkabri rolled the letter to Zafadola tightly and dropped hot wax on the overlapping leaf. It cooled like clotted blood on the parchment as the king leaned forward with practiced experience to press his signet into the wax. Alkabri handed the letter to Don Umar.

"The king's will be done," Don Umar said, bowing deeply to his monarch before he left.

The Palatine Council had concluded its business. The standard-bearer carried the official Sword of Fealty back to its silver encrusted coffer and closed the lid with a substantial thump. He bowed slightly as he walked out. The tapestry near the doorway fell silently back into place.

The day's events had tired Alfonso. He pulled off the mantle of office with relief and ran his hand roughly across his perspiring neck. A slight breeze rustled some of the remaining parchments on the table, but the room was still hot and oppressive. At that moment, the chamberlain entered with wine and crystal goblets.

"Ah, the good wine from Jerez de la Frontera," the king said with satisfaction. He raised his goblet and held it to the light.

In the company of his most trusted advisor and secretary, he could allow himself to reflect on his burdens.

"Life should measure out problems one at a time," Alfonso said, staring down into his goblet with morose intensity, "not all at once, in a jumble. I handle problems best if they are one at a time. Do you think years of experience will sharpen my response to many problems at once?"

"The years will come, whether we invite them or not," Don Garcia answered with a laugh. "If the Almohad Caliph Al-Kumi dogs your heels on the frontier, you will deal with that challenge. If the monks demand a rigid Latin Catholicism, you will deal with them. For the moment, concentrate on the biggest threat. Both Alkabri and I will bolster your decisions."

"Too many things are happening at once," the king sighed.

"You must deal with the paramount threat, Alfonso,"

Alkabri warned. "The biggest worry is what the Caliph will do next. All else is dependent on that. If you meet that challenge, then with the help of the Almighty, the other problems will solve themselves."

The king sighed and took another sip of wine from his goblet. The delicate glass, a gift from the Emir of Seville, sparkled in the light.

"I hope you are right, Alkabri. The different threads of my problems are so intertwined. I cannot figure out where one problem ends and the next begins."

"That is why a wise king gathers advisors around him," Don Garcia reassured him. "The Almohad problem will answer the Cluniac problem, which answers the Karaite problem. It is all as logical as one, two, three."

"You have solved the Karaite problem," Alkabri said gently. "The heretics have left your realm. Now, this mean-spirited little legate would devise slander against the Jews and make you think that the Karaite problem could lead to a Jewish problem. I assure Your Grace that there is no problem among your Jewish subjects. We will always be loyal to you. I will not give substance to this afternoon's slander by even repeating it."

"No need, dear friend," Alfonso interjected. "I can see a lie when it is a lie."

Alkabri reached forward and refilled the king's goblet.

"You have done admirably well in seeing through deception, Your Grace," he said. "In spite of the duplicity of your half-brother who sits on the throne of Portugal. At least, the western front is peaceful."

"But is it secure?" the king asked. "I should have crushed the villain at the first sign of treachery, even if he is my blood."

"Discretion has its own merits, even for a warrior, Your Grace," Alkabri said, stroking his cheek with his index finger. "The masterful secret negotiations of my Jewish countryman Joseph Ibn Kamaniel on your behalf have made the western frontier peaceful. Indeed, it is almost as safe as Burgos."

"Peace on all sides," Don Garcia mused. "That is what we seek, Your Grace. Ramirez in the east has expressed his loyal vassalage. Zafadola, after that small setback in the south, is as strong as ever in your behalf. That still leaves the threat of the Caliph Al-Kumi at Gibraltar. That is why discretion is again of utmost importance."

King Alfonso paused with his hand outstretched around the stem of the goblet. New plans were brewing.

"Battling the Moors from North Africa is wasteful," Alkabri explained. "But the greater tragedy is that it divides the realm along the lines of language. If we are not careful, we could play the kingdom into the hands of your Cluniac advisors."

"Let me clarify," Don Garcia suggested. "Bernard is constantly demanding the elimination of the Mozarabic rite. I had thought his obsession was merely a pompous attitude of the churchmen. Now I see a graver danger. The defeat of the caliph opens up Castile for the worst violation."

Don Garcia encircled his goblet in his hands by way of demonstration. "You see, there is the enemy without, and the enemy within," he continued. "If we defeat the caliph and his cause of Islam, we are unprotected from the enemy within—those who make this realm a dour copy of the Monastery of Cluny."

"I had not thought of the situation in so many words," the king admitted.

"Nor I," Alkabri hastened to add. "You realize that I hold little sympathy for this caliph. He is a murderous Berber who slaughtered my own dear brother. Still, I will agree that this ongoing warfare holds the monks in check. A major defeat of the caliph would probably encourage a wave of Cluniac reform in the realm."

"And that is why we must not jump from the cauldron into the fire," Don Garcia concluded.

King Alfonso nodded, deep in thought.

"I must not completely defeat this . . . this Caliph Al-Kumi, even though his raids become more daring with each day. Just look at the latest! Who would have thought that his men would dare to ride as far north as Calatrava? It is unthinkable!"

"But to send an army south to defeat him could make you little more than a puppet for the politics of Bernard and his Church superior, Peter the Venerable," Don Garcia reminded him.

"What then will I do?" queried Alfonso. "I must act! To sit and wait is unbearable."

"Inaction is unthinkable," Alkabri agreed. "The situation in the south is intolerable. I fear the fanaticism of this Al-Kumi, Your Grace. He is worse than the Cluniac monks. Wherever he conquers, he imposes forced conversions to Islam on my countrymen, and his spies are everywhere. If they spot a class of children being taught by a rabbi, they burn down the house. Threats from this butcher are not to be taken lightly. He would no doubt persecute the Christians of your realm in the same merciless way. Where will it all end?"

"It will end with the efforts of another secret envoy," Don Garcia suggested. "We tried it in Portugal, with some success. We have learned from our mistakes. We will try again in North Africa. We will give the brutish Moor a taste of peace that will make him think he has found Paradise on earth. Then he will stop the raids on Christians and Jews of Andalusia."

"May it be the Will of the Almighty," Alkabri said fervently.

"And I will truly be the Guardian of All Religions," King Alfonso said, savoring the truth.

The king, turned suddenly to face his advisor. "But there is a flaw in your thinking, Don Garcia," he said. "If the caliph is as fanatic and bloodthirsty as Alkabri says, what does he care for peace? Perhaps, our hope for peace is just a shadow."

"But there is a chance, Your Grace, that we can make it to his advantage," insisted Don Garcia. "Until now, we have been obliged to react to the caliph's initiatives. He presses forward at one weak spot on our frontier, and we rush soldiers to push back. Then he bides his time for a few days and pushes forward at another weak spot."

"And so it goes, year after year," King Alfonso agreed. "We move forward. He disappears."

"Now we can take the initiative," Don Garcia promised. "The war must be costly to him as well. I have plans to end this war, at least for a while. If wisdom guides us, we are poised to usher in an era of peace and prosperity for Castile and all of Spain.

"And we all have a part to play. Alkabri, you must think of someone for a secret mission to the caliph. Joseph Ibn Kamaniel did his best when he negotiated in Portugal. Now we need someone with even greater skills. He must be a man of courage and great moral integrity. He must be adept at the subtleties of the Muslim ways. He must grasp the threat of the monks and see through their ploys. Above all, he must be a man we can trust to undertake this mission."

"Does such a man exist, Alkabri?" King Alfonso whispered.

Alkabri fell silent as the immensity of the project dawned on him. He pondered the many people whom he could propose for the mission. His gaze wandered to the king's astrolabe, and he absently reached out to pick it up as he thought. Each person who entered his mind had some drawback which could jeopardize the success of this bold plan. He toyed with the pointer on the astrolabe and examined the gilt inlays surrounding the outer rings.

"But of course!" he exclaimed. "Why didn't I think of him immediately?"

Don Garcia blinked at Alkabri's enthusiasm.

"I will seek out the negotiator we need," the secretary continued. "He is a rabbi of great wisdom and much practical experience. He has travelled widely and can read the face of a man as he reads the stars at night. This astrolabe brought him directly to mind."

"Who is the man?" King Alfonso queried. "Do I know him?"

"It is Rabban Avraham Ibn Amram," Alkabri answered

brightly. "You might very well know of him. His fame as an astronomer precedes him. He is the right man for this mission!"

"Then summon him immediately," King Alfonso directed, retrieving the astrolabe from Alkabri's fingers.

Don Garcia watched the secretary slyly.

"Was not this Ibn Amram the rabbi who chafed you during the Karaite expulsion? I recall that you walked around in annoyance for days."

Alkabri colored at the memory.

"My personal feelings are nothing in this matter," he said. "We had a difference of opinion, yes. That did not close my eyes to the true greatness of the sage. If you want a negotiator who can deal with unblinking honesty, Rabban Ibn Amram is your man."

The decision was made. King Alfonso rose to leave, motioning to the chamberlain who quickly opened the door to his private study.

"Inform me as soon as this Ibn Amram is in Burgos, Alkabri," the king called over his shoulder. "Both you and Don Garcia have much to do."

CHAPTER SEVEN

The Royal Audience

TUDELLA, NAVARRE
AUTUMN, 1139

IN THE MONTH OF *MARCHESHVAN*, THERE WERE NO FESTIVALS to enjoy. The *Yamim Noraim* and the rain-spotted meals of *Sukkot* were just a fond memory to Ibn Amram and his student. It was time for new directions. With the aid of his father-in-law, Ibn Amram's commentary on *Koheleth* was taking shape. Ibn Amram looked forward to its completion, and he joyously contemplated his next undertaking.

He was discussing the concluding text of *Koheleth* with Joseph one late afternoon, when a messenger arrived bearing a document written in Alkabri's fastidious hand. With dark foreboding, Ibn Amram read that the king commanded his presence in Burgos without delay.

"It appears the king wishes to speak with me on an urgent matter, Joseph," Ibn Amram murmured. "Yet there is no hint of what it is all about."

"Perhaps Alkabri will be able to reveal the reason," Joseph suggested.

"No doubt he can, no doubt he can. When we last parted, I felt sure he would want little to do with me for a long time. Yet here it is only a few weeks!"

"He calls upon you in the name of the king. Perhaps it is pertaining to the Karaite expulsion. Or perhaps the French monks have nearly convinced the king to expel all Jews and Alkabri wishes your alliance."

"We must go at once. It is the Will of Hashem."

"I will prepare the horses and provisions," said Joseph.

"And I must tell Naomi that I am leaving once again."

Before daybreak the next day, the two men left Tudela, bound for the capital. On the way, Ibn Amram expounded further on *Koheleth* and described the piercing insights of Yerucham Halevi. Joseph was astounded that Ibn Amram never uttered another word of speculation about his impending meeting with the King of Castile. And when Joseph once dared to raise the question, Ibn Amram replied crisply, "Hashem will show us the way. We must wait and see."

On their arrival in Burgos, they went directly to Alkabri's house, only to find he wasn't home and could not be reached. Arrangements had been made for them at a nearby inn, however, and they were to await his instructions. Ibn Amram and Joseph dutifully made their way to the inn. They waited one day, two days . . . without word from Alkabri or the king.

At last, there was a rap at the door. It swung open, and Alkabri plunged into Ibn Amram's room, accompanied by his bodyguard.

"The king apologizes for the delay," Alkabri announced, "but now he is ready to see us!"

His breath was quick, almost labored. He had evidently run up the long flight of stairs. Ibn Amram nodded, closing the manuscript he had just been studying.

"Whether it is a delay of two days or two weeks, we are ready."

With his student, he followed Alkabri and the guard down the steep stairway and directly across the broad plaza to the imposing summer palace.

A choirboy from the cathedral noticed the arrival of the Jews and skipped across the paving stones in the direction of the chancery.

"Pah!" Alkabri exclaimed, spitting on the ground in distaste. "The walls have eyes and ears. I warrant before we reach the antechamber, more spies of the archbishop will note our arrival."

A porter stood at attention at the inner door. Alkabri motioned to him and strode past him. More guards snapped to attention within the cool confines of the great hall. The banners of many emirs were on display, with those of Zafadola most prominent.

"King Alfonso has held audience with his most loyal emir," Alkabri explained. "Now his own Minister of Finance must wait! Take heart at this precedence, Rabban Ibn Amram. The revenues of Castile must stand in abeyance while the king confers with you."

He rapped sharply on the door while the guard stood close at hand. Presently, the hinges squeaked, and Raoul, the king's confessor, appeared in the narrow space between the door and the jamb.

"The king will see Ibn Amram now," the confessor said, eyeing Joseph Vitale with displeasure. "Only the rabbi, if you please. Not the boy or the secretary."

Alkabri wiped his hand across his forehead and stepped back, grasping Joseph by the shoulder.

"Come!" he said tersely. "No time for us. So be it, Raoul."

The old master of court intrigue turned on his heel before the door could close in his face. The choirboy, sitting beneath the banners in the great hall, peeked out, hugging his knees in expectation of great news. Alkabri walked briskly down the corridor, glancing at the youngster with aversion.

"What do you hope to see?" he asked sternly. "Go practice

your prayers, boy. There is nothing here for you."

The boy instantly fled down the long passageway.

Within the royal chamber, a curious pantomime was in progress, unseen by either the choirboy or by Alkabri. Raoul had stepped back from the door, almost hidden in the cowl of his coarse-woven cassock. He motioned the rabbi to the table where King Alfonso sat. Behind the king, guiding his finger along complex tables, stood Don Garcia. Ibn Amram held back for the space of a single breath, but Raoul nodded and gestured vigorously to approach the throne.

Not a sound came from Ibn Amram's boots as he approached the great oak table, as the king examined a particular page in a massive sheaf of parchments. Ibn Amram stopped, four paces from the edge of the table and waited. From the corner of his eye, he could see that Raoul had retreated to a small table at the far wall where he immersed himself in what looked like a small prayerbook.

A snuffling at the king's feet surprised Ibn Amram. A hound, no doubt, but the rabbi did not bend his head to look. Alfonso let his hand drop casually past the arm of his throne to touch the unseen animal. The snuffling ceased.

More minutes passed while the king followed the visual cues of Don Garcia's index finger. They pored over the columns of figures with meticulous perseverance. A small pictorial illumination of exquisite execution caught Ibn Amram's eye. He would have liked to draw closer to examine the artistry of the page, but he remained frozen in his place until the king should break the silence.

"Yes, rabbi, I am preoccupied with this astronomical chart," King Alfonso said at last, without looking up. "It is a matter of considerable importance to my future. If we could anticipate the motions and influence of the heavenly bodies, we could with greater certainty administer the empire."

The king's eyes followed Don Garcia's forefinger as it traced the sequence of numbers on the page, checking and double-checking the figures. The Royal Advisor drew his hand from the page and straightened to look for the first time at Ibn Amram. His gaze was piercing and not altogether trusting. Meanwhile, the king continued to scrutinize the last column on the chart, unwilling to tear his attention from the mystery therein.

Ibn Amram stared down at his boots, sensing the impasse of their first meeting. He felt that somehow he must advance the conversation, yet every instinct warned him against seizing the initiative. The outthrust chin of King Alfonso suggested that he was not in the best of moods. There was no encouragement from Don Garcia.

At last, Ibn Amram dared break the strained silence. "May I?" he asked in a quiet, yet confident voice, raising his hand ever so slightly in a gesture of reaching for the manuscript.

A man of lesser stature may have instantly felt the sharp tongue of Don Garcia, but the Royal Advisor remained silent. The hand of the King of Castile wavered over the manuscript, then pushed the work toward the rabbi. Ibn Amram hunched over the tables, studying one column in particular. His right hand fished within the folds of his *burnous*, and he withdrew his own notebook. The king watched through slitted eyes as Ibn Amram attempted to verify a series of algebraic calculations from the manuscript.

"It will take more time to check which year we are in, according to this table, Your Majesty," Ibn Amram said guardedly. "The numbers unfortunately are duplicated, but they suggest that there would be much slaughter in every country that should happen to be under the sign of the Sheep and its columns. It would happen in the twelfth year of the sign of *Machbereth*."

"You lie!" hissed King Alfonso. "The tables of Thabit Ibn Qurrah have no duplication. You struggle to answer thus because you cannot understand the work of the Master Astrolabist of Baghdad! You are a false and deceiving Jew!"

The blood drained from Ibn Amram's face. He reeled from the harsh words and put out his hand to the table to steady himself. It was as if the windows opposite him were rotating slowly in the wall. Strangely, it was the calm eyes of Don Garcia which gave him renewed courage.

"I would never lie to His Majesty," he struggled to whisper. "My devotion to your rule stands as my witness."

The king smiled sardonically.

"The words of a poet! Shall we trust this poet, Don Garcia?"

The Royal Advisor folded his arms across his chest and surveyed the shaken rabbi.

"We hear the words of a master poet, Your Grace; the truth candied with honeyed words." Don Garcia turned to Ibn Amram and dropped his folded arms to his sides. "Be cautious of your fate, Ibn Amram. Alkabri has spoken highly of your skills. Yet we hear nothing but banality from your explanation of this astronomical table."

Ibn Amram swallowed hard. "If it please His Majesty," he responded, almost choking on his dry tongue, "the truth is governed by natural processes, not my words. If this duplication were valid, the slaughter would have been in conjunction with the year of your coronation. But such was not the case."

The shadow of a smile crossed the king's lips. He turned his face to the window for a moment, under the pretense of stroking the hound's head.

"You have answered my challenge, rabbi. Now show me the duplication."

Don Garcia immediately shifted a chair so that Ibn Amram could sit at the table. He pushed aside some of the loose pages and twisted around the parchment covered with columns of figures. For a brief moment, Ibn Amram saw the challenge melt into avid interest as the king's eyes followed his finger in a zig-zag across the lines of numbers. His finger slowed and stopped at the offending notation, so small as to escape many an astronomer of the realm. But Ibn Amram was no ordinary astronomer. The science of the stars had been taught to him from early childhood.

"There is the error," he said to the king. "Undoubtedly, a copyist working by poor candlelight repeated the numbers. It throws all subsequent numbers awry. An unfortunate error!"

Don Garcia, intensely interested in this startling discovery, twisted the page from Ibn Amram's grasp to see for himself the erroneous item. There was a slight nod of the head, a mute recognition of error transmitted from tutor to student. Ibn Amram observed with fascination the subtle relationship that bound Don Garcia to the youthful King Alfonso.

The king's smile could no longer be hidden. But the edges of his mouth turned down in an ironic twist.

"You have passed the test for the moment, Rabban Ibn Amram. We shall discuss this matter again. Raoul!"

The confessor arose and motioned Ibn Amram to the door. The sage blinked in surprise. He realized he had been peremptorily dismissed, but he was uncertain whether his performance had pleased or displeased the king and his powerful advisor. He retreated with backward steps from the king, who was now hunched over the table with Don Garcia, unmindful of the rabbi's presence. The heavy door swung open, and Ibn Amram found himself in the darkened corridor. The guardsman smiled, his teeth shining fiercely in the dim light.

Two days later, Ibn Amram's audience with the king was repeated with much the same perversity. The king kept Ibn Amram waiting for a painfully tedious interlude, then lashed out with vicious words at Ibn Amram's alleged ignorance of Thabit's methods. When Ibn Amram carefully explained his reasoning, the king was mollified as before. Their meeting was concluded with the king and Don Garcia listening raptly to Ibn Amram's explanation of an alternative to Thabit's method. Then they abruptly dismissed him. These meetings were becoming a trying experience for Ibn Amram.

"I think he is testing you," Joseph said one night, upon hearing all the details of Ibn Amram's latest audience with the king.

"It seems obvious, Joseph," Ibn Amram agreed. "The third meeting might very well be decisive. The king must make up his mind whether or not he will trust me. For now, the two of them toy with me, test my reactions and appear alternately satisfied and dissatisfied, leaving me completely in the dark."

"What does Alkabri say of this matter?" asked Joseph.

Ibn Amram lifted his bread soaked with soup to his mouth.

"Alkabri has explained that he cannot reveal the king's motives. Apparently, they are contemplating a mission of considerable immensity. I might be the man to undertake the mission. Then again, I may not be right for it. I can only surmise that the care expended in these tests denotes a gravity beyond the ordinary in the objectives of King Alfonso."

"Sometimes, a ruler presents a dilemma of unattractive alternatives," Joseph commented. "My father has often been tested by Count Henri. The options were dire. This king has the same subtlety as the Count."

Ibn Amram once again had two full days to ponder the king's motives. The third test began in much the same fashion as the first and second. The only difference was that the Legate Paul, not Zafadola, had first held audience with the monarch.

Paul lingered by the door in apparent conversation with a pious chamberlain. But his eyes expressed great relish at what he perceived to be the plight of the hapless Jew.

"The expulsion will soon begin," he gloated under his breath.

Ibn Amram tried to ignore the taunt. The confessor Raoul was not present for the third meeting, and the chamberlain also stepped into the corridor at Ibn Amram's entrance. The sage was completely alone with the king and Don Garcia.

"You may pour me a goblet of wine," the king commented, gesturing to the carafe to the left of his hand. His eyes dropped to a manuscript where yet another series of Thabit's calculations were expressed in a fantastical design of interwoven arcs.

"Rabban Ibn Amram," the king went on confidentially.

"The rule of the stars has fascinated me from the day Don Garcia first sighted the Red Star for me. I have gathered in my court the ablest stargazers in the realm. But we have labored with imperfect tables, as you can see." The king's voice now resonated throughout the room. "I want perfection! For that, I will send you to Tunisia to gather the finest astronomers. Alkabri has assured me that you have conferred in the past with Tashpin, the King of Tunisia. Is that so?"

Ibn Amram answered pensively.

"The King of Tunisia is schooled in this science. He has granted me an audience on a number of occasions." Ibn Amram sighed at the thought. "But I have not seen him since he became the Chief Minister to your enemy Caliph Al-Kumi."

"He will see you now," King Alfonso said flatly. "You will see to it that he will arrange with his caliph for your safe passage in all the Muslim lands of the Almohades. There, you will find the best men of science from Marrakesh to Fostat and bring them back to Burgos. Money is no object. Under your guidance, Ibn Amram, Master Astrolabist of the Realm, they will create new tables."

He smiled at the immensity of the undertaking. Even Don Garcia seemed to be taken aback by the novelty of the project.

Ibn Amram nodded in silent agreement, relishing the pursuit of such wisdom. Yet he wondered how such a bold plan could be feasible at a time of continuous warfare between King Alfonso and the Caliph Al-Kumi. Somehow, a piece was missing from the ambitious plan.

He glanced across to Don Garcia and sensed an inkling of something bigger, as yet unrevealed. To question Alfonso further was a ripe temptation. But the impassive face of the king stilled his words.

"You may go now," the king said. He motioned to the door.

The tedious testing of Ibn Amram was to continue. Alkabri commiserated with his uneasy situation but had been sworn to secrecy. Long discussions passed between Ibn Amram and

Joseph considering what reasons the hostile caliph might have in granting safe passage to a Castilian Jew gathering together the best astronomers of the Muslim world.

These were trying times for Ibn Amram and Alkabri, but for Joseph Vitale, they were days of youthful joy. Don Umar, the king's Commander of the Garrison, was back in Burgos, fresh from his victory at Calatrava. He had taken an instant liking to the quiet youth from Champagne, and Joseph admired the soldier's knightly skills. When Don Umar offered him lessons in the art of Spanish horsemanship, the proposition was greeted with unalloyed enthusiasm.

On blustery autumn afternoons, when leaves were whisked from swaying trees by brisk winds, Joseph and Don Umar could be seen together making their way to the corral. Mounted on the big black stallion with a white star on its forehead, Joseph learned the dizzying technique of the *caracol*, a half turn to the left and then to the right. The high-spirited stallion seemed to dance on air.

Day after day, Joseph's competence increased. Yet one afternoon, in a moment of frenzied joy, a reckless motion caused the stallion to panic and kick, sending Joseph sprawling to the ground. Don Umar rushed to his side as he writhed in pain.

It was but moments later when the great oak door of the Palatine Council resounded with three sharp knocks. King Alfonso and Ibn Amram looked up. The door swung open to reveal Don Umar.

"A thousand pardons for this intrusion, Your Majesty," the commander said hurriedly. "The lad has been injured by my stallion. I have asked Abdul to treat him in the infirmary."

Ibn Amram leaped to his feet, obviously distraught. The king noticed his alarm and motioned to the door.

"Yes, go with Don Umar," he said. "You may confer with the Court Physician, if you wish. Whatever your friend needs, he will have."

They hastened down the rain-dampened corridors, their

footsteps echoing like a dull reproach for their slowness. At the sight of the red streamers hung from the pole outside the infirmary, Ibn Amram broke into a run and burst through the doorway.

"My poor Joseph! How is the boy?" he cried.

The Muslim doctor looked up from his ministrations.

"It was just a chance kick," he answered. "Perhaps a rib is cracked. We shall know by tomorrow when I remove these bindings." His fingers struggled to twist the end of the bandage for a suitable knot. "Hold this while I pull, would you, good man?"

Ibn Amram quickly held the end with his left hand while he wiped the droplets of perspiration from Joseph's brow.

"It is a vicious pain," he said in sympathy. "Yes, I know, Joseph. With every breath, it is as if your lungs were on fire. Do not try to talk. Just lie quietly and calm your breathing. Breathe gently, Joseph, and the pain will lessen." His right hand brushed in soothing rhythms across Joseph's forehead.

"I dismounted on the wrong side," Joseph whispered. "What a foolish thing to do! I don't blame the horse. He had every right to kick me for my foolishness."

"You must recover your strength, Joseph, then return to the horse with a carrot," Don Umar advised. "I know that his big heart is broken at what he has done. He never meant to kick you. But a horse is not always sensible."

No one in the infirmary had noticed that the king had followed them unannounced. He surveyed the scene from the open door, glancing back to see if he had been followed. Then he quietly entered, closing the door behind him.

"A good horse is part of the passage to manhood," Alfonso declared suddenly. There was a flurry of bows and nods as he continued. "Joseph will survive this injury with greater wisdom than he mustered at this morning's dawn. But we cannot wait for him to heal and join us on our journey. Don Umar, are you ready to travel with us to Pamplona?" His glance took in Ibn Amram as well.

"Do not look so bewildered, rabbi. My liegeman Garcia Ramirez will be in excellent humor. The fifth day of the week marks the confirmation of his son Fernando as his successor. My presence at the Cathedral of Pamplona will speak volumes on the importance of an untroubled succession in Navarre. And peace in Navarre ensures peace for Castile."

"Yes, Your Grace," Don Umar responded. "I will certainly go to such a momentous celebration. We would not want anyone to trouble the peace in Navarre at such a time."

"And me, Your Majesty?" Ibn Amram queried. "What do you wish of me? What can an astronomer do for you in the capital of Navarre?" He wondered if this were the secret mission.

The king strode past Doctor Abdul to survey the variety of jugs and bottle containing tinctures, unguents and dried herbs.

"In the midst of political turbulence, the rule of the stars is a steadying influence," he said simply. "When warfare is like a night of uncertainty over the land, I look to the stars with the same confidence as a sailor who relies on them nightly. I want you to be at my side."

He turned away from Ibn Amram's searching gaze to examine a bottle of camphor oil. How could he express to the sage his fear that the coming solar darkness might contribute to problems with some of his vassals? How could he explain his moral defeat at the hands of his Portuguese half-brother and his vulnerability to the raids of the Caliph? His mind strained to find a reason for these failures. It felt logical and comforting to say that the stars dictated his losses, as if men were fools by heavenly compulsion.

The look of doubt that played across the monarch's face was not lost on Ibn Amram, but he would not comment on it. He had yet to see a coherent connection between the proposed astronomical tables and the strategy of war. But he was resolved to follow Alkabri's advice to wait for King Alfonso to issue his command.

"Then it is resolved," the king concluded. "Tomorrow we take the north road to Pamplona. We should have a suitable contingent, Don Umar."

"May it be your will," Don Umar answered, withdrawing his sword a fraction from its scabbard and driving it back with an authoritative snap. "The royal carriage will be in the plaza before you have finished your morning prayers."

CHAPTER EIGHT

Journey into the Unknown

BURGOS, CASTILE
AUTUMN, 1139

MORNING ARRIVED WITH A TOUCH OF FROST IN THE AIR. THE horses were champing and snorting, anxious to be off. The grooms hastened from one to the other calming the high-strung beasts. Don Umar and Lieutenant Ricardo marshalled a group of seasoned knights, with many lances bedecked with fluttering pennants and the fiery optimism of warriors on their faces.

The full contingent of *caballeros* led by Don Umar on the black stallion did not fail to attract the attention of the churchmen. Archbishop Bernard glided among the crowd of peasants pushing to catch sight of their monarch. He conferred with a priest who hung back in the early morning shadows.

When King Alfonso stepped from his private chapel, a cheer rose from the crowd. Bernard scowled when he heard the heartfelt shouts expressed in Arabic.

A groom, perched at the back of the royal carriage, unlatched the windowless rear door. Pausing with his foot on the rail, King Alfonso exchanged a few words with Don Umar, then disappeared into the coach. No sign of the occupant was visible from anywhere along the length of the carriage, although Archbishop Bernard walked the entire distance to catch King Alfonso's eye. From front to back, intricate arabesques of embroidery covered the tight linden slats of the arched roof.

"Don Umar!" the archbishop called out impatiently. "Be so good as to tell our king that I will personally bless his carriage for the journey."

Don Umar nodded, handed his reins to his lieutenant and climbed into the carriage. The door swung open, and King Alfonso leaned out, accepting the archbishop's benediction with ready assurance.

The smile of superiority faded from the churchman's face when he noticed Ibn Amram emerge from the crowd.

"What business have you with the king, Jew?" he sneered. "Do not be sullen with your superiors. Speak up!"

"The purpose of my business is still hidden by Providence," Ibn Amram answered.

He rapped lightly on the door of the carriage. Don Umar opened it and bade him enter. From inside the carriage, Don Garcia motioned to the cushion beside him.

"This is not the way of an expulsion," Archbishop Bernard said to his colleague. "Let us leave at once before the common folk assume we are blessing the Jew."

He bowed his head and smoothed his scapular across his chest. The crowd moved away in deference to let him pass to the abbey.

The knights of the royal contingent formed a tight phalanx. The coachman flicked his whip and whistled to his team, which lunged forward, ears pressed tightly against their heads. As the wheels of the great carriage began to roll, the groom leaped back onto the narrow railing that hung below the rear door, looked back to the cheering crowd and waved his hat in salute.

The interior of the huge carriage was like a royal military tent. Lavish silks hung from the great arch of the body. A lamp with a neatly trimmed wick hung from the central lodge pole, casting shifting shadows across the folds of silk.

The king and his commander engaged in a leisurely discussion of the strategy that was used to break the siege of Calatrava, but Don Garcia was unusually taciturn. Ibn Amram leaned back against the pillows and waited. The road became bumpy, and he winced as the jolting sent a flash of pain through his back.

A throng of people had recognized the royal carriage and pressed forward in adulation. The knights shouted warnings to the peasants to make room for the royal carriage.

"*Viva el Rey!*" they shouted in a frenzy. "Long live the King!"

Within the carriage, the conversation had turned to the Caliph Al-Kumi, and Don Garcia had at last become more animated. It was evident to Ibn Amram that he was not simply travelling to Pamplona to attend a ceremony of state. Clearly, he had been brought into this carriage in order to participate in a vital conference, away from the eyes and ears of the palace.

King Alfonso finally looked at Ibn Amram quizzically. "Shall we benefit from your poetic words, rabbi?" he asked Ibn Amram. "Alkabri assured me that you have a way with words. Would your words convince a treacherous Berber?"

"My eloquence is best engaged when I fully know your plan, Your Majesty."

King Alfonso and Don Garcia exchanged glances. Don Garcia edged forward to sit lightly on his cushion, dominating the lamplight within the carriage.

"We have brought you with us today so that we may speak in utmost privacy," he began. "When you journey to Tunisia and word of His Majesty's plan for new astronomical tables reaches the caliph, he will see Alfonso in a new light. He is not a learned man, this Berber, but he will understand that a king obedient to the rule of the stars is less likely to plot warfare."

"But you are at war with the caliph," Ibn Amram insisted. "Don Umar has recounted the fierce battles at Calatrava. This is not child's play."

"Ah, but we shall not be at war," Don Garcia continued in a confidential tone. "You will carry a treaty of peace from King Alfonso to the Caliph Al-Kumi!"

The immensity of the plan overwhelmed Ibn Amram. Alfonsine astronomical tables were to be merely the culmination of a longed-for peace.

"But what makes you believe this victorious caliph will ever agree to peace?" Ibn Amram questioned.

"He harries our every step, but he can never paralyze our forces," Don Umar interjected. "He strikes and then he falls back, just as he did at Calatrava. He fights with volleys of arrows but shuns conventional warfare. The caliph harasses me, but he will never defeat me in a real battle!" The sincerity of Don Umar's words was eloquent.

"In short," Don Garcia explained, "the primitive Berber stands in awe of our methods of warfare. The *cabelleros* of Castile have been taught new ways by the French knights. They were invincible in the last Crusade. The caliph fears their lances and their armor. In time, all our knights will wear armor instead of just chain mail."

Don Umar waited, gauging the reaction of his ruler. "If a new Crusade were invoked against the Moors, the caliph would be overrun by fearsome knights from Burgundy and Blois. A Moorish archer could never stop a French knight in full armor. That thought alone must strike fear into the caliph's heart!"

"And permits us to negotiate from a position of strength, Rabban Ibn Amram," King Alfonso interpolated. "For the caliph, the alternative to peace is wretched. Every garrison in

Castile manned by Franks! Every road patrolled by Franks! A horrible thought."

"Of course, he will never know that it is likewise a horrible thought for us," Don Garcia added. His ironic smile invited Ibn Amram into the intrigue against the French monks.

"You see, if there were ever a Second Crusade, and we pray fervently that it should never come to pass, Bernard would have his fondest wish. Whether His Majesty desired it or not, Castile would come under the thumb of the French monasteries. Cluny would rule Spain."

Don Garcia watched the puzzled expression on Ibn Amram's face dissolve into slow comprehension. Then he continued.

"Caliph Al-Kumi knows that the Church's plans to control all of Spain are a serious threat to his dynasty. If His Majesty promised him he would curb the monks and thwart their plans of taking Andalusia, the caliph could not fail to see the advantages. Even if he would not agree to a lasting peace, he may well accept a ten-year treaty."

"A clever stratagem!" Ibn Amram exclaimed in sincere admiration. "Do you expect that he will sign readily?"

"It is difficult to tell," Don Garcia responded soberly. "There is so much about him we do not understand."

"But surely, peace would better serve his purposes now, just as it would mine," the king argued. "There is so much we could learn from each other. The wisdom of the stars is just one of many things we both prize."

"There is yet one more inducement," added Don Garcia. "If His Majesty and the caliph could join hands in suppressing Cluniac reforms in Spain, they could also ally to insure the Caliph Al-Kumi's dynasty. He is an Almohad and passionately wishes to hold back the rival Almoravid Muslims. The unity of the king and the caliph in these matters would be a supreme advantage to both."

"I can surely see," Ibn Amram responded thoughtfully, "that such an alliance would settle religious conflicts and bring stability to all. All, except, of course..."

"The Jews?" Don Garcia interjected. "Do not think for a moment, learned rabbi, that this peace will not help your people as well. Why, you do not even know what dangers lurk all around you!"

Ibn Amram's eyes formed narrow slits. He dared not ask the countless questions which suddenly thronged his brain.

"I believe we should tell him," urged King Alfonso. "Perhaps the rabbi's mission will prove more successful if he is fully aware of its consequences."

"I would do my utmost to serve my king, in any event," Ibn Amram protested.

"Yet it would be beneficial for you to be aware," Don Garcia intoned darkly, "that if the caliph is defeated and Cluniac reforms sweep this land, the Karaites would be invited back to Castile in an instant."

"Why would the churchmen favor Jewish heretics?" Ibn Amram asked in alarm. "What do they care about our internal struggles?"

"The French monks are in accordance with the fundamentalist philosophies of the Karaite sect," Don Garcia speculated. "Yet I believe they have a more sinister motive in restoring them to the realm. Alkabri assures me that to strengthen the Karaites would undermine all Jewish influence in Castile. With the Karaites back, the Jews would once again be fighting each other and the Cluniacs could then urge expulsion of *all* Jews–Rabbanite and Karaite alike–to restore peace and bring unity to the realm."

"And line their own pockets with confiscated property," added Alfonso slyly. "The possessions of the Jews would, of course, go to the Church."

"Ponder your position well, my friend," Don Garcia smiled. "Peace with the caliph may mean more to you than you thought!"

Ibn Amram's mind reeled. Could it be true? Could the churchmen bring the Karaites back and later banish all the

Jews? Ibn Amram keenly felt the injustice of the Karaites expulsion, yet it was over and done. Now that they were gone, could the Jewish community tolerate their return?

What if the king and Don Garcia were only threatening such a result in order to make sure that he go to Tunisia and put forth his best effort for their peace treaty?

Each question brought another in rapid succession. Ibn Amram turned to look out of the window to avoid the gaze of the king and his advisor. The passing landscape became blurred.

A change in the sound of the wheels made Don Umar suddenly attentive.

"What is happening, Rodrigo?" Don Umar asked, leaning out to the driver.

Rodrigo stood up in his seat and peered into the distance behind them. Then he shouted something to the young groom clinging to the railing at the rear.

"There is a dust cloud behind us, Don Umar," the driver answered, pointing with his whip. "We cannot yet tell if it is a horse and rider or another carriage."

"It is merely another traveller on his way to the Pamplona festival," remarked the king lazily.

"Be it another traveller or not, I will accompany the carriage on horseback," Don Umar responded. "Stop the carriage, Rodrigo. I will take command of our contingent."

The harness jangled in protest as the coachman reined in the team. The brake squealed on the front wheel. In a twinkling, Don Umar reached for the iron handle of the rear door, opened it and sprang to his waiting mount. The groom slammed the door shut as Don Umar directed his men into defensive positions.

The driver whipped the horses briskly, and they struggled to regain speed. Ibn Amram fell into silence as he thought about his experience on the road to Toledo when the elder Rikuv had played his dangerous pranks. He was glad Don Umar had accompanied them.

The carriage continued its headlong pace, careening wildly past the limestone cliffs on either side. As they slowed to approach a mountain valley, the sound of the carriage behind them reached their ears for the first time. It was a cumbersome trader's wagon of the type that carried goods from Merida to Leon. On the road to Pamplona, it was a strange sight. And the speed of its breakneck approach proved it was empty, or almost empty.

The noise of clattering stones and hooves reached a crescendo, then died away as the trader's wagon passed them.

"The Devil take them!" the king cursed. "We are well rid of their company." He extended his arm to steady himself against the lodgepole of the carriage. "I hope that Rodrigo can maintain his speed all the way to Pamplona."

The sense of danger had passed. The king talked casually about the Pamplona festival and whiled away the moments by nibbling sweetmeats from a glass container. He looked up when the carriage slowed again. Angry shouts from the knights echoed through the air.

"It is a tree," Rodrigo called down. "Apparently a tree has fallen across the roadway, though I do not understand how the trader's wagon bypassed such a massive trunk."

King Alfonso rose and opened the rear door, flooding the interior with the grey light of a cloudy day. Don Garcia rose as well and tugged gently at the monarch's sleeve.

"It may be a trick or a trap," he warned. "How did the trader's wagon pass a fallen tree?"

The king nodded, feeling with confidence for his sword. Don Umar's horse appeared suddenly at the side of the carriage.

"Stay back, Your Grace," he warned. "It is unnatural to find this tree. No sign of bad weather, and a tree should fall? I say, keep within the carriage."

There was no high ground for the commander to take at this blind corner of the road. The eastern edge of the road dipped with a sickening drop to cliff sides below. The western side rose abruptly into forests of dense pine. Some of the knights had already dismounted and were laboring to shift the tree trunk. Don Umar guided his stallion around the tangle of branches, shouting commands and encouragement to his men.

A sudden gasp and a shake of his hand warned the men to fall into silence. Don Umar rose in his stirrups and surveyed the endless ridges of pine above him. A flash of white had caught his attention. He lifted his hand to shield his eyes from the glare of the sky. Another flash! A blackbird, hidden in the shadows far up on the cliff, had suddenly taken flight, displaying his brilliant white shoulder patches.

Don Umar was squinting into the distance to see why the bird had risen with a startled flutter, when a single arrow aimed at the blazing red and blue escutcheon on his shoulder almost knocked him from his horse. A volley of arrows streamed from the trees above them. One knight, struck in the neck, died instantly. The remaining knights rushed to regain their mounts and defend the royal carriage.

Reeling in his saddle, Don Umar managed to control his stallion and shout hoarse commands to his men. Three of them attempted to break through the roadside thicket on horseback to intercept the raiders. Their noisy advance brought squawks from the blackbirds, but no further arrows from the attackers. Less than a third of the way up the cliff, the underbrush stopped their pursuit.

King Alfonso, true to his warrior instincts, had leaped from the carriage to be with his men.

"Poor fellow," he sighed, breaking off the arrow from the neck of his fallen knight. The other soldiers were now returning from the underbrush. The king motioned to them to retrieve the horse of the fallen knight and strap the body across the saddle.

Presently, Don Umar returned, his leggings and chain mail tangled with brambles.

"They have fled, the cowards!" he spat. His face was white

from the loss of blood.

"Don Umar!" Ibn Amram called out, hurrying to the commander's horse as he was about to fall from the saddle. "Swing your leg down on this side. Yes, like that."

Ibn Amram eased the dizzy soldier to the trunk and quickly ripped a strip of cloth from his own *burnous* to fashion a tourniquet.

"Well done, Ibn Amram," the king complimented. "Have Don Umar brought into the carriage. In Pamplona, a physician will staunch the flow of blood." He turned to Don Umar. "Rest easy, old friend! I am angry enough for both of us. This treachery is without doubt the work of that half-witted half-brother of mine. My blood boils when I think that anyone like that could call himself King of Portugal! If it were not for his Norman mercenaries and the direct protection of the pope, I would execute him for this insolence!"

"How can you be sure this is the work of Aphonso Henriques?" Ibn Amram asked. He did not want to express a suspicion based on a fleeting image, but he had caught sight of a pale face in the open window of the trader's coach and it had looked remarkably like someone in Alfonso's own royal court.

"I am sure Aphonso Henriques masterminded this ambush," King Alfonso snapped. "The dog! It is his style. Ever since we were small children, he has been an underhanded cheat. He swallowed the lies fed to him by his teachers. They made him believe he is my equal simply because Urraca was likewise his mother. But he was not born to the purple. He takes it by cunning, like a thief. Then he runs to the Pope for protection."

Don Umar managed to smile as Ibn Amram helped him to his feet.

"His Majesty has strong opinions of the Count of Portugal," he said. "And they are well justified. The man is devious beyond measure."

"He is," the king affirmed. "More devious than the Serpent. He has taken to calling himself Knight of the Roman Pontiff. I do not know which title galls me more, his claim to kingship or his claim to knighthood!"

Don Umar's lieutenant took the reins of the black stallion, and the door to the carriage closed. Rodrigo whipped the team into motion.

"Mark my words, Don Umar," the king said darkly. "When I have assured peace with the caliph on my southern flank, I will deal with this ingrate to the west. Portugal will be nothing. She will be my vassal to the end of days."

Don Umar's breathing was labored, but he struggled to contribute his thoughts. "This ambush is part of a plan to stop us from bringing more vassals to King Alfonso's empire. Aphonso Henriques is livid at the number of Alfonso's loyal supporters—Ramiro of Aragon, Ramon Berenguer of Barcelona, Garcia Ramirez of Navarre, Guillame de Montpellier, Alphonse Jourdian de Toulouse. He would try to stop the empire with an arrow!"

"He failed today, and he always will," King Alfonso said fiercely. He called up to his driver. "Faster, Rodrigo! Faster! Don Umar needs treatment as soon as possible. And I do not want to miss the running of the bulls."

"Yes, Your Majesty," Rodrigo answered, slapping his thigh in anticipation. "When I was a young man, I also used to run through the streets, just inches from the wicked horns of *el toro*! If the bulls finish their run and reach the bull ring before we get there, it would indeed be a pity."

He flicked his whip again, and the horses broke into a wild gallop up the curving road.

As they entered the narrow streets of Pamplona, a barricade of human bodies lined the cobblestone streets where the bulls would soon plunge into the crowd. Old men of the capital, now no longer able to kick up their heels in the path of the furious beasts contented themselves with the proximity of danger. When they saw the carriage of the King of Castile, a roar of enthusiasm rose from the crowd.

"El Rey! El Rey de Castila! Viva el Rey de Castila!"

The chant continued and the men dared to move from the safety of the limestone walls to wave their arms and cheer their emperor. Alfonso stepped to the front of the carriage and looked out, raising his hand in appreciation of their hearty applause. With the deafening noise and stamping feet, Rodrigo struggled to control his high-strung team.

"I will take that alley," he muttered, pointing to a narrow lane on the left. He shouted instructions to the groom mounted on the nervous lead stallion. The carriage wheels turned sharply over the cobblestones, sending a violent shiver through the axle.

Once freed from the crushing throng of celebrants on the main street, Rodrigo made good time up the back alley. Ahead, the tower of the cathedral was clearly visible above the roofline of the houses and the tall beech trees that lined the central plaza.

"Whoa," the coachman suddenly shouted, standing up to better control the reins. From out of nowhere, a heavy wagon had entered the alley. It was the same wagon which had passed them on the road. Its driver skewed the wheels directly into the path of the royal carriage.

The lead stallion whinnied with a piercing high-pitched sound, more like a woman's scream than an animal's cry. Ibn Amram and the other passengers lunged forward.

For an instant, as the merchant wagon lumbered around the corner, Ibn Amram thought he again recognized a face at its window. The same face! The face moved back as quickly as it had appeared, but the pale image remained etched on Ibn Amram's memory.

"Whoa," the coachman shouted again at his horses, as the spirited team nearly collided with the trader's wagon just ahead.

"We could have overturned because of you!" the groom shouted at the negligent driver of the clumsy vehicle. The driver did not seem to pay attention.

Don Umar raised himself with difficulty and pried open the rear door.

"Ricardo," he called out to his lieutenant. "Get rid of that wagon! You know what to do." His right arm dropped from the handle, and Ibn Amram eased him back onto the pillows.

Perhaps the driver of the trader's wagon sensed retribution was inevitable. The heavy wagon speeded up and lumbered heavily into a lane on the left. For a long moment, the trickster was lost from sight, but Rodrigo followed it down the twisting alley.

Suddenly, the wagon came to a halt. To the left, the bloated carcass of a mule blocked the passage of the heavy vehicle. To the right, a cartful of barrels had overturned, spilling olive oil over the cobblestone street. Two goats were now engaged in an angry head-butting battle over which could claim first rights to the oil. With each whirl and butt, one or the other was sent sprawling over the slippery stones.

The driver of the trader's wagon could not pull past these obstacles. He shouted and cursed the goats, desperately trying to steer his horses around the mess as the sound of Ricardo's contingent came closer and closer. The king's knights were suddenly upon him.

"Get down, driver!" Ricardo commanded, swinging at him with a club.

The man fell headfirst from the seat and screamed in pain.

"Where are your passengers?" Ricardo demanded. He prodded the canvas with his sword. "You carried the archers, didn't you? Who are your masters? Have they fled down the alley?"

"They are gone," the driver moaned, clutching his bloodied face with his hands. "Have pity on a poor sinner. I did as I was commanded. I bear no ill will to the king."

"So you knew he was the king!" Ricardo said. His words had a dreadful finality. The tip of his sword slashed the traitor with swift justice.

The other knights fanned out through the labyrinthine

alleys in pursuit of the passengers and their mysterious master. Hoarse shouts and the violent clatter of axed shutters funnelled through the narrow streets. But the search was fruitless.

Rodrigo watched the scene impassively, waiting for a sign from his ruler to continue. When the trader's wagon had been removed, Alfonso signaled and bade him reach the cathedral with all due haste.

"Through here is a shortcut," Rodrigo assured him. "There is still time to pass directly through the main street. But we must be fast."

He pulled his hat tightly onto his head and whipped his team into furious action. The carriage rocked and listed at a frightening angle, sending up a shower of stones at each dip in the road.

As they entered another narrow road, there was a fanfare of brass horns from the plaza. The running of the bulls had begun. The quick-witted Rodrigo cursed his luck and turned adroitly into the next alley. It was a desperate move that snapped the trace of the carriage as it struck a nearby wall. The carriage grated along the length of the wall, slamming its great weight into a corner post.

Inside, the lamp on the lodge pole spun violently in a tight arc, struck the roof of the carriage and snuffed out the flame.

"The door! The rear door!" the king commanded in the sudden darkness.

Ibn Amram managed to crawl through the chaos of cushions to the rear and feel along the vertical surface of its embroidery for the metal latch. It seemed to elude his anxious fingers, and he hissed in frustration. At last, his fingers touched the cool metal, and he pulled up on it sharply, sending a harsh stream of daylight into his eyes.

The groom assigned to the rear door was caught up in the excitement of the street. The first wave of young men had already passed, leaping in fear and exhilaration ahead of the bulls let loose in the plaza. Then a second wave of youths appeared from the far end of the street.

"You can almost feel the breath of the bull on the back of your neck!" the young groom exclaimed.

He seemed ready to leap down from his perch to run with the youths. But his exaltation was instantly overshadowed by the grim reality of the bulls as they clattered into the cobblestone street. The bellowing and heavy breath of a dozen rampaging bulls resounded between the stone walls like myriad devilish echoes.

One gigantic beast lost his footing and crashed heavily into a barred door, splintering the oak like an eggshell. He rose heavily to his feet, snorting his fury. The rest of the herd passed in a sustained drumroll of hooves. Now the giant was alone and more dangerous than before. He spied an old man cringing at a rain spout near a broken barrel. The lone bull lowered his head and rushed to take his revenge.

Other men scattered in abject fear, but the old man was petrified until the bull reached his unresisting body. Then he was tossed like a limp rag doll over the bull's neck. Except for the dull thud of his body, the wounded man made no sound. As the bull whirled around, a brave companion ventured out and pushed the old man into the gutter, away from the slashing horns of the maddened animal.

For a moment, the bull paused, head upraised. Then his bloodshot eyes focused directly on the open door of the royal carriage. His nostrils flared, and as he bellowed his fierce warning, his fleshy tongue seemed to fill Ibn Amram's eyes.

Wordlessly, the king pulled his entranced groom in from the rear railing and latched the door again.

"Rodrigo," he called out softly. "Move ahead. Our position is vulnerable."

There was a sudden furious grunt and a jolting crash against the rear of the carriage. The groom wept in fear, crossing himself all the while. Again the bull charged the carriage, jolting it forward like a toy. An ominous splintering sound came from the rear axle.

"Rodrigo, forward!" the king yelled.

But the terrified horses were hopelessly tangled in the broken trace. Again, the bull charged the rear of the carriage. The groom screamed as a wicked horn slashed through the wooden door. It wedged for a moment, glinting in the dim light, before the bull could pull it free. A beam of light poured through the hole where the horn had torn through.

Grabbing the royal banner which hung from the front of the carriage, Rodrigo leaped to the ground, waving the silk flag like a cape. The king felt for his sword, unsheathing it to meet the danger.

It was a moment of desperate courage. Rodrigo could not anticipate the speed and fury of the bull. A slashing horn caught his mantle and gored him. The king leaped to his driver's aid, but before he could reach the crumpled form, a young man appeared at the end of the street. His hoots and taunts infuriated the bull far more than the fallen figure of the coachman. With a bellow of renewed rage, the bull clattered down the street.

"*Mi Rey!*" the old man in the gutter groaned, extending his hand towards the monarch. "My King!"

"Go and check on him," King Alfonso said to his groom.

He bent down over Rodrigo while Ibn Amram applied a bandage to a bloody gash on the man's chest. The coachman, dazed, tried to get back on his feet.

"*Mi Rey!*" he whispered. "Are you safe, Your Majesty?"

CHAPTER NINE

Skirmish at Dawn

SARAGOSSA, ARAGON
AUTUMN, 1139

"WHY ARE YOU SO DESPONDENT, *MORI?*" JOSEPH ASKED. "IS IT the rain? Look! I have built a roaring fire to drive away the chill of the night."

With the remarkable resilience of youth, Joseph had fully recovered from his injury in Burgos and now thrilled to be included in Ibn Amram's mission to the desert king. The King of Castile had provided them both with fine horses to make the trek to the seaport of Tarragona. They had already made excellent progress. Soon they would pass through the town of Saragossa. Somehow, Joseph did not feel even a twinge of fear, even though they were in territory disputed by the Spanish Christians and the Muslim conquerors. He trusted implicitly the long experience of Ibn Amram to travel unscathed through hostile lands.

Crouching in his tiny makeshift tent, Joseph was exceedingly proud of his handiwork. He had to hold his head very low because the tent pole which he had fashioned from a dead branch was quite short. His mantle, suspended loosely from the tent pole, was weighted with heavy stones on the ground.

"Warm your hands, *Mori*!" he called out. "The heat will make you feel better."

Joseph pushed his sleeves up to his elbows and extended the palms of his hands toward the crackling pinewood fire. His face was flushed and happy, from both his pride and the sudden heat of the fire.

The pine pitch in the bark popped fiercely in showers of sparks that seemed to transfix the falling rain in suspension. Each time a gust of wind blew into Joseph's tent, the fire popped and crackled, sizzling defiantly at the sweeping veils of rain.

Ibn Amram nodded mutely. His head was hunched over the gruel in the pot, he rocked ever so slightly on his heels, as he would in prayer. The stones on which he placed the pot were not yet hot, but he continued to stir the gruel in an absentminded way.

Joseph watched from his ingenious shelter, trying to follow Ibn Amram's gaze up the dirt road to where the horses were tethered. The youth's eyes were consumed by the beauty of the fine-boned Andalusian steeds. He sat in rapt attention, gazing through the swirling rain to see the brilliant black manes and the flowing tails of these noble creatures. Rarely had he seen such horses in Laon. Here was a horse to make Henri of Champagne himself envious!

But Joseph could tell that his teacher did not look at the horses, even though their black coats were magnificent in the rain. Ibn Amram's gaze was far beyond the trees.

"Ah, excuse me, young son, for my preoccupied thoughts," Ibn Amram responded, as though awakening from a dream. "It may seem improbable, but at this moment, I was thinking of the craft of poetry. My talents, of course, are but a dim shadow of the brilliance of our greatest poets, but I enjoy the exercise. Do you know what makes a good poet, Joseph?"

Joseph stared anxiously at the pot of gruel. He was very hungry and worried that the food might burn. He drew back in relief when he saw that Ibn Amram was about to stir the pot.

"It is like every craft," Joseph answered. "The good poet is a good craftsman."

"Exactly," Ibn Amram continued, rousing himself with enthusiasm. "With the rules firmly in mind, the poet attacks the subject with all the skill of his language. It takes many years of diligent practice to achieve greatness."

"How fortunate we are to know the greatest of them all. Yerucham Halevi by far exceeds his nearest rival in piety and poetry," Joseph added with genuine admiration.

Ibn Amram shivered in recognition of the name, as Joseph had so quickly brought the conversation to the one person who dominated his thoughts that evening.

"Yes, the master poet is Yerucham Halevi. I ponder his works tonight, because it pains me to think about him directly. Who would have thought he would undertake a journey to Jerusalem at a time like this? How much I wanted to change his decision! But how could I? How dare I?"

Joseph nodded wordlessly. They had just been in Tudela, preparing for the mission to Tunis, when the merchant Chalfon of Damietta paid an unexpected visit. He was so unlike a messenger of holy ideals. Short and pudgy, with a complacent girth that spoke amply of fine meals in his home in Egypt, Chalfon at first appeared far removed from any ideal. Yet in the long evening hours, as he recounted his travels, he waxed enthusiastic over Zion. Bathed in the dim light of Yerucham Halevi's *sala grande*, Chalfon had transcended mundane matters. His tongue painted magnificent pictures of the Holy Land that enraptured the Poet of Tudela with an irresistible longing.

Joseph swallowed his dry bread with difficulty, thinking about that stirring encounter.

"Truly, I, too, would have made plans to go to Zion on the

spot," the boy mused. "But then, I must return to Laon to aid my father in his holy work."

Ibn Amram looked up suddenly with unmeasured pain on his face.

"And Yerucham likewise has commitments! How could he leave us all? How could he leave the Jews who depend on him?"

"But how can anyone keep a man from fulfilling his life's dream? He has written that his heart is in the east, but he is in the west. Surely, he meant it with his entire soul, not just as a poetic concept."

"But to leave now, Joseph? Just when his people need him to clear their minds of Karaite heresy and to restore their favor with the nobility! I have argued time and again that he must continue in his service to the Navarrese nobility. It is only through his influence with the royal houses of Iberia that we ensure the security of our people. But no, he has fallen under the sway of this Chalfon of Damietta."

The intensity of Ibn Amram's feelings surprised Joseph. Ibn Amram was not a man moved to fits of passion. Reason was the keynote of his life, and that was what had endeared him most to Rabbeinu Vitale.

"You miss him already," Joseph said gently, watching his teacher carefully.

"Who?" Ibn Amram asked sharply. "I? Miss him? Why, we have not even reached the sea. How can I miss him when neither of us has left Iberia?"

"But he will leave shortly, Master," Joseph continued, scouring his pot with a piece of bread. "His destination is irrevocably Jerusalem."

Ibn Amram grated his teeth at the thought.

"The timing could not be worse," he said. "The Crusaders hold the Holy City. Life under their misguided rule will be a penury for a man of distinction. If he is convinced that the golden age for us is over in Castile, why not simply settle in Egypt? You know I have spoken at length with Rav Maimon, the *dayan* of Cordoba. He assures me that he will take his entire family to Egypt if the Caliph Al-Kumi seizes the area. He is certain that the Fatimid caliphs of Egypt will give us shelter from this storm of fanaticism that troubles Spain."

"Egypt is not Jerusalem."

"No," Ibn Amram admitted softly.

He looked down again quickly and resumed his eating. Time passed in a mournful hush.

"Your silence speaks volumes," Joseph noted. "Again, you are thinking of Yerucham Halevi. And you have not yet admitted that you miss him."

"Perhaps I do," Ibn Amram said, looking away. "We had reached a significant point in our work on *Koheleth*. Like the pilot who guides the ship past the shoals, he was moving me past difficult interpretations that vexed my optimism. I am an astronomer, yet it was the Poet of Tudela who fixed a firm sighting on the stars and charted my course. I wish we had reached the end. We needed more time. Yes, I miss him . . ." His voice trailed off to a whisper.

"You will feel better in the morning," Joseph said, injecting an extra measure of good humor into his voice. He drew his feet up to avoid a puddle. The mantle, stretched above his head was drenched, but it carried most of the water away from him.

The resinous wood of the campfire quickly burned to embers, and its noisy spitting and popping were replaced by the dull dripping of rain in the pine forest.

The following day, there was a beautiful panorama in the distance as they travelled. Dry tableland gave way to the rich greens and yellows of the grasslands of Aragon. The fields were excellent for cattle grazing.

"I think there must be a huge herd in the distance," Joseph exclaimed, squinting at a huge dust cloud that rose above the crest of the Ebro valley. It was impossible to tell just how big the herd was, but by the time they had travelled to the crest of the valley, Ibn Amram could tell that this herd was like none he had ever seen near Tudela.

"I hope the *vaqueros* are not driving that herd across the bridge," he said. "We could lose an entire day while they drive them through."

Ibn Amram elected to stop for *Minchah*, and he turned the horses loose to graze on the stubbles of grass. An occasional updraft of wind in the valley carried the lowing of the many cattle like a persistent rumbling of rapids from a distant river. At the entrance to the Ebro valley, the first fortifications of Saragossa were clearly visible, guarding access to the bridge.

"Let us continue quickly, before the herd can reach the bridge," Ibn Amram exclaimed, concluding his prayers with a final bow to the east.

He strode back to his horse and adjusted the reins while Joseph steadied the stirrup.

"Such an animal," he said in wonderment at the size of the horse. "I can see for miles from his back."

Few horses in Castile stood seventeen hands high, but King Alfonso had selected just such a mount for his esteemed envoy.

They cantered easily down the trail that led to the valley. Normally, the stock route was the trail for a few meager herds of sheep. But this time, it was overburdened with thousands of long-horned cattle. The dust was blinding.

Ibn Amram sucked his teeth in vexation while he rose in his saddle to survey the huge herd.

"This is the worst possible timing," he said to Joseph. "When hundreds and hundreds of head of cattle are funnelled onto a tiny bridge, it can take days to clear the road. Then there is always the danger of a stampede as the cattle push and shove to escape the confined area. That would be a calamity for us, Joseph! The traders in the port of Tarragona are hastening to set sail before the autumn gales. If we miss them, we just might have to wait until spring."

"But that is unthinkable," Joseph cried.

"*Hola!*" Ibn Amram called out, trying to catch the eye of the nearest herdsman. "*Hola, vaquero*! Can you stop the herd to let us cross the bridge?"

The dusty man turned in his saddle and arched his back to lift himself up to his fullest height.

"You're mistaken," he said disdainfully. "I am not a cattleman. You speak to the Officer of the Guard of Saragossa!"

"A thousand pardons," said Ibn Amram. "I should have instantly recognized your position by your lance of authority."

The officer glanced up at the war-torn pennant that had hung from his lance for years and then looked back at the two travellers. The sight of the magnificent charger which Ibn Amram rode evoked his respect.

"Don't mention it, *Senor el Rabi*," he said with a toss of his hand. "This is not the donkey of an *imam*. How did a preacher of the Jews get such a horse when the preachers of the Muslims must ride donkeys?"

The inquisitiveness of the officer put Ibn Amram in a difficult quandary. On the one hand, he needed to maintain a deferential tone toward this man in the hopes that their way across the cattle-clogged bridge could be hastened. Yet he could not reveal the secret mission he had undertaken for the king.

The officer's stare was piercing, waiting for any sign of subterfuge. Ibn Amram decided upon honesty.

"You are most perceptive. I usually ride a pony, but this noble steed is the gift of a man of the army. He will, I assure you, take back such a fine gift when I return to him. And I will be content once more with my humble pony. You can understand my embarrassment, can you not?"

Apparently, the officer could appreciate the embarrassment of an itinerant sage on a royal steed because he laughed outright at Ibn Amram's discomfiture.

"Then take pleasure in your horse while you can, *Senor el Rabi*," the officer said, turning to whistle orders at his foot-weary guards.

"It is the pleasure of the open road," Ibn Amram persisted, drawing nearer so that the officer could hear him clearly above the noise of the herd. "This horse becomes impatient if he waits at the roadside. Our business south of Saragossa is most important, but this is the only bridge for miles. Can you not stop the herd for a brief moment and let us through?"

"I see you have spent your years acquiring grey hairs over your books and not in the field," the officer responded, glancing down at Ibn Amram's boots and leggings. "What do you know of stopping a herd of thousands of animals? Do you think I am like Moses and can turn the tide by raising my arm?"

Well pleased with his witticism, the officer raised his arm to the unseeing cattle.

"You could turn them aside for a short while," Ibn Amram said. "There is grassland by the river's edge. They could graze for the afternoon and that would let us move across the bridge." He watched in trepidation as the huge herd came closer and closer. It was like an avalanche in slow motion, all the more painful because he could see his chances slipping away with each step the cattle took.

The smile instantly left the officer's face.

"Do you take me for your stable boy, *Senor el Rabi*?" he asked gruffly. "The cattlemen have left their summer pastures in Aragon. Now they must begin the long drive south to the *mesetas* of the Guadiana. No one can turn us aside."

"I know the protection of your armed contingent is a custom of the land," Ibn Amram said, smiling to placate the mounting anger of the officer. "But I do not see any reason for your rush. On whose authority must you drive these cattle without a rest for grazing?"

"By my life, you are a daring Jew!" the officer responded, levelling his lance at Ibn Amram. "Do you take me for a mere guard? I am the law incarnate. My men quiver at every command. I am judge, jury and executioner! Do not mock my authority, Jew. Wherever I ride with this herd, I carry with me the full authority of Saragossa."

"Forgive me again," Ibn Amram answered gently. "I did not realize such power rested with you."

The pride of the officer was something to work on. Ibn Amram made sure no one else was nearby to hear what he was about to say.

"I suspect you are answerable only to the *Commandador* of Saragossa," he continued, looking with new-found respect at the officer. Ibn Amram leaned forward in his saddle in an engaging conspiratorial fashion.

The officer glanced over his shoulder to ensure that none of his men were within earshot.

"The statute of the town charter makes us answerable only to the King of Aragon," he replied proudly.

"It is an excellent policy. I wish these simple-minded cattlemen could understand what power rests on your shoulders. If they only knew. If they had even an inkling of that august power, they would respect you as the Officer of the King!"

The officer leaned forward, caught up in the thought of his regal powers. He heaved a sigh of disappointment at the panorama of the stock drive, without a single vestige of pomp and ceremony.

"Perhaps," Ibn Amram continued confidentially, "you could stop the drive and assemble your men properly for full military honors before the massive movement across the bridge. Think of the honor! The *vaqueros* lined up respectfully, with thousands of head of cattle behind them, waiting for you and you alone to give the word to proceed. Your men dressed in their military best. Lances at the ready! Horses snorting in anticipation! And there, at the center of everything, overshadowed only by the sun, you sit mounted on an excellent warhorse!"

"Yes, yes!" the officer interjected with delight. "It must be a horse like no other. A horse that would make a *caballero* sick with envy. Black and glistening! Quick, *Senor el Rabi,* you must let me borrow your horse."

"Bravo," Ibn Amram declared, gathering up his reins in preparation to dismount. He patted the horse's cheek and rubbed his fingers across the animal's silky-smooth ear.

Joseph sat open-mouthed on his own mount.

"You shall have your steed and your moment of glory," Ibn Amram continued. "Don't forget what you said about Moses. When you gather everyone around you, lift your lance high. Not until you drop your arm will they begin."

He stepped back and mounted the officer's tired pony. Overcome with sudden emotion, the officer brushed away a tear from the corner of his eye and kissed the royal animal. His hand trembled as he climbed up into the saddle. For a moment he paused, immensely proud to be seen on the noble black stallion.

"*Salud, Senor el Rabi*," he answered before galloping off to the cattle.

He was in a mad rush now to stop the surging herd, and he whistled commands impatiently to his guards and *vaqueros*. The cattle were pressing closer to the river bank, but the skill of the officer brought them to a halt. The noise of the many hooves dwindled, and in its place a constant lowing and bellowing of bulls rose on the wind.

"That was a masterful ploy, *Mori*," Joseph commented breaking at last from his silence. "But have you not made a mistake in giving away your magnificent horse? The officer will be on the north shore of the river while we cross over to the south. It would take a day or more before he can return the beast."

Ibn Amram waved away Joseph's concerns with a smile and a toss of his head.

"I feel better already with this little pony," he confided. "Trust in Hashem, not in a beautiful horse. A simple teacher like myself should ride a simple pony."

A pained expression crossed Joseph's face, but Ibn Amram was quick enough to catch it.

"Do not worry, Joseph," he said. "I will not give away your

horse to the officer. Not just yet!"

He climbed up easily into the saddle of the officer's pony and crossed the tumble of rocks on the hill to the dusty flatland of the valley.

Excited by the proximity of the water, the weary cattle milled about on the muddy embankments, raking each other with their long horns and bellowing their abuse at the overworked cattlemen. The herders, too, were dreadfully tired. But it was not a time to relax. They shouted their exasperation at the slow-moving beasts, grumbling as well over this inexplicable delay and the foolish whimsy of the guards to pause in their passage over the bridge.

The herders were anxious to complete this part of their journey, for experience had taught them its dangers. The nearby forest could serve as cover for raiders who abounded in the area. Archers positioned in the forest could easily take aim at the slow-moving procession in its trek across the river.

The officer's pony obviously knew every rock and boulder of the terrain. Ibn Amram tried to guide it down the embankment towards the bridge, then realized that the pony was more skillful than he.

"Look how sure-footed this creature is in a rocky jumble, Joseph," he called out. He let go of the reins to let the animal find his own way.

"The herders were right," he added thoughtfully. "This bridge is open to ambush. No wonder an armed guard is necessary to see the herd safely to its destination."

Both of them hung back, sensing a morbid fear. But the pony forged ahead. There was nothing to do but trust in Hashem and ride past the forest. Ibn Amram carefully scanned the dense woods for any sign of life. Something about the stillness of the trees made him uneasy.

"*Mori*, the road lies that way, to the south!"

Joseph rose in his stirrups to point to the distinct edges of the muddy road skirting the woodlands.

Ibn Amram pressed forward resolutely into the tall grasses

to the east. Like an undulating sea of gold, they rustled at his passage then closed upon him again, almost hiding him from view. Were it not for the full-sized mount he rode, Joseph might have circled in vain to pick up Ibn Amram's trail.

"I thought you were in a hurry to follow the road, *Mori*," he said, pushing aside the luxuriant grass from his leggings to stare at Ibn Amram.

His teacher signalled silently to dismount and led the way on foot.

"I do not like the look of the forest, Joseph," he whispered. "Leave the horse here and we shall survey our vantage point in relative safety."

With infinite caution, Ibn Amram eased his large frame through the grass, scarcely daring to bend the blades. The wind stirred the hillside into a sinuous rhythm that masked their pathway.

At the crest, he dropped to his elbows and motioned to a fortress in the distance. Its main gate was open and lounging outside the walls were many soldiers of the garrison, watching the herdsmen and their guards.

"The officer is putting on quite a show, I see," Ibn Amram noted, nodding in amusement at the stiff-necked militarism on display in the wetlands of the river's edge.

The grouping of the cattle took great pains. Some beasts were stubborn and had to be beaten with whips to fall back into the herd. Others made a dash for the river and were lassoed by the nimble *vaqueros*. The officer was almost satisfied with the deployment of his troops and his massive herd. Rising in his saddle, he sat like a noble general raising his arm to an army.

He never had the chance to drop his arm and experience the thrill of watching everything move at his command. Muslim archers in the woods loosed a deadly volley of arrows at his proud form seated high on the royal saddle. Most found their mark. Some struck the black stallion which bolted in fright, dragging the hapless officer in his own stirrups.

"Poor man," Ibn Amram sighed, ducking back out of sight. "He never savored his one moment of glory."

No heralds of war announced the call of battle. The scene shifted suddenly from peace to chaos. The raiders rode in fierce abandon across the stone bridge, picking off the guards with arrows from their longbows. Some of the herdsmen managed to escape by clinging to cattle which broke into a stampede.

With noisy whistles and ear-splitting cracks of their bull whips, the Muslim forces broke rank and attempted to encircle as much of the maddened herd as possible. The raiders had captured a truly remarkable prize, a huge herd worth thousands of *dirhams* in the cattle market of Merida.

Bobbing up their heads hastily to survey the battlefield, Ibn Amram and Joseph could clearly see the vanguard of the raiders head for the fortress with flaming brands swinging overhead, determined to lay waste to the fortress or, at the very least, burn its granary. Without provisions, the outpost would have to be abandoned for the coming winter. The setback for the King of Aragon would be a victory for the caliph.

Ibn Amram and Joseph slithered back down the hill and plunged headlong through the tall grass. Their horses awaited, their ears perked forward in anticipation but otherwise showing no fear.

Ibn Amram seized the reins and led both animals into the relative shelter of a rock formation.

"It is an ambush, all right, and a very well conceived one at that!" He clambered onto the saddle of Joseph's horse and watched the action below the ramparts of the fortress. "Oh, now the raiders have thrown Greek fire onto the wooden walkways. Everything is on fire. Look, the *Commandador* has sent for help!"

With a hand over his eyes to squint into the brilliant blue sky, Joseph followed the direction of Ibn Amram's hand to watch a brace of white pigeons rise higher and higher, circle gracefully and then head southward to Saragossa.

"If the Muslim raiders can break through the main gate of the fortress, they will fight the Christian defenders in hand-to-hand combat. They might even destroy the grain silos. But whatever they intend, they do not have much time to do it."

Joseph felt for a handhold on the rock face and climbed up to watch what Ibn Amram saw. He felt horribly sickened at the sight of the dead and wounded on that plain and at the gate of the fortress. Some men were thrown like toy soldiers onto the ground in grotesque postures.

Suddenly, the main gate was thrown open and a squadron of *caballeros* in full armor emerged. They whirled deftly through the Muslim archers, scattering them like geese at the sight of the fox. It was a blur of action as defenders whirled and feinted while the attackers drew back and regrouped.

"The raiders have given up," Joseph cried. "They are running for cover across the river."

It certainly looked like an ignominious rout. The Aragonese knights had broken the back of the vanguard, scattering it to the four winds. Now they relentlessly pursued the leader of the raiders and his wounded lieutenant.

Ibn Amram shook his head in disbelief.

"You are familiar with the warfare in Champagne, Joseph," he said. "The Moors fight a different battle. You see? It is a, a feigned retreat!"

His hand clenched Joseph's arm in a vise-like grip. The raiders had encircled the overconfident knights and now slashed them frenziedly with their scimitars. Both sides suffered heavy losses, but the dust of an approaching contingent of mounted *caballeros* and foot soldiers from Saragossa meant that the raid was over.

"Heaven help us!" Ibn Amram exclaimed. "The Muslims are retreating into this very plain!"

He clambered down from the saddle and whirled around to look for a hiding place.

"We must escape! We must outrun them!" Joseph cried,

pulling the reins of the pony and horse and heading down from the rock.

Ibn Amram shook his head. "The raiders have years of practice and know every inch of this terrain. Every rock we stumble over, they leap over. It is useless to run."

Rooted to the spot like two statues of stone, Ibn Amram and Joseph waited with wild-eyed fear as the sounds of battle and retreat drew nearer.

"Again, it is a *rebato*," Ibn Amram whispered. "Perhaps the raiders will lead the knights away to another location."

Time seemed suspended. The raiders retreated in the opposite direction across the plain. Ibn Amram and Joseph watched in relief as they disappeared.

The sound of a horse's whinny took them by surprise. A pony appeared at the crest of a small hill, laboring under a heavy weight. The battle-weary Muslim who led the pony instantly caught sight of the two travellers.

"Halt!" he commanded. "Don't move a muscle."

The Muslim's eyes widened in surprise as Ibn Amram ignored the sharp command and hurried forward to the pony's saddle.

Draped across the saddle was a young man badly burned and sobbing deliriously. The sage loosed the *burnous* which was tangled tightly around the boy's neck and raised him into the saddle.

"Here, support him upright," he said to the surprised Muslim. "With his head forward like that, he chances a massive hemorrhage from these burns."

The man complied, wrapping his strong arm around the youth.

"You are *al-chakim*, the doctor of medicine for whom I prayed," the Muslim said.

Ibn Amram nodded. "I know the rudiments of the science."

"Thank the Almighty!" the raider cried fervently. "But there is no time at the present for my son's medical treatment.

Quick! Mount up before the Christians catch up."

His pony wheeled heavily as he shouted to a cluster of his raiders pounding along nearby. He seemed to be in command.

"Abdullah!" he yelled, as the contingent passed. "Take Yakub and double back to the bridge. Draw off these cursed knights!"

His commands, accompanied by hand signals jostled his son who moaned piteously. Abdullah swung his scimitar in the direction of the knights.

"You come with me," the leader commanded Ibn Amram. Again the youth moaned.

More screams carried on the wind from the bridge. The raiders had left their wounded on the field of battle. The dying already attracted vultures which circled on the updrafts.

Ibn Amram hastily followed and Joseph had no choice but to pursue them through the underbrush. Their headlong dash stopped suddenly as the raider halted near a meager stream. He stood in his stirrups and listened intently before he dismounted.

"We can wait here until the Christians have tired themselves out in pursuit," the Muslim declared. "Can you do something for my son Achbar?" He lifted the lad gently down from the saddle. "Can you salve his burns?"

Ibn Amram looked around at the withered plants that clung tenaciously to the edge of the pitiful stream.

"You asked for the skills of medicine, not the skills of magic," he replied. "If your son had the gout or suffered from the tertian fever, I could brew a suitable tea for each ailment." His hand pointed out each herb in turn. "But I see nothing here which can be mashed into a poultice for burns. I am sorry to disappoint you."

While the father wailed and beat his chest, Ibn Amram, tore a strip of cloth from his mantle and soaked it in the stream. He placed it across the ugly burns that disfigured the face of the young man.

"How did this thing happen?" Ibn Amram asked. "I have

rarely seen such bad burns on a soldier."

"It was the Greek fire," the Muslim answered. "Achbar held a pottery flagon. It is easier to lob the missile over the walls of a fortress if you hold the narrow neck. But as he lifted it over his head, the neck broke and the fire engulfed him!"

"So I can see," Ibn Amram said with compassion. "If only I had a soothing unguent for these wounds. The slightest abrasion will cause him to bleed profusely. Come closer, Joseph. What do you propose we do?"

His fingers gently spread the damp cloth across the boy's face.

"There is so much pressure," Achbar whispered, wincing at the feather-light touch of Ibn Amram's fingers.

His words became a tirade of childhood reminiscences as the delirium carried him into another consciousness.

"If I could find a way to lessen the pressure on the poor boy's head, the burns would heal," Ibn Amram said. "Does that not sound familiar to something we learned in *Gittin*, Joseph?"

A flash of recognition crossed Joseph's face, and he turned back to the plain to search methodically along its sun-baked banks.

The raider watched this interchange in complete bewilderment.

"I do not understand your words, *chakim*," he said, "but I can see that you and your lad are both People of the Book, and the Prophet has honored you for that learning. As true as my name is Ali Banu Hajaj, I will repay your compassion if you can save the life of my boy."

Joseph returned gleefully with a sprig of myrtle.

"It is just as you said, *Mori*," he called out. Remembering at the last moment that Christian knights might be nearby and discover them, his voice dropped to a whisper. "It is *hadas*, as aromatic as the *hadas* of the Holy Land."

Ibn Amram leaned forward slightly, taking care not to disturb the young man's head balanced on his knee.

"The mystery is revealed, Banu Hajaj," he said to the raider. "Along each leaf of this myrtle is a series of circlets, each containing a drop of myrtle balm. We prepare the leaves like so and then apply them to the wound."

His strong fingernail broke the circlets of oil. As he rubbed the thick leaves into a crude paste, a heavy fragrance engulfed them.

"Thank the Almighty," Banu Hajaj exclaimed, likewise forgetting for the moment the need for silence. "I have found a Jewish *chakim* for my boy!"

"That will do for the present," Ibn Amram said, well pleased with his makeshift medicine. "If you can locate a farmyard with chickens, a few eggs would do nicely as a salve. Or we could use butter, if the farmer's wife has churned any. But then, we are getting ahead of ourselves. First, we must get out of this place."

"For your kindness, I would let you go now, *chakim*," Banu Hajaj declared. "But I cannot risk your telling the *caballeros* of my whereabouts."

His hand moved as a sign of their imprisonment. Although Ibn Amram and Joseph were not in shackles, the control which the Muslim exerted was as tight as a band of steel.

"No, you must stay with me. I could not allow you to talk with the *Commandador* of the garrison Gonzalo de Ruiz." He spat on the ground in anger.

"Then we shall leave with you," Ibn Amram said firmly. "I do not want to see more bloodshed today. Here, give me a hand with your son, Banu Hajaj. If we can get him up into Joseph's saddle, the extra weight will be better carried by the stallion than by our ponies."

Making plans for their departure appealed to the Muslim raider. For the moment, he was able to put aside thoughts of his losses and concentrate on the good fortune his men had in waylaying such a major herd of cattle. His mathematics failed him when he tried to estimate the money this herd would bring in the stockyards of Merida.

"Never mind," he said, brushing aside the particulars of the coming transaction. "It will put many silver *dirhams* in our hands. And then we will return to the frontier towns, to Albarracin, Teruel and Segrobe to buy the weapons and armor we need to fight these Christian knights."

"You mean you buy your weapons from Christians?" Joseph asked in surprise. The battle over Spain was becoming more and more bizarre to him.

"But of course," Banu Hajaj answered, casting a lurid grin in the general direction of Saragossa. "What better way is there to meet a knight on the field of battle than with the very same armaments that the craftsmen of Toledo have made for him? I know exactly what kind of body armor the hateful Gonzalo de Ruiz wears. I know the length and thickness of his lance. I know the weight of the armor he uses on his warhorse. For the moment, he has the advantage. But when I bribe the armament makers with heavy silver *dirhams*, they will give me the same or better. Money is everything to these Christians."

"I thought the knights were motivated by the love of Heaven and the fear of Hell," Joseph contended.

He struggled to keep Achbar upright in the saddle as they descended a steep incline.

"That is what they would have you think," Banu Hajaj scoffed. "I know the superficial piety of this Gonzalo de Ruiz, his love of titles and all the trappings of knightly respect. But when it comes to the welfare of his eternal soul, he hires a private chaplain for a pittance. You know, I once kidnapped the chaplain. Yes, I, Ali Banu Hajaj, almost trapped the prideful Gonzalo in his own confessional, but the chaplain cried out at the last moment!"

His laugh was vulgar and ribald, delighting in exposing the hidden weaknesses of his arch opponent.

"Why do you hate him with such bitterness?" Ibn Amram asked.

"The man is a savage," Banu Hajaj retorted. "If he stood

here this very moment, I would spit in his face. His father was of the lowest scum, and he wrongs the pure blood of his mother!"

After this tirade, Banu Hajaj fell silent, panting at the exertion of his emotions. The rest of the party fell silent, too, until an orange haze could be seen on the horizon. Ali Banu Hajaj whirled around. All color drained from his face.

"That son of a swine!" he cursed between clenched teeth. "Gonzalo de Ruiz is burning out my men from their stronghold in the hills. The dog! And to think he is my half-brother! I cannot tell you the pain it causes me, *chakim*."

"Brother? But how can this be?"

"Yes, it is true," Banu Hajaj answered, ruefully shaking his head. "My mother was a woman of precious virtue. I never understood how she could marry Martin de Ruiz when my father was killed. And that dog of a Christian raised Gonzalo as a Christian too. Son of a dog! Oh, forgive me, mother."

"War brings great sadness," Ibn Amram said quietly. "Did you ever see your mother again?"

"How could I?" Banu Hajaj asked with open hands. "Her husband demands that I convert to Catholicism. I accused him of abducting my sweet mother, and he laughed in my face. He turned to my own brother and pointed at me. 'Remember that face well, Gonzalo,' he said. 'That is the face of your worst enemy. He would steal your mother from under our noses if we aren't careful!' Then he spat on me and Gonzalo did likewise.

"I swore to take my revenge on them! I committed myself to my personal *jihad*, a holy war against these idolaters. And it will not be fulfilled until Gonzalo de Ruiz is slain!"

A tiny mountain stream had broken through a patch of red clay and stained its course like a tracery of blood. Ibn Amram knelt beside the water to rinse Achbar's bandages. He pinched more myrtle leaves between his thumb and forefinger, grinding them back and forth across the leathery leaf until the oil became a soft paste that oozed under his fingernails. Then he spread the unguent across the linen and returned the bandages to Achbar's face.

"Good lad," Ibn Amram said. "You didn't wince even once this time. It must be having some effect."

The sun was low in the sky, reminding Ibn Amram that he had not taken a sighting in a number of days.

"This will only take a moment," he explained to Banu Hajaj and extricated the astrolabe from under his coat. While he positioned himself to take a good sighting, the Muslim leader sauntered down the hill to check for edible berries.

Beneath the simplicity of his passions, the complexity of Banu Hajaj's life lay heavily on Joseph's mind.

"The fury of a brother wronged spills more blood than a king's ambitions," Joseph remarked quietly to his master. "Blood feuds justify the worst obscenities of war."

Ibn Amram nodded, still involved in his sighting on the sun. "This violence gives soldiers a taste for more violence. They cannot live without it. If you think Banu Hajaj is fanatic, you can imagine what his brother is saying to his troops right now. And when one wins and the other dies, can we really think these violent men will revert to a life of peace? Or will they continue their violence by finding a new enemy?"

"That is what Yerucham Halevi said," Joseph agreed. "He said that the reconquest is the beginning of the end. Either the Christians will win or the Muslims. And then they will turn the full force of their attention against the Jews."

The thought crossed Ibn Amram's mind that such an evil decree might be averted if his mission to the caliph were a success. If only an accommodation could be found between Muslim and Christian, the lands of Spain would be blessed with peace. Jews of the realm would no longer dangle over the precipice of war and politics.

He struggled to hold his astrolabe steady for an accurate reading.

"The king is tolerant and his influence may extend to other kingdoms," he remarked. "He may then enlighten Garcia

Ramirez of Navarre and all his other vassals. That is the promise of our age, if peace prevails and I can strengthen his hand to stop mindless superstition."

The sighting was never completed. Ali Banu Hajaj rushed up the hill and grasped the astrolabe, almost flinging it to the ground before Ibn Amram could stop him.

"What are you doing, foolish man?" the Muslim screamed. "Are you deliberately signalling to the garrison of Saragossa or are you so blind that you don't see the flashes?"

"Oh, my heavens!" Ibn Amram gasped, realizing at last that the shiny bronze astrolabe had sent flickering flashes of sunlight back to the fortress on the river.

"Perhaps they did not notice!"

"Perhaps chickens have teeth!" Banu Hajaj answered maliciously. "You should know that Gonzalo de Ruiz is combing the hills for us. He does not give up that easily. He will ride for days without sleep if he thinks he can catch me at my campfire. He is a relentless bloodhound, and you have just signalled the trail he should follow."

In a spasm of anger, he reached for his scimitar.

"Father!" Achbar called out from the shade of the rocks. "The People of the Book meant no harm. Remember that you promised him compassion in return for the compassion he has shown me."

He fell back, exhausted by the effort of speaking. Ibn Amram rushed to his side to cool his burning lips with a sip of water.

"You are right, my son," said Banu Hajaj. "But it does not lessen our danger. Nightfall is near and we're on an unprotected hill with the river to the north and the grainfield of Mendosa to the south."

"If there is a grainfield, is there a granary?" Ibn Amram asked suddenly.

Banu Hajaj shrugged while he tried to remember the details.

"There is a large granary by the new road. And then, there

is the old Roman granary near the ruins of the old Roman road. It is nothing more than a huge cavern, but it is well hidden."

"This granary," Ibn Amram began, "is it a suitable hiding place?"

"It is excellent! There is only one entrance and we are the only ones who know about it."

"Only one entrance?" Joseph echoed in astonishment. "We would be fools to enter that silo. It could become a perfect trap!"

"That is exactly what Gonzalo de Ruiz would think, too," Banu Hajaj answered. "The more I think about it, the more I am convinced that the knights would never bother to search every nook. The most obvious hiding places are the ones which tired soldiers overlook."

"You may be right," Ibn Amram said, rising to his feet and twirling the damp cloth to cool it. He applied it again to the youth's face.

"There is little else we can do now. At least, a Spaniard's lance is a poor weapon in a silo."

"You are right, *chakim*," Banu Hajaj declared, touching the hilt of his scimitar with clear meaning.

A violet haze was slowly descending with the dusk onto the barren fields. Banu Hajaj hurried to lead the way to the granary.

"Ah, there it is, Achbar," he whispered.

"But where is the door?" Joseph asked.

"There is no door, but there are still overhanging fronds to keep out the rains. They were planted hundreds of years ago, and the branches are as thick as your wrist."

"Can you guide us in with safety, Banu Hajaj?" Ibn Amram asked, controlling any sign of anxiety in his voice.

"I admit that I likely could not," the Muslim answered. "It has been many years since I was here."

"Then I shall be the guide," Achbar whispered painfully. "I will tell you where to walk, if you tell me what you feel on the walls of the cavern."

They stepped forward into the profound darkness, Banu Hajaj and Joseph supporting the youth on their arms while Ibn Amram led the horses. The vines overhanging the entry fell back into place, and the pony whinnied in distrust of the sudden darkness.

"I know how you feel, old fellow," Ibn Amram whispered. The darkness was like the utter lack of light he had experienced when the sun had disappeared in Languedoc. How quickly light could be snuffed out! The cavern made him think about the impending celestial darkness and that thought, in turn, saddened him greatly. As for now, the dangers of the cavern menaced them. Who knew what would greet them in the bowels of the earth? There might be mountains of grain to thwart every footstep like the great sea of sand in Tunisia. Or the cave might be barren with no corner to hide in if pursuers lit a torch. The darkness depressed Ibn Amram, but he declined to express his thoughts.

"It is warm in here!" Banu Hajaj exclaimed, his voice echoing back from a distant wall. "You will not catch a fever here tonight, my son."

Unlike the field which had quickly cooled off, the cavern was hot and dry, with a dusty taste that lingered in everyone's throat. Joseph scuffed his boots along the worn floor, feeling for any hidden obstacles. There were none.

"There isn't any grain at all. It must be very large," Joseph whispered, appalled by the echo that returned to his ears.

"Over there, Joseph," Ibn Amram whispered from behind. "The echo points us to your right. You will find a broad rock. And I suspect it will be vertical by the intensity of the echo."

More scuffling sounds of boots followed. Achbar coughed on the dust which they raised, and the sound rebounded from the walls like the mournful hooting of a barn owl.

A horrid sensation of a physical presence directly in front of his face made Joseph wince. He extended his hand into the blackness that was almost palpable. But his hand touched nothing. He waved his hand violently from side to side, convinced that something was there. Only a hot wind touched the tips of his fingers.

Standing so near to Joseph, Ibn Amram could feel the contortions of his arms.

"It is a deceitful sensation of the darkness," he explained. "We think that there is something oppressive when really there is nothing at all. It is an absence. A great void that lurks before us, mocking our eyes. We simply must press forward and disprove the mockery."

"Whoa, boy. Easy, old fellow," Ibn Amram said in soothing tones to the black stallion.

Even the animals did not like the darkness, sensing exactly what the boy had felt. Ibn Amram marvelled at the sensation in the cavern, so much like the superstition that gripped the poor folk of Languedoc during that frightening eclipse.

He tried to remember if it was six summers ago or seven. The darkness had fallen in the late afternoon. It had been almost palpable, like the darkness of this silo, and men in their ignorance had stampeded out like a herd of mindless sheep, trampling anything that stood in their way. He had felt an immense sadness at the fears and frailties of man on that afternoon. But now, so many years later, he could comprehend those fears in the oppressive darkness of a silo in Aragon.

"Ah, I have found it at last," Banu Hajaj said. The echo had almost ceased. Ibn Amram worked his way forward and likewise felt the warm rock face against his palm.

"Now we turn left," Banu Hajaj advised. "Do you remember, Achbar, how we played here when you were a child and the darkness was a test? We will go perhaps fifty paces, then the floor will slope. That marks the end of the silo. It is a suitable place for us to hide."

Before they had reached forty paces, Banu Hajaj paused to test the echoes. Banu Hajaj counted out the paces which they took.

"And now the floor slopes," Joseph advised as the count neared fifty.

Ibn Amram led the animals around the perimeter of the small room fashioned in rock. He spoke in soothing tones, assuring them that the darkness and stillness were quite natural. Then he tethered them together at the far end.

"We must get some sleep," he said. "From my own experience, I wake up earlier than I should when I have no stars to gauge the passage of time."

Ali Banu Hajaj was near the far wall. The sound of his hands scraping lightly, wiping through the fine sand was faintly discerned.

"But first we both have our own prayers to attend to, doctor," he replied.

A softer sound followed. Perhaps it was the sliding noise of a small prayer rug laid on the floor.

Ibn Amram by reflex motioned to Joseph, then realized that no motion could be seen. He reached out and touched the boy's shoulder, then rose to his feet.

"*Vehu Rachum*," he sang in a quiet voice that was just loud enough to reach Joseph's ears. Would there, indeed, be mercy for the remainder of the night?

A heavy hand fell on Joseph's mouth, stifling any possible cry. He opened his eyes in fear and, to his abject surprise, found that he could see. Unlike daylight, a light in the silo flickered. Ibn Amram's ruddy face seemed to waver, like the flame of a candle. His mind told him that the light was playing tricks with his eyes. Crouched above him, Ibn Amram motioned imperatively for total silence. In the far back, the hazy light of a torch lit the huge outer room of the granary and fantastical shadows danced on the rock roof. Banu Hajaj was fastening coats and blankets to the head of each pony. His motions had the stealth of the leopard. Achbar had not yet awakened.

Ibn Amram motioned to Joseph to keep his head down, and he then crept across the sloping floor to silence any possible sound from the Muslim youth, just as he had done with Joseph. A faint sound reached their ears, and an acid scent tickled Joseph's nose.

He crept on knees and elbows across the floor, placing each with meticulous care and testing the surface so that no sand should scrape or grate under his weight. Catlike, Joseph inched forward so slowly that he felt dizzy at the prolonged vision of russet shadows. At last, he reached the rock from which Ibn Amram was peering cautiously into the outer room.

A knight, dressed in a full coat of chain mail, brandished a smoky torch which he thrust before him repeatedly. In the ghastly light, the saffron lacquer of his mail glowed like diabolical gold. His footsteps were not cautious, and he occasionally kicked a pebble, which he cursed under his breath. It might take minutes or it might take hours; but it was simply a matter of time before he would stumble upon the recess in which they hid.

Ali Banu Hajaj had already drawn his scimitar, but he remained by the horses. Although the cave was pitch black except for the smudgy light of the knight's firebrand, the night was evidently giving way to a grey dawn. The first bats were returning to the silo. They fluttered in erratic patterns without a sound.

The knight became terrified.

"Get you hence, spawn of Satan!" he shouted, waving the torch at the darting creatures. "This must be a temple of idol worship. Pagans go into caves in the rocks and into holes in the earth. The bats and the moles are their only companions. Begone, Mephisto's minions!"

He swung his torch more violently and almost extinguished the flame, to his utter terror. His heavy footsteps echoed without pause back to the entrance of the silo.

"We have been saved by the cave dwelling bats," Ibn Amram said with a nervous sigh.

"Not so," Ali Banu Hajaj replied in the enveloping darkness. "The cave dwellers have saved the life of this one Christian." His scimitar grated with grim authority as he returned it to its scabbard.

The pause while they waited to see if the knight would return with his comrades was painfully long. The horses were becoming restless, and Banu Hajaj controlled them with difficulty.

"Strange, isn't it, that we did not notice the acid smell of the bats last night?" Joseph whispered.

"When danger stalks in the night, your ears become the chief organ for your safety," Ibn Amram answered. "Your nose lost all importance. With a new day, our worst fears are behind us and the sensations we lost last night are retrieved as a strange novelty."

"Then let us leave this silo now," Banu Hajaj remarked. His voice echoed eerily, as he walked ahead into the large chamber.

Their footsteps were cautious. The blackness was as impenetrable as it had been at night, but a glimmer of green hinted at the location of the vines.

"Do not look directly at the green," Achbar cautioned, pulling Joseph back by the arm. "You will fatigue your eyes in straining to see what is not yet there. Rather, you must look indirectly. Cast your vision to the left and right and watch for a glimmer of movement at the edges of your vision. You still see it?"

Joseph blinked again and looked away. The green glimmer seemed to dart at the edges of his outstretched arm.

"It is there," he whispered. "We have come the right way."

Ali Banu Hajaj eased forward like a feline predator and touched the fronds of the vine with the tip of his scimitar. They rustled then fell back in place. He waited quietly, then thrust his scimitar through in a deadly stabbing motion. The tip met no obstruction. He waited again, as patient as a leopard in a tree. Slowly, he eased the fronds aside with his weapon and a brilliant light filled the opening of the silo. The stallion stamped his approval.

The game of cat-and-mouse was not yet over, but it was

almost won. Banu Hajaj handed the reins of the two ponies to Joseph and crept into the brilliant sunshine, slipping from rock to rock to reach the promontory. His dusty cloak and hood blended with the dry landscape, making him one with the rocks. Again imperturbable in his stealth, he gained high ground, waiting for any sign of movement in the panorama of stubbly fields and rocky *mesetas*.

At last, Banu Hajaj was satisfied. He leaped down from the rock and threw back the hood of his garment. His stride was the epitome of supreme self-confidence.

"We have succeeded, doctor," he said, strutting up to the horses like a rooster. "Gonzalo de Ruiz may be persistent, but he does not have the tenacity of Ali Banu Hajaj. I shall live another day to fight him."

Ibn Amram mounted his pony and motioned to Joseph to do likewise.

"You live by your wits, as do all warriors, Banu Hajaj," he remarked. "With your cleverness you could have served as the vizier of any one of the Muslim kings of Andalusia, instead of being a commander of these ragtag raiders. Why do you fight this battle when you could live a life of comfort in the city?"

The question was pointed, and for a moment, the raider seemed undecided. He laughed raucously.

"You would have me serve the corrupt *muluk* of Badajoz or maybe the *muluk* of Huelva?" His laughter rose again in coarse mockery of the idea. "They are nothing but greedy pretenders. All the Almoravids are like that! No luxury is too ostentatious for them. They refuse to give up their pleasures. And the worst of it is that they mock the truly pious reformers as unlettered barbarians who descended from the mountains with the zeal of a new faith. They dare to mock the Almohad caliph!"

"It is a hot dry wind blowing north from Africa," Ibn Amram observed. "Your caliph represents a kind of Islam that has not been seen in Iberia for many generations."

"It is not a kind of Islam," Banu Hajaj responded, rising in his saddle so that his eyes were at the same level with Ibn Amram's. "There is only one Islam. It is only we Almohads who still believe in the absolute unity of Allah. We are proud of our beliefs and our holy name."

"Certainly, your Caliph Al-Kumi is proud of the name Almohad," Ibn Amram said.

"It is the only name," Banu Hajaj replied with the simplicity of an ascetic. "We will blot the Almoravid names from the memory of Andalusia. In no more than a generation, the Almoravids will be forgotten." His smile contorted into a sardonic leer. "Is it not much like the name of the Karaites, doctor? Will anyone remember the name of your heretics in another generation?"

The thrust was so unexpected that Ibn Amram literally jumped in surprise.

"The analogy is spurious," Ibn Amram said flatly, trying to avoid signs that the thrust had found its mark. "Islam conquers with the sword. As you call us People of the Book, you must know that the Book and not the sword is in our hands. I do not deny that the Karaites are heretics. But we will win them over with the Book, not with the sword."

"As you will, *chakim*," Banu Hajaj answered. "I know that a book did not drive them from Castile. But that is no matter at the present. You will see in time that the fortunes of man are determined by the sword. I wish you well as you journey to the sea. But you might be stopped by other Muslim raiders. Here, take this!"

He reached within his *burnous* and drew out a scrap of parchment.

"It bears my sign for a safe journey. In the presence of an Almohad it could prove a valuable talisman."

Ibn Amram exhaled quickly and took the parchment offered to him. He sensed a passing motive of contrition on the part of Banu Hajaj.

"A valuable talisman?" he echoed. "And what will it be if I meet Christians on the road?"

Banu Hajaj reined in his pony tightly, obliging the creatures to wait patiently.

"I think you know the answer already," he said. "Treat it as you treat the instruments of the stars. In the presence of those who hate your science, it is wisely out of sight!"

The ponies of Banu Hajaj and Achbar slowly ascended the hillside. Ibn Amram looked up at the dust that drifted on the wind, then down at the scrap of parchment still in his hand. He fumbled for the catch on his money pouch and tucked the note away.

"We have received more than we anticipated on this leg of our journey, Joseph," he said. "We have seen brother pitted against brother. And did you notice the gall of the fellow in making his comparison to our own Karaite affair? My heart is troubled!"

Banu Hajaj's jibe about the Karaites brought them quickly to Ibn Amram's mind, but not as a faceless abstraction. They appeared almost in flesh and blood in the person of Yissaschar Rikuv. Where was that misguided boy? he wondered. The lad's twisted smile and livid anger vexed his memory. Yet the cool depth of Yissaschar's eyes offered a bewildering solace, an intimation that this heretic, for one, might be saved from his own notions.

Joseph turned his stallion towards the river.

"Remember what you told me. The river road is long and winding. You will have plenty of time to think about a solution to the problem of the Karaites. But for now we can wash and be thankful that we have lived another day to bless the Merciful One."

CHAPTER TEN

The Black Monks

TARRAGONA, ARAGON
AUTUMN, 1139

"*HOLA, PESCADOR!*" IBN AMRAM CALLED OUT TO THE FISHERMAN wading in the shallows of the Francoli River. "Fisherman! Have you caught anything for two travellers?"

The edges of the net were hanging from the bank into the water, and a large fish was flapping around inside. The fisherman whacked at the movement with a short club, sending showers of water into his own face. He wrestled the unruly fish into submission and managed to raise it, still squirming, though he held it firmly by the gill.

"Ah, a greenback tench," Ibn Amram murmured. "That will be tasty. How much to conclude our transaction?"

"One *dirham*," the fisherman answered sullenly. "And it should be a *dirham* of silver, if you please."

Joseph rolled up his leggings and waded into the weedy shallows to examine the fish. It was not quite so big as it had first seemed. Something else was lurking in the net, not quite as rambunctious as the first fish.

"A good price, *pescador*," Joseph said, holding the coin just beyond the man's reach. "You said it was one *dirham* for the pair?"

The old man scowled but lunged forward again with his club, sending a great splash of water this time over Joseph.

"As you will, *hombre*. Whether it is one fish for a *dirham* or two. The Francoli is full of fish. What I don't catch today, I will catch tomorrow."

He handed the fish roughly to Joseph and reached immediately for the coin, testing it with a hard bite between his molars.

Joseph turned with his hands full and clambered back up the embankment. He threw the fish onto the grass, and while he wiggled his toes to dry his feet, he filleted the fish.

"How much further is it to Tarragona?" Ibn Amram called out to the fisherman.

"On such a mount, you will reach the seaport by tomorrow afternoon, if you follow the new road."

"And that is the new road over yonder?"

"That it is, *hombre*." The fisherman went back to drying his nets.

"We have made good time for the past three days, Joseph," Ibn Amram said, unhooking his saddle bag so that Joseph could slip the fish inside.

"No Muslim raiders have stopped us, and no Christian *caballeros* have challenged us. I must remember this peaceful route for the future."

He headed for the road which had recently been slashed through a dense copse of cork oak. There was no need for haste. With some fresh fish to savor, both of them were looking forward to their warm dinner. With the nip of late autumn in the air, both had their eyes peeled for a suitable place to camp.

There were times on their long trip when Ibn Amram and

Joseph relished the comfort of an early camp. A leisurely conclusion to the day's ride compensated for their hectic pace. But plans for a peaceful evening can often go awry.

The horse and pony had been given their fodder, the meal had been prepared and eaten and their *Mishnah* was open, all before the sun had settled below the topmost branches of the high trees flanking the river. Ibn Amram's forefinger drew their eyes down to the page and soon they were immersed in Torah.

The black stallion snorted, warning of the arrival of a stranger at dusk. They looked up and beheld a ghastly sight.

"Oh, save my eternal soul," the man sobbed, weakened by a savage beating. Both his eyes were swollen, and his scalp was caked with dried blood. His coat was ripped and muddied. Ibn Amram leaped to his feet and rushed to the man's aid.

"Poor man," he whispered with compassion. "Who has beaten you?"

"Only you can stand as witness to my expiation," the man sobbed, oblivious to the question. "My time is near, and my pure soul longs for its freedom."

He choked on a mouthful of blood, but Ibn Amram turned his head quickly and thumped him vigorously between the shoulder blades to relieve his labored breathing.

"Do not talk," Ibn Amram warned, taking off his coat and rolling it up as a pillow for the man. "You are in no condition to talk."

He tried to lower the man's arms to his sides and make him rest, but the delirium was frantic.

"I see the heavens opening for me!" he raved, waving his arms in rejoicing. "Above are the eighteen angels. They beckon me through each of the seven heavens, through green pastures, cool waters, the gentlest breezes! I feel it! I feel it within! Neither hot nor cold, nor thirst nor hunger. I see outstretched a holy cloth of light. They beckon me to wrap myself in it!"

His words became incomprehensible as he babbled on.

Then his head crooked to the side, and he fell into a deep sleep, broken only by his heavy breathing.

Joseph reached forward and felt the man's forehead. "It is not hot, *Mori*, and yet the poor man raves as one with a terrible fever. I have never seen such a strange malady."

"Nor have I," Ibn Amram commented, rising to step back and contemplate the man. "Here is an enigma. A well-dressed man travelling in Aragon, apparently assaulted by ruffians. He does not repeat the details of his beating, as is common when someone suffers at the hands of highwaymen. Rather, he steps beyond the here and now to strange visions. It makes me uneasy. But when he regains wakefulness, I am sure we will learn more."

Joseph prepared a poultice of myrtle which Ibn Amram applied to the man's face. They returned to their *Mishnah*, but the stranger disturbed their study with his labored breathing.

Later that night, in the weak light of the waxing moon, Ibn Amram saw the man stir. The man sat with his elbows on his knees and his face cradled in the palms of his hands.

"What is wrong?" Ibn Amram asked gently, unnerved by the man's crying.

"I am hungry," he answered. "And that is proof that I have not been released from this evil body. My travail of expiation must continue."

"Shall I get him what remains of our supper?" Joseph asked. "It is still in the pot."

The man shuddered and drew back as Joseph approached.

"It is meat! I am sure it is meat. Oh, I cannot stand this punishment!"

Joseph was dumfounded. "No it is not meat. It is fish. Greenback tench caught today in the Francoli. You will like it, sir, if you taste a morsel."

"Fish, you say?" The man had instantly lost his aversion for the meal and drew forward again. "I can eat fish, you know. It is not a fruit of generation."

He dipped his fingers into the pot and greedily drew up chunks of fish and gruel. His motions were furtive, like a hungry wolf throwing food back into its gullet without chewing a morsel. Even his eyes were wolf-like as he lunged forward for each bite then threw the food back into his throat with a swing of his neck.

When the meal was finished and the beaten man had drunk great gulps of water to down the chunks of fish, they sat opposite each other with the campfire flickering between.

"You were hungry," Ibn Amram said in understatement.

"That I was. Most hungry. A sure sign of continued punishment." He belched as punctuation to that thought.

"There is something I do not understand," Ibn Amram said, looking at the pale eyes which squinted past the swollen eyelids and the wrappings of the bandage. "You called the fish a fruit of generation."

"Oh, no, just the opposite!" the man replied, instantly alarmed. "Fish do not procreate, you know! They arise spontaneously in the sea or in the river. That is not generation, and that is why we can eat fish."

"I thought you were a Catholic who does not eat fish on Friday," Joseph suggested.

The man laughed a grim laugh of hatred and regret.

"To think that I might be mistaken for a Catholic. What a precious thought! You speak to Henri du Mans, and I am a Cathar, one of the truly pure."

"Oh, a pure Catholic," Joseph muttered. "There are many kinds of monks these days."

"You do not understand, boy," Henri du Mans retorted. "We are the true church, although the Catholics hate us for our wisdom."

"And who beat you?" Ibn Amram interjected.

"It was a coincidence on the road. I was accosted by a evil-eyed beggar who cursed me and then asked me for alms. I walked away from him, but he followed me. And then the black monks came over the crest of the road. They seized my arm and demanded that I give alms to this vile creature. Oh, they cannot run roughshod over Henri du Mans. I told them of their mortal sin, and they beat me so badly they almost released me from this life of suffering."

Ibn Amram answered sternly, "Your ravings sound absurd to me. No wonder the monks beat you."

"Forgive me if my words spill with impetuosity, *Monsieur le Rabbin*," the Cathar answered. "I suspect that you would rave, too, if you felt the club of Christianity across your back. As for your teachings, I have just one thought to tell you. The snake was right!"

"What do you mean?" Ibn Amram said coldly.

"I am surprised at how little you know of your own Bible, *Monsieur le Rabbin*," Henri du Mans continued, undaunted by Ibn Amram's cold stare. "We accept that there is a hidden truth in your Bible but, poor bird, you do not realize that Satan has caught you and your ancestors in his snare. Noah, in his simplicity, thought that the world was saved by the Almighty. He did not know that the work was done by the Devil."

"Your words are a sacrilege!" Ibn Amram flared. "Your Cathar dogma is heretical nonsense."

"You cannot silence truth forever," the Cathar responded, raising his voice another octave. "The snake of the Almighty cannot be silenced. Where did evil come from, *Monsieur le Rabbin*? You cannot answer, can you? You dare not answer!"

"I cannot answer a fool," Ibn Amram answered quietly. "Your obsession with evil leads you to deny the good. Yes, there is evil. But there is far more good than evil. The Master of the Universe is Master over all, even what appears to you as evil. Do you not understand that simple fact, Henri du Mans?"

"You are trying to equivocate, *Monsieur le Rabbin*," the Cathar shot back, squinting at Ibn Amram through swollen, bloodshot eyes. "You see evil all around you, and yet you try to tell me it is not there! I can assure you that Satan is proud of you for perpetuating his lies about the goodness of creation. When the final judgment comes and the Creator overcomes the evil of Satan, only pure souls will rise up to the spiritual world. For your obstinacy, you Jews will be condemned to this hell forever!"

"According to your thinking, there is not one Master of the Universe but two. And what we call good, you call bad. I feel sorry for the churchmen who must contend with such a strange heresy as yours, Henri du Mans."

"Do not be complacent, *Monsieur le Rabbin*. I don't have to remind you that you Jews have your problems with Karaites. Do you really think Karaites will be simple-minded sheep to be herded out of Castile and sent to other lands?"

"Your words are an evil bluff, Henri du Mans," Ibn Amram answered, permitting his voice to rise in anger. "We have our arguments with the Karaites, but their Torah is our Torah. They would never alter the holy text. They already accept the Written Law, and one day, they will accept the Oral Law. So don't try your petty games with me. I will not stand for it."

"Ah, I have touched a tender nerve and the rabbi jumps," Henri du Mans mocked. "You would like to pretend the Karaites have never had contact with the pure Cathars. But many of them have already taken the first step to enter the perfection of Catharism. We will convince them yet that their Written Law is a hoax."

"You lie!" Ibn Amram roared. "I cannot take another word of this endless gutter of falsehoods."

"You cannot prove me wrong," Henri du Mans said, drawing back from the fire as he saw Ibn Amram advance. "You Rabbanites have driven the Karaites from Castile, and you pretend that the expulsion will end the problem. Do you truly believe they will disappear into thin air? No! They will join with us and bring everlasting purity to the world!"

"The road to Tarragona is well supplied with kindling for a campfire," Ibn Amram advised, his voice now icy cold. "I would advise you to leave our campsite at once."

Henri du Mans rose to his feet, then tripped and fell when he saw a club in Ibn Amram's hand.

"Take it," Ibn Amram said. "You will need a walking stick for your journey tonight. Do not pretend I would have hit you with it. That is not the way of Judaism." His outstretched arm was steady, his gaze unyielding.

"You have shown me an unexpected kindness," the Cathar said, taking the stick and testing it. "I will give you some advice in return. Take the Roman road that runs past the amphitheater if you are going to Tarragona. Do not take the new road, unless you wish to encounter the black monks!"

He turned slowly and shuffled away.

Ibn Amram stood with his hands on his hips for many minutes until he saw the figure lit by moonlight disappear over the crest of the distant hill.

"I did not understand why we could not seem to concentrate when the man was here," he said to Joseph. "Now, I wonder if Henri du Mans is really a man or a *shed*, a demon created out of fire and air."

He shivered at the thought and returned to the smoldering embers of the campfire to wrap himself in his blanket.

"Do you really think the Karaites are in league with the Cathars?" Joseph questioned.

"Do not trouble your mind with that taunt," Ibn Amram advised. "We have experienced the evil of a misguided Karaites, but we have also conversed with those whose motives are good. Enough of this Cathar! We must sleep now for our trip tomorrow. It will take longer to reach Tarragona if we follow the Roman road as he advised."

The next day dawned with a penetrating drizzle that soaked their blankets and their spirits.

"Do you really think it is necessary to follow the Roman road, as the Cathar advised, *Mori*?" Joseph asked, reluctant to undertake the arduous circuit through mud and brambles. He had already climbed up into his saddle and was surveying the grey expanse of forests.

"The race is not won by the swift," Ibn Amram answered, tightening the girths of his saddle. "It will be a slower journey by the Roman road, but our safe arrival will be more certain."

He mounted and pushed ahead into the trees, ducking the many low branches. Snorting and foaming from their exertion, the horse and pony picked their way gingerly along the rough gravel laid so many years before by the slaves of the Emperor Hadrian. It was a straight road, cut through the forest with the dexterous confidence of a conquering army. But the years of neglect were now showing. Saplings pushed up through the roadbed, and some sections were completely washed out by spring floods.

"Be careful at the washouts," Ibn Amram warned. "The gravel underneath is flinty and a danger to the hooves."

They had almost reached the Roman walls of the seaport when Ibn Amram's warning bore bitter fruit. His pony stumbled on a sharp stone of the broken roadway, splitting his hoof. Ibn Amram quickly dismounted, shaking his head in regret.

"We will have to walk the rest of the way and then sell this pony in the market. Here, help me shift these saddle bags to the stallion. He is able to carry the extra weight."

His fingers fumbled with the thongs of the saddlebags. They walked along in silence, thinking more of the voyage on the Mediterranean that would take them to Tunis than the inconvenience of the split hoof.

The sight of a huge tent surrounded by black-frocked monks outside the old Roman amphitheater arrested their attention, bringing them both back to the present.

"Do not pause in your footsteps, Joseph," Ibn Amram whispered. "And above all, do not try a futile escape. There are too many of them!"

It was a shocking discovery that the man he saved from a mortal beating had deliberately misled them. With a sickening twist to his stomach, Ibn Amram realized the fullest implications of the Cathar's parting words. A perfidious deception! The black monks had not met the Cathar on the new road. Their encampment was right here on the Roman road.

A big-boned novice, still sunburnt from his days behind

the plow, caught sight of the two travellers and dropped his buckets to accost them.

"Halt!" he shouted. "Stand and be counted before Prior Matthew!"

Blocking the road with his great size, the youth pointed to a carriage where books and tables denoted a mobile office of sorts.

"What have we here, Bartholomew?" the prior asked, looking up from his quill. "Is it infidels you have caught? They look like infidels."

"No, *Senor el Prior*," Ibn Amram answered in a Castilian overlaced with nuances of Arabic pronunciation. "I am a Jew of the Realm. We are both Jews."

"Does a Jew talk like a Muslim and dress like a Muslim?" Prior Matthew retorted. His Castilian was heavily overlaid with the accent of Cluny. "Truly, this is yet another matter which the abbot must raise with the king. Your reasons for travelling on this road are unclear. You are not merchants, because you have nothing to sell. I suspect you are infidels or spies of the infidels. You will not leave until the abbot hears of this."

Ibn Amram stepped back from the table and eyed the open road.

"We must leave now, Master Prior," he stated with civility. "Our business takes us to Tarragona."

"Are you deaf?" the prior answered, turning back to his parchment. "You will leave when the abbot decides you can leave. Tether your horses. You will be called."

The equerry proved to be a pleasant young man, the son of an equerry of the royal house of Burgundy. He was currying the horses of the abbot's carriage, but he instantly dropped what he was doing and walked over to Ibn Amram when he saw how his pony limped.

"A nasty split," he muttered, examining the hoof with a gentle hand. "But I have the remedy."

With practiced skill, he crouched beside the animal,

whittled at the damaged hoof with a strong knife and daubed unguent on the split.

"Thank you, young man," Ibn Amram said, watching the procedure with keen interest. "I am sure the creature would thank you, too, if he could talk."

"Oh, they thank me in other ways, traveller," the young monk responded, examining the ankles of the pony. "They know when someone shows them a kindness. Here, the thong of your headstall is worn. If you have a moment, I can fashion a new one."

Ibn Amram's glance was rueful.

"I don't seem to be in a hurry now. But I had hoped to reach Tarragona before evening. They say I must tarry here until the abbot will see me."

"Your delay is momentary," the monk explained. "The bloodletting of Brother Peter will not take much longer."

Joseph felt some surprise at such radical treatment. "Why does the abbot need bloodletting?" he asked. "Is he at the door of death?"

The equerry of the abbey crossed himself at the thought. "By the grace of the Almighty, the abbot will lead us in prayer this evening. He suffers from catarrh, and the bloodletting eases his coughing. You will see."

Joseph looked back with apprehension at the billowing fabric of the tent. The great entourage of the black monks seemed totally unconcerned about the surgery. Monks and numerous novices busied themselves with the mundane tasks of feeding this virtual army.

"Thank you again," Ibn Amram said. "We will wait near the tent. If they see us, they will be less likely to forget to call us." He motioned to Joseph.

The flap of the great tent opened and a well-muscled man stepped out. His strength apparent by his bare arms, he finished wiping his bloodied hands on a towel, then flung it onto a table.

"Brother Peter will see you," he said, gesturing to the tent flap emblazoned with a silk cross. "His health is restored."

Within the darkened confines of the tent, a delicate man sat propped on a travelling divan.

"Thank you, Cantor Jerome," the abbot said fastidiously. "I will be better able to eat the goose flesh if you slice it into smaller portions."

The cantor, foregoing his normal duties of communion for the sick, prepared the delicacy for the abbot's discerning palate. Three men with books and parchments open on a trestle table watched the signs of the abbot's returning health with great interest.

The abbot noticed the two travellers and snapped his fingers to gain the cantor's attention.

"Brother Peter the Venerable, Abbot of Cluny," the cantor intoned.

"Your excellency," Ibn Amram answered, drawing closer to the smoky light of the taper beside the divan. "I am Avraham Ibn Amram and this is Joseph Vitale. We are Jews of the Realm."

"As Matthew has expressed," Peter the Venerable noted, nibbling at his slice of goose. "But you realize doubts may be raised as to your true identity as well as your true reasons for travelling this road. It has been known to happen."

"We are Jews of the Realm," Ibn Amram repeated.

"It is a moot point," Peter the Venerable responded with a shrug, tasting another portion of goose, then putting it back on the plate half-eaten. "The Council of Toledo is quite succinct. You are serfs in perpetual subjection to the Holy Church."

"Your excellency," Ibn Amram responded in measured tones. "That memorable phrase was expressed by the Church hundreds and hundreds of years ago. The more recent laws of Castile are quite clear. We are Jews of the Realm. We are Jews of the King. No matter whether we live under the authority of other dignitaries or under that of monasteries, we belong to the king alone and to him alone we owe our service."

It was a daring retort to the prideful traditionalist of Cluny, but well within the laws, as it expressed the exact wording of Alfonso's charter. The abbot grimaced and snapped his fingers. The cantor brought a goblet of wine.

"There is a dangerous drift to accommodation of subversive elements in the Kingdom of Castile," Peter the Venerable said darkly. "It is a threat we will deal with shortly. For the moment, you are safe, Jew. The will of your king protects you from investigation. But only if you truly are a Jew. These are troubled times we live in. Jews seek exemption from our authority, and heretics hide under the same prayer shawls. Let us think of the alternatives. If you are a Jew, you are a thorn in my flesh. But you might be a Saracen, or even a Karaite!"

Peter watched for Ibn Amram's reaction over the lip of his goblet.

"I can assure your excellency that I am neither a Muslim nor a Karaite. I was born a Jew, and I will die a Jew."

"Then you will be spared my invective, for the moment," Peter the Venerable answered. "Too bad you are not a Karaite. We would have much to discuss."

His delicate frame was suddenly wracked by a deep cough that seemed to tear him from within. A red-haired monk leaped to his feet and slapped the abbot on the back.

"Thank you, Robert. My breath has returned," Peter the Venerable managed to say at last. "These are my three translators, Jew. Robert of Ketton, Herman of Dalmatia and Peter of Poitiers. Peter is also my notary. They are three wise men, but they have not been led by the star of Islam."

He laughed at his private humor while the three translators nodded inscrutably at the two travellers.

"Have you ever read the Koran, Jew?" Peter asked.

"I have seen the book," Ibn Amram answered guardedly.

"Do you know what it says of Jews in its pages?" Peter motioned to the Englishman, Robert of Ketton.

"My master is entranced by my translation," Robert announced with shy pride. "He has discovered that the Saracens, unlike the Jews, do acceps some of the basic elements of Christianity."

"What has this to do with me?" Ibn Amram asked, vexed by the badgering tones of the translator.

"It is simply this," Peter the Venerable said sternly, leaning forward on the divan. "We root out the brambles and thorns of heresy. We are the zealous husbandmen of the Church, and our mission is to tend a garden run over with weeds. A heretic is no more than a lapsed Christian. We must cultivate him with all our skills of husbandry. Are you a heretic, or perhaps a hypocrite?"

One of Ibn Amram's shortcomings was his unwillingness to give an inch to an adversary. With a few mollifying words, he might have appeased the abbot who was more concerned with his own health than with two Jews who happened to wander on this road in Spain. But the abbot had raised Ibn Amram's ire.

"Look within your own monastery before you look at a Jew, your excellency," Ibn Amram answered coldly. "Your black monks profess to follow the Rule of Benedict, but white monks have personally told me that you admit a novice after only a few days. Sometimes even after a few hours!"

"Well, who are we to keep a worthy novice waiting for a full year?" Peter the Venerable sputtered, falling back into the divan. "How dare you accuse us of not keeping the rule? We follow the higher rule of Christian charity! In this way, we seize our young men before they have a chance to reconsider and fall back into the ways of the world."

He was again doubled over with coughing. Robert of Ketton thumped him between the shoulder blades.

"Your monastery is filled with misguided young men, without probation or training," Ibn Amram persisted. "And they are most certainly without charity. It is not Christian charity to beat a man as I have witnessed just yesterday."

Peter the Venerable stared long and hard at the unyielding Jew before he turned and conferred with Cantor Jerome.

Their whispers were a low mumble that carried to no one else's ears.

"My cantor concedes that such might be the case if you refer to the Cathar," the abbot said at last. "Such men are capable of goading even the pious to acts of violence. I am told that a few monks, ennobled by their crusading spirit, saw fit to strike him."

"The cowl does not make a monk," Ibn Amram observed drily.

Peter the Venerable, suddenly red-faced, leaned forward and raised his arm. His rasping cough doubled him over again, delaying his response. Robert pounded him again on the back.

"Again you blaspheme the Church and its servants! Somehow I doubt you are a Jew. Your brazen attitudes suggest most clearly to me that you are a Saracen. Look in his clothing, Robert, for signs of his faith. Check his pouch!"

Ibn Amram stepped to the far side of the table.

"You have no right to search the king's Jew," he declared.

"The king's Devil" Peter wheezed, almost overcome with rage. "A subverter of the Christian truth who won't make the slightest step toward accommodation. It's a tragedy that the wrong people were expelled from Castile. If you Rabbanite Jews had been forced into exile instead, I believe I could've been successful with the Karaites. They don't bother themselves with the insolence of the Oral Law that contradicts our teachings. Reveal your identity and purpose in travelling to the sea, insolent one, or consider the future when I replace your kind with the more sensible Karaites."

The abbot's taunt had hit its mark, leaving Ibn Amram confused for the moment. Already Robert of Ketton had stepped forward, delving nimble fingers into his pouch. The sensation brought Ibn Amram instantly to his senses. His mind raced at the proportions of his problem. Secreted within his pouch was the note from Ali Banu Hajaj. With three translators in the tent, the contents of the message would be clear. It would be hard to dispute his connection to the Muslim.

He feared most keenly for Joseph's safety, remembering his solemn promise to his old friend in Laon to safeguard the boy throughout his stay in Iberia.

"My master has asked to see your personal possessions," Robert of Ketton insisted apologetically, as Ibn Amram pulled away. "I will not damage any of your property, Jew."

"But you will not be able to see clearly in this poor light," Ibn Amram answered, grasping a new idea to lead them to safety. "Let us step outside into the light of day where you may see more clearly how innocuous my possessions are."

He turned on his heel, and before Peter the Venerable could object, he had exited from the tent. Joseph followed close on his heels.

It was almost darker outside than within the tent. The evening sun had dropped below the horizon, and now a chill purple pallor outlined the shapes of the many black monks eating their meal.

"I will be gentle," Robert insisted. "But you must place your possessions here on the table."

"Yes, you must," the cantor agreed. "The Saracens have been known to hide their Korans in the folds of their *burnouses*." He gazed fixedly at the many folds of Ibn Amram's garment. His concentration expressed his sense of suspicion.

The translator stepped forward and reached for the pouch, but in that instant, the folds fell aside and the bronze astrolabe glinted in the dim light.

"Aha! What's this?" the cantor demanded, reaching for the forbidden instrument. "So we were right!"

"It is nothing! Remove your hands," Ibn Amram commanded.

"Give it here! Peter the Venerable must know of this!"

The cantor pressed forward, fumbling to hold onto Ibn Amram's garment. Prior Matthew from the other side was all thumbs and caught up his fingers in the sleeve, pulling with great force. But the sleeve he caught was the cantor's. More hands tried to grab at Ibn Amram. Oaths were shouted at the immensity of the Jew's crime, and a young monk was dispatched immediately to the abbot's tent bearing the telltale astrolabe.

"Run, Joseph!" Ibn Amram warned in Hebrew. "Run to the stallion and ride like the wind to the harbor! Hide somewhere in the warehouse. I will meet you there soon."

Ibn Amram pointed hurriedly in the direction of the road, then dodged into the deepening dusk.

In the sudden tumult of darkening shadows, Ibn Amram eluded the hands of the cantor and the thronging monks and ran to the nearest shelter. The old Roman amphitheater towered above him and within its confines, he would surely find alleys and corridors to elude even them.

With the hubbub by the tent, Joseph slipped unnoticed past the mules and the horses tethered under the trees. The equerry never even saw him unhitch the horse. By the time anyone noticed his silhouette on the towering stallion, it was too late to stop him. Only the bony monk Bartholomew dared to step into the road to stop Joseph, but Joseph deftly turned the *caracol* taught to him by Don Umar and sped off. By the time he had disappeared past the copse of oak, Ibn Amram had disappeared through the arcade of the amphitheater.

But Bartholomew, outraged at the incident, was organizing a mob to deal with the offender even more firmly than they had dealt with the Cathar.

Ibn Amram realized that speed alone would not save him from the infuriated monks. He would have to match wits against a dozen or more men. The pale moon did not greatly benefit his needs, casting only the faintest light into the deep recesses of the main corridors.

The noise of heavy footsteps was coming closer. Ibn Amram scurried hastily down the main corridor. It was enough that he should be out of sight. With that simple objective reached, he could then formulate a coherent plan of escape.

He would rush ahead and hope to pry open the gates of the arena. They did not look very formidable. But then, what would he do in the open arena?

Ibn Amram shook his head at the unpleasant thought and eased down a ramp leading toward the gloom of the arena. Above him, he detected two monks on the upper tier, dodging back and forth as each shadow promised to be a huddled form of a man. Their cudgels were ugly in the pale moonlight. Ibn Amram could hear each dull thud as they brought the clubs down upon any moving shadow.

He swung his shoulder with ease towards the darkness and groped his way down the ramp. With no light in the dank cellar, Ibn Amram had little idea where he was going or where the ingenious passageway would lead. He instinctively made mental notes on the frequency of left and right turns in the passageway, hoping that if he had to, he could retrace his steps. He had no trouble remembering every twist of the damp corridor.

He moved forward with renewed confidence. Again, the corridor curved to the left, and now the floor inclined gently up again to a higher level. A fresh breeze struck Ibn Amram full on the face, but as yet, no light entered the dim recesses.

His hand felt along the rough hewn walls, then paused at the unmistakable coldness of iron. Both hands reached to the right. His thumbs and forefingers encircled the bars, feeling from top to bottom.

"What could it be?" he muttered. "The underground entrance of the ancient gladiators?"

Visions of an idle wealthy class of Romans came to his mind. He could almost hear the conquering Edomites above him, ranked in endless rows of seats as they watched the "players" in their deadly circus in this proud outpost of ancient Rome.

And then the awful truth of those players flooded Ibn Amram's mind. Hot tears flooded his eyes. Such players did not act out a jolly role in a play to be re-enacted over and over again. No, these players had one role and one performance. "We, who are about to die, salute you!" The doomed gladiators of Tarragona must have pronounced these words with terrible finality on this very spot.

Ibn Amram whirled back to the bars and grasped them firmly in his two hands. With the fullest exertion of his strength, he raised the gate and eased it open a crack. The hinges were mercifully silent. Then he twisted under the gate, easing it ever so gently back to its original position. He leaned against a wall as voices approached.

"He is not down here, I tell you, Brother Bartholomew. Only a madman would venture into this hole! We are wasting our time and endangering our good health in this dampness."

Footsteps told Ibn Amram that the monk was attempting to retreat back up the ramp.

"Do not give up so quickly, Brother Matthew," Bartholomew responded. "If we find him here we will have him all to ourselves."

His voice echoed down the passage, making Ibn Amram blink in the darkness. Bartholomew swung his cudgel, suddenly striking the iron bars in the darkness.

Ibn Amram did not cry out. But Brother Matthew did! The fearsome noise and bloodthirsty threats of Bartholomew were too much for the poor fellow. Ibn Amram could hear Matthew's footsteps racing up the ramp. There was a long pause, and Bartholomew reluctantly followed his colleague.

A faint sound reached Ibn Amram's ears, unlike the clattering cudgels and hollow footsteps of the monks.

"Ah, it is but a heavy rain", he thought to himself. "That will force my pursuers to seek shelter in the arcades."

Gambling on the most intrepid path to freedom as the safest, Ibn Amram hastened down the ramp to the vast playing field of the amphitheater. Over his shoulder, in the southern arcades, he could hear the raised voices and heated words of some of his pursuers. Evidently, they were of mixed opinion on the chase, some wishing to call it off and return to their comfortable bivouac. Others, however, were made of sterner stuff. Their angry voices reverberated in the darkness.

"The Jew will not escape us!" they shouted, spitting out each word with malicious venom. "We will follow the cursed astrolabist even if the Second Flood drowns us!"

Ibn Amram froze in his tracks, then slipped unnoticed behind a forlorn statue of a huntress whose arms were broken. The group of monks was too close for comfort.

"I tell you, he is nearby," one whispered. "I can smell him. Brother Matthew always said I have a nose for this sort of business."

"Nonsense," the other retorted, his teeth chattering from the driving force of the cold rains. "You smell the horse dung on your own boots! The only way out for the Jew is at the break in the battlements to the south. The others are right to lay in wait there. We will wait here until they catch him and then contribute our cudgels to his enlightenment. Beside, it is dry under this roof!"

A fierce gust of wind ripped across the open expanse of the arena, twisting curtains of rain in precarious patterns. The faint moonlight was almost obliterated by the sheets of rain which tore again and again into whirlpools of wind and water. Ibn Amram slumped back against the pedestal of the statue, trying to suppress a groan. The rain was icy cold and penetrated every layer of his *burnous*. A distant fash of lightning followed by a dull crash of thunder sent the monk with the discerning nose scurrying after his brother.

Again, the field was plunged into darkness, all the more oppressive after the brief flash of light. Ibn Amram rubbed his eyes and blinked to accustom his sight again to the deep shadows. In that momentary flash of blue light, Ibn Amram had noticed another ramp at the far side of the arena. If he could climb over the jumble of broken stone columns, the ramp could lead to his escape.

He picked his way through the rain-slick rocks, grasping with his fingernails for a firm handhold and crouching low to balance his weight. He clutched his mantle more closely to his neck to slow the steady trickle of cold rain down his neck. The temptation was strong to look over his shoulder at the high arcades behind him. He knew the monks were there, probably crouching behind seats and lurking behind columns. But he held his head low to the ground, knowing that his pale face in the moonlight would flash his presence like a beacon.

Another flash of lightning, much closer than the first, banished the darkness in a sudden burst of blue. It was as if it had seared his eyeballs. Ibn Amram flinched, squeezing his eyes shut to press out the thrust of pain. But in that interval, he spied a slight movement in the wall. His heart froze. He dared not move his hand nor a single muscle. His head was bowed in an awkward posture, but he dared not raise it.

"Do not advance, lowly one," Ibn Amram whispered. "Remain in your shelter."

The viper near his left hand tested the air with tentative confidence. A slow undulation passed down his glistening ribs. Dark clouds passed overhead, dimming the light from the moon until the movement of muscular coils was like a strange phantasm of the imagination. The cloud passed, sending more torrents of rain in its path. The moonlight waxed stronger by degrees, and Ibn Amram watched mutely as the viper positioned himself in the deep break of the rock, safe from the gusty wind.

Another flash of lightning dazzled both man and snake, driving the serpentine back into his safe recesses. It was too soon for a blessing; the probing head ushered forth from the rock again, still twitching the tongue that tested the air.

Ibn Amram dared not move his hand, even though the rain trickled down across his wrist, prompting an almost insatiable itching sensation. He must ignore it! The darting tongue was closer now, aware of the warm smell of man, just inches away. The viper was confused by the convergence of the warm smell and the cold gusts of rain.

"Be still, lowest of the low," Ibn Amram intoned in a deep baritone whose nascent melody seemed to hypnotize the curious viper.

Again, lightning seared the heavens with an electrifying shock. The instantaneous crash of thunder deafened Ibn Amram. He had to swallow twice to relieve the pain and pressure in his ears. But he dared not turn his eyes from the viper. He had no further interest in the cringing monks whose murmurs carried to him from the seats of the southern arcade. He could only watch in mounting horror as the viper rose again, grey and rain-swept as the rocks themselves, to test the air for the breath of the man.

Ibn Amram would gladly have ceased to breath if the snake would only withdraw its head from the proximity of his face, but his fear made his breath labored. With each exhalation, the viper wavered in a tight arc, drawing nearer and nearer to the source of the warm breath.

"You lowliest of creatures!" Ibn Amram continued slowly in his rich hypnotic voice. The notes of each word formed a soothing monotony that charmed the viper. "You crawl on your belly in darkness. You are destined to grovel through dirt all the days of your life. May every man who sees you strike at your head in disgust. Begone, vile offender!"

The slow chant had reached a crescendo as the torrents of rain subsided. The viper drew back into his crevice. Ibn Amram, breathing a tortured sigh of relief, pulled back his vulnerable left hand and slumped back against the column.

He hadn't noticed the electrifying effect his words had on his pursuers in the arcade. The superior acoustics of the amphitheater had carried his every threat and whisper to the furthest extremities of the building. Unaware that the voice in the darkness was that of Ibn Amram, panic had stricken the cringing monks. Their frenzied cries broke the silence.

"I tell you, Brother Matthew, it is a curse from Heaven!"

"We should never have seized that astrolabe," another whispered from the shadows.

"The Angel of Death has cursed us with an eternity of torment! Oh, I do not want every man who sees me to strike at my head!"

More murmurs and scuffling noises followed. Then a new voice rose on a tremolo of fear.

"It is the Devil calling to us! I recognize his voice!"

"No! It is the Jew conversing with the Devil. I hear them both!"

"The final darkness has come. The astrolabe has brought the darkness on our heads, mocking us at night instead of during the height of day!"

A sudden deadly bolt of lightning crackled and spat above their heads. Immediately afterwards, the utter darkness seemed deeper than ever.

"Aiee! Save me, save me!" a young monk screamed.

His shrieks were followed by a pandemonium of voices as the other monks pushed and shoved to be first to flee from the accursed amphitheater.

"Darkness! Darkness everywhere! The sky will be rent! The firmament will fall!"

Their superstitious voices died away as they rushed back to their bivouac to inform the abbot of doomsday at night.

Pelted by rain and dazzled by lightning, Ibn Amram shook his head in wonderment at the gullibility of men. He felt no rancor for the benighted monks. He only felt a terrible tiredness sink into his bones. He hoped Joseph was safe in the stables at the docks of Tarragona. His chin sank onto his chest and he stared aimlessly at the crevice where the viper had retreated. He thought he saw the forked tongue again.

"You have brought about an astonishing rescue tonight," he whispered listlessly. "I suspect there is a lesson to be learned, but I am simply too tired to dwell on it tonight!"

He shifted his weight and rose heavily onto his right knee before raising himself slowly to his feet.

CHAPTER ELEVEN

Tempest at Sea

TARRAGONA, ARAGON
WINTER, 1139

"MORI!" **JOSEPH SHOUTED IN DELIGHT, RACING FROM BEHIND** the bales of wool and nearly bowling Ibn Amram over with his welcome. "I feared you would never arrive. How did you escape? Did they hurt you? Oh, tell me everything that happened since we parted!"

"Yes, you will hear all the astonishing details, Joseph," Ibn Amram answered jovially, picking the youth up in a bear hug and dancing on the dock in celebration. "But first, let us locate a ship to Tunisia. Then we can marvel at my escapades."

His responsibility for negotiating a peace pact for all of Iberia came again to his mind, and he looked around with a keen sense of urgency. A few minutes of inquiries brought him to the berth of a ship bound for Tunis.

The captain's partner, an elegant Lombard banker with black flowing hair and impeccable manners, was caught up in an argument with an Italian trader. Neither man was voluble, but the intensity of their words caught Ibn Amram's attention. He also noticed from the distinctive hat which the Italian trader wore that he was a Jew, and when he heard the banker address the trader by the name of Mar Elijah of Otranto his observation was confirmed.

Ibn Amram waited until they had finished their business, then he approached the Jew.

"*Shalom aleichem,*" Ibn Amram said. He introduced himself and Joseph, and when they had exchanged formal greetings, he inquired whether the trader would be a passenger on the ship.

"With the help of the Almighty, I will be a passenger," Mar Elijah answered with obvious satisfaction. "I had anticipated a dreary passage in which I would see nothing but sea and sky, but the Master of the Universe has granted me good fortune and placed me in the company of an illustrious sage. My teachers Rav Yeshaya and Rav Menachem often mention your insights during their *shiurim*. In particular, we were all delighted last year to receive the first draft of your commentary on *Iyov*. We labored long hours over it, Rabban Ibn Amram. It is a masterful illumination into suffering and divine justice."

"Thank you, Mar Elijah," the sage responded, shifting his feet uncomfortably at the sudden compliment. "We can never presume to understand the cause of our afflictions. Did you know that I have begun a commentary on *Koheleth*? Yes, Joseph and I will be spending more time on it during this voyage. You are more than welcome to join us if you have the time. My copy is safely tucked away in my saddle bags."

"Excellent," Mar Elijah said, grasping both of Ibn Amram's hands and pumping them up and down in delight. "I suggest you conclude your arrangements for passage with the captain while I look after my departure taxes with the berthing master. Oh, and by the way . . ." His manner became confidential as he stepped back to whisper in the sage's ear. "If your finances are at all stretched with the price of passage, leave the transaction to me. Enough said, Rabban Ibn Amram! Our voyage to Tunis will be fruitful."

He walked briskly up the dock, neatly sidestepping the burly black sailor who heaved a massive ingot into the ship.

The time for departure was fast approaching. The neap tide had filled the basin of the harbor to its maximum. The sandbars to the western edge of the harbor entrance were almost invisible, only occasionally sending a ripple of foam across the smooth water to warn of their presence.

The captain, dressed in a flowing black cape that made him look almost like a Cluniac monk, walked briskly from the warehouse to the gangway and crossed the trembling plank in just three paces. He motioned to his passengers, then began a hurried conversation with his swain. At each question, the swain pointed out respective locations of cargo and provisions. The captain was satisfied.

The ropes dropped, and the swain turned to the hold and shouted down a sharp command in a foreign tongue. Like an insect's antenna, a single oar reached out and lodged hard against the timbers. The boatswain flicked his whip for encouragement, and the prow of the ship at last eased away from the dock, heading toward the limitless expanse of sea ahead. The boatswain motioned for the steady beat on the gong to begin.

"*Buen viaje!*" the berthing master called out as the distance between the dock and the stern widened. "Good voyage and good speed."

"Mercy, have pity on us!" the captain exclaimed as soon as they had cleared the headland. He squinted into the brilliant expanse of shimmering sea, pointing out the distinctive sail of a corsair in a northern cove. "Is it a pirate waiting to board us?"

Anxious eyes turned to the cove, but the corsair made no attempt to tack into the wind. The steady sweep of the oars soon distanced the trading ship from the warship. The captain breathed more easily.

"Gentlemen, I pray that safety lies on the edge of the horizon," he said to his three passengers. "The sight of our sail will soon be swallowed up by the sea, and we can keep a sharp eye for that jib sail on the corsair."

The steady beat on the gong continued, a sound that would seep into the recesses of everyone's consciousness before the trip was over. The mallet struck the bronze plate with a commanding blow, and before the echo died away, the gong reverberated again its insistent command to the slaves.

Ibn Amram retreated to the furthest edge of the stern in an attempt to escape the penetrating sound. He shifted his position on the coil of rope so that Joseph could sit beside him. Mar Elijah came over to them and appeared agitated.

"I do not wish to bring bad news so early in the voyage," he whispered, "but I think I see a glimpse of white on the horizon. It just might be the corsair, pursuing us at a distance."

"In truth?" Ibn Amram exclaimed, rising to his feet to look. Mar Elijah motioned him to his seat again.

"Do not vex the crew with our suspicion," he suggested. "They might heave my iron ingots overboard to gain speed, all for nought. If it is the corsair, there is little we can do."

"Are our lives in jeopardy?" Joseph whispered, staring fearfully into the distance.

"We have nothing to fear this trip," Mar Elijah said jovially. "The pirate will see that we carry only iron and wool. There is no profit for him in these commodities. But my return trip with spices and glass could spell danger. I will have to glean every snippet of information on the movements of this corsair. I might have to take another route to foil this piracy!"

"I hope you are right," Ibn Amram declared, shaking his head. "And I wish the criminals who sail the high seas are as logical as you. Then we could anticipate their actions. But the evil of this world is a caprice that blows as inconstantly as the westerly wind."

At sunset, Ibn Amram's words proved true. They were below decks in the cramped quarters assigned to paying passengers when a hubbub of voices arose from the bow. The tempo of the beating gong increased, and the ship lurched to starboard, sending Ibn Amram's manuscript skittering from the table into his lap. Joseph jumped to his feet.

"What is that? The corsair?"

The larboard slaves strained mightily with their long oars, while the starboard side waited for the command to join their mates in pulling fiercely at the oars. The lookout stood balanced at the bow, almost toppling over the rail. His extended left arm pinpointing a menacing shape outlined by waves curling to left and right.

Mar Elijah stepped to the larboard rail and peered into the deepening shadows of waves and storm clouds. An undulating form rose and fell in the calm waters. It drifted like a sleeping sea snake in sailors' yarns. But there was no head or tail. Mar Elijah shivered at the eerie sight.

"What is it, boatswain?" he whispered, afraid to awaken the sleeping creature.

"By my life, it is a derelict ship floating keel up," the boatswain answered. "A victim of the sea or a victim of the pirate corsair. We will never know which. There are no sailors left to tell us!"

He motioned to the black man beating the rhythm for the oars, and the tempo increased significantly.

The water between the ship and the hapless derelict seemed to breathe like a viscous jelly, heaving up and down like the chest of a sleeping man. Not a single wave broke the surface. The sight appalled the captain.

"She will sink at any moment now. It is her dying breath!" he exclaimed. "Gently, men. Gently. We don't want her to take us down with her."

The men on board stared in terror at the derelict, suddenly aware of their own danger. If the derelict plunged like a rock at this moment, it could swamp the deep-laden ship, pulling it into the depths, too. The gray sea that separated the two showed no transparency at all. The opaque surface seemed to mock them, shuttering their fate for a long moment.

The larboard oars were feathered, scarcely breaking the water with their gentle stroke. Another sweep and the derelict bobbed past the stern, almost touching it in a pathetic gesture of entreaty to the healthy ship.

"Now, ship oars, men," the captain called, walking lightly from his rail to the stern.

His footsteps lacked the bounce of his previous confidence. He hung his head in despair, as one who helps lower a dear friend into the yawning grave.

The overturned hulk was caught in an irresistible force from which there would be no retreat.

"She has breathed her last. Her sails will never fill again with the sea wind," the captain whispered.

He retreated from the stern rail, as if he feared that the death grip on the hulk would reach out and take him too.

The smooth waves paused. The oily surface of the sea trembled for an instant, and then the derelict was gone. A wall of foam surged up like a boiling kettle. As the foam subsided, it swirled in delicate eddies. The captain sighed and crossed himself, muttering a silent prayer.

"Let us proceed," he said dully, returning to his rail. "And a double portion of wine for the lookout. He has saved us from a watery grave."

The beat of the mallet on the gong resumed.

The sea became choppy that night. In the dull light of the swaying oil lamps in their cabin, Ibn Amram could not shake the last pathetic images of the sinking ship.

"Rivers flow to the sea, yet the sea is not full," Ibn Amram said in sad reflection. "She had to claim that pitiful ship and her men. The water of many rivers was not enough. It is taken up by the clouds and returns again in an endless cycle to the sea. But those sailors can never return again."

"Today's adventure has tinged your accustomed confidence with bleak pessimism," Mar Elijah commented. "Here, I have the answer to raise your spirits."

He leaned over to his trunk and withdrew a dark green carafe stopped with a cork.

"It is the good wine of Jerez! Let me pour you a glass, Rabban Ibn Amram."

"Ah, but you are a lover of life," Ibn Amram retorted morosely. "I'm sure you believe that if an honest day's labor can reward us with a crust of bread and a sip of good wine, we should be happy."

Mar Elijah nodded benignly. Ibn Amram smiled and sipped his wine.

"The final words must ring in our ears, in spite of all adversity and all pleasures," he said. "What are those final words of *Koheleth*, Joseph?"

" 'When everything is considered, fear the Master of the Universe and keep his commandments. That is man's entire duty,' " Joseph answered.

"When we are young, we think sadness cannot touch us," Mar Elijah conceded. "The good things of life were guaranteed by my loving parents. Then my father died. I had never experienced sadness before. It tempers the pleasure of living. It makes the wisdom of *Koheleth* accessible."

Joseph cast his eyes down to the half-empty glass in his hand. He knew in his heart that he had never been touched by the sadness of *Koheleth*. It was for him an intellectual exercise, and he had nothing to contribute.

He took another sip of wine and thought briefly about the sunken ship. He could not really imagine what anguish the crew had suffered before their ship capsized. He could only remember the shiver of fear that had tickled the hairs on the nape of his neck as he thought about sea serpents and other monsters.

The flame of the oil lamp was becoming more and more smudgy as the rough seas shook the lamp from side to side. Ibn Amram leaned against the bulkhead, steadying his throbbing temples with his fingertips.

"Come, *Mori*," Joseph advised, rising to give his teacher a hand. "It's time to retire to our bunks. If you close your eyes, you will feel better."

Mar Elijah cupped his hand around the lamp and blew out the light. His footsteps to his bunk were silent. In the darkness, the creaks and groans from the timbers were rhythmic. The gong was at last silent as the slaves slept.

The gale did not subside. Everyone slept fitfully, with an arm braced and a knee wedged against the bunk. If any of the passengers had dared go on deck, he would have seen that the long, low ocean swells had shortened into treacherous troughs. More and more whitecaps flickered in the penetrating light of the moon.

Daylight brought no relief. The gale brought sheets of rain scudding across the turbulent sea. The helmsman fought the obstinate handle of the tiller as the ship slid down the side of each mountainous trough. At every peak, the ship teetered as the helmsman called out blessings and imprecations in a jumble of tongues until the tiller dug deep again, like a ploughshare in spring mud. With arrogant skill, the ship rode the danger like a *vaquero* on a bucking bull.

The captain, clinging to his rail midships, raised his hand in anger at the skies.

"West Wind of Winter!" he shouted. His voice was shredded into ribbons. "You are a barbarian! By heaven, if you were a man . . ." His clenched fist conveyed what his words could not.

His three passengers clung to the railing as well, each immersed in his own prayer. Mar Elijah chanced to look up, soaked and sputtering in the cold rain and spray. He watched the foreshortened sail billow tightly against the taut lanyards. The canvas had held admirably all night in a sea that would have snapped an oar like a brittle straw. One moment the sail was there, a white emblem of hope against the black sky. Suddenly, it was gone, confiscated by the ruthless wind.

"The sail! The sail!" Mar Elijah screamed in complete disbelief, pointing to the canvas that flashed into the murky clouds like a huge sea falcon.

Sailors rushed from their positions and swore at the bad luck. The captain shouted orders and poured curses into the winds. Mar Elijah aided the helmsman as the waves tried to wrench the tiller out of their hands.

"The worst is past!" he shouted at the sailor, pointing to a patch of grey in the sky. The helmsman nodded, then nodded toward a spot further to the east. A blotch of white rode quickly on the distant waves, followed by another fleck of white.

"It is a Genoese merchantman," he observed, "followed, if I am not mistaken, by the corsair!"

All eyes were fastened on that distant drama.

"Thank Heaven, our sail is gone. It would have announced our presence like a clarion," the captain said.

He motioned to the boatswain, and the relentless tempo of the rowing gong began for the first time that morning.

"Cursed luck, she has seen us! She changes her course," the boatswain muttered. His face, smudged with dried salt, turned pale.

For long pauses, the corsair hove into view, then retreated behind the grey billows. Every time the pirate ship disappeared from sight, a collective sigh was breathed on the deck of the Spanish trader. Then the corsair would reappear from the misty clouds, fulfilling everyone's worst fears.

"She will soon be able to draw alongside," the boatswain said.

They could almost sense the swaggering work on deck, the readying of grappling hooks and swords for the ultimate capture.

"Faster!" the Captain commanded, turning to the black slave who struck the gong. "I want triple time! Faster, I say!"

The slave rolled his eyes in disbelief, then complied with the impossible order. The reverberations echoed across the deck like a death knell. The cries of pain from the hold multiplied. The boatswain raised his whip and flicked it across the bare back of any oarsman who dared complain. The cries of agony increased.

Ibn Amram was convulsed at the rail with revulsion at the brutal treatment. He slowly made his way forward.

"In the name of compassion," he pleaded with the boatswain, "you must stop this murderous tempo!"

The boatswain pushed him roughly aside.

"Begone, soft-heart," he shouted. "Our only hope of survival is the muscle of these men. Would you treat a mule with carrots if he balked?"

"But these men are not mules! They laugh and they cry like you and I!"

"Doddering fool," the boatswain sneered and pushed Ibn Amram again.

His whip flicked across the shoulder of one of the slaves. The slave stiffened in pain but was too exhausted to cry out.

The frieze of faces was imprinted indelibly on Ibn Amram's mind. A row of tired Nubians plied the oars. On the backstroke, a muscular giant with an ugly welt of the whip on his back glanced at Ibn Amram. His haggard face registered an indefinable sorrow. In that instant, Ibn Amram knew that he did not see a simple black man at the oar. In spite of the pain and the injustice of his lot, the slave worked with a quiet nobility.

Ibn Amram had seen that spirit before, in the eyes of Alfonso, King of Castile, in the eyes of Ibn Tashpin, King of Tunisia and in the eyes of King Henry of England. The slave, whom the boatswain abused with word and whip, was not just a strong herdsman from Dongola but, without a sliver of doubt, a prince of that kingdom.

The realization registered on Ibn Amram's shocked face. And in that flash of knowledge, he knew that the prince saw his insight. The wordless interchange was severed brutally by another flick from the boatswain's whip.

A flood of indignation swept over Ibn Amram. He wanted to leap at the throat of the insolent boatswain and pummel him with the handle of his own whip. He wanted to race to the unsuspecting captain and shake sense into his empty head. Still, the triple time for the oarsmen continued, and the corsair drew closer in spite of their best efforts.

"The sail of the Genoese merchantman is almost past the horizon," Mar Elijah commented ruefully. "It is evident that the corsair has bigger fish to fry, and we are that fish!"

The sound of her flapping sail reached their ears on snatches of the wind. The pirate ship's men were positioned at her bow, but as yet, no signs of boarding were seen.

"Is it possible?" Mar Elijah shouted, jumping to his feet. "She is tacking. The corsair is tacking!"

The captain expressed the same surprise and crossed himself profusely. Their pursuer fell back into the grey shadows of the gale, lingering long in the cloud before reappearing far to stern. The angle of her sail proved that the prize had been knowingly relinquished.

"I do not understand," Mar Elijah said. "Her spies roamed the streets of Tarragona to collect information on our cargo. She lay in that cove to await our departure, and she followed us halfway to Tunisia. Now she has given up the spoils without any attempt to capture. It doesn't make sense."

"It is not the first time I have experienced someone following me," Ibn Amram said, squinting into the sudden sunlight. "Pursuers may fall back for reasons best known to them and retrace their steps at a later date. For now, I am glad to see the last of them."

The smile that had begun to broaden suddenly froze. The corners of his mouth turned down as he noticed something that now robbed him of any joy.

The gong had ceased. A stillness filled the hold where only moments before men had screamed and groaned as they pulled at the heavy oars.

"You there," the boatswain ordered in the foreign tongue. "Pick him up!"

Four slaves clambered heavily up the slippery steps,

dragging one of their mates by the wrists. Joseph's hand flew to his mouth in shock.

"He is dead! That is the one the boatswain beat and whipped so mercilessly."

The poor man's head lolled awkwardly to the side. His eyes were open but unseeing.

"Yes, that is the one," Ibn Amram said, choking on his words. "The boatswain boasted that these slaves came from Dongola. Little does he know that he beat a prince of Dongola to death."

"Shall we administer the last rites?" a sailor asked the captain.

"Don't be ridiculous," the captain scoffed. "They are heathens. His soul cannot be saved now. Heave him overboard!"

The boatswain jerked his thumb, and the four slaves pulled the heavy body closer to the ship's side. The black giant in death was not easy to handle. His body was smeared with the refuse of bilge water, and his supple arms and legs were contorted like the limbs of a rag doll.

"Look lively and kick him over," the boatswain commanded, raising his whip as a threat.

One of the slaves levered his shipmate overboard with his foot. The body caught on a broken board and hung like carrion before a wave washed up and carried it away.

"Don't stand there dawdling instead of rowing!" the boatswain screamed. His whip snapped another warning.

The four slaves trudged back to their positions without a single glance back at the sea that had swallowed their prince. The beat of the gong started afresh, and all was as before, except that one position was empty.

Ibn Amram rose unsteadily to his feet and felt his way with outstretched hand along the side of the sodden bales of wool.

"I must consult *Koheleth*," he said softly. "I must seek its wisdom."

When Mar Elijah and Joseph joined him in the cabin, Ibn

Amram was immersed in his manuscript. He looked up briefly and motioned to the empty bench on the opposite side of the table.

"I have seen the tears of the oppressed with none to comfort them," Ibn Amram said at last. "That black slave blinked back the tears, but I could see them. If his village had been devastated by floods, he would have stood tall and rebuilt his ancestral home. If his herds had been struck down by famine, he would have ridden north to the great markets of Egypt to barter for their replacement. No matter what calamity came from Hashem, he would have borne his lot with grace."

"But the boatswain is just another man, no better than the black prince," Joseph objected.

"Exactly!" Ibn Amram agreed, thumping the table with unaccustomed ferocity. "The prince suffered at the hands of another man. Can you imagine how a man born to nobility feels when an inferior man dares raise the whip to him? I believe it was too much for him and death overcame him."

A silence fell over the cabin as Ibn Amram's words sank in.

Ibn Amram awoke to the first rays of dawn with great joviality. He busied himself in the crowded cabin, tidying their possessions, warming the remnants of the previous night's tea over the lamp and readying his *tallis* and *tefillin* for their morning prayers.

Mar Elijah was pleased with the renewed confidence the sage showed.

"As soon as we finish *Shacharis*, we shall go up on deck and watch for the first signs of Tunis. The isthmus is unmistakable," he said.

In a dazzling haze of blue sky and shimmering sea, the peach-colored buildings of the old city of Tunis rose proudly on the hills of Bir-Kassa like jewels mounted on a tiara.

"I see the city," Joseph cried, standing up at the beaked prow. "But I don't see a single ship. Where are they all, Mar Elijah?"

"Not at this end of the bay," Mar Elijah answered, squinting into the distance. "The quays are more sheltered at the end of the bay, where the lagoon is shallow and reedy. You will love Tunis, Joseph. It's a beautiful city that delights the eye with pastel colors."

"Already I see colors like ripe fruit," Ibn Amram said, joining in the conversation.

"Some of the houses are as pink as alabaster," Mar Elijah noted. "And the palace of the king is as yellow as burnished gold. Then there are the many blues. The blue of the sky, the blue of the Mediterranean, and yet another blue of the Bahira, the Lake of Tunis. It's on the other side."

The captain, a prideful man, reappeared on deck. He had doffed his salt-encrusted sea cape in favor of an unbleached linen *burnous*. The sailors quickly complied with his last-minute orders and dismantled the remnants of the mainmast, where the sail had been lost during the storm.

"He will not admit to his calamity at the hands of the west wind when he meets his comrades at dockside," Mar Elijah whispered. "He will speak only of his victories, never of his defeat."

Joseph smiled at the thought.

"That is the way of the sailor, confidence is everything," Mar Elijah remarked, his finger upraised. "If he never admits to bad weather, the trader in Tunisia will trust him with a load back to Spain. If he says he had been caught in the storm, they would think twice about giving him their business."

"And now we will find more business from the seafarers of Tunis," Ibn Amram interjected, pointing to two small boats vying for the advantage of reaching the Spanish trading ship first.

The captain of each stood in the bow, gesturing madly at the trader. Each wave promised to pitch them headfirst into the bay, but they hung on to lanyards like spiders, trying to be the first to hail the visitors.

"Ahoy, trader!" the first captain called out from a distance.

"You are the trader, no?"

Ibn Amram shook his head and pointed to Mar Elijah.

"Trader!" the captain persisted, motioning his oarsmen to veer closer. "Is your business only in Tunisia, or are you going to Egypt? I have much skill in following the coastline to Pelusium or Damietta. Let me take your wares to Egypt. You will have much profit if you hire my ship!"

"Thief and son of a thief!" the second captain swore. "I saw this trader first. He is mine, I tell you! Go steal from the old women in the market as you usually do."

His oarsmen pulled hard to enter the fray, but the first captain shouted hoarse commands and curses. His men spiked the maneuver with their oars. Sailors on both vessels immediately plucked up belaying pins and made ready to start a fierce battle over the prize.

"Stop it, or neither of you will carry my goods to Egypt," Mar Elijah warned. "Tomorrow, we will talk. You will find me in the Jewish quarter by the Gate of Bab-Souika. For now, go!"

The first captain shook a heavy wooden pin in the general direction of his competitor but grudgingly complied with Mar Elijah's wishes.

"No sooner do you arrive in this port than the sailors are anxious that you should be off," Ibn Amram noted.

"It is all the same to me," Mar Elijah said. "I will dispose of some wool here in the *souk* of Tunis. As for the leather, it is not as fine as the leather of Cordoba, but it is very good all the same. All the rest is signed for Ashkelon."

"Ah, that is an important town for us, now that the Crusaders have made the Holy City into a Christian kingdom. Many of my former students have fled the sacred walls of Jerusalem for the safety of Ashkelon. I hear it is a refuge for many Jews."

As the ship drew closer to a quay in the reedy lagoon, they watched a fisherman standing crane-like in the shallows, fishing with a crude spear. Ibn Amram watched with distraction the sudden thrust of the man's spear. The unanswered problem of the Karaites was suddenly uppermost in his mind, jabbing his thoughts like the spear in the water.

"Tell me, Mar Elijah, would you be able to conduct a discreet inquiry while you are in Ashkelon?" he asked.

The trader of Otranto nodded without any hesitation.

"If you could," said Ibn Amram, "consult with the *Av Bet Din* and determine if the Karaites of Ashkelon have shown any signs of compromise towards *Torah Sheb'al Peh*. I have recently been involved with an influential Karaite of Burgos. He has now fled to Jerusalem. I would dearly like to know if we could influence him to return to the fold. Oh, and there is one other. One by the name of Rikuv is most offensive, but his son Yissaschar holds promise. Inquire into the fortunes of this Rikuv family, Mar Elijah, and send me a note at your earliest opportunity. I long to know what has become of them."

"Certainly, Rabban Ibn Amram," Mar Elijah agreed. "I can consult the leaders of the Ashkelon community, and travel to Jerusalem. While I'm there, I can buy goods from the Far East in the *souk* of Jerusalem. You don't inconvenience me at all!"

Ibn Amram embraced him without a word. The die was cast to make yet another overture to the renegade sect.

"And if you could inquire about my father-in-law, perhaps," Ibn Amram added haltingly. "I do not wish to inconvenience you, Mar Elijah. Not when you have been so kind with everything. But Yerucham Halevi is constantly on my mind. Perhaps he has reached Damietta as he proposed. Or perhaps he has already arrived in Jerusalem."

"Consider it done!" Mar Elijah interjected. "There is absolutely no inconvenience. It is on my way, and I am honored that you would ask me to extend to you such a small favor. Enough said! Tonight you will eat with my friends in the Jewish quarter. Tomorrow you can pursue your business with King Tashpin while I negotiate with these sailors."

CHAPTER TWELVE

Intruders in the Palace

TUNIS, TUNISIA
WINTER, 1140

IBN AMRAM STEPPED UNSTEADILY DOWN THE GANGWAY. "IT'S good to stand on solid ground at last, Joseph," he said. "I'm afraid my knees are still shaking from the voyage."

Joseph reached out and took his arm. The sights and sounds of the harbor assailed them, and a troop of barefoot children clamored for their attention. One beat a tambour with relentless vigor, while the others danced and clapped in glee. Ibn Amram smiled at their antics, reached into his leather pouch and drew out a handful of dried grapes to give the entertainers.

"Don't give them any more!" a sunburnt sailor warned. "You will never be rid of them." He shook his fist at the children. "Enough! Don't bother the good doctor."

The little urchins retreated to the end of the quay, where they resumed their free-spirited march. Joseph tried to give the sailor a hand, dragging the heavy saddle bags down the gangway. The horse and pony had been sold in Tarragona, and their possessions were crammed into the bulging bags.

"We shall spend the night in the Jewish quarter," Ibn Amram mentioned. "If you could bring that bag to the end of the quay, we would be appreciative."

The sailor glanced back as the boatswain bellowed commands to his shipmates, struggling to unload the heavy iron ingots.

"I will do more than that, doctor," he answered, dragging the bags to the edge of the warehouse, out of sight of the boatswain. "I will help you take them all the way to the gate. It is adjacent to the *souk*, doctor. We can buy oranges to refresh out dry throats!" He glanced meaningfully at Ibn Amram's pouch.

"As you will," Joseph responded. "Your service is appreciated."

Once at the gate of Bab-Souika, the sailor showed little interest in hurrying back to ship. He relished the sweet oranges.

"Show me the house where you are staying, doctor," he said. "I will bring your bags to the door."

He sucked the last drops from the rind then threw it to a mule tethered by a doorway.

The houses of the Jewish quarter were built around one central courtyard. The outer walls were formed of mud and straw. The windowless expanse of mud gave little evidence of the location of the house of Mar Elijah's friend Aaron. Skilled in mathematics, Aaron lived in the Jewish quarter but travelled daily to the royal palace where he worked with the Finance Minister of Tunisia.

"Ah, there you are," Mar Elijah called out from behind a sturdy iron gate. It swung easily on its hinges. "Come in. Can you drag that bag down this narrow corridor?"

The women at the well nearby drew their veils more tightly across their faces as they watched the foreigners enter the house of the mathematician.

Aaron the Mathematician was a tireless host. He counselled Mar Elijah on the best tactics of negotiation with sea captains. He also provided him with letters of introduction; the signature of the royal mathematician carried much weight everywhere along the North African coastline. To Ibn Amram, he offered insights into the successes and setbacks Tashpin had suffered in his maneuvering to be independent of the caliph.

"For the moment, it is a stand-off," he confided. "The Caliph Al-Kumi recognizes the popular appeal of the Almoravid king, but he disdains what he calls the lax religion of Tashpin's palace. For his part, King Tashpin concedes that the forces of the caliph are supreme and works faithfully as his chief minister."

"It is a position of great authority," Ibn Amram noted. "Many Muslims would aspire to that honor, but few can attain it. Let us hope that Tashpin has a civilizing influence on the hot-headed Almohad caliph."

The next morning, Aaron escorted his guests from the Jewish quarter to the royal palace. They entered the royal gardens in silence under the watchful eye of a silk-robed guard. A tiled pathway meandered through delicate date and pomegranate orchards. Ibn Amram reached up and touched first one rare delicacy then another, without breaking them free from their stems. He sighed and let his right arm drop heavily to his side.

"With what vexation of spirit did King Solomon wander through his gardens and orchards, Joseph?" he asked. "Every kind of fruit tree lined his path. At arm's length was any delicacy which his palate could enjoy, yet his taste buds no longer relished the exotic fruits, even those his many slaves tended hourly. I believe it was a scene that rivalled the beauty of the Garden of Eden, yet his soul found no serenity there."

Joseph was pained to discover that his master's thoughts were again so bleak, especially when he needed all his mental energy to greet the powerful King of Tunisia.

"Must you struggle even now to analyze the problems of *Koheleth, Mori!*" he entreated.

Ibn Amram straightened, nodding to his student in agreement.

"This royal garden helps me feel as the king must have felt in his garden as he struggled with eternal questions. In all my years of poverty I have never been able to feel like a king. Should I now squander the chance? But don't worry so, young son. Though I may feel pain, I do not forget the opposite. Just because of darkness, we don't forget the day."

"Think of the orchards of Andalusia which we saw on our trip to the south," Joseph suggested, brightening at his master's changing mood.

"It wasn't the first time I walked for hours there, you know," Ibn Amram said. "Did I ever tell you of the time I travelled to Cordoba with my son Yitzchak? He was so young then. Most of the time I carried him on my back. And when we were tired, we crossed into the orchards. We had to duck, the boughs were so heavy with fruit. My feet ached and my back was weary from carrying my child, but my heart was gladdened. Though it did not belong to us, how much we enjoyed the shade of that orchard!"

He stopped at an aged fig tree, laden with ripe fruit. A guard paused at the edge of the orchard.

"Take, take!" he urged. "You are a royal guest."

Ibn Amram smiled and broke a fig from its stem, spreading the ripe fruit open for himself and his student.

"Though I do not own this orchard," he continued, "I am invited to share its wealth."

They ate the fig slowly. A courtier appeared on the pathway and motioned to them.

"The king will see you now!" he commanded.

They followed him up a pathway lined with cypresses and oleanders that had bloomed all summer. Amongst the greenery, a pair of peacocks strutted, and in the leaf canopy above their heads, they heard nightingales flutter.

The courtier walked down the long colonnade and entered a waiting room, motioning for the youth to wait inside.

"I must leave him with a book to read," Ibn Amram responded, hastily digging into the folds of his garment to withdraw their *Mishnah*.

The courtier bowed and entered another room with Ibn Amram close behind. A heavy-set sentinel dressed in a coarse vest and baggy pantaloons stepped forward from the shadows of the corridor. His dark silhouette made Ibn Amram jump.

"It is all right," the courtier said to the guard. "This is the envoy from Castile."

The sentinel drew back again into the deep shadows of the columns. Pushing aside a tapestry, the courtier led him into a large room with dazzling contrasts of shape and color. Each delicate column of the arcade overlooked the garden courtyard and was topped with the most startling pattern of white and black stones. Every wall was plastered and finished in patterns of exquisite lace work that made the great hall of the palace appear as incorporeal as a dream.

A meeting of magnificently attired men was taking place at the far end of the room. One of them wore a caftan fashioned from gold cloth, an unmistakable sign of kingship, yet his turban was of simple cotton, embroidered in subtle threads of burgundy. He was speaking to his chief advisor.

"And what says Ibn Azzoun?" asked the king.

"He is still jealous of Seddrei Ibn Wezr and El Batrougui," the advisor answered, shifting his foot to sit more comfortably on his cushion. "None of them has the stomach to war against us."

A courtier made ready to say something to the king but drew back instantly when he noticed the advisor's frown. The advisor was more than a general. As chief administrator of the palace, he was the sole intermediary between the king and his sheiks, the lesser princely authorities of the court. He knew that his policy of accommodation towards the nobles of Spain met with some resistance from the hot-headed sheiks.

"I am honored that you accept my decision, Your Grace," the advisor remarked to the king. "I am convinced that Ibn Azzoun of Jerez, Ibn Wezir of Beja and El Batrougui of Niebla will never join forces against us. Of course, some would disagree!" His glance at the impetuous sheik cast daggers at his court opponent. "And my strategy was correct with the King of Cordoba. Yahia Ibn Gania is now at the end of his resources. Even Zafadola of Saragossa cannot help him now! He must open his arms to the army of the caliph. Our victory is written in the stars!"

The impetuous sheik leaned forward again to whisper a harsh remonstrance about hostages. The King of Tunisia motioned him quickly to silence, casting a meaningful glance in the direction of the envoy.

"The Almighty be praised," he said serenely. "We have no need for hostages at this time, Achmed. Time is in our favor."

He stretched luxuriously, extending from the folds of his caftan an elegant pointed slipper which was elaborately varnished. With a slight nod of his head, a youthful attendant was quickly dispatched to the brazier where nuts were roasting. The youth selected a few with nimble fingers, placing them on a brass tray for the king.

"Yes, time favors us," the advisor agreed. "But we must strike now, when we have utmost advantage. Ibn Gania can now provide us with a base of operations. Four sails will be sufficient to move our men before the winter winds bottle us up in the harbor."

At these last words, the advisor frowned at the envoy. He had no wish to give the envoy of his Christian enemy any advantage. He turned deliberately on the cushion to adjust the heavy silver brooch which fastened his tunic. It was a sign of office.

"What does the envoy of Castile think?" the king asked suddenly.

A courtier motioned Ibn Amram to a vacant pillow at the

periphery of the assembled men. The king nodded again to the youth who scurried behind the circle of seated advisors to offer the tray of roasted nuts to Ibn Amram.

"Is time on the side of the Prophet and his people?" the king challenged Ibn Amram.

Ibn Amram hesitated, noting a vexing playfulness in the king's voice.

"Do not be embarrassed by power," the king cajoled. "After all, it is as the proverb says: To the dog who has power, men say, 'My lord dog.' "

His eyes creased into a smile, but his lips remained a tight enigma.

"Your Grace," the sage responded. "Avraham Ibn Amram does not come to your realm as a pawn of power but on a mission of peace. I have spent too many years immersed in the holy Torah to lose my vision in the presence of power. But I delight in praising the Almighty who has given of his glory to mortals."

He glanced in sincerity at the King of Tunisia and his court and recited the blessing in Hebrew.

The inscrutable smile on King Tashpin's lips widened.

"Your reference to the pawn whets my appetite," he said. "This meeting has come to its end. Bring out my chess board. I will engage the envoy of Castile in battle!"

He snapped his fingers, and the youth scurried to the tapestry to confer with another attendant. For a moment, the advisor paused on the cushions, then he rose to his feet, bowing to his king. The other sheiks bowed simultaneously before leaving the hall.

Ibn Amram felt manipulated into an uncomfortable position, but he did not yet have a clear sense of the king's motives. Aaron the Mathematician had warned him that the king weighed many of the most crucial affairs of state according to the outcome of a game of chess. For that reason, the board was not housed in the palace itself but within the chancery, as a sign of its importance.

Presently, a clerk from the counting house appeared in the doorway, bearing the royal chessboard and pieces. The sentinel waved him into the hall.

Without a word, the king motioned to the open area on the rug in front of him. Again he snapped his fingers to the youth, calling for refreshment. While the clerk meticulously arranged the ivory and ebony chess pieces on the board, the king held up his chalice, motioning to the youth to likewise fill the chalice of the envoy.

"It is cool and refreshing, Ibn Amram," King Tashpin said. "Juice of the palm. And not fermented, as my caliph would suspect."

The corners of his lips turned down again as he thought of the dour Caliph Al-Kumi, encamped somewhere to the south with nothing but a tent over his head. His dynasty promised a return to the simple values of Islam, most notably an observance of abstinence in all its varieties. Wine and alcoholic beverage were forbidden in the caliph's empire.

As the clerk withdrew from their presence, the king leaned forward to concentrate on the first move of the game. His eyebrows furrowed in thought. Ibn Amram watched in fascination as the king's hand wavered above the chess pieces.

"There!" he said, deciding at last on the knight. "I begin with my favorite! He is a savage warrior, overleaping six squares with ease."

Rabban Ibn Amram watched King Tashpin closely, wondering if this apparent ferocity was not an elaborate guise. His words expressed violence, yet his hand did not tremble at all. He placed the piece on its new square with strange gentleness. Ibn Amram had no taste for the blood of battle, even when it was transposed into mental dexterity.

"This game has a superiority over all others because it is a faithful view in miniature of the needs of man," he observed, moving his pawn.

"It is," the king responded. "Chess is a game of war where

men lie dying on the battlefield while kings strive for victory."

The knight pushed further into Ibn Amram's defense.

"For some, chess is war," Ibn Amram conceded, moving another pawn. "But for the able ruler who understands its intricacies, chess is a parable of political government. Justice is the foundation of chess. Victory is built upon worthy rules and honorable judgments. For those with vision, chess is founded upon truth and law."

The king smiled, withdrawing his knight to a less aggressive position.

"You confound me, Ibn Amram," he said. "Many are the times I have played with my advisor, and he always insists that the goal is to ravish and destroy the enemy. Do you suggest that the advisor is wrong?" His smile was impenetrable.

"The advisor has led men in the heat of battle. Like the Norman warriors who press forward when lesser men would retreat. He would command, 'Boldness, more boldness, always boldness!' "

The King of Tunisia shivered slightly at the mention of Normans who vexed his fleet from their Sicilian stronghold.

"Do not speak to me of Normans and their brutal ways, Ibn Amram."

"I doubt they play this game," Ibn Amram answered drily. "But I know that King Alfonso plays chess well. The prudent winner takes glory from this game. Players come together in peace to play chess, and they leave it in peace."

Tashpin sipped slowly on his palm juice, reflecting on Ibn Amram's unexpected words of peace during a game of war.

"You do not see hatred as the basis for this encounter between enemies?" he asked.

"Perhaps when lesser men take up the pieces," Ibn Amram said, daring to smile at the thought. "I have known lesser men to become furious at losing the game. They will pluck up the pieces and hurl them at their opponent. War on the board quickly transforms to war on the battlefield."

"But not for the King of Castile and the King of Tunisia?"

Again, Tashpin's smile was perplexing, as if he were being led to a novel idea while overleaping the preliminary arguments.

Ibn Amram nodded, advancing yet another pawn to open up a path for his most powerful piece. His finger rested gently upon the tall ebony figure.

"The king sits on a throne of justice." he said. "He is recognized by his people as an impartial judge who loves truth. His power has been given to him by the Master of the Universe who alone is above this able monarch. Next comes his viceroy, obedient even to the most demanding wishes of the king. Over there stands the priest. The king does nothing without consulting him. And flanking the priest, for the proper balance of temporal power, is the general. He is guided night and day by the rule of law."

"It is a pretty parable which you have drawn from the board, Ibn Amram," King Tashpin commented. His hand reached out to touch Ibn Amram's black king. "Here stands the King of Castile. Then this white king must be the Caliph Al-Kumi, ruling over the vast empire here to the south. Who is his viceroy? No, don't tell me! Let me guess. It must be me, since no other *muluk* is as powerful as I. Who is the black viceroy? It must be Zafadola. The black priest is Bernard. And the general is Don Umar. Am I correct, Ibn Amram? Have I grasped your analogy?"

"Yes," Ibn Amram noted. He moved into a bold position that threatened to split the vanguard of the white forces. "As for the other pieces, they are too numerous to name individually. They represent in totality the many lords and sheiks of the realms who command cities and fortified outposts. They are the leaders of thousands, of hundreds, of fifties and of tens. We can include in their number the judges of each city, and the mayor and his councilors as well. Each works for his own happiness while aiding the happiness of his neighbor."

King Tashpin nodded in recognition of the parable.

"Each sustains the other," he breathed in quiet reflection.

"And the Master of the Universe looks down and blesses the work of their hands," Ibn Amram said.

King Tashpin looked at the board whose groupings were now tilted in favor of the black.

"The parable must stand on its own merit," he said tipping over both the black and the white king. "No one will win this war. But both shall live in peace."

At last, seizing the initiative, Ibn Amram expressed in its entirety the bold plan for peace which King Alfonso wished to propose to the Caliph Al-Kumi. King Tashpin sat in quiet reflection, sipping the last drops of his palm juice, and only rarely interrupting Ibn Amram to clarify some details.

"It is indeed a bold plan," the king commented, rising to his feet and motioning to his attendant to open the tapestry for them. "So much depends upon a third party to your negotiations. I know all too well the importance of third parties, even at the height of war. When I drove the Almohads from their mountain retreat at Tinmal, my flank attack would have crushed a lesser man. But the caliph countered with outrageous courage and directly entered the plain. My Almoravid warriors beat a hasty retreat, leaving both Al-Kumi and myself with equal strength. He could have pursued me and waged a horrible battle of attrition in the great sand sea, or he could relent and let me go.

"But I did not count on the tribe of the Guezzoulas. My own trained warriors, all of them! Yet they sided with the caliph at that moment, ensuring him victory. So I made my peace with the great conqueror and became his vassal. All because of a third party."

"There is no third party in our negotiations," Ibn Amram insisted. "I need only an introduction from you to the caliph. I have been given authority to negotiate directly with the caliph on behalf of the King of Castile. The paper I take back to Burgos will be binding."

"You forget about the Cluniacs and their Burgundian knights," Tashpin noted drily. "They are the third party in this affair. I do not trust them, and frankly, I do not think Al-Kumi will either."

"But we must at the very least try," Ibn Amram said in entreaty. He followed the king through the airy arcade and out into the lush garden. "Peace will let both participants divert these ghastly energies of war and death to the noble exploration of science. King Alfonso has an abiding love of astronomy, and he would combine the wisdom of your kingdom and his. Think about the implications for your children and children's children. The master astrolabists of Tunisia would be able to travel in peace and safety to Burgos where we can mutually explore the mysteries of the stars."

"You are a dreamer," Tashpin responded, deep in thought. "But the dreams are good! Come, Rabban Ibn Amram. Walk with me in my garden."

The bodyguard, who had watched every move of his king, dissolved into the deep shadows within the palms of the garden. A strange solitude came upon the two men. Only the scolding of a finch, bobbing its head from its leafy cover, could be heard.

The garden below the high crenelated wall of the palace was cultivated to resemble an oasis. A fig tree thrust its gnarled branches up against the bleak expanse. At its roots, hidden pipes conveyed water that bubbled into a deep pool. By the waterside, a sad-eyed gazelle hung its head, in spite of the caresses of a young boy who hung on its neck.

"Is he still sad, Yakub?" King Tashpin asked, leaning down to pat the boy on the head.

"He is, Father," the boy answered, renewing his energies to hug the disconsolate creature. "Since his sister died, he has not been the same."

"Feed him a morsel of sugar cane," the king advised, walking on. "He will get better."

They passed the body of the female, half-buried in the shifting sands of the garden. Ibn Amram glanced down in passing.

"Have the blackbirds plucked out the eyes?" he asked.

King Tashpin glanced back, shaking his head slightly.

"It is the work of one of my wives. The desert people have told her that she will have eyes as beautiful as the female gazelle if she takes them. It is the way of the desert."

For him, the gazelle was not worthy of a second glance. He continued up the path.

A sound of bells and chanting reached their ears. King Tashpin paused at the top of the stairs, rising on tiptoe to look over the top of the wall at the foot of the garden. A bodyguard appeared out of nowhere and assumed a protective stance behind his king. His hand rested lightly on his scimitar.

"It is nothing but a desert mystic and his followers," the king observed, squinting into the glare of the setting sun. "They come down from the hills of Bir-Kassa at dusk to demonstrate their healing power to the faithful. They are nothing but harmless mystics."

He turned and walked back into the arcade. A haunting voice carried on the evening air from the minaret nearby. In the intervals between the penetrating swoop of the *muezzin's* voice, the persistent tinkling of bells continued. But the tumult of shopkeepers and buyers in the bazaar had ceased.

King Tashpin and Ibn Amram turned back to the great hall. The bells and chanting penetrated even to the inner chambers of the palace.

"Do the mystics not go to evening prayer with the rest of your people?" Ibn Amram asked, looking out past the columns of the arcade. The evening sky was turning a deep purple. Soon it would be night.

The king hastened to the waiting room, anxious to join the faithful in the mosque.

"The mystic is without law," he explained simply. "We tolerate his eccentricities as long as he does not draw too many of our young men from our rituals. Ah, I see your companion is still immersed in his reading! The time has come for us to part, Ibn Amram. I will think at length on your proposal, and when I am ready I will summon you again. May Allah remain with you!"

He turned abruptly to leave. As he neared the hanging tapestry covering the doorway, a commotion broke out in the dim corridor beyond. Voices of alarm and clashes of steel resounded from the distant rooms. The advisor rushed into the room, almost tearing the tapestry from its hangings.

"Your Grace!" he exploded. "Followers of the mystic have scaled the walls! With my own eyes I saw their cunning. One moment, they whirled in mystic ecstasy, plucking at their beards and stabbing at their chests. The next moment, they rushed through the orchard where my archers could not reach them. Then they climbed the walls into the palace. Do not leave here!"

He left as suddenly as he had entered, leaving three guards to surround the king.

"This is not the way of a mystic," the king said, shaking his head in wonderment. He drew back into a room where a pale light glowed from a single lamp suspended from the center of the ceiling. "These mystics may ignore the law, but violence towards the faithful is unthinkable!" He paused in mid-thought, glancing wildly at Ibn Amram and his student. "But what if the object of their violence is not the faithful of Tunisia but an envoy, the envoy of an enemy? Is it possible?"

He strode quickly to the open window spanned by the arcade, then drew back, aware of his vulnerability.

"Who leads them? Did you see the leader who scaled the wall?" he asked a burly guard.

"A man unlike the rest," the guard said, sorting carefully the strands of his memory. "The man was agile as a cat, and his skin was pale, as pale as goat's milk!"

"He is not a mystic!" the king declared in a trenchant voice. "He is a foreigner to our land! Summon my advisor immediately. The foreigner must be caught, not executed. And you! Conduct the envoy to my private apartments for his own protection. No foreigner would know how to penetrate the corridors of my private apartments!"

With an abrupt wave of the hand, he bid the guard take Ibn Amram and Joseph. They had not the shortest pause for breath. Joseph, wide-eyed in fright at the turmoil within the palace, clung to Ibn Amram's sleeve. The guard, slow of tongue but quick with his scimitar, strode past files of guards behind the shadowy columns.

His upraised scimitar glinting in the poor light of smudgy torches was the badge of his authority. The columns narrowed into a perplexing maze. Through dexterous maneuvers with his weapon, the guard was able to determine in the dark which direction to take. He plunged quickly through the winding corridors.

"Quickly! We must not lose him, Joseph!" Ibn Amram whispered, pulling his student along through the darkness.

His sharp ears focused on the tiled floor where the guard's heavy footfalls echoed. They caught up with him just as he reached a wooden door. The guard was feeling the hobnailed pattern on the surface of a door, as if to identify it. Then he pounded seven times. The door opened.

"Hide them, Ishmael!" the guard commanded, stepping back at once into the darkness and pulling shut the door.

Ishmael, huge in his bloated corpulence, smiled benignly at his two charges.

"The pillows!" he commanded. "You will like the pillows. Under, like so."

He lifted two huge pillows and the flesh that hung in folds from his broad arms wavered to a tempo all its own.

He pushed both Ibn Amram and Joseph down and proceeded to cover them with a barrage of silk pillows. The mountains of pillows grew higher.

"Uph!" Joseph groaned, feeling an overpowering weight on his legs. "The giant has sat on me, *Mori*! I shall never walk again!"

Nor was Ibn Amram able to evade the corpulent shelter that Ishmael devised. A broad arm was flung across his back, and Ibn Amram was pressed into submission beneath a quivering mound of pillows.

No sound of battle reached their ears. Only muffled snippets of faint laughter penetrated the edges of the pillows, drowned out again as Ishmael shifted his position.

At last, the weight was released, the pillows thrown aside. The slow-witted guard was back, torch in hand, leaning forward to peer at the two Jews.

"The danger is past," he announced. "You will come with me. The king will see you in the hawking room."

The torch cast spectral shadows from each column as they wound their way back through the twists and turns of the hallways. He led Ibn Amram and Joseph up a whitewashed corridor to a narrow flight of stairs.

Gruff words were exchanged by the guard and another sentinel at a door at the top of the stairs. The tall sentinel motioned them past the door and around the heavy tapestry. He touched his lips to indicate silence.

At the far end of the soundless hawking room, Tashpin stood near a sturdy wooden perch. A peregrine falcon sat calmly on the perch, deigning to let the man touch her feet and claws. Occasionally, she blinked in response to her master's tender words.

"My pretty," King Tashpin murmured with surprising gentleness.

All four walls of the hawking room were hung with heavy tapestries, blotting out all exterior sights and sounds to enable the complete concentration of the bird. In the narrow spaces between each tapestry, a torch was hung for the evening. In the glow, Ibn Amram could make out lavish depictions of hunting scenes. On the far wall, the tapestry captured the excitement of a boar hunt with mastiffs in hot pursuit. On another, the scene was alive with brilliant colors of a stag hunt. But the most exquisite tapestry of all was hung on the wall behind the falcon's perch. It represented the king's love of hawking and falconry. It seemed to bathe the entire room in a wash of sky blue where birds flew free.

"She is a beautiful bird," Joseph whispered to his master. "Count Henri of Champagne has a hawk, but there is no comparison."

Ibn Amram nodded in agreement, motioning with a finger that they should remain silent until spoken to by the king. He strained his ears to catch any phrases which the king spoke to the bird.

"The walls are so dense in this room," Joseph whispered. "There is no possibility whatever for enemies to penetrate these four walls!"

Ibn Amram waved his student into silence.

The king stepped to the side of the noble bird and released the leather straps from the bird's ankles.

"Watch my lovely falcon fly to the bait," he announced, suddenly acknowledging the presence of Ibn Amram and Joseph.

He strode past them to the far side. Directly in front of the tapestry at the far end, he halted and turned with his gauntleted left arm upraised.

"My lovely! Come!" he commanded, clucking an enticement with his tongue while his right hand revealed the furry back of a dead mouse.

The falcon leaned forward in delight, opening and closing her strong beak before spreading her wings and following an arc that dipped down and then sharply up just in front of her master's hand. She alighted with the slightest flutter of feathers on King Tashpin's gauntlet. Like an inquisitive child poking into a parent's closed hand for a surprise, the falcon thrust her beak into the space between thumb and forefinger to rip away shreds of the mouse.

"My lovely is a bird of battle," the king remarked proudly. "But the mystic and his followers have no fighting spirit. They only prattle about paradise in the hills of Bir-Kassa. I would never have expected them to launch a revolt. Or would they?"

"Your tolerance is commendable, Your Grace," Ibn Amram

noted. "Where I am from, those who would challenge the accepted Christianity are relentlessly pursued."

"Rumors have reached me of evil bloodshed in Languedoc. The monks destroy Cathars in the name of the Church. Hah! They call them heretics and infidels. They even dare call us infidels! They will learn who is the heretic and who is the true believer when the caliph reconquers all of Andalusia!"

"Meanwhile the mystics are a thorn in your flesh," Ibn Amram commented.

"If the advisor had his way, he would behead every offender on the spot," the king answered, deftly tying the falcon with one hand. "I have tried to reason with them, and I have followed the principles of compassion and kindness."

King Tashpin was suddenly distracted by a sudden agitation which the falcon expressed. She lunged towards the tapestry on the right, screaming defiance. Tashpin stared suspiciously at the ripples within the hanging tapestry. But he said nothing and walked on, as if nothing had happened.

The three of them walked back again to the far wall. Before they could resume the baiting exercise, the tapestry at the entrance way was pushed aside, and the advisor entered. He entered into a soft conversation with the king. Both men cast suspicious glances around the room.

The youthful master of the hawks appeared in the doorway, dressed in leather tunic and heavily gauntleted. The king strode silently to the master of the hawks, who took the falcon from his hand. The boy disappeared into the corridor, and the advisor stepped into the shadows near the entranceway. The king returned to the center of the room and silently drew his scimitar.

"Could it be that I have sent my falcon to her roost before the hunt is done?" he asked in a piercing voice. "I think I see the motions of a mouse. Ah, it would elude my blade!"

He struck past a tapestry toward the wall. The blade clanged sharply on the bare stones.

"The mouse is quick," the king bantered, much to the satisfaction of the advisor. "He has scurried away to his mouse hole."

Tashpin worked his way down the room, striking with apparent random intent at the tapestries, yet knowing that the suspicious ripple was further along.

"My falcon would love this sport," King Tashpin said, talking indifferently to either the advisor or the invisible opponent. The scene of the boar hunt spread out before the fingertips of his left hand.

"How now? A rat?" he roared, striking the tapestry with a violent blow. The entire length of the tapestry shivered from the intensity of his attack. Closer he came to an offending bulge that had moved to the very end of the tapestry. A discernible shaking enveloped the edge and shook the silk fringe.

"Or is it a mouse? A large and horrid mouse?"

The tapestry convulsed in wild trembles as the hidden conspirator threw himself from behind his cover and grovelled at the king's feet.

"Oh, please, your lordship," groaned the pale-faced man. "I would not! Oh, I could not!"

Ibn Amram's jaw dropped in total amazement to see his adversary from Burgos in the rags of a mendicant Muslim. It was too shocking for words.

"You!" he exclaimed.

King Tashpin whirled around. "You know this man?" he asked imperiously.

"I do. It is the Legate Paul."

"You worm!" the king spat on the shaking legate. "Speak! Who sent you here? What is your purpose?"

"Oh, I cannot speak. Put the blade away," Paul begged, shaking uncontrollably. His eyes rolled in abject fear, and his tongue caught on his teeth as he babbled unintelligible words.

"You will speak now," King Tashpin said coldly.

His blade lifted up the legate's chin and pressed tightly

against the pale skin of his throat. Strange gurgles of convulsive fear came from Paul's lips, but he dared not move a muscle.

"I will talk!" he spluttered. "Anything! I will tell you all my spying secrets. In Pamplona. On the corsair. At Bir-Kassa. I will tell all! Just spare me."

The king withdrew his sword and glanced meaningfully at his advisor who took up a position behind the legate. Ibn Amram shivered to see King Tashpin examine the wicked blade of his scimitar and wipe away a drop of blood which had been drawn from the churchman's neck.

"This man is in league with the Devil!" Paul declared, raising a trembling finger to point at Ibn Amram. "I know it, and the archbishop knows it! We almost stopped him at Pamplona with a heavy carriage. But his luck remained with him. The evil luck of a stargazer in league with Satan."

"It would seem to be true, Your Grace," Ibn Amram agreed. "A carriage blocked the path of the royal carriage. Our lives were in jeopardy because of this man. I thought I recognized him at the window."

"And did you recognize me on the deck of the corsair?" Paul shot back, regaining his strength through his anger. "I saw you! I watched your every move. But I could not determine your motive. I had to follow further to be assured that the mission was to this Muslim. Now I know!"

"You know nothing!" King Tashpin retorted. "You only know that a Jew from Spain has come to Tunis. He is not the first Jew to whom I have granted an audience. Nor is he the last."

The scimitar drew nearer to Paul's throat again. The legate quivered anew.

"You see what I mean about third parties," King Tashpin said tiredly to Ibn Amram.

"Kill him," the advisor urged with a guttural snarl. "There are no accomplices to tell the tale."

Ibn Amram sprang forward. "No, spare his life!" he pleaded.

"Death for death is not our way."

The king stroked his fine eyebrow with his index finger.

"But what shall I do?" he mused. "I cannot possibly set this spy free. He might yet achieve success on behalf of his cursed archbishop. What am I to do?"

The advisor's lips narrowed to a quill edge, and his teeth gleamed in the torch light.

"He is strong and young," he commented. "It takes a strong arm to scale the walls as easily as he did. Let him expend some of that energy as a slave at sea. Sell him to a ship captain."

The index finger paused in midstroke. A smile creased the corners of the king's lips.

"You will learn the ways of submission in shackles," he said to the legate. "And you can thank the Jew for saving your life."

"Your head would be spiked on the battlements if it had been my choice," the advisor taunted, lifting the legate by his collar and shoving him into the corridor.

As the sounds of their footsteps carried down the long corridor, the king regained his accustomed poise.

"Again, I have met adversity and conquered it," he commented, sheathing his scimitar. "Your wise counsel was instrumental, Ibn Amram. I can see now why the King of Castile has entrusted you with this mission. Yes, I have decided. Tomorrow, I will send a rider to the caliph to obtain his permission to send you to him. Soon you will meet Caliph Al-Kumi!"

CHAPTER THIRTEEN

The Sands of Fury

TUNIS, TUNISIA
WINTER, 1140

MORE THAN A WEEK PASSED AFTER THE DEPARTURE SOUTH OF the royal messenger and still no word came back to Tunis. Ibn Amram bore the tension of waiting with agitation and unrest, wondering if the great Caliph Al-Kumi would grant him an audience to hear the proposal of the King of Castile. Ibn Amram knew full well that a treaty between King Alfonso and the Muslim caliph would do more than just bring peace to Christians and Muslims. It would give the Jews of the land peace at last. Furthermore, it would check the strutting power of the churchmen from Cluny. Could it be true, as King Alfonso had maintained, that the fanatical Cluniacs would use their stranglehold on a united Christian kingdom to expel the Rabbanite Jews? If the peace plan fails, such a Christian victory might just be possible, and with it would go the Jews' destiny.

In the meantime, Ibn Amram refused to let his anxiey mar this remarkable opportunity to conduct more sightings on the sun and moon. The algebra which had eluded him in the cities of Castile and Navarre was now making sense, thanks to the unstinting efforts of Aaron the Mathematician.

Aaron the Mathematician had provided Ibn Amram with another astrolabe to replace the one so rudely confiscated by the black monks on the road to Tarragona. The new astrolabe was similar to his own, although it lacked the fine detail the Arab craftsmen had bestowed on the instrument. Yet its precision was equal, and his sightings continued as before. Ibn Amram's fame as an astronomer was growing in Tunis.

Ibn Amram savored the paradox of his situation. At a time of political uncertainty, while the future of three nations and religions hung in the balance, the weeks spent in Tunis had been a time of great personal discovery for him.

One night, the messenger finally returned from his arduous trip. Ibn Amram was summoned immediately from the Jewish quarter. An evening meeting with the king was unusual; a meeting this late at night was almost unheard of. The Minister of the Palace ushered Ibn Amram into the room where a single hanging lamp was augmented by the glow of torches held by attendants.

"The caliph will see you in the badlands south of the salt lakes, at the oasis of Bir Khanafis," King Tashpin informed him.

His index finger had been tracing the arch of his eyebrow, a sign of agitation. At his side, a goblet of palm juice to calm his nerves was half empty.

"For that, you must begin the trip as soon as possible," the king continued. "Even now, my men are assembling the camels and camel drivers to accompany you on the caravan. One more matter! The officer of the port has reported a serious business to me. The captain of a ship has suffered a sudden revolt. Five sailors in the docks have been killed by renegade Christian slaves. Most of these Christians are now under control. Some fell overboard and drowned in their shackles. But it seems that three swam to safety in the lagoon. The search for them goes on at this very moment. They will be found and hanged!"

"Is one of the three the Legate Paul?" Ibn Amram asked.

"He is a slippery genie," the king muttered through clenched teeth. "The captain cannot imagine how he loosened his irons. With the help of Allah, he will be found. But you will leave before he can interrupt this mission." He twisted on the cushion to catch the attention of a heavily armed guard dressed in an oversized *burnous*. "Bachir! You will accompany the envoy to the Jewish quarter where he can gather a few possessions. Let nothing stand in your way."

The man selected as Ibn Amram's interpreter and guide bowed in response, rising silently to his feet. His leathery complexion bespoke a long intimacy with the wild winds of the Sahara.

"As you command," he said.

"The boy . . . my student," Ibn Amram ventured to interject. "May I take him, too?"

"Take whomever you please," the king said, dismissing him. "There will be enough camels for all."

The guard retreated to the columns of the doorway, beckoning Ibn Amram to hurry. They plunged into the night, breathing deeply of the brisk air that carried a tang of the Mediterranean. Striding quickly through the narrow street, Bachir led the way to a scene of quiet urgency outside the doors of the royal stable.

Awakened from their sleep, the camels twitched and stamped their displeasure. Their handlers looped braided ropes through the nose-rings, dodging the hooves of the irritable beasts. Young attendants, still rubbing their eyes from their abrupt awakening, scooted with their torches toward the stable hands who loaded the provisions. Other stable hands, dressed in the livery of the palace, tightened saddle girths for the many riders of the caravan. Guards, drivers and attendants were already mounting.

The provisions were now ready, and Ibn Amram reluctantly mounted. Torches were quickly doused in a rain barrel. The entire assembly was plunged into darkness, broken only by the faint light of the new moon. The street to the north was transformed into an eerie spasm of febrile shadows.

"Move on!" Bachir shouted.

The handlers whistled their commands, and the caravan lumbered heavily along the alleys toward the Jewish quarter and Bab-Souika.

"You there," Bachir shouted to one driver whose bale was slipping at a dangerous angle. "Tighten the load. We cannot afford to lose the salt for the black traders."

The rest of the caravan squeezed by as the tribesman feverishly undid the knots and retied the ropes. Little time was lost when the caravan rounded the corner of the quarter and stopped outside the iron gate of Aaron's home. Joseph was ready, pacing back and forth on the other side of the gate.

There was no time to lose. Bachir chided them for even a moment's pause. Joseph mounted the small camel provided for him, and the caravan clattered off. They soon passed under the high arch of Bab-Souika and into the darkness of the coastal road.

"There is no time for leisure," Ibn Amram whispered to Joseph. "The Christian slaves on one of their ships have escaped. They may be the same men who followed us here to Tunis. They would stop at nothing to destroy this mission."

Joseph nodded silently, glancing apprehensively at the fishermen's shanties at the edge of the beach. Bachir whistled sharp commands to his guards, and they fanned out from the caravan, roaming along the flat beach for any sign of intruders.

During the long hours spent in crossing the coastline to Wadi el Metiana, Bachir was very tense. He crossed and recrossed the path of the lead camel, peering into the mud hovels of the fishermen to search out any enemies. Few words were spoken. All the guards had unsheathed their scimitars.

Yet the camels made surprisingly good speed on the hard-packed shingle, wave-worn from centuries of the Mediterranean's abuse. Before the first gray light of dawn broke across the horizon of the east, the caravan had reached the bluffs of El Metiana, and Bachir could breathe a sigh of relief.

"We have crossed the most dangerous part," he explained to Ibn Amram. "The Christian slaves could have been anywhere along the coastline. But they will never penetrate the interior. Now we are among my people. They are always near if we need them."

He added a short whoop of delight and whipped his camel into a cumbersome gallop. The cold light of dawn revealed rocky plateaus to the west and bare rocky outcrops to the east of the *wadi*, the dry river bed which was a deeply eroded gorge. Into its depths, the entire caravan now descended, swallowed up by the lingering darkness of night in the steep walls of the *wadi*. The shallow water flew in curtains to either side of Bachir's mount. The other camels of the caravan hurried to keep up with his progress.

Ibn Amram cast an eye to the nearly perpendicular walls of the *wadi*.

"It's not like an *arroyo* of Spain," he explained to Joseph. "The *wadis* of Africa are worn by centuries of torrential rain. There are no forests like ours to soak up the rain. It simply ravages the land, rushing in terrible flash floods through these river beds. For the space of a few hours, a quiet *wadi* can become a place of extreme danger. Do not forget that, Joseph!"

His student clung to the jouncing saddle with his left hand while pointing up to the harsh rocky wall.

"What is that horrible noise?" he called out. Cries like infants in distress echoed sporadically along the length of the river bed where Joseph pointed.

"It is nothing," Ibn Amram replied. "They are jackals, nothing more."

"Allah be praised," Bachir interjected. "We have made

good time in this *wadi*. You see the mountain in the distance?"

His unwavering finger pointed out a peak that rose far above any other hill. The great peak of Zaghouan at this time of the morning was subtly shaded in delicate tones of lilac, from the deepest purple of its fissures to the pale mauve of its crag.

Ibn Amram nodded and pointed beyond the mountain to the towering black clouds forming in the east.

"We will have to hurry if we hope to reach Kairouan before the rain," he said.

Bachir responded instantly and rushed ahead to hurry the lead camel. Ibn Amram twisted around in his saddle to ease his tired back and to talk to Joseph.

"It feels as if I have been a wanderer all my life," he sighed. "Always moving from place to place. Always driven by bad weather or bad people! I can't tell you how delightful the prospect is of no longer being condemned to wander. Think of it, Joseph! Peace with the caliph. We shall have a safe haven for our people. Yerucham Halevi would be proud of my mission."

Joseph sensed a certain pang in his teacher's voice.

"I am sure we will be successful," he responded. "No one can resist your persuasion."

Ibn Amram had a substantial portion of the journey to think about his possible success. By early afternoon of the third day, the hot sun was hidden behind grey clouds, and a damp wind presaged a winter storm. From the low-lying *wadi*, the land had risen almost imperceptibly to a vast craggy plateau. A few acacia trees still clung tenaciously to the edge of the plain, but the tamarisk had relinquished the land to the spiky grass that anchored its roots in the barren soil. Astonished by the sight of the caravan, half a dozen gazelles flicked their tails in alarm and leaped behind the boulders.

The first cold drops of rain came with no warning, striking the plain with such force that each drop created small dusty clouds at impact. Then the sheer force of the sudden rain soaked the dust and formed a thick mud. In the violence of the downpour, all bearing of direction were momentarily lost. The horizon was invisible in the swirling rain. The camel drivers shouted and whistled to keep the caravan together. The guards, previously so talkative, hunched over their saddles in silence. A linen *burnous* offered no protection from the cold and intense force of the driving storm.

"We are fortunate to be following this new *wadi*," Ibn Amram called out, peering from under the sodden hood of his *burnous*. "But don't ride too close to the edge, Joseph. The water is rising quickly, and a flood may soon start."

The significance of his words was largely lost on the young traveller from Champagne, unfamiliar with the weather of North Africa. The rain abated as quickly as it began, and for the moment, attention was diverted to a noisy argument between Bachir and one of the camel drivers. The young driver was from a tribe other than Bachir's and dared to question his commands. The other drivers sat impassively and waited for Bachir to exert his full authority.

"We cross now!" Bachir commanded in Berber. "This is the place to cross in safety!" He pointed angrily at the waters boiling up over the rocks of the ford.

"In safety?" the driver screamed, tearing at his turban for effect. "The waters are rising with every word we speak. I cannot promise I can control my camels in such a depth."

"I did not ask for a promise," Bachir said coldly, throwing back his hood from his head. His hair was plastered flat against his skull, giving him a fierce, hawkish appearance.

The obstinate driver cast his eyes down and flicked his whip, urging his camel into the ford. A faint gleam of a smile crossed Bachir's mouth.

"We cross now," he repeated to the other drivers, raising his voice louder to be heard above the roar of the water. An old driver pulled abreast of Ibn Amram, resigned to crossing the churning undercurrent that ripped across the rocks.

"Allah will provide," he said, gaining strength from his

simple statement. "Don't worry! It is written."

His camel snorted in fear but pushed gamely into the water.

The first five camels eased into the water, their bales swaying violently. Snorting and braying their displeasures, they rose hastily from the white water. Suddenly, the sixth camel stumbled and fell to his knees. The full force of the water struck the bale lashed broadside to his back and tipped the miserable creature headlong into the stream.

"Aiee!" the young driver screamed, terrified by the rushing water and thrashing with all his might to find a handhold. The camel shook him free, and in desperation, he floundered for a rope hanging from the bale.

"My son, my son!" the old driver shouted, leaping from his camel and plunging into the mud. The canvas bale was just beyond his grasp. "Heaven help you!"

The boy clawed his way to the upper side of the heavy canvas as the bale moved downstream.

"Quickly, Joseph," Ibn Amram commanded. "Double back along the bank. We can catch him where the *wadi* turns."

"But what can we use for a rope?" Joseph called out in frustration, scrambling down from his high saddle.

"The reins!" Ibn Amram shouted back. "Pull off your reins, and we will tie both pairs together!"

Bachir looked on disdainfully from the other side of the *wadi*.

"Don't let go of the bale!" he shouted to the driver.

Coughing and sputtering in each wave of muddy water, the young man tried to hold on. By slow degrees, Joseph edged closer to the drowning man. The lad's father was in a paroxysm of fear, muttering uncontrollably.

The bale was slowly sinking. The young man showed few signs of having the strength to let go and swim for shore. Joseph carefully negotiated the muddy washout to reach him. Spitting away the mud and wiping the stinging ooze from his eyes, Joseph managed to crouch by the torrential waters.

"Here, man!" Joseph shouted. "Grab the rope when I throw it to you!"

His face a tableau of fear, the driver shook his head vigorously. "If I grab it, I will have to let go of the provisions for the caliph. We must save the bale or Bachir will have me killed!"

He glanced to where Bachir stood waist-deep in the water heaping curses and insults upon him.

"Then I must grab the bale for you," Joseph decided. "Between the two of us, we should be able to bring the thing to this stone. Are you ready?"

The young man blinked in disbelief. He had already resigned himself to clinging to the bale until the waters subsided, or until he drowned. With Ibn Amram holding the leather thong, Joseph threw himself into the water, forcefully inching his way toward the driver. Reaching the precious bale, he deftly tied the end of the line to it and reached out to the young man.

"*Inshallah,*" the boy's father breathed, almost collapsing.

"Now we must pull together," Joseph warned. "If either of us trips, the bale will be lost forever. It might take us down, too."

Two of Bachir's guards had retraced their steps and now stood beside the *wadi* aiding the old man and Ibn Amram in pulling the load ashore. Arm over arm, the four men struggled with the great weight. The waters were still high and the force of the water powerful, but the bale was coming closer. It danced capriciously on the waters as they pulled it steadily toward them.

"Tie it! Yes, tie it around the bale," Bachir shouted, suddenly taking charge. "Now we will all pull together, and I can ask this dog of a camel driver how he managed to lose the goods meant for the caliph."

The young man clawed his way up the mud to the top and fell into the arms of his father.

"Speak, dog!" Bachir commanded, looking down at the

piteous tribesman who had fallen to his knees in the mud.

"My lord," the driver implored. "I never meant to fall. The camel is young and inexperienced. He tried to regain his footing. It all happened so quickly."

"I shall remember your face," Bachir replied sardonically, looking at the disconcerted countenance of Ibn Amram. He looked back with renewed coldness at the inept driver. "I shall remember it. And if you ever fail me again, I shall sell you to the traders from Ghana!"

He turned to his guards and whispered a few words. They dragged the monstrous bale, now oozing muddy water like a bizarre sea sponge, and tried to lift it again onto the trembling camel.

Joseph now managed to follow the same path taken by the driver and clawed his way to the top of the muddy *wadi*.

"I almost drowned!" he sobbed.

"Heaven forbid!" Ibn Amram soothed him, wiping the mud from his face. "And thanks to Hashem, you have escaped from the *wadi* with nothing more serious than the indignity of this mud. Here, we shall wrap you in my sleeping blanket."

They went unnoticed as Bachir strode back to the lead camel to berate his guards. "What luck," he groaned, shaking his head, "to be at the head of fools and idiots! Do you think this camel can carry the caliph's linen and half the water of the *wadi* as well? Open the bale, simpletons, and wring out each piece!"

He stamped his foot, and the guards cringed at his rebuke. Then he turned on his heel and returned placidly to his camel.

From beneath the folds of the blanket, Joseph made a face at Ibn Amram, expressing his shock at Bachir's volatile outburst. But the fierceness of the Berber blew as strong as a hot desert wind and then died out just as suddenly. Back in the saddle of his favorite camel, Bachir stroked the creature's ears and calmed himself. He looked back at Joseph with newfound compassion.

"You are soaking wet, young man," he commented. "You

did better than all of us. Now you shiver. We must dry your clothes before the chill of sunset reaches the plain. If it were just that fool driver, I would let him suffer. But not you! You cannot see it from here, but there is a small fort to the west. It is big enough to build a fire in comfort and dry our things within it. The caliph will prefer dry linen. We will camp there this evening and reach Kairouan in the morning."

Almost hidden from view in the protective embrace of a wind-worn hill, the fort bravely accosted the travellers as they approached. A clumsy wall of sticks plastered with mud was the semblance of fortification. Bachir rode forward and was immediately greeted by a horde of desert urchins dressed in rags.

A call was raised, and soon the entire community of the fortress was massed at the main gate, applauding the arrival of the caravan. Bachir leaped down from his camel and shook his damp *burnous* into some semblance of presentability.

"Come with me," he said, motioning to Ibn Amram. "The chieftain of this fort will be delighted to show his hospitality. He must decide who will show hospitality to you. If he did not decide, the men would fight for the honor."

Palsied but sharp-eyed in the central tent of the enclave, the old chieftain held court with practiced skill. He motioned his guests to the rug on the other side of the smoldering fire and snapped his fingers for food and drink. An old woman, unveiled and curiously marked with a blue chin tattoo, returned with an earthenware dish of *couscous*.

Bachir exchanged a few words in Berber with the chieftain, and the old man shook his head in delight to hear Joseph's exploits.

"Fire! More fire!" he said appreciatively, gesturing to Joseph to draw closer.

A young girl staggered into the tent with slabs of dried camel dung in her arms. She crisscrossed the slabs in the fire which burst into hot flames.

The fire and the burning sensation of palm wine soon left

Joseph feeling dizzy and disoriented in the smoky tent.

"It is good, isn't it?" the chieftain said. "Tonight you will sleep like a baby. Here, show them their quarters. They can share with your magnificent camel."

The chamber selected for Ibn Amram and Joseph was little more than a cattle shed, roofed with heaps of brush and excavated to the depth of a man's knees. But it was enough to escape the cold night air and the damp puddles of the winter rain. Bachir's camel snorted appreciatively, dipped his head and knowingly entered the cabin. Ibn Amram shrugged and followed suit.

"Your bedding within is dry," Bachir called after him. "Sleep well. Our day will start before dawn."

With that he returned with the chieftain to the tent to discuss tribal matters over the dregs of palm wine.

By degrees, the Spanish envoy was coming to realize that the customs of the desert people were considerably different from the luxurious ways of Spanish Muslims. Theirs was a simple life reflected in simple tastes.

The harsh land was a panorama of opposites, often reflected in the customs of the Berber people. In the fort, Ibn Amram experienced the unstinting generosity of desert hospitality. In the city of Kairouan, he saw at first hand the lessons of blood revenge.

Installed at the outskirts of the city was a curious assembly of black traders, marvelously coiffed in beadwork and feathers. Their leader, more outrageously tricked out in ostrich feathers than his followers, sat on his heels until Bachir approached.

"You have brought it?" he asked with no pretense at cordiality.

"The weight of a man," Bachir answered. "Equal weight for equal weight as promised. Where is the gold?"

Silently, the two men fell to concluding the negotiations. A simple scale was borrowed from the rice merchant and into its pans were placed slabs of salt from the king's quarries and bags of gold dust from the trader's realm. The pans wavered for a long moment before both parties were satisfied that the trade of salt for gold was exactly equal. Bachir gestured to his guard who lifted the gold dust from the scale. The trader from Ghana watched the pan with salt plunge abruptly to the ground. He nodded with satisfaction.

"It is good to trade with an honest man," he declared.

Bachir nodded. A malicious smile twisted the corner of his mouth as his eyes searched the crowd behind him for the unfortunate camel driver who had fallen into the *wadi*.

"You! Son of a dog! Come here!" he commanded.

The young man approached with trembling knees.

"I have warned you," Bachir hissed. "The man who fails me deserves to be a slave! It is the law of blood revenge. Pain for pain! Have you failed me?"

The young tribesman rolled his eyes in fright and wrung his hands.

"My lord," he pleaded. "Do not trade me to the black man of Ghana! I have not failed you since the terrible day in the *wadi*. I have curried your camel each and every evening! Have pity on me. Avert your revenge!" He fell to his knees and wept at Bachir's feet.

Ibn Amram stepped forward, visibly moved by the tribesman's plea. Bachir noticed his movement out of the corner of his eye and in his own subtle way balanced the ferocity of his punishment with the ingenuous desire to maintain the admiration of the Spanish envoy.

"Enough," Bachir laughed, reverting to the language which Ibn Amram understood. "That's enough. Let the law of blood revenge stand as your warning."

He pulled the young man roughly to his feet and pushed him back. The camel driver's father quickly grabbed the young man's shoulders and pulled him into obscurity at the back of the crowd.

"Revenge is good! The spirits tell us so," the black trader noted, biting his upper lip in a strong display of emotion.

"Only through revenge is manhood proven."

Here was a man after Bachir's own heart. Bachir nodded his assent and touched the pommel of his scimitar with fierce meaning.

The Ghanaian rose to his feet, kicked the dust from his ankles and walked to his donkeys. Bales of ivory, ostrich feathers and satchels of gold dust were tended by his white slaves. He gestured disdainfully to the tightly lashed provisions on a donkey. When the slaves responded slowly to his silent command, the trader cuffed him with the butt of a switch fashioned from a rhinoceros tail.

An ebony box, waxed and polished, gleamed in the trader's hands as he returned to Bachir's side.

"Revenge is sweet," he declared, stroking the smooth surface of the black box.

The men of the caravan gathered at a respectful distance, their eyes glued to the mysterious box.

"The King of Ouagadougou heard my plea," the trader continued, caressing the lid of the box with a strange abstraction. "I called for satisfaction for my entire family. The man who dared kidnap my son told his lies, but the king would not listen to him. He gave me satisfaction!"

His fingers punctuated the statement by reaching to the top of the lid and drawing it back. As one man, the group of men assembled around the trader drew in their breath. On top of dried grass lay a human hand, withered and twisted.

"Revenge is sweet," the Ghanaian repeated. He tilted the box for Bachir and Ibn Amram to see more clearly.

Ibn Amram jerked back in surprise and disgust, but Bachir did not notice the rapid motion. He, too, had moved but his movement was forward, avidly fascinated by the morbid shape. Silence hung like a fog while he surveyed the surface of the severed hand.

"A hand for a hand and a head for a head," Bachir said. A motion caught his attention and he glanced at the shocked face of Ibn Amram. "Revenge is good, rabbi!"

"Yes," the trader agreed. "Sweet like the apricots of the oasis."

Ibn Amram looked down at his boots. When he looked up, the eyes of both men were rivetted on him, but he did not avert his gaze.

"Hot anger leads to revenge," he agreed, deliberately avoiding any further glimpse of the frightful box. "What is the blood avenger? Is he the executioner? I say no! He is the one who must hunt down the guilty man and bring him before the judge."

Bachir, irritated almost beyond measure by Ibn Amram's cool words of rebuke, spat on the ground and then ground his foot into the spot.

"The judge?" he exclaimed. "Ha! I have seen the judicial magistrate of Tunis, but I call him an old woman."

Ibn Amram shrugged, mindful of the delicate balance he had to maintain. "Man is quick to anger," he commented. "But a man must not die unless he has stood trial. And if a man were to kill his neighbor by accident, the Merciful One has decreed that he will flee to a city of refuge. It is the law of the Almighty, not the law of blood revenge."

Bachir stared at Ibn Amram, clenching and unclenching his hands. He grew impatient of this well-reasoned appeal to a higher authority.

"I will not be lectured by a Jew," he declared flatly. "Enough! For the rabbi, it is the court of law. For the warrior, it is the sword!"

He turned his back on Ibn Amram and continued his meticulous inspection of the hand. Ibn Amram motioned to Joseph and diplomatically withdrew from the circle of men. The Ghanaian, strutting like a rooster, could not contain his delight at besting a teacher of the book. In an ecstasy of self confidence, he reached into the box, lifted out the hand and raised it to his lips, kissing it hungrily with a loud smacking sound. His followers drew back in horror.

The city of Kairouan was suddenly a painful oppression

for the hot-blooded Bachir. He nodded abruptly to the Ghanaian and hurled guttural commands at his guards and drivers. The caravan was marshalled again, though little was left of the waning daylight.

"We will encamp in the hills to the south," he shouted to Ibn Amram. "I have had enough of cities of refuge."

A pall had been cast over the fragile friendship which Bachir had established with the Spanish envoy. They rode in silence the entire next day.

It was a time of troubled reflection for Ibn Amram. He sought to master the algebra which would unlock the mystery of the coming solar darkness. If he could only find the key to this understanding he could make the unknown known. He could dispel the rampant superstitions that were a blight on King Alfonso's reign. Ignorance and narrow-mindedness were at the heart of the darkness of Castile.

The brutal pace of their journey left little time in the evenings for their customary discussion of *Koheleth*. Joseph could see that Ibn Amram needed to concentrate on his algebra in order to prepare for the coming eclipse. Ibn Amram seemed to be in a hurry to complete his computations soon. With each sighting of the sun, he appeared more and more vexed.

The dawn of the next day of the week brought a cruel surprise. The *chamsin*, the hot wind of China, blew out of the east, sickening both man and beast with its heat.

"Like a forge!" Joseph exclaimed weakly. "As if you had pressed your face towards the red hot coals of the blacksmith's forge."

"We will do well to begin at once," Ibn Amram urged Bachir.

Bachir scowled, drawing his *burnous* across his neck as a gust of hot wind blew an eddy of sand their way. Unexpectedly, his dire expression broke into a smile.

"I will take you to the oasis by nightfall," he said. "Even if it means we must drive our beautiful camels into the ground."

True to his word, their pace that day was unrelenting. The salt lake rose up on the horizon, but Bachir refused to turn the caravan towards the brackish water for a rest. Ahead of them, formless yet forbidding, was the great sand sea of Tunisia.

The camels soon mired down in the sand, climbing hill after hill with greater effort. Bachir cursed their luck and dismounted to let his animal find his way.

"When I was a young man, I tracked my enemies in the sand," he said to Ibn Amram as they drew abreast in their struggle to climb a treacherous dune. "At night, I could see each footprint like a beacon in the dark. Then in the morning, the *chamsin* would erase every mark, like the chalk scribbles from a schoolboy's slate. But not before I had read and memorized the message of my enemy. No man can escape me in the sand sea. Only the sea itself laughs at me."

Neither man could speak any more. The struggle to climb up the shifting sands was simply too great. Panting and gasping for breath, they would clear the crest of each hillock, only to survey a continuation of the same white sand. They lay on their stomachs and grovelled up the shifting surfaces like lizards. For hours they saw nothing but endless ridges of white sand.

Bachir struggled up one more slope expecting to see another just ahead. But the white wavelets had ceased. He gave a whoop of joy. The sand was a vivid yellow, hard-packed and promising a fast journey. The eastern edges of the smooth hillocks of sand were tinged with a rich umber hue.

"We have found our footing at last!" Bachir crowed. "I recognize this land. My camel will recognize the firm footing, too."

He threw himself into the saddle and motioned triumphantly to the east. Speed that whipped the edges of a desert *burnous* was a delighful change from their arduous trek. The guards became talkative again. Their pace was now feverish. Bachir was committed to finding the oasis before nightfall.

Bachir had another reason to command and cajole the

utmost speed from his flagging men and camels. A sand storm was rising from the east, ugly and green-edged as it stirred the sands. It dared them to move forward into its abrasive embrace.

Somewhere in the dim outlines of the storm was a verdant oasis. There, in the eye of the storm, or later in the strange still of the desert night, the caliph would meet them. The sight of that longed-for oasis was suddenly obliterated by swirling sand.

Bachir choked on the sand, dismounting suddenly to regain his breath. His camel pinched tight his nostrils and prepared to wait out the worst of the storm. But Bachir would have nothing of a delay. He teased the creature's ears and pointed deliberately into the face of the storm. The animal leaned forward, testing the sand as a blind man tests the terrain. His nostrils flared as each gust subsided.

"Come on!" Bachir commanded.

The other camels grudgingly rose to their feet, encouraged by the switches of their handlers. The caravan trudged after Bachir's camel even when he veered capriciously to the north.

Trudging blindly behind Bachir, Ibn Amram felt the heavy bronze astrolabe strike his thigh rhythmically. Here in the sand storm, the instrument meant nothing, and he was reduced to following a clever beast. The position of the sun was blotted from the sky.

They moved on slowly as the winds swirled about them. At the crest of a hillock, Bachir turned and motioned to Ibn Amram and Joseph to catch up with him. They hurried their camels to the top and followed the line of his finger, pointing below to the valley. A verdant miracle of fertility dazzled their eyes.

"Like the Garden of Eden!" Ibn Amram breathed, overcome with emotion. "Blessed be Hashem, we have found the oasis!"

CHAPTER FOURTEEN

The Way of the Desert

BIR KHANAFIS, TUNISIA
WINTER, 1140

"THERE IT IS," BACHIR SAID PROUDLY. "BIR KHANAFIS!"
They stumbled blindly through the grove of date palms. The camels broke free with a bizarre braying and plunged into the fetid mire of the first stagnant pond. Bending their knees into the mud, the camels and the drivers drank greedily.

Ibn Amram pulled Joseph away from the pool and headed deeper into the palm grove, looking for fresher water.

"It will be *Shabbat* soon. We must prepare ourselves," he said to Joseph, glancing up at the waning sunlight. The last orange glow from the western edges of the sky turned to muted ocher, leaving everything in dull shadows.

Joseph had foraged in the grove of date palms and returned with a bag of palm hearts to mince with their *couscous*. It was a meager meal, but neither of them complained. Grateful to have reached the oasis before the *Shabbat*, Ibn

Amram sang his favorite *zemirot* composed by Dunash Ibn Labrat a century earlier. His deep baritone carried across the sand, and even Bachir and the camel drivers paused to listen.

"Why don't we sing your own *zemirot*?" Joseph asked.

Ibn Amram pushed away his empty platter and shook his head with distinct humility.

"The old songs are the best," he concluded.

Another offering from Dunash Ibn Labrat carried on the still air of the oasis. The songs and the fire died out almost simultaneously.

Ibn Amram and Joseph spent the next day in refreshing contemplation of *Koheleth,* adding new insights with each passing hour. The threats of the desert, their impending meeting with the caliph, even the thorny problem of the Karaites seemed distant. But as the day stole silently away and the twilight stars sparkled in the crisp night air, Ibn Amram's mind was seized once again by his momentous mission to the caliph. There had been no word of when he and the caliph would stand face to face.

For many days, the question of the arrival of Al-Kumi remained unanswered. Bachir could not begin to guess when the wily caliph would make his appearance.

"Perhaps he is out there even now," he suggested, squinting into the harsh dazzle of the sand dunes. "He waits and contemplates our actions. No matter! We will wait as long as he waits."

Daily routine became a deadly tedium. Peaceful hours spent under the shady leaves of the apricot trees did not seem to calm Ibn Amram's distressed spirit. He seized every opportunity throughout the sunny mornings and afternoons to take precise sightings on the sun. What had been a science was rapidly becoming an obsession.

It was the coming celestial darkness that intrigued and vexed him. A throbbing at the back of his head told him that if he could pinpoint its exact coming–if he could only predict the darkness with utter accuracy–the ignorant peasants could be prepared for it. It could be explained to them as a natural occurrence. There would be no fear, no terror, no bloodshed.

The *chamsin* had ceased to blow. The rolling hills of sand were sharply defined like a crystalline image. The watchman had stared into those maddening shapes for days, seeing nothing. But the fourth day of the week brought a belated change. He sounded the alarm on a high-pitched horn. The other guards were instantly on the alert.

"It is the retinue of the caliph," Bachir announced with satisfaction. "They come from the east. They will encamp in our midst."

The drab camels were at first spectral, like moving sand dunes on the horizon. Soon they came closer and their silhouettes showed the rounded forms of heavy bales. With the sun high in the noonday sky, tribal greetings were at last exchanged. The swarthy attendants set about to erect the silken tents for the great caliph. They struggled proudly, disdaining any offer of help from Bachir's men. At last, ready and guarded at all four points by Berber warriors, the tent stood strangely empty.

Their waiting continued. The cook prepared a sumptuous meal for the caliph. But Al-Kumi did not come. The following morning dawned like the previous one. Guards became snappish during the tedious anticipation. When the vigil was almost unbearable, horses appeared on the horizon.

There was no mistaking the dour Caliph Abd Al-Kumi. He shunned the glistening chain mail of his warriors in favor of a simple desert *burnous*. His linen turban was even simpler than that of King Tashpin. Even the brooches of his garment were a plain bronze instead of the gold preferred by the sheiks of Tunis.

In all this simplicity of attire, two distinct features set him aside as the emperor. His Arabian charger was a magnificent animal, blue-grey and dappled like the subtle moonlight of a forest glade. His troops ranged on either side, but he remained steadfastly at the vanguard as the horse pranced through the sand. Feathers of the desert pheasant adorned the headpiece of his imperial eagle.

Bachir walked slowly to the edge of the encampment and thrust out his arm in traditional greeting.

"Come in peace," he shouted with ritual reverence.

The caliph delayed his response until he was easily within earshot.

"The Almighty should grant you peace," he replied.

He dismounted with the assurance of a warrior. Bachir walked forward and they entered into a secretive conversation, glancing once or twice over the horse's mane in the general direction of Ibn Amram. The eagle still sat placidly on the caliph's left hand.

The caliph walked past the Spanish envoy without a second glance. The attendants immediately undid the sashes which held the tent flaps securely closed. Bachir bowed as he retreated from the tent. He beckoned Ibn Amram with a nervous gesture.

"He will see you now," he whispered. "Immediately! Before he has even washed his hands and feet."

Ibn Amram nodded apprehensively at this impetuous behavior and entered the tent opening, bending deeply to clear the scooped flap. It took a moment for his eyes to become accustomed to the dim light of the tent.

"Who are you?" the caliph demanded.

He was flanked by a minister in full military attire. The warrior's hand was on the handle of his scimitar.

"I am Avraham Ibn Amram," the sage replied. "I have been chosen by Alfonso, King of Castile, to carry a proposal to the great Caliph Abd Al-Mumin Al-Kumi, Emperor of the Faithful."

Al-Kumi leaned back into the cushions, momentarily satisfied by the deference. But an undercurrent of vexation was visible on his face. He snapped his fingers to a boy who approached with a brass laver to wash his feet.

"Envoys and more envoys," he muttered, without explaining his words. "I am plagued by envoys from Iberia. Where did you last see this King Alfonso?"

"Why, in the palace of Burgos, of course," Ibn Amram answered. "He has sent me on a difficult journey. From that palace, I travelled many days until I reached the palace of the King of Tunisia, your faithful *Hajib*."

"Palaces and more palaces," the caliph scoffed. "I have met envoys who would rather spend their days in the mausoleums of Lisbon instead of the living desert. Tell me, envoy. Are you only impressed when your patrons live in great stone palaces?"

An eye as steady and as unblinking as the eagle's orange eye was on Ibn Amram. He paused to think, wondering what Lisbon had to do with his mission.

"Palaces are built of stone," he answered carefully. "A great leader cannot lead stones into battle. A mighty emperor counts the warriors in his empire, not the stones of his dwelling."

The caliph leaned sideways and extended his other foot to the boy.

"An artful answer, envoy," he noted. "I spurn the luxury of castles and palaces. The King of Castile might think his dwelling will last for a millennium. But I know better than the Christian. I am a child of the mountains and a man of the desert. I know the power of wind and of sand as no spoiled princes could hope to know. Envoys come prattling to me of power, but I know better. They would teach me their lessons, but I know better. The lesson is for me to teach them. Tell me, envoy, how long will the pride of man last?"

The directness of the question startled Ibn Amram. The caliph's manner of testing was totally unlike the subtle games which King Alfonso or Tashpin had used. He averted his eyes from the black inscrutability of the caliph's gaze.

"Some wise men of another age said that pride lasts forever, that everything around us is the vanity of pride," he answered slowly.

"Come, be precise," the caliph demanded. "Do not talk in

circles when you can be clear in calculation. Is it a year? Is it a decade? Is it an eternity? How long does it take the winds of the desert to dislodge the most tightly mortared walls of man?"

"In a storm such as we encountered, I suspect the stones would start to crumble in just a few years," Ibn Amram answered, following the caliph's lead wherever it might take them.

"Would a decade be sufficient to topple the stone walls of man?" the caliph pressed. "Would anything remain standing after twenty years facing the fury of the desert? I see you have thought little about this question, safe as you have been in the cities of Castile. Tell me, envoy, is this Alfonso a fool?"

Ibn Amram recoiled at the insult.

"If I may speak for the Spanish king," he said distinctly, "there are ruins enough in Burgos. He does not have to look for them in the desert. The Tower of Queen Urraca still stands as mute testimony to past sorrows. King Alfonso knows better than to trust his future to the thickness of his walls."

The caliph's exclamation in Berber was harsh but grudging in its approval of the envoy's answer. The wall of his tent billowed with a sudden blow of his scimitar.

"I think I like you, envoy," the caliph noted, badgering Ibn Amram with a sour smile. He sheathed his scimitar and drew his legs ceremoniously back under his *burnous*. "Perhaps I will come to like your king, although he is my enemy. For now, you must cast your eye around you and see the way of the desert. My name is spread through the fame of my eagle and the speed of my horse. These are the true symbols of my empire. If Alfonso has sent you to spy on my castles and fortresses, you will look in vain. Tomorrow, my horse and my eagle will test you as they have tested me. I leave you with this fact–the Caliph Al-Kumi has learned the secrets of the great sand sea. I will last longer in the shifting sand, longer than any of the envoys my enemies dare to send south. These sands, which are the walls of my palace, will remain forever a mystery!"

The caliph snapped his fingers. Ibn Amram's audience was concluded.

For the rest of the afternoon, the caliph did not stir from his tent. A variety of warriors and ministers came and went.

Ibn Amram waited, but he was not called again. He returned to the afternoon *shiur* with Joseph. The lad was doing well, learning with acuity and gratefully making the most of the hours Ibn Amram spent with him. Ibn Amram rolled up their manuscript of *Koheleth* at the close of the *shiur* and sighed.

"You know, Joseph, I can usually tell humbug when I hear it. Take that pompous heretic Henri du Mans, for instance. He showed his true colors as soon as he opened his mouth. And the Abbot Peter, much of what he says is nothing more than pious puffery, though I must concede that an inner fire burns in his eye. But the caliph! Many a Spanish nobleman would dismiss him as a simpleton. Yet I am troubled by him. There is more to him than angry outbursts and impetuous will. Perhaps the way of the desert by which he lives is the key to his mind and his actions."

"Is it not merely a simple understanding of the sand and the sky?"

"I fear it is more than that, Joseph. For years the Spanish royalty, their ministers, their envoys have overlooked it. They have treated the Almohad warrior as though he were a rebellious Christian nobleman. Joseph, if I can watch the Caliph Al-Kumi carefully and learn every nuance of his mysterious doctrine, I could advise the king with far greater success."

At dawn the next morning, Ibn Amram and Joseph began their morning prayers. It was a time of thoughtful introspection for the sage, when he could bind the straps of his *tefillin* with undistracted intention. Here beneath the overhanging boughs of the apricot trees he was able to pace back and forth, immersed in *Shacharith*.

The caliph, too, was an early riser. Walking to the tether

line to check on his horses, he noticed the white of Ibn Amram's *tallith* within the dark shadows of the trees.

"Ho! Envoy!" he called out with a jocular familiarity almost unseemly for an emperor. "What do you think of my castle?"

He stood with his hands on his hips, his back to the sandy landscape and his face an enigmatic shadow. A pause ensued while Ibn Amram concluded the last words of his prayers. Then he turned quickly to face the caliph.

"I think it will last longer than any other man's," he answered. "But it is not by what men will judge you."

"Then I will let you judge my true value this morning," the caliph added. "Come to my tent when I have finished my prayers and we shall ride to the hunt."

The horses, one chestnut and one gray, were waiting when Ibn Amram approached the tent. The nomadic sheiks in the caliph's retinue eyed the Spanish Jew with new-found respect. Bachir motioned in vain to catch Ibn Amram's attention, but the caliph had already stepped forth from the tent. His imperial eagle flapped its wings nervously in expectation of the hunt.

This was certainly a sport to which the horses were well accustomed. The gray almost pitched Ibn Amram from his saddle as he bolted forward in pursuit of distant quarry. The undulating hills were eaten up by the swift-footed beasts. Still, the caliph did not talk. He held his left hand forward, letting the great eagle test the wind.

Gradually, the pace of the caliph's horse slowed, and the caliph held aloft the eagle, coaxing him with whisperings.

"He is a magnificent bird," Ibn Amram commented, watching the astonishing breadth of the eagle's wingspan and wondering what prey he could find on a windswept sand sea.

"Yes, magnificent is the word," the caliph agreed, extending his left hand still further. "He is proud to survey my realm. It is his realm also. Ah, he spreads his wings and prepares himself for flight. He is like a golden *menorah* which I hold up in praise of Allah."

The simile was unexpected. Ibn Amram watched the wind flutter the pinion feather of the noble bird, poised like a living candelabra.

"The short-sighted man would think the bird provides my meals," the caliph said. "But that is not so. He nourishes my heart with his freedom and his captivity. It is not what I get from my eagle but what I give to him that makes me an emperor."

"I do not understand," Ibn Amram dared say. "But then, I never have been a master of hawking."

The caliph turned slightly in the saddle, appreciative of Ibn Amram's interest but also condescending in his explanation, aware that here was man as shortsighted as the rest.

"This eagle did not come to me trained as you now see," he stated, reining in his horse so that the eagle could test the air. "I myself was his teacher. I remember the first time I laid eyes on him, crouched low in a trader's wicker basket. He uttered strange cries of protest and longing. I called him Rochi, my soul. He did not yet understand. Again he shrieked, but I answered gently, feeding him a tidbit of snake. He hated his captivity, and he hated me. But I persisted. His anger was greater than my soul, and it would consume me. But I stroked each wing with the gentle touch of a feather."

"You mastered the eagle with a feather?" Ibn Amram asked incredulously.

"Just so! At first, he could not understand my purpose. But he saw the light of the sun rise to the fullness of noon and sink to the evening with no stop to my gentle stroking. My voice lulled him. Rochi... Rochi... All night the stroking continued. I spoke to him as I speak to my precious children. He could not understand, but his anger was less and less."

"How does that make you his master?" Ibn Amram asked, intrigued by the absolute loyalty the bird showed his handler.

"I bent his will to mine with the gentlest touch of my hand. I would not let him sleep. It was torture for his proud spirit. He never left my side. I watched his eyes flame with the fire of all wild creatures. Then I named him Ayuni, my eyes. Soon, the fire burned to an ember. Sleep took hold of his senses. He had to close his eyes. It took two days and two nights and all morning of the third day, but I never let him sleep. Nor did I sleep, for that matter. I was nearly dead, but in the end, envoy, I won him to my heart. He knew I had outlasted his proud will and the weight of sleep on his eyelids made him trust me. From that moment forth, Ayuni was mine."

"A pretty tale," Ibn Amram said, drawing back again as the eagle broke the calm with a fierce beating of wings.

"And a lesson for wise men," the caliph added. "Do not believe the stories that I, Al-Kumi, am an impetuous leader. My patience is legendary. That is how I master a bird and how I master a man. Can you resist, envoy?"

"You would stroke me with a feather?" Ibn Amram asked.

"I would bend you to my will," the caliph said sternly. "You and all the other envoys who dare come into my desert."

He reached into his leather pouch and withdrew a morsel of viper which he fed to the eagle. A flicker of wings at that instant appeared over the smooth topped hills nearby. An unsuspecting wagtail was flying back to the oasis.

"Ayuni!" the Caliph whispered. "Hunt him down."

His right hand deftly freed the bird's legs. The eagle crouched and threw himself heavily into the air, gaining speed from each stroke of his massive wings.

Ibn Amram stood up in the stirrups, fascinated by the life and death struggle enacted before his eyes, and the apparent symbolism which the caliph sought. The small bird, aware of the fast-closing form of the swooping eagle, dropped rapidly to within a wing beat of the ground, skimming a hair's breadth above the rocky dunes.

Once, twice, the great eagle swooped to the kill, then flitted past his elusive prey. Fierce cries of frustration expressed his ire. The wagtail flew on.

The caliph called to the eagle, holding up his right hand with another morsel of snake. The eagle circled effortlessly on the still air and flashed back to his master. The outcome was not exactly as the caliph had intended. His eyebrows were furrowed in frustration.

"It is not always by force that the battle is won," Ibn Amram commented, settling back into his saddle. "Strategy must match strength."

The caliph was understandably irritated by the failure of his eagle, but he tried to hide his feelings by involving himself completely in the task of retying the bird's feet.

"We shall try again," he responded. "If not today, tomorrow. One battle does not make a war. I am poised with boundless lands to the south and a loveless land across the straits to the north." He stroked the wings of his nervous eagle and called him again by his pet name. "Who shall give ground to the conqueror?"

Ibn Amram looked carefully at the face of the caliph. He did not see the hard lines of his frequent scowl. The eyes were softened into a wistful gaze as he examined the feathers of his prized bird.

"Perhaps the time has come to discuss the question of giving ground," Ibn Amram declared. "There have been bad feelings for years in Andalusia. Part of the ill will is probably brought on by the Christian zeal of the king's advisors. They do not always represent his enlightened attitudes."

The caliph's face hardened into a scowl.

"I see you are not a hunter," he said with muted derision. "An envoy through and through! So be it! We shall talk today. You apparently have not waited these many weeks just to see a wagtail elude my eagle."

He kneed his horse with masterful pressure, and the creature responded with delight, racing with the wind in his mane across the rippling hills.

When he reached the tethering line, shaded by the miraculous greenery of tall palms, the Caliph Al-Kumi whirled around, clearly upset over an apparent loss.

"What is it, master?" a young squire asked, racing forward

to take control of the caliph's reins.

"The pig! Where is the pig?"

The boy heaved a sigh of relief and pointed to the dense underbrush behind the caliph. A young boar whose broad ears were intricately dyed in blue snuffled in the shadows.

The caliph was immediately reassured and mimicked the guttural snuffles to attract the pig back amongst the horses.

"Bring him out!" he commanded. "Turn his head! This will bring him out!"

He reached into his leather pouch and, to the consternation of the jealous eagle, proffered a tidbit of tasty snake to the wayward pig.

"Come back, young one," Al-Kumi called.

The pig resisted all enticements. The squire kept prodding it with a stick.

"You belong with the horses," Al-Kumi commanded. "What would happen if the spirits came to the paddock in your absence?"

The pig was unconcerned with that danger and squealed loudly in rebellion.

"He is in league with the demons, you know," the caliph said confidentially to Ibn Amram.

They watched the boy tie the hind legs carefully to the tethering line. The horses ignored the presence of the pig.

"I have heard the spirits late at night when the horses are asleep," said the caliph. "It is then that they try to enter my beauties and make them mischievous."

"Ah, you invite them to enter the pig instead," said Ibn Amram, suddenly realizing the value of the squealing boar.

"They have taken him over many times already, as you can see," the caliph agreed. "With each day, he becomes more restless and obstinate. Do not look at his eyes, envoy. They are the entrance way of the spirits to your soul."

Ibn Amram dismounted, quite happy not to look more closely at the furious boar.

"His tusks are growing," he said. "Soon he will sever the

rope with a twist of his head. Then he will make his escape."

"That is as it should be," the caliph said, likewise turning his back on the squeals. "Soon he will escape into the badlands and take the spirits with him."

For the moment, Ibn Amram's poise and self confidence were shattered. During their wild ride back to camp, he had rehearsed the topics he wanted to present to the Muslim emperor. It was a logical and persuasive presentation he had in mind. Now, the boar and the evil it represented to the caliph distracted him. The way of the desert left him baffled.

The harsh laugh of the caliph suddenly reminded him of the lusty roar of Ali Banu Hajaj on the battlefield of Aragon. Visions of the fierce battle, Ali's badly burned son and the suffering Spanish knights on the blood-soaked plain brought his mind back to his mission. Peace. He must urge peace, no matter what the Almohad warrior would answer.

The time was upon him. There was not a moment to lose. Already, the caliph squatted comfortably upon his cushions and called for refreshments. The attendant with the huge fan of ostrich feathers eyed the Spanish envoy expectantly.

"Proceed," the caliph demanded darkly. "Perhaps you will fare better than the previous envoy."

"Alfonso, King of Castile, has chosen me to convey the plans of a special peace," Ibn Amram began, inwardly decrying the convolutions of his speech. "He respects your growing power. The Almohad dynasty is an active participant in the affairs of the Mediterranean, as well it should be."

The caliph looked up at him, arching an eyebrow in displeasure at the abstractions of these flowery words.

"You did not come here to tell me something I already know, envoy," he remonstrated, setting the carafe of palm juice back down on the brass platter.

"I am struggling with my thoughts," Ibn Amram conceded quietly, leaning forward. "I wish to speak plainly. From your perspective, old opponents can become valuable allies. The King of Tunis is living proof that Muslims, even Muslims from different tribes of the mountains, can unite in a common objective. But to Alfonso, old opponents do not always become allies. They simply remain grudging combatants, grating on his abilities to govern."

"You are doing it again, envoy," the caliph said sharply, watching him over the rim of his goblet. "Do not talk in circles. Who are these opponents? The Jews? I bent the Jews to my will in Guadalajara, until that Jewish advisor managed to spirit them out of the city. I asked you once if Alfonso is a fool, envoy. His blind trust in that Jew makes me wonder!"

Ibn Amram blanched at the ferocity of the caliph's attack on Alkabri.

"I refer to the Cluniac monks," said Ibn Amram. "Spain is filled with monks. They hamstring Alfonso's court."

"He should cut off the hand that opposes him!" the caliph said fiercely. "Alfonso is a fool to trust such people. That dog of a Jew and now this dog of a priest Bernard! I know all, envoy. A thousand spirits of the worst sandstorm could not begin to compare with how this vile man rubs my skin. He rubs me raw, envoy, and I will see his head upon a pike when I conquer Toledo."

"He rubs Alfonso the wrong way, too," Ibn Amram nodded. "But Alfonso has assured me that the monks can be controlled. Bernard and his followers came from Cluny. They can go back to Cluny, if the politics of Iberia are right."

"You mean if the Muslims loyal to me are subjugated to the will of the Spanish king. Isn't that what you mean, envoy?"

"Not at all! Consider the outcome of such a black day. With no one to oppose the expansion of the monks into Granada, they would be intoxicated with their new power. With no Almohad dynasty to the south to balance their power, the scales would tip in their favor, and they would even dare overrule the will of the king himself. It would be worse than a crusade."

"You see only your side of the game, as if it were a game of chess. No more and no less. Do you think you are the only envoy? I must make strong my will and my forces for the final push. It will come soon."

"You do not need to strengthen your forces. There is an alternative to war!" Ibn Amram declared fervently.

He reached under his *burnous* and withdrew a document in Arabic, written in the neat hand of Alkabri.

"King Alfonso sees with a clear eye your power. But he is sick of war. He has seen his finest knights killed or maimed in battles with your warriors. This fighting cannot go on. It is an ugliness on the face of the beautiful land of Spain. The people deserve peace. What does it matter if one more village or one less village swears allegiance to the Prophet?"

"What are you talking about, envoy?" the caliph demanded. "Come to the point!"

"I am talking of peace. Here, let me show you. The appendix of this document includes a map. You see? South of the Guadiana will be yours in perpetuity. North of the river will remain in Alfonso's hands. All raids will cease. The land will be peaceful once more."

"It is a trick," Al-Kumi hissed, staring suspiciously at the neat calligraphy with slitted eyes. "Is this a race to see which document I will sign first?"

"I do not understand," Ibn Amram stammered, totally at a loss for words at this strange outburst.

"The peace plan, envoy! I am talking about the peace plan with this same map. Not just similar to the one that Aphonso Henriques' envoy brought me last month; it is identical! Your king is in league with his half-brother! Do these kings of the peninsula take me for a fool? With how many documents will you try my patience?"

He threw the empty goblet at Ibn Amram. It struck the envoy full in the chest, falling heavily into his lap.

The attendant with the ostrich fan had stopped his movements and drew back into the furthest recesses of the tent. The minister stepped forward, his scimitar drawn.

"But surely the King of Portugal did not devise the self-same plan!" Ibn Amram cried. "What treachery could have brought this map to the hands of Alfonso's hated brother?"

"His envoy was most persuasive," the caliph said coldly. "The outcome is simple. The King of Portugal and the King of Castile take my empire and divide it between them. Didn't your king explain this to you? How did you come to serve such devious men, rabbi? I would have thought that a man of the Book would have spent his time with holy manuscripts, not Spanish schemers!"

Ibn Amram felt shocked and betrayed. His mind was reeling. How had the Portuguese found out about his secret mission? How had they managed to send an envoy to Tunisia on such short notice? But the evidence was now irrefutable. He fell back into the cushions, almost toppling onto the floor of the tent.

"I am certain that King Alfonso was no party to a secret pact with the Portuguese. His half-brother is his sworn enemy," Ibn Amram asserted.

"Your words say one thing," the caliph interjected. "Your face says another."

"He acts for the good of all people. He wants a new age of enlightenment in his realm. Like you, he has a fiery enthusiasm for the mysteries of the world. Alfonso has appointed me his court astronomer. Once we have peace, he wants to bring the best astronomers together in his court!"

Al-Kumi's out-thrust jaw and flashing eyes expressed unbridled malice.

"You are either a dreamer or the most devious schemer!" he declared. "Everyone knows Christians know nothing of astronomy. The only astronomers are the Arab starmen in my realm. Do you think you could just march through my empire and gather together these men of science for your own purposes?" His laugh was caustic.

"Not for my own purposes," Ibn Amram vowed. "For the good of humanity. What does it matter if an astronomer is a Muslim, a Christian or a Jew? The truth of the stars is eternal!"

"With you as the greatest astronomer of all," the caliph hissed. "You would make the study of the stars your own realm. You are envious of the pope's miter, rabbi! You want one of your own!"

"I have not been bought, if that is what you mean," Ibn Amram retorted. The color rose dramatically to his cheeks, and he swayed in anger before the caliph.

"As you please, envoy. I have heard enough of your prating of peace. Now you will know the full fury of the desert. At least, you are not a simpering fool like the Portuguese envoy. But my disgust is the same. Carry this Berber message to your Christian master. *Ladaua id-nar daim teka!*"

"What do your words mean?" Ibn Amram asked weakly.

The caliph spat out each syllable. "The enmity between us will never be extinguished! Carry that message, envoy. You leave tomorrow!"

Ibn Amram staggered from the tent, groping in a miasma of dazzling sunlight to find his way. Joseph rushed forward to aid him as he stumbled towards the hills, but he pushed his student away.

All afternoon he paced through the sand dunes, muttering to himself and compulsively taking sightings on the sun. By nightfall, a fever laid him low. Bachir summoned his guards, and they carried the envoy back to this blankets.

"The celestial darkness," he mumbled, as though obsessed with his sightings. "I cannot avert the evil. I see the shadow of the darkened sun spreading over the land. Darkness is coming, and there is nothing I can do to avert the evil."

"He has wandered too long in the sun without sufficient food and drink," Bachir commiserated with Joseph. "Tend him carefully tonight. We will take him back to Tunis when he is well."

CHAPTER FIFTEEN

Treachery Revealed

VALENCIA, ARAGON
SPRING, 1140

IBN AMRAM STRETCHED PAINFULLY ON THE OAK BENCH IN THE *beit medrash* of Valencia. The seat was uncomfortable, but the diversity of manuscripts in the main synagogue of the capital of Aragon provided a welcome challenge to the scholar's mind. Much of his intellectual daring had been dampened by the failure of his mission to the caliph.

"You think I am chastened, Joseph?" he said. "Perhaps you are right. Chased from the desert by that impetuous madman and chastened by my many failures."

"I'm glad you chose the port of Valencia," Joseph commented. "Yes, it will be a longer trip overland to Burgos, but we run fewer risks of bumping into the Cluniac monks again. It will take two more weeks, but we will carry the news to King Alfonso safely."

"Pah! What news?" Ibn Amram exclaimed, settling again

over his notebooks of grammatical rules.

The door grated on its hinges, and the black-frocked Rabbi Nathan of Valencia entered, timorous to be in the presence of the great biblical exegete and grammarian. Joseph drew back from the table, nodded in deference and exited through the door to the *beit knesset*.

"Sit, sit," Ibn Amram said jovially.

"It is a great honor to personally receive your precious insights into Hebrew grammar," Rabbi Nathan said. "I bless the day I casually mentioned news of the Italian trader Mar Elijah. Little did I know he was a friend of yours and that you would wait for his return to Valencia."

"Yes, I will wait," Ibn Amram agreed in a dull monotone, as one trapped in a series of events beyond his control. "It will be easier on my poor back to travel with him in his carriage than to chance my aching bones to horseback. And then, there is news from Jerusalem I hope to hear."

"*Be'ezrat Hashem*, may your news always be good."

Rabbi Nathan squeezed carefully into the position beside the mass of manuscripts. The discussion began.

The days in the port city settled into a pattern of study and prayer for Ibn Amram, an excellent remedy for one convalescing from the rigors of desert travel. The lingering fever had almost left him. Yet Joseph stubbornly kept a sharp eye on his teacher, especially when the Mediterranean sent a bone-chilling draft through the narrow streets.

They had been walking home from the synagogue one late afternoon when their conversation again turned to Mar Elijah. Ibn Amram repeated the details of the trader's persuasive abilities and the chances of his success in the company of Joshua ben Judah, the old Karaite adversary transplanted from Castile. Joseph noticed a distinct chattering of the sage's teeth and knew they must quickly find shelter from the windy street. Ibn Amram made a gruff pretense of ignoring his frailty, but Joseph cast his eyes for a sign of a Jewish household at this margin of the Jewish quarter.

Just a few steps from the *beit knesset*, the Jews mingled freely with the Muslims. The first door bore the ambiguous sign of the hand of Fatima. But the second door had a *mezuzah* on the door jamb. Joseph pulled Ibn Amram by the arm, and they ascended the steep stairs. He pounded loudly on the door with his fist, hoping the resident had not already left for *Minchah*.

"That's all right, young son," Ibn Amram declared as they stood in front of the door. "No one is home. I'll just pin my cloak more tightly around my neck, and we shall continue."

He turned slowly and reached for the balustrade to descend the stairs. The door opened a crack, and a wizened old man peered into the waning light.

Ibn Amram's illness gave Joseph Vitale the boldness to take charge of the situation.

"Good man!" Joseph commanded, stepping forward with his master's hand tucked firmly into the crook of his elbow. "My master, Rabban Ibn Amram, suffers a chill. I have here the rootstock to make him a soothing tea. May I partake of your fire and some water?"

His right hand withdrew the canvas pouch of dried herbs as further evidence of their good intentions.

"Enter," the old man answered in a quavering voice. "No teacher should be outdoors in this wind."

His slippers shuffled on the worn tiles as he led his two visitors into the *sala grande*. His gnarled hand, twisted into a parody of human fingers by many years of damp weather in the mountains gestured to the cushions.

"Rachel," he called. "Boil the pot of water again. We will make tea for this teacher and his student."

Joseph watched them inquisitively as the two old people negotiated the archway with painful slowness. They leaned on the surface of the credenza, then shuffled out of sight into the kitchen beyond the doorway. Joseph turned his attention again to his teacher, massaging his hands to restore the circulation.

Ibn Amram's eye shifted from the dark doorway to the *tallith* hung on the wall. Its edges were yellowed by the occasional shaft of sunlight, and dust exaggerated the folds traced at the bottom edges. His gaze was intense.

"*Ure'isem oso*. And you may look upon it and remember all the commandments of Hashem, " Ibn Amram quoted.

Joseph alternated his gaze from the doorway of the kitchen to the *tallith* which held some mystery for his teacher. He searched his master's face in vain. His shivers had stopped almost completely.

"If the Torah says we should look upon the prayer shawl, here is the literal fulfillment of that command," Ibn Amram explained. "Not worn, but mounted on the wall."

Joseph had never seen anything quite so strange. It seemed a veiled affront to the *mitzvah* of *tzitzit*. He started to open his mouth to speak, but Ibn Amram raised a finger to his lips. The old woman returned with a small brass pot. She manipulated the wire handle with both hands.

"Put the rootstock there, young man," she said. "It will steep on the hearthstone."

Her husband, taking the cue, pushed the brick closer to the remaining embers and carefully extricated the handle from her interlocked fingers.

"You carry your years with grace," Ibn Amram said, drawing his cloak around his shoulders to avoid a sudden shudder. "May you live to a hundred and twenty."

"Life has been good to us, young man," the woman replied, returning to her cushions on the far side of the room. "We have many fine children and many blessed grandchildren. But they do not visit us as they did in the past."

"Oh?" Ibn Amram asked quietly. "The children are busy with the problems of their own generation?"

The old man shook his head. "No, moved away. All of them. Not a single relative left here in Valencia. But the Jewish community cares for us. The neighborhood women ensure that we have a hot meal every *Shabbat*."

"They are a blessing on our old age!" the woman interjected.

"The Torah commands us to treat those less fortunate than ourselves with justice," Ibn Amram commented, still eyeing the *tallith*. "A comfortable home, a warm meal and no one to bother you. These are truly blessings of old age. Tell me, no one bothers you, do they?"

"Not at all, young man," the old man assured him. "Here is peace and quiet. We do not live a lie. We simply keep our privacy to ourselves. Don't we, Rachel?"

A peaceful pause ensued while Ibn Amram's gaze again lingered on the *tallith*. The sight bothered Joseph.

"But why do you have a garment on the wall?" Joseph ventured to ask, breaking the silence. "Aren't you afraid your neighbors will misinterpret your motives?"

"What is there to misinterpret? Your master has grasped the truth of the *tallith*. We have fulfilled the *mitzvah*." The old man raised himself to an upright posture on his cushion, staring down any suggestion of impropriety.

"It is as I indicated while our hosts prepared the water," Ibn Amram suggested congenially. "This is the literal observance of the commandment."

The old man shrugged, as if to ask what other possible fulfillment of a *mitzvah* could be imagined by the faithful.

"Ah, you are a Karaite," Joseph breathed.

"I have never denied it," the old man answered with simple dignity. "But no one has ever come to my door and asked me to state it. I must repeat, we do not live a lie."

"But the Karaites were expelled from the realm!" Joseph persisted. "How did you evade the ban?"

"Age provides its own perspective," the old Karaite noted, drawing his feet under his *burnous* and fastidiously sipping his tea. "The trip to the sea was a painful misery for young and old alike. Would my dear Rachel have survived? What has she done for which she must die?"

"Our host has a point, Joseph. I doubt that either he or his wife has committed any sin punishable by death."

"I did not mean to stand in judgment of you," Joseph said contritely. He raised his cup to occupy himself during the pause.

"It is as it should be," Ibn Amram stated. "Do not stir up troubled waters. Let the madness of the world pass you by."

"*Amein*, young man," the old man said, touched by an inner chord of meaning which Ibn Amram's words amplified. "*Amein.*"

Their words ceased peacefully in the silent room. The woman poured more tea for everyone and then sipped it quietly, savoring the interlude. The fire had died out, leaving nothing but a wisp of smoke. Ibn Amram rose to his feet.

"We have reached an understanding," he said. "I bid you good day."

For Joseph, it was a curious interchange at the door. Something beyond words had passed between his teacher and the old couple. The old man clenched Ibn Amram's hands in his arthritic grasp and only reluctantly released his hand as Ibn Amram stepped back.

A gust of wind whipped Ibn Amram's *burnous* into a sudden frenzy, and he waved a hasty good bye. His right hand rested lightly on Joseph's shoulder, more as a reassurance to his student that he would not trip in the half-light than as a real need on that breezy evening.

"There are various strategies of survival," Ibn Amram noted, hastening his pace as he noticed activity in the courtyard ahead. "Some victims of oppression can hope for better times at the end of a long road. But this old couple would surely have died on the trip. For the moment, no one is harmed by the dissimulation."

"But they are still Karaites," Joseph persisted.

"He is a man, just like you and I," Ibn Amram answered. "He is warmed by the same summer sun and cooled by the same winter winds. If his brow is feverish, he can be healed by the very same remedies as you and I."

Men from the docks were hauling heavy cases from the street to the *patio* beyond the iron gate. Ibn Amram clapped his hands in delight and strode forward, leaving Joseph in a flurry of footsteps to catch up.

"Who has come to visit Rabbi Nathan at this late vigil?" he inquired.

The stevedore gave the case an extra push with his foot, then sat down on the edge to catch his breath. "Mar Elijah has returned," he answered. "With the bounties of the East!"

A candle appeared, wavering in the night air. Behind it was a familiar figure.

"Ah, Rabban Avraham," the trader said effusively. "Rabbi Nathan has told me you were waiting. I must treat you to a taste of the East, *tamar hindi*, the date of India."

He eyed the numerous cases and motioned to a smaller one, wedged between the wall and the others. His servants struggled to open the clasps. Tucked between the glass of Syria and some manuscripts was a bag, carefully rolled and tied with ribbon. Mar Elijah evidently enjoyed the ceremony. His thin dexterous fingers withdrew the succulent tamarind pods, and he used them as a pointer, motioning Ibn Amram up the stairs.

They entered the study, where Rabbi Nathan was already poring over a text Mar Elijah had brought from Jerusalem. He snapped the work closed and stood up when Ibn Amram entered.

"Mar Elijah has given us all the first fruit of the new season," he said respectfully. "It is a time for blessing and renewal."

Ibn Amram nodded, intoning the blessing on the first fruit with rhythmic stress. The thought of renewal hung heavily on Ibn Amram's mind. He sighed and tasted the tamarind, chewing absent-mindedly.

"I see you have deep thoughts," Mar Elijah said, settling back at the table to watch the sage.

Ibn Amram shook his head to shake away his pensive

mood. "I was recalling my life in Tudela. My father-in-law lived right next door. It took seventeen paces to reach his front door, another six paces to reach the table where we studied together." He sighed again.

Mar Elijah coughed, attempting to open a difficult topic. "I checked along my itinerary," he said at last. "At Damietta, at Ashkelon and at Jerusalem. To date, there is no word of Yerucham Halevi in the Holy Land. I did not have the opportunity to speak with traders from Baghdad. I am humbled at my oversight."

"Oh, no, it is not your responsibility to worry over this," Ibn Amram hastened to say. "My father-in-law always follows his own timetable. I will check again in the summer. One cannot hasten news from distant corners of the world."

Another pause ensued. Mar Elijah shifted uncomfortably in his chair. "I had hoped to bring you some kernel of good news. At the very least, I thought news from the *Av Beit Din* in Ashkelon would be encouraging. Unfortunately, he has found the new Karaite leader to be both learned and recalcitrant. Their meetings ended in failure. A stiff formality now cloaks any further contact in a veneer of etiquette. Their words are courteous. Their intentions are not."

"It is just as well that you reveal bluntly what happened," Ibn Amram said, glancing across at Rabbi Nathan with a forced smile.

The rabbi, noticing the effect of the news on the sage, had begun to leave. Ibn Amram motioned him back to the table.

"There is yet a moment before *Maariv*," he said. "We can polish a few principles of *dikduk*. Please stay, Rabbi Nathan."

For the moment, Mar Elijah had lost the impish delight that traced the corners of his ready smile.

"I did not want to see failure heaped on failure, Rabban Avraham. You deserve better from your *sheliach*. I wanted to be a messenger only of good tidings, and now I have set your teeth on edge with the bad news of Joshua ben Judah."

"I had hoped for some success in channeling the energies

of the Karaites along more constructive paths," Ibn Amram admitted. "Are all my efforts met with failure?"

Mar Elijah's face brightened. "Not at all. If we must count our efforts with their leader a failure, we can take comfort in our influence on individuals within his community. You spoke of the Rikuv family, and I deliberately asked the *Av Beit Din* to seek them out for me. It was a tumultuous meeting, I can tell you. The old man scowled at me throughout, but the young one dared contradict him. Yes, his son did not sit silent."

Ibn Amram's face caught some of the enthusiasm the trader radiated.

"You mean there is hope yet for Yissaschar?" He clenched his fists in strong emotion. "Tell me all you know."

"I know the young man is burdened with shame at how he treated you. When he discovered I would meet with you in Spain, he asked me to carry a message: 'Don't think the worst of me. I spend my days with my own people, but at night I venture from my father's roof to visit the Jewish community. It is too early to reveal what I have learned, but I can say with certainty that I have learned.' Those were his words, Rabban Avraham."

Ibn Amram grinned broadly at the news. "My intuition tells me the boy has joined a *shiur*, perhaps in *Gemara*. A rabbi of Ahkelon will be his guide. In a world of waywardness, it is comforting to know that a confused boy can find his way. The Rikuv youth reminds me so much of my own son! I would it were so . . ." His words trailed into silence as he thought of the temptations of Baghdad.

"It will all be for the best," Mar Elijah said, settling back into his chair.

Ibn Amram glanced down at the tamarind pod and dug out more of the soft flesh.

"The cycles of life are dictated by Hashem. We cannot speed them although we can hope to foretell the movement, like the cycles of the moon. When I was younger, adversity was a constant companion. I laughed in its teeth. I weathered the worst storm! Now, I am not so sure of myself. I have had serious setbacks in close succession. Now I lean more frequently on my student's arm, and Joseph grows stronger from my weight!"

The young man drew back further from the candlelight, embarrassed by the reference. With his arms encircling his knees, he busied himself with the tamarind and watched and waited.

"Do you know, Mar Elijah, I have missed the sighting of the dawn for two successive mornings?" Ibn Amram continued. "It is not like me. I used to rouse myself before the first light of dawn and feel at one with the universe. I reached out to it with my astrolabe and charted each star as though it were an old friend. Where is my enthusiasm? The signs are leading us to darkness, and that depresses me."

"Don't be morose," Mar Elijah said. "The stars are neither optimists nor pessimists. They move at the behest of Hashem. Carry that message to your king and you will have done all a man can do."

The next morning, Mar Elijah made ready his carriage for the trip to Burgos. He had a staggering array of Syrian glass to show the Castilian merchants. And Ibn Amram had the bitter news of his failure to persuade the caliph. The roads of Castile were awash with the spring floods and patches of crocus opened saffron flowers through the lingering snow. But harbingers of the sun brought no joy to the eyes of Ibn Amram. Despite the warm spring sun on his back, he thought about the dreary day of darkness.

On their arrival, they noticed that a festive mood seemed to have enveloped the streets of Burgos. Children had flung off their winter cloaks and clapped in delight as a minstrel entertained the crowd in the plaza. A bear, bedecked in brightly colored ribbons and manacled in iron shackles, attempted to dance to the music.

The royal palace rose from the promontory overlooking

the city square. Nothing had changed. The walls still thrust impassive thickness to the sky. The darkened slits of windows at the second story still blindly overlooked any activity below.

"But the lilacs are about to bloom," Ibn Amram noted with an edge of dejection to his voice. "Look at the size of the buds, Joseph. Flowers are breeding from the dead land. In this way does Hashem promise hope even when despair lingers."

As they approached the castle, he averted his gaze from the carousel where the children of the courtiers played. The sound of the brass rings dangling just beyond their fingertips reached their ears. So did the laughter of the children.

Alkabri had relayed the news of the envoy's arrival to King Alfonso. The sage winced as a royal trumpeter announced his presence with a flourish. The attendants swung open the massive doors. At that moment, the self-doubts which nagged at Ibn Amram's confidence vanished. He felt strangely calm.

He regretted that the treaty of peace so carefully crafted by Don Garcia and Alkabri remained unsigned. But his emotions were plucked from despair by the bright face of the young king. Here was the next generation to rule Spain, groomed from childhood by the enlightened Don Garcia and now clearly able to make wise decisions independently. The longings of a teacher welled up in Ibn Amram's heart. He had come as a political envoy, but in truth he had a more precious insight to share as a teacher with his student.

Don Garcia cleared his throat to catch the attention of the king. Don Umar glanced up from the table and smiled broadly at Ibn Amram. But he too remained wordless, waiting for Alfonso to break the silence.

Alfonso turned away from the window where he had been watching the children on the carousel.

"Greetings on your return, Ibn Amram," he said. "I trust you have savored the delicacies of the caliph's oasis?" His eyes searched the dark circles around Ibn Amram's eyes and the sunken cheeks, scarcely hidden by the sage's full beard.

"I have eaten pomegranates in season and the dates of a

bounteous harvest, Your Grace," Ibn Amram replied.

"The sweetness of the land does not agree with everyone," Alfonso said cryptically. His right hand motioned to the chair across from Don Umar. "It is the same for the palate as for the blank of our eye. Too much sweetness numbs the tongue until sweet and sour are one. And light exhausts the eye until the blank sees nothing in the spaces between the brilliance. When I stand at the window with my astrolabe, the spring sunlight frustrates me. I squint to find the truth, but I am dazzled. Ah, we will speak further about the sun. What happened in the desert, Rabban Ibn Amram? Do you bring me news of victory?"

The envoy glanced down at his hands before he began to speak.

"The mission was almost thwarted before I even reached Tunis," he answered dully. "A corsair followed us, intent as we thought, upon pillage. But the pirate ship turned tail at the last moment. Eventually, we learned the appalling truth. The Legate Paul was on that ship, spying on my movements. Later, he dared attack the palace of Tashpin, but he was caught. Tashpin consigned him to a slave ship, but we heard later that he had escaped."

Don Garcia smiled grimly, but said nothing.

"Of that, too, we will speak further, Ibn Amram," the king responded impatiently. "You eluded the legate. What happened in the desert?"

"I cannot hide the truth," Ibn Amram said in a voice so low the king was forced to step closer to hear him distinctly. "There was no victory. The caliph was congenial for days on end. I thought we had reached an understanding, for he sought to teach me the ways of the desert. But when our discussions reached the peace plan his fury overleaped all bounds.

"I was astonished by the strange news he blurted in his anger. The peace plan had been copied. Aphonso Henriques had sent an envoy to the caliph before I ever arrived at the oasis. The plan put forward by the Portuguese was a duplicate down to the last jot of the map. The caliph was convinced that the kings of Iberia are playing games to mock him."

Alfonso's cheeks turned a deathly gray. "There has been a rumor of this treachery," he said.

"The Portuguese, that miserable schemer!" Don Garcia erupted.

"Give me leave to organize a siege, Your Grace," Don Umar declared, standing up to unsheathe his sword. "I will starve the ingrate out of his fortifications. Portugal will again be the vassal of Castile."

"We will not be hasty in our response, Don Umar," King Alfonso ordered with surprising restraint. "That matter can wait. But tell me, Ibn Amram, is everything lost? Will the Caliph Al-Kumi bring darkness over my reign? Will his savagery disrupt my rule?"

"My mood was indeed black when the caliph dismissed me, and there was no way to snatch the thread of our negotiations. I was left in a twilight of doubts. Then, much later, I realized he had given me something which he could never take back. He had revealed the inner workings of his mind and his people's sense of destiny. This is what he calls the way of the desert, and this crucial knowledge I can share with you."

The king blinked. "I have no wish to visit the great sand sea. What good is this way of the desert to me?"

"A wise king is forever learning," Ibn Amram answered. "You have learned much in the company of Don Garcia. He has taught you to weigh the strengths and weaknesses of others, from the monks of Cluny to your proud vassals of Andalusia. Just as you have mastered the subtleties of action and discourse to live in peace with Zafadola, so a new set of rules must be mastered to make peace with–or vanquish–this Almohad emperor. Make no mistake, he is as unlike the worldly Moors of Andalusia as night is from day."

"Do I wish to deal with the night?"

"Does not night follow day? It is a certainty that one day you will have no choice, and you must be prepared."

King Alfonso's voice rose. "Must I be schooled in how to speak to a barbarian?" He drummed his fingers on the table. "He has already rejected my proposal of peace. It seems Don Umar's knights are the only answer."

"Do not misunderstand Caliph Al-Kumi's simplicity, Your Grace. His life is primitive in its comforts, but it has made him strong. He learns wisdom from every speck of sand. He believes the weak will always be vanquished by the strong, just as the wind and rain blot out all trace of man. And retribution is more than justice to the desert people; it is duty and honor as well. You must always remember this."

"Then he must live by the sword, and there is no hope for peace," Alfonso sighed.

"That may not be true. He is not like other warriors who think their swords control the world. He comprehends a certain inner harmony and timelessness. As he has seen the sands shift countless times, he knows that when the time is right, peace will reign."

"You have learned much in your stay with the chieftain, Ibn Amram. Shall I persist in my attempts at befriending him then?"

"In the future, perhaps. But beware. The way of the desert mandates a lavish reception for all visitors, but do not mistake such cordiality for friendship. While you are in his tent, you sip palm juice and are treated with great honor. But once you step outside you are no longer his guest, and he is free to attack you with bloodthirsty ferocity. This is to be expected."

"I do not understand."

"In short, the desert has its own morality, its own honor and code. You cannot deal with this Berber as you would with a Spaniard."

"Nor can I deal with him as I would a Cluniac, a Jew, a Karaite or even the other Muslims in my realm," mused the king.

"Each new insight brings another, my king. In time, I will be able to reveal everything to you. There will yet come a day when this Almohad will no longer be a mystery."

The king leaned forward, unclasping his fingers. "Will there be time for more talks, Ibn Amram? I mean before the great darkness descends. My calculations seem to show it will be very soon, but I cannot tell for how long it will last. Have you succeeded in your study of the sun? Can you tell me if the sun will be blotted out long enough for me to lose control of my kingdom?"

Ibn Amram noticed an almost child-like blinking of Alfonso's eye and an uncontrollable twitch of his fingers. Don Garcia shifted nervously and leaned forward to listen.

"It is as we anticipated," Ibn Amram replied. "All that remains to be seen is when the darkness will reach Castile. But have no fear, Your Grace, my calculations show that it will not last more than a few moments. The shadow of the sun will pass over Spain, and then the light will return."

Alfonso was visibly relieved.

"We must tell the people, Don Garcia. Word must reach the people, so they will not be alarmed when the darkness begins."

"We cannot do that until we know when it will happen, Your Grace," Don Garcia answered. "To try to explain it to them now will only raise apprehensions, I fear."

"That is true," King Alfonso admitted. "Rabban Ibn Amram, it is imperative that you inform me at once, as soon as you know when the darkness will begin. At that time, we will assemble my people and calm their terrors. At last, they will understand that the astrolabe is not an instrument of the devil but an instrument of truth."

The chamber door squeaked on its hinges, and King Alfonso's confessor entered.

"His Excellency, Bernard of Toledo chafes in the antechamber. He tells me that with his own eyes he has seen the Jew enter to confer with you. He demands an audience."

Alfonso clenched his teeth.

"Let him enter, but be quick about it!"

The fat man swayed into the room, redolent of moral umbrage. In tow, the Legate Paul squirmed under Bernard's heavy hand.

"I am shocked and saddened that you would keep me waiting," the archbishop intoned. "Did we not agree upon the order of business for your council? Do you not remember that ecclesiastical matters must always come first?"

"What is on your mind, Bernard?" Alfonso said abruptly. He did not motion the clergyman to any empty chair.

"That Jew is the Deceiver!" the archbishop declared, drawing himself up to his fullest height and pointing a dimpled finger in the direction of Ibn Amram. "He has humbled the papal legate in Tunis, knowing full well that Paul travels under the privileges of the Holy See. He has mocked his authority, robbed him of his signet ring and incited his pitiful mistreatment at the hands of an infidel. Alfonso, hear my words. I demand the sternest punishment for this odious Jew!"

King Alfonso rose abruptly and stepped around the edge of the table. The legate drew back behind the bulk of the archbishop.

"You were in Tunis? I do not remember giving you authority to cross my toll bridge on your way to the south," King Alfonso warned. "And where is this ring? Just how did the envoy pry a ring off your finger?"

His left hand darted out and bent back Paul's wrist, quickly extending all four fingers in the process.

"Oh, please! You will break the bones," Paul squealed. "The ring was on my index finger. You can even see the pale circle. That proves its forfeiture to the hated Jew. He used it to bribe Tashpin."

"It proves nothing," Alfonso hissed, releasing the thin wrist. "Do you take me for an idiot? Do you think a signet of the pope would influence Tashpin?"

"He took it! The Jew took my ring!" Paul trembled in self-righteous rage. "There is nothing he would not dare do."

Paul broke free of the archbishop's protective grasp and ran to the window.

"Beware of the Jew and his accursed astronomy!" he shouted. "He will dare the heavens to stand still. He will banish the sun if you pay him enough. He has evil miracles waiting to be unleashed by his incantations."

"There is a difference between miracles and nature," Ibn Amram said. "There is no incantation that can stop the movement of the sun and the moon."

"His words are like the peace pact brought back from the desert," Paul answered. "An empty promise!"

King Alfonso stared suspiciously at the legate. "How do you know so much about miracles and peace pacts? You have over-reached yourself."

The legate stood, open-mouthed by the window, opening and closing his lips like a carp in still water.

"Don Umar, bring him to the herb garden," said the king. "Rabban Ibn Amram as well. We will lay this question to rest."

With a single gesture, the king indicated that his council should remain in the throne room. Bernard made a move to follow Paul, but Don Umar blocked his movement.

"You are a man filled with deceit," Paul taunted, as they followed the darkened passageway that led down to the gardens behind the palace. "A Jew will never rise above his lies until he renounces his obedience to the perversions of Torah. I will have you banished from this land, if it is the last thing I do."

They pushed past the vines that darkened the archway and entered an overgrown orchard that bordered the garden. A broken walkway led through the trees. King Alfonso pointed to the left.

The garden sloped past a dishevelled planting of savory, sage and hyssop in the old herb garden planted for Queen Urraca.

"It once was very beautiful," Alfonso said pensively. "I

remember it as a child." The fountain had long since ceased its display of bubbling water, and now weeds crept along the edges that once had been flower beds. "The queen had excellent gardeners from Andalusia. This garden shows their art, or what is left of it."

"There is also a great deal of science to be discovered in this garden," Ibn Amram added.

"The Jew would reduce everything to logic and science," the legate responded hotly. "He would make everything and everyone in this world a subject of his scientific scrutiny. Ha! Little good it did him in the desert with his doomed peace plan! Could he offer logic to the caliph? Could he explain why he brought forth the same map as the Portuguese?"

In that instant, Paul's eyes bulged from their sockets. He was aware all too late that his words spelled death. Don Umar lunged for him, seizing him roughly by the shoulder.

"How did you know of a map? Speak, you dog!"

Alfonso's fury transcended the boundary of hot words and had imploded to a quiet intensity.

The legate quaked. "It is a known rumor! N-Nothing more than a rumor in the streets of Burgos, Your Majesty!" he stuttered. "I meant no harm. I know nothing about maps or plans. The Jew made me say it."

"I cannot put into words my disgust for a traitor," Don Umar sneered. "Aphonso Henriques can sit in his court and gloat, but at last we know the truth. If I am pleased about anything, I am pleased that you are a child of your passion, legate."

"Yes, it has made my judgment easier to reach," Alfonso added thoughtfully, giving a meaningful nod to Don Umar, whose fingers tightened their grip on the legate's shoulder. The knuckles were white, but the hand was as steady as a rock.

The legate stared at the cold eyes of his monarch and then whirled to face Ibn Amram. Ashen-faced, Ibn Amram watched the wild gesticulations of the legate, bereft of his senses in his desperation to save his own skin.

"Dona Urraca, my own mother, used to sit and make her lace in that summer house," Alfonso said, pointing to a ramshackle structure at the edge of the herb garden. "It was a place of beauty and peace until the townsfolk came with bloody rebellion in their eyes. Now I see it only as a place of death!"

He stepped forward to the path that led to the summer house. Don Umar followed, dragging the pathetic Paul.

Ibn Amram turned away from that final vision of the whimpering legate clinging to the edges of the door jamb. Ibn Amram left the garden, but not before a stifled scream arose from the summer house of Dona Urraca.

CHAPTER SIXTEEN

Darkness over Castile

TUDELLA, NAVARRE
SPRING, 1140

"I MUST UNDO MY BELT A NOTCH!" JOSEPH SAID WITH A LAUGH. He leaned back in the chair, smiling as Naomi Ibn Amram again pushed the bowl of *madroteh* towards him.

"You must eat," Naomi insisted pleasantly. "I would not want my husband to take you back to your parents looking like skin and bones."

Joseph threw up his hands in mock horror at the onslaught of more food, but he did not resist a third helping.

"And you, my husband," Naomi continued, turning gently in her chair to face Ibn Amram. "Why do you not set a good example for your student?"

Ibn Amram poked listlessly at his meal. "Oh, I am sorry, but these sightings have lately distracted me. All signs point to a celestial darkness that will envelop Castile in the very near future."

"What will happen?" Naomi asked.

"Oh, the people will not even notice the change, at first. They will not even recognize the dark shadow of the moon that will transform the brilliance of the sun to a crescent. They might first notice a chill wind which makes them shiver and draw their cloaks more tightly around their shoulders, but they will think it the cold breath of the changing season. They will not even look up!"

"Then how will we know the darkness has arrived?"

"We will know when the last edge of the sun's scimitar is sheathed in the darkness of the moon, when all that remains of the sun is a mere shadow. Then the darkness will come swiftly. The animals will sense it first. Then men will rush into the darkness, like their beasts."

"It sounds frightening," Naomi said.

"My father and I learned a *Gemara* about eclipses," Joseph added shyly. "It says the blocking of the sun is a bad sign for the entire world."

"Yes, it is a *Gemara* in *Sukkah*," Ibn Amram concurred. "The occurrence is compared to a human king who prepares a feast for his servants and places a lantern before them to light up the feast. But he becomes angry with them and decides to remove *the lantern and let them sit in darkness.*"

"Leaving them in darkness as when the Karaites snuffed out our lanterns," Naomi sighed.

"It is true that we must be mindful of the warning the eclipse portends," Ibn Amram continued. "But it is only a warning, not a punishment in itself. And yet, for those who study the stars, it will be a wondrous event. Stars which are always hidden in the daylight hours will appear prominently in the darkened sky. Many astronomers have suggested to me that the brief moment will reveal signs otherwise hidden from the eyes of man. I do not know. But I hope to be ready. I have been saving a piece of smoked Egyptian glass which will shield my eye from the blinding rays. Through it, I hope to look to the sky directly and see with my own eyes the beams of light which I am told shoot forth from the face of the hidden sun. In the midst of the greatest darkness, there is a hidden light. So it was when Hashem came to Moshe Rabbeinu in the thickness of a cloud. And then the radiance! Behold, the skin of his face shot forth beams."

Neither Joseph nor Naomi grasped just where these beams would appear, but they never doubted the mystery the sage would soon be privileged to see. Joseph shivered.

Ibn Amram looked towards the window where a cricket hummed on the sill.

"The night air was not silent a year ago," he commented. "How well I recall the angry words that filled the air."

"Now the Karaites are gone," Naomi responded. "The big house at the corner of the street still stands empty, a rebuke of the high-handed treatment which the Jewish community meted out to the strangers. It saddens me every day to see its sightless windows, like eyes without vision."

"Sometimes I wonder if I could have done more in my meeting with Joshua ben Judah," Ibn Amram mused. "There was the beginning of a rapport. I told you about the old Karaite couple in Valencia, didn't I? There should have been better ways to deal with the Karaites, even if they are renegades."

"Don't vex your soul with the past, Avraham." Naomi's eyes glistened with tears held back. "Abba will pick up the thread where it lays tangled when he reaches Jerusalem."

Ibn Amram's hand fluttered to his chest. "I feel a pinch in my heart whenever you mention Yerucham Halevi. Yes, he could change the course of history, if anyone could."

"Don't overlook that the Karaites were their own worst enemy," Joseph said. "They seemed to delight in making enemies."

"Enough said. What is past is past," the sage replied. "Now I am immersed in my sightings which will culminate in a decisive sighting very soon. And then, who knows? After the darkness, there may be little left for me to do in Castile. It just might be the right time for the two of us to take the long awaited journey back to Champagne. What do you say, Joseph? Are you ready to see your parents again?"

His student nodded. "My father will have many things for me to do. His last letter mentions a growing fear of another Crusade. The knights of Champagne are more headstrong with each passing day. But so far, praised be Hashem, they have not menaced us."

"What does Rabbeinu Vitale think will happen?" Ibn Amram asked. "Will Count Henri permit fanatics to take up the cross and harass our people?"

Joseph shrugged. "It's a long ride to Troyes, and my father would never attempt it. But he has his envoys, and they regularly hold audiences with the Count. It helps that our most frequent envoy is the merchant who provides Henri with fine English wool. Henri is not like the King of France. He knows the value of his Jewish merchants. He would never let the Crusaders steal our wealth."

"With the help of the Almighty, I hope your words ring true!" Ibn Amram said with sudden vehemence. "I look forward to seeing my old friend again. Meanwhile, I must see to my current task. We will get to bed early tonight. Tomorrow will be a fateful day, if I am not mistaken."

He dipped his fingers in *mayim achronim* and began *Birkat Hamazon*. The supplication for restoration and sustenance rang a note of hope in an otherwise somber meal.

True to his word, Ibn Amram was up and about very early the next morning. *Shacharith* was concluded in the first gray light of dawn. The horses were saddled before the glow of dawn appeared on the horizon. In the plain, he assumed his accustomed position using his established sight posts.

Ibn Amram stood as still as a statue during the sighting. Now he swung his arm down decisively to his side.

"It is enough!" he declared. "There is no time to waste. We must ride directly to Burgos and inform the king!"

"The time has come, hasn't it?" Joseph said.

Ibn Amram nodded, as they mounted their horses and

urged them to a swift canter. He glanced over his shoulder at the rising sun. There was an anxious haste to his movements. Joseph felt a fearful prickling on the nape of his neck.

They rode in silence. The landmarks came and passed in quick succession as the two travellers pursued their goal of reaching the capital in the early afternoon. Ibn Amram leaned across and offered Joseph a chunk of cheese and the waterskin. There was no time to lose in stopping for a meal.

A sentry post loomed into view, emblazoned with the royal banner. Its crimson eagle heartened Ibn Amram. Joseph slowed his mount to let the sentry observe their lack of weapons. A nod of the head sent them hurrying on their way.

"Hurry!" Ibn Amram called out as he spurred his horse on. "We must reach Burgos before the darkness begins and lies threaten our people."

"Will there be lies to combat?" Joseph asked as he caught up and drew alongside. "Will they dare accuse the Jews of bringing on the darkness?"

"It is too early to tell. By word and by deed, we must be alert. Alkabri has wisely suggested that the king's council go out to calm the people when the darkness comes."

"What will King Alfonso do when he learns that today is the day?"

"Alfonso can be forceful and articulate. He will speak in the plaza, showing the people that darkness is neither magic nor retribution."

The two travellers lapsed into silence, watching the road wind through the fields. The walls of Burgos were clearly visible in the distance. So, too, was a growing crowd of townsfolk, surging onto the south road. Flashes of black in the midst of the crowd told of the presence of black monks. Ibn Amram slowed his pony to a trot.

Townsfolk and peasants on the way to the market place were milling about on the south road, fascinated by the sight of the monkish glory. A huge tent emblazoned with the cross was already pitched at the crossroads. To the side stood a massive carriage. Ibn Amram tried to guide his horse through the crowd, but a hand shot out and stopped him.

"You there! Come hear the words of Peter the Venerable. He has wisdom to share with all Castilians!"

A brawny monk had reached up and grasped the reins, easily controlling both horses with his single pudgy hand. Ibn Amram dismounted.

"I have heard the abbot before, in Burgundy," he said drily. His wrist twisted at the reins to pull them free.

"What now, insolent one?" cried the monk, his face flushed with moral indignation. "Do you dare avert your ears from the words of Christian holiness?"

A knight with a brilliant silk emblem was attracted by the growing argument.

"Does the villain hamper your progress, brother?" he asked, staring suspiciously at Ibn Amram's flowing *burnous*. His eyes caught sight of a faint sign of the rash which the sage had suffered in the last bout of his fever.

"Here! What is this?" His mailed glove reached out suddenly and tore at the neck of the *burnous*, revealing a pink rash just above the edge of the *tallith katan*. "I have heard of this affliction. My own brother saw it with his eyes."

"It is nothing but the tertian fever," Joseph called out.

Ibn Amram waved him to silence. "Have a care, knight," he warned. "I am a Jew of the Realm."

"These Castilians," the knight hissed, drawing his fingers more tightly into the garment bunched up in his fist. "I don't care if you are the lackey of Saint Sebastian. I know your disease, leper! You have wandered through the Holy Land, tainting Christian relics with your disease. Now you wander through Castile to spread your evil on more Christians."

Ibn Amram staggered back, both from the violent shove the knight gave him and from surprise at this fierce outburst. The knight spat in disgust on the palm of the glove that had held the *burnous*, then wiped it on his sleeve. The impressionable monk was wide-eyed in fright.

"Lepers!" he whispered hoarsely to his brethren. "Lepers from the East!"

Ibn Amram glared at him sharply and drew back the neckline of his garment.

"You would not know leprosy if you saw it." His eyes were narrow slits of unspoken intensity. The sage sniffed disdainfully and pulled the neckline of the *burnous* back into place. "Besides, there is no leprosy in the Holy Land," he added.

"Again you lie!" the knight responded, stamping his foot in fury. "All Jews are lepers. From the time of Moses, the greatest leper of all. Why do you think the Jews were expelled from Egypt? Don't let him twist his words, brother. The Jew knows I will cut off his devilish tongue if he darts it at me. Be strong, brother!"

The brawny monk almost danced from foot to foot in mental anguish. He could clearly see that the rash had none of the signs of leprosy. But the anger of the knight was contagious. Now he was chastened to silence as the Abbot of Cluny launched his diatribe in the distance.

"Hush, Sir Knight," the monk whispered. "The great abbot will hear us."

In the background, the voice of Peter the Venerable carried with the practiced skill of the orator.

"Let us build in the secret place of our hearts," he intoned. "There we will find silence and peacefulness. We will have unceasing recourse to the solitude of our inner heart. In the midst of tumult, we shall find inner peace."

Standing on the dais which had been lifted down from his carriage for the address, Peter the Venerable carved his vision with a majestic sweep of his arm. A cough rose from his chest, and he was momentarily doubled over in pain. The crowd murmured sympathetically.

"Do not look so smug, Jew!" the knight warned, shaking his fist at him. "The abbot's cough is nothing but the catarrh."

Ibn Amram pointedly turned his gaze away from the knight, moving as far back as he could until the bulk of the young monk stopped him from moving further. The wheezing interval on the dais continued. The sympathetic murmur changed to weighty embarrassment. Whispers were heard here and there, stifled by the actions of monks who moved through the crowd.

Drained from the exertion of his coughing, the abbot finally raised his head and sipped from a goblet that the prior offered. When he spoke, he was filled with spleen and needed a topic which would give free rein to his frustrations. The subject was stargazing. Peter the Venerable roundly cursed the false science of stargazing and snapped his fingers to orchestrate the necessary aversion.

On cue, a burly monk stepped from the tent with a fearful Moor, presumably an accursed stargazer of Andalusia. With each condemnation of the science which Peter the Venerable uttered, the monk punctuated the intensity of the words with a violent shake of the Moor's shoulders. Soon, the poor man's teeth were chattering in his head.

"For them is divine retribution coming!" Peter the Venerable proclaimed, raising a thin finger and pointing it at the Moor. "He has dabbled in this forbidden mystery. He and others like him."

Ibn Amram shifted his weight uncomfortably from one foot to another and waited. The monks stood shoulder to shoulder behind him.

"False doctrine!" Peter the Venerable cried shrilly. "Everywhere I look, I am beset by false doctrine! I have just completed an arduous trip through Toulouse. I could not find inner peace. No, my heart was troubled. Everywhere I looked, I saw the signs of the Cathars and their impious dogma. I brandished the holy sword with relentless vigor. I will not be satisfied until I have rooted every Cathar from the weed-infested garden of Toulouse. Their tribulations will be unending!"

A fierce gleam lit his eyes until he was again racked with a paroxysm of coughing. The crowd applauded with loud shouts, egged on by the numerous monks in their midst.

Joseph watched a glazed look of total absorption cross the eyes of the young monk. He shouted himself hoarse with the rest of them. He was immersed in the vitriol of his abbot. The twisted reins of the two horses had slipped from his hand. Joseph edged closer to take hold of them.

"With the banishment of the Cathars, Toulouse will again be a bastion of the True Church," Peter the Venerable continued. "Now I have come to Castile to continue the holy work. I see with my own eyes the inroads of Muslims and Jews who practice their arcane science with impunity. They subvert the gospel with their false scribbles. But they do not reckon on Peter the Venerable! I will chasten the sinners! Look! He quakes in his boots when I stare at him. He recognizes the fire of Christian justice! And there are others like him, steeped in their sin. Look at what I confiscated from the Deceiver himself on the road near Tarragona."

He held up a bronze instrument that glistened in the early afternoon sun.

Joseph was shocked by the startling sight, drawing in his breath wildly. For an instant, he could see the face of his master turn a ghastly white. The instrument in Peter the Venerable's hand was the astrolabe of Ibn Amram.

The monk holding the reins was suddenly aware of Joseph's hand twisting the reins free. He whirled on Joseph, striking him suddenly, then shook the lad heavily by the collar.

"Release him, I say!" Ibn Amram shouted, pulling a beefy arm away from Joseph's neck. "I warned you that we are Jews of the Realm!"

The sharp-eyed abbot caught sight of the fracas in the back of the crowd. The sermon was disrupted. He bent over to confer with his prior. One face was distressingly familiar to the churchman.

"Ho, brother!" he shouted so that his voice would reach. "Bring that Jew here!"

"Fly, Joseph," Ibn Amram whispered in Hebrew. "This

delay could ruin everything. Fly to the king and warn him of the darkness coming at the very start of the second vigil of the afternoon. Tell him he can assure his people it will be brief. Remember! The second vigil!"

Joseph nodded, ducking down to elude the eyes of their captor. The reins in the monk's hands controlled Ibn Amram's horse, not Joseph's. The lithe youth catapulted into the saddle of his horse, roughly kicking the other horse in the ribs with his right foot. The animal stepped back in surprise onto the monk's foot. While Ibn Amram's captor danced on one foot, Joseph's horse easily outdistanced the monks on the periphery of the crowd.

"The Deceiver himself!" Peter the Venerable proclaimed in his most caustic voice. He gestured to the crowd with a twirl of his wrist. "Satan met me on the road outside Tarragona. I wrestled with him. It was a conflict of biblical proportions, good Christians. But the Deceiver could not throw me to the ground. Before he scampered into the night darkness, he dropped his worst weapon. Now he returns to interrupt my sermon!"

"I had no wish to be present for your sermon," Ibn Amram answered. "Your monk detained me against my will. I have business in Burgos."

"Burgos! Tarragona! The Deceiver is everywhere! And you master this evil instrument. Do not deny it, Satan!"

He held up the astrolabe for the edification of the crowd. The crowd roared its approval. Ibn Amram stood in weary desperation. Now, at the last moment, his plans to aid King Alfonso were slipping away. He had intended to coach the king on how to explain the solar darkness to his fearful subjects. Now the king was on his own, with nothing but the slimmest of warnings from his student.

Ibn Amram searched his mind for a strategy. His eyes fixed blankly upon the astrolabe, the instrument whose every function was second nature to him and a marvel to others. Now it was extended before his eyes like a badge of shame.

"Well, Jew?" Peter the Venerable taunted, buoyant with his discovery. "Are you tongue-tied? Has the cat bit your lips?"

Again, the abbot gestured meaningfully with the astrolabe to the townsfolk. Their cheers grew wilder, as if they sensed the smell of blood in the air. The astrolabe was almost touching Ibn Amram's nose now. Peter the Venerable dared the astronomer to take it. The sun glistened provocatively from its burnished surface.

The moment was one of the longest of the sage's life.

"Good citizens!" Ibn Amram exhorted, rising to the occasion. He cast a sidelong glance at the sun, perceiving what the townsfolk ignored. A dark shadow had already begun to make its bold passage towards the edge of the sun. The darkness had begun. "The Charter of Burgos has given you freedom. No longer are you indentured as slaves to a capricious master. Do you value your freedom to act in accordance with your own true will? Do you value your freedom to think as free men?"

The prior was beside himself with rage.

"Do not be misled by this rhetoric!" he shouted, trying to elbow Ibn Amram away from the dais. "We are all servants of the Church and of His Holiness the Pope. Remember the title of the pontiff and then fall on your knees in submission to his will. You are the servants of the Almighty."

He bowed his head, watching from the corner of his eye the effect his words had on the crowd. Some did indeed prostrate themselves at this call to submission. Others exchanged looks of surprise at the novelty of Ibn Amram's words. Ibn Amram folded his arms across his chest, waiting for the disorder to subside, while he gazed to the southeast. The planet Venus stood out in brilliant relief against a sky that was rapidly assuming a greenish pallor.

"Value your freedom!" Ibn Amram called out above the hubbub. "It is a blessing of the enlightened reign of King Alfonso that you can achieve that of which your grandfathers only dreamed."

Ibn Amram felt a faint chill in the air. With supreme effort, he resisted the temptation to glance up again at the waning crescent that moments before had been the radiant sun. Throwing back his head as he spoke, he caught sight of brilliant Jupiter. To the west, a rusty glow in the spreading green hinted at the presence of Mars. It was all as he had anticipated. Yet all eyes were upon him, and the people were as yet oblivious to the changes high above their heads.

"This truly is an enlightened age," Ibn Amram continued, hastening his words for fear that the darkness envelop them before he had finished. "Would you want to step back into the darkness of ignorance and slavery after such progress?"

The prior stepped forward again to menace Ibn Amram into silence. The burly monk was already clambering up onto the dais to add his weight to that threat.

"Mark my words, stargazer," the prior shouted hoarsely, "Yours is the evil of the demagogue as well as the evil of all your other false sciences."

He raised his hand towards the astronomer, but just then Peter the Venerable again doubled over with coughing. The convulsions were severe, and both monks stepped away from Ibn Amram to steady their abbot.

"Let him speak!" the crowd demanded, surging forward. "Let the Jew speak!"

"I will ask the question directly!" Ibn Amram stated loudly, stepping to the very edge of the dais. "When the darkness comes, will it bring evil on your heads?"

The surging crowd became an ebb tide of uncertainty. Many swooned at these words. Others fell to their knees and prayed in abject fear.

"Please, let it not bring evil!"

"Release us from this dreadful judgment!"

"Save us!"

"Save us!"

"You evil man," the prior whispered. "Are you trying to sow chaos in the land?"

He reached out, still supporting the frail abbot and tried to grab Ibn Amram away from the crowd.

"There is no evil in the heavens!" Ibn Amram shouted, gaining strength. "What man can anticipate is surely a natural occurrence. I will tell you that before my words are finished, the light from the sun will be blotted from the heavens."

At this statement, the entire crowd, including the abbot, fell to its knees, crossing themselves and moaning in panic.

"But wait," Ibn Amram continued, gesturing for silence. "Know that the darkness will be fleeting. The gentle moon will ride her path as always, giving back the light she momentarily coveted. The tables of science prove that fact. Now your own eyes can affirm what science has foretold!"

For a moment, the sage looked with compassion on the uplifted eyes of the townsfolk below him. Against all hope, they sought to believe his words, craning their necks to see him more clearly in the midday dusk. Their eyes rolled up to stare in blinking confusion at the preternatural gloom.

As the darkness deepened and a chill wind whipped the air, the animals tethered near the roadway whinnied in terror. Rising on their hind legs, they kicked and tugged until the tether line snapped. With wild shrieks, the townsfolk rose to their feet and stampeded after their animals.

"The sky is falling! It's falling," they screamed.

Many ran with their hands over their heads, as if to deflect the gigantic shards of sky which they were convinced would crash down upon them. A death-like calm had stilled the wind.

The image of hope was broken. The prior could no longer hesitate. The abbot motioned with his hand, and now the burly little man lunged for Ibn Amram's collar. In the deepening shadows, his arm became entangled with that of the monk, and they scuffled fiercely, each thinking the other was Ibn Amram. As the darkness grew more profound, the burly monk began to look about him in terror. At last, he lost all interest in the Jewish stargazer and threw himself to his knees, clasping his hands together in moaning supplication. Halfheartedly, he grasped the sleeve of Ibn Amram's cloak.

"Will the light ever return?" he pleaded.

Ibn Amram stared down the distracted monk and pried his shaking fingers from his arm.

"Be still, my son," Ibn Amram soothed. "The light is almost returning. The Will of the Almighty stands only as a reproach, not as an ultimate punishment in these shadows."

His fingers eased the white-knuckled grip away from his sleeve. He was free at last to reach for the square of smoked Egyptian glass. There was not a second to lose.

The hood of his *burnous* fell back from his head as he raised the glass to his eye and beheld the majestic crown of the darkened sun and the eerie ring of fire surrounding it. But wait! Ibn Amram stared more intently, scarcely believing his good fortune to be present at such a mystery.

Even through the smoked glass, the corona of the sun was dazzling. Ibn Amram wiped away the tears with his sleeve and squinted again at the secret normally hidden by the full brilliance of the sun. At first, he was not sure, but it appeared that the aura of the sun was not uniform but shot out horns of splendor. He blinked away tears, almost overcome by the radiance of this heavenly crown. Seconds before, the aura had seemed like one continuous band, but now he saw the mystery of a hidden light. The crown was shot through with iridescent streamers, fanciful horns that shimmered in distant solar winds. The people had been so wrong. This was not a dying sun, but a dancing sun, dancing to an unheard music. Rising and falling, shooting and turning, the rays of the sun danced in constant praise of the Creator! Ibn Amram had seen what few men dared to see and shared in that secret.

With a tremor, he remembered the words of the *Gemara*. Though magnificent in its mysterious glory, the snuffing of Hashem's lantern must not be ignored. Blinking back more tears, he lifted his trembling voice.

"Remove the lantern," he breathed.

"Here now! The magician himself in our midst. Hear his devil's incantations!"

The light had begun to return, and in the green haze, the prior spotted Ibn Amram hurriedly returning the smoked glass to his pouch and rushing toward the nearest horse. Unlike the lithe Joseph who could hop onto a horse like a springing cat, Ibn Amram had only managed to get one foot into the stirrup when the prior dragged him down.

"You would imprison us in darkness as Moses did to the Egyptians, would you? I heard your incantation myself. You would keep us in a dark house for the rest of our lives."

Already the silhouettes of stately trees at the roadway loomed into view from the confusing obscurity of the previous moment. Far to the south one could still hear the sounds of animals stampeding in frenzy.

The abbot was sprawled in a chair. His personal confessor dabbed at his perspiring forehead with a cloth and uncorked a bottle of smelling salts.

"Oh, my heavens, the Devil himself," the abbot sighed, spying Ibn Amram pinned between the prior and a monk. He waved his hand for more air. The confessor accommodated him by fanning him with a towel.

"I am not the Devil, as well you know," Ibn Amram retorted. "I am a Jew of the Realm, no more and no less. Ignorance compounds ignorance in these troubled times, but you should not make a natural event transcend its natural boundaries with talk of the Devil!"

"Cease your babbling, Deceiver, or I will personally dampen the enthusiasm of your tongue," the prior warned. "The abbot will speak and you will listen."

Raising himself from the chair, the abbot stared long and hard at the rabbi, trembling at what he saw. A bout of coughing followed, more severe than any before.

"Guard him well, with the other," the prior commanded, and two young monks seized Ibn Amram by the elbows. "At the moment, the abbot requires the ministration of his bloodletting. When that is done and the abbot has rested, we will deal with these evil men."

They yanked Ibn Amram along roughly until they reached the wagons filled with provisions. The furthest, broken and slatternly, had evidently once held bales of hay and bags of flour. The monk shoved Ibn Amram onto a makeshift bench, linking a shackle tightly around one ankle. A Muslim, beaten and bruised, looked up from the shadows then let his head nod again on his chest.

"We will be back, Deceiver! Do not try any tricks." The monk let the canvas flap fall into place, plunging the dusty interior of the wagon into shadows.

"What reason did they have for imprisoning you, my friend?" Ibn Amram asked quietly.

"I have gazed at the stars and the moon in the outfields of my village," he answered. "The monks dreamed up horrible stories about my motives. They spread a rumor of withered grain and blasted harvests. They would not listen to reason."

"Why did the field attract you?"

"My studies show a power of the moon over the spring crops. As the moon controls our tides, so she exerts a subtle influence over the sprouting of the first grains of the land. With a better knowledge of the waxing moon, farmers could pick the best days for planting."

"A sensible study," Ibn Amram agreed. "It is a shame your work was interrupted by the monks. Have they made you suffer?"

"Their torture is severe," the Muslim responded, rocking in response either to his pain or the memory of the pain. "But they could not break my spirit."

"Those they cannot break, they kill," Ibn Amram said simply. "In the name of truth and religion, they murder the good, the gentle and the brave. It matters not to them."

"And you, rabbi," the Muslim continued, taking closer interest in his fellow prisoner. "Why have they taken you?"

"For much the same reason, my friend. I have studied the moon for years, but now my special interest is the sun and the convergence with the star *Machbereth*. Day after day in my sightings, I could see the mathematics bringing me closer to this fateful day when the sun's light was blotted from the sky."

"You anticipated the eclipse?" the Muslim said in great admiration. "You must have a remarkable astrolabe. With whom did you study the rule of the stars?"

"My father was my teacher," Ibn Amram said wistfully. "And in his advancing years, he was tutored by a mathematician of Saragossa, Ahmed Ibn Muhamad."

The Muslim jerked around in surprise. "It is a small world, rabbi. The stargazer of Saragossa was my uncle. He introduced us all to the discipline of his astrolabe, but most of my brothers were more adept than I. I have been content to limit my impoverished skills to the study of the moon."

"Your humility should not go unnoticed, my friend," Ibn Amram said. "But the monks will reward you in a way that neither of us will appreciate. Where have they gone? I hear nothing from their tents."

"Our keeper told me of their intention to hold a mass of thanksgiving. The abbot has taken them to the Cathedral of Burgos. But they will return for dinner and vespers. What will happen to us then?"

"I do not know," Ibn Amram answered. "We can only wait. I wish I had my leather purse, but someone in the scuffle pulled it from my belt. It contained a few herbs which could ease the swelling of your cuts and bruises. Never mind. When our keeper returns, I will demand the return of my belongings."

They fell into silence, gazing at the dull light that crept past the ragged fold of the canvas. Dusk was approaching.

In time, the sound of many feet and rhythmic chanting reached their ears. The flap was thrown open, but the monk in the dim light was not the meek young man who had left them but the harsh prior.

"We have found the evidence, Deceiver!" he chortled. "Your lies and deceptions will fall on deaf ears now that we hold the evidence in our very hands." He unclasped the shackles. "The two of you, climb out of the wagon and come with me!" He motioned derisively with his thumb.

"What is it that the fool has found?" the Muslim whispered.

Ibn Amram shrugged in confusion, following the form of the monk as best he could, in spite of the hoots and jeers the hot-headed monks showered upon them. On the grassy flatland where the open-air kitchen had been established, a large group of monks was already gathered. They hung their heads in fear and loathing as they saw the Muslim and the Jew approach.

"Look what we found in the saddle bags of your horse, Deceiver!" the prior gloated. "You thought you could play an old shell game on us, pretending your hands were empty while you hid your black magic in the saddle bags. But we are more clever than you. Look at it all!"

His fingers brushed open the pages of Ibn Amram's manuscript, revealing columns of mathematical notations.

"What is it, Jewish Deceiver?" the prior demanded. "Speak or you will be sorry."

"Good Master Monk," Ibn Amram chided. "It is nothing but mathematics. Of no more mystery than the columns of figures which traders record in their ledgers of account."

The prior twisted the manuscript this way and that, anticipating a hidden alphabet to spring forth from the finely traced numerals. He expressed his frustration with a hiss and shoved the book under the eyes of the Muslim.

"The Jew will talk in circles. What do you know of this mathematics?"

The Muslim blanched at the sight of the neat figures and stared in wild fascination at Ibn Amram.

"By the love of Allah, it is the lost manuscript of Al-Magriti! I have not seen this work in decades!"

"You see? You see?" the prior crowed with joy. "How much more damning can the evidence be, my brothers? Al-Magriti, the stargazer says. Al-Magriti, indeed! And who is this vile Al-Magriti?"

The Muslim bit his lips for his impetuous answer. "I know him as a wise mathematician. Nothing more."

"Hah! Another deceiver. Hold tight to both while I send word to His Eminence. The abbot will see with his own eyes the forbidden mathematics of this hateful Al-Magriti. I warrant there will be justice done before this day is over."

The prior and the monk locked arms and marched proudly to the tent of Peter the Venerable. The sides of the tent billowed lazily, like a great bird settling down to roost for the night.

No sooner had the prior entered the tent than he left in haste, rolling up his sleeves at the same time.

"The abbot is delirious!" he whispered. "The black magic of the stargazers has plunged him into a choleric rage."

A copper bowl and leeches were readied for the bloodletting. Ibn Amram strained to see above the shoulders of the monks who held him.

"Good Master Monk," he shouted. "Do not conduct yet another bloodletting. You surely have reached a balance of the humors with the first bloodletting today. You will gain nothing with another!"

The prior stopped in mid-stride, glancing back at the rabbi with a strange mixture of loathing and admiration.

"You dare tell me my job?" he asked. "What do you know of medical practice, stargazer?"

"I know enough that the middle way is the right way. Medicine always requires an equilibrium. Take too little blood from the sick man and the humors will be dominant. Take too much and your patient will be bilious and downcast."

"I myself would advise an herbal treatment to induce transpiration," the Muslim put in. "Our physicians no longer trust in bloodletting."

"Muslim doctors! Heretics!" the prior shot back angrily. "Lock him in the pillory. Let him suffer for his taunts!"

The prior glanced meaningfully at a collection of boxes ranged haphazardly beside the benches. He pointed to the longest one, and three monks went scurrying to open it and assemble its contents.

While the monks ate their meal, the Muslim stargazer stood painfully on the pillory, his arms stretched up to the fullest extent and bound in leather straps. Ibn Amram was chained in full view of the device and left to contemplate this piteous lesson.

"Do not faint, good man," Ibn Amram whispered. "When the arms are raised, the breathing is labored. Concentrate on each slow breath and ignore the taunts of these ruffians."

The meal was finished and vespers began, followed by a late-night vigil at the abbot's bedside. Still, the monks did not release the Muslim from the bondage of the pillory.

"Poor man," Ibn Amram commiserated. "Be strong and think of eternal wisdom, unsullied by these fools. Your studies are not in vain. What is learned is an accomplishment that can never be taken from you."

During the night, the Muslim's pain reached a numbing intensity, blotting out all other perceptions of the conscious world. He lolled awkwardly from the leather thongs which held his wrists. His hands had long lost all sensation.

A youthful monk took pity on him in the third vigil of the night, bringing a gourd of water to slake his terrible thirst.

"Hush," he warned. "Be quiet or they will find that I treated you well. That would mean a grim punishment for me. Be strong until dawn. I have it on good authority that they will cut you down in the light of the new day."

He cast a fearful glance at the uneven shapes of monks sleeping in their blankets under the benches. Without another word, he retreated to the shadows of his own corner.

CHAPTER SEVENTEEN

The Hidden Lights

BURGOS, CASTILE
SPRING, 1140

IBN AMRAM WAS AWAKENED BY A GNAWING SOUND WHICH seemed quite near him. It was not precisely like the sound of a rodent, yet it persisted with the same nibbling rhythm. Shaking himself awake, he saw a monk sawing at the lashings that bound the Muslim's wrists. The thong was severed by a final cut of the dull knife and the moongazer fell flat to the floor, unable to bear his own weight on his cramped legs.

"Oh, help me!" he groaned, his arms still thrust grotesquely above his head, although he lay in a heap.

"The abbot had a horrid visitation in the night," the monk said gruffly. "Not the Blessed One, but Satan tricked out in the clothes of a stargazer. His Eminence takes the vision as a warning and divine judgment. You will no longer pollute the minds of good Christians. Your end in the capital of Castile is decreed."

The prior hurried them off to the wagon. The monks' encampment was soon to be a memory. The mules were brought forth from the halter line, braying in anger as the wagons were readied. The great tent of the abbot no longer resembled a white bird. With the ropes loosened, the tent sagged like sour dough.

"Take this," the young monk whispered, appearing suddenly at the flap of the wagon. He pressed a piece of bread into Ibn Amram's hand. "May the Almighty have compassion on your soul," he said.

He crossed himself in anguish, then disappeared. Sounds of muleteers carried on the air, and the driver of the prisoners' wagon whistled his commands to his team. The monks were on the move.

Ibn Amram's companion sat huddled in a corner, his knees pressed against his chest while he rubbed his wrists.

"Do you think we are bound for a dungeon in Burgos?" Ibn Amram asked. His accustomed equanimity of spirit was returning, and he broke the crust of bread in two, offering half to the Muslim.

"Would it were so," the Muslim moaned. "If they imprison us, my family can call on all my brothers to amass the money needed to pay the fine. But I tell you, rabbi, this is not a good sign. At the snap of the abbot's fingers, he holds the powers of life and death. Remember, too, he just returned from Languedoc where Cathars were not merely imprisoned."

"What is our fate then?"

"I speak of extirpation. That is the favorite word of these monks to justify their killing. They want to root out what they think is evil."

Ibn Amram sat silent as the wagon jostled across the bridge of Burgos. There was no need for further words.

"Here, you! Get out of the wagon!" The brake squealed on the wagon wheel, and the driver immediately flicked open the flap to order them out. A gap-toothed monk beckoned them as one would motion to dogs.

Above them, a bright spring sun revealed no caprice of the recent eclipse. The sky was pristine blue. Behind them, the Cathedral of Burgos thrust its towers skyward in august solemnity. The square was largely vacant of passersby, except for the monks and a structure they were assembling.

"Put them on, both of you," the gap-toothed warden snarled. His hand held ill-shapen smocks of rudely woven wool. A flash of red caught Ibn Amram's eye as he started to unfold the smock to see just what was attached.

"Did I ask you to inspect it, vile Jew?" the monk screamed, striking Ibn Amram on the cheek. "Don the garment without question, as you know you will be judged for all eternity!"

Ibn Amram puzzled over the design in crimson. His eye surreptitiously travelled to the smock which the Muslim now wore. It likewise bore the same design.

"The tongue of the Devil!" the monk exclaimed. "Let the world know your sin and let Mother Church judge you accordingly."

Their shackles burdened their footsteps, prompting more harsh words and shoves from the warden. The smooth white paving stones of the plaza gleamed with startling purity. Halfway to the structure, their plodding footsteps were hastened by the drumbeat of assembled monks. Ranged along the stairs of the cathedral, the monks with festive tambours beat a rhythm that attracted a growing crowd. It signalled a diversion that Ibn Amram could guess with horror.

For an astronomer who reached up with longing to the sights of the sky, the steps which took him and his Muslim counterpart to the center of the plaza were a descent into vertigo. Ibn Amram felt as if he stood on the edge of the world and one false step would tip him over the brink. The azure sky which had always spread its light and warmth like a canopy for him was now a tangible enemy, pressing its steely-blue jaw down upon him with relentless force. He could not raise his eyes to the cloudless cover yet the fearful delusion became even stronger.

"Here, you! Stand straight when you approach His Eminence!"

The warder shook the Muslim like a rat and pushed him past the two benches where various officials of the Abbey of Cluny sat. Before them, sitting delicately on a straight-backed chair upholstered in crimson broadcloth sat the sole accusatory. Peter the Venerable raised a finger, motioning them to stop.

"I have pondered at length the appropriate time for this inquiry," the abbot began, pausing to ensure that a cough did not break his modulated voice. "I have weighed the advisability of a postponement for the purpose of assembling more copious confessions and denunciations. In the end, I chose haste. As I have said many times, an unweeded garden runs riot in the fertile spring."

The officials at the bench nodded in approval at this well-worn metaphor. The edge of a smile crossed the abbot's mouth.

"We must extirpate, we must root out these noxious herbs from the garden of Christendom," Peter the Venerable continued. "Not for us the sins of the laggard. With vigor and courage we have applied our hands to the task. First witness, step forward!"

All eyes in the crowd fastened upon a meek man, a member of the Cluniac Order who approached the abbot, throwing himself onto his knees in submission.

"Speak, Brother Jerome," the abbot commanded. "Reveal the dark secrets of this vile Jew at our encampment near Tarragona."

The monk crossed himself in fear. "I do not usually find myself charged with the responsibility of examining the possessions of strangers. I am a simple man, Brother Peter. I am more comfortable in raising our assembled voices in praise than in raising a cloak in discovery."

"And what did you discover, Brother Jerome?"

Shivering in fright at the memory, the monk blurted out

his words with compelling sincerity. "His instrument, Brother Peter! It was a bronze instrument of the heavens, designed by the Devil to negate the divine order of celestial harmony. He tried to wrest it from my fingers by turning his back on me. That was the moment I saw the bulge in his cloak. He tried to hide it, but I recognized the evil. It was the tail of the Devil!"

The murmurs of the expectant crowd subsided into a low sobbing fear. The monks armed with tambours began again their relentless drumming to exorcize the evil. The abbot waved the tambour players into silence and dismissed the agonized Jerome.

"Brother Bartholomeus, you are next."

The big-boned monk strode to the center of the plaza and bowed to his master. His finger was raised in confident denunciation.

"That is the Devil himself," he hissed. "We followed him into the ruins of the Roman amphitheater near Tarragona. There in the dark, we overheard his worst secret. He held colloquy with the snake. Yes, the devil snake incarnate! I shall never forget it!"

"Appalling!" the abbot agreed, staring down the astronomer with fastidious derision. "There is a third and final witness at this inquiry, but first, I will give you this opportunity to confess and abjure your sins of stargazing and black magic. What have you to say, Jew?"

Ibn Amram, haggard from the vigil of the night, stepped forward and raised himself his fullest height.

"I say you have overstepped your authority, Abbot Peter of Cluny," he said hoarsely. "Every citizen of Castile knows that a Jew of the Realm is exempt from canon law. We are subject to one authority in this temporal world and that is the Monarch of the Realm. In matters of treason, disorder or mercantile injustice, a Jew is subject to the will of King Alfonso. In all other matters, the Almighty alone is the Judge of our destiny."

The abbot coughed violently at the surprising intransigence of the rabbi. Both Bartholomeus and Jerome hastened to his side to support him. The crowd drew back in alarm at the mysterious powers the Jew seemed to hold over the abbot. The beat of the tambours resumed.

"Audacious black heart," Peter intoned. "Know this day that you stand judged . . . as soon as I regain my breath."

"Your Eminence," Ibn Amram said pointedly. "You promised a third witness. I have not heard his testimony."

"Nor shall you, vile Jew!" the abbot said, red in the face from the pounding Jerome had delivered between his shoulder blades. "Canon law stipulates that a witness may deliver his evidence in utmost secrecy to the accusatory. And so I have!"

"You are both the witness and the accusatory?" the Muslim broke in, finding his tongue at this astonishing revelation. "Lead them away! Let the tambour beat the time of their last heartbeats on this earth!" The abbot regained his composure and leaned back into the chair.

A jumble of horrid images beset Ibn Amram's eyes as they were marched towards the stakes. The kindling was prepared. A monk stood ready with the firebrand. But even now, Ibn Amram disdained to believe in this unthinkable end to his life. Just the previous day he had been buoyed on an irrepressible wave of joy. The eclipse had confirmed his deepest understandings of the Divine plan for the world. The brightness, he knew, had achieved greater clarity because of the darkness. He had felt more alive than ever before. Now a vain and wilful churchman would drag him down to the blackest reality. His life would be snuffed out by caprice. He saw, and yet could not comprehend, the scaffolding, the timbers and the stairs, well-worn by the footsteps of the condemned.

The monk to his right shoved him smartly. The youthful one to his left seemed different, extending his arm so that Ibn Amram might lean upon it ascending the stairs. He loosely lashed Ibn Amram's arms while the surly monk attended to the ropes at his ankles, drawing them cruelly tight.

"If you are possessed of the Devil, may this fire consign you to the sulphurous depths of choking brimstone!" the monk tying his wrists called loudly. In an undertone, he added, "If you are but a rabbi, may we seek forgiveness for our sin."

Ibn Amram nodded weakly, seeing the distraught look in the young man's eyes. Both monks stepped back to survey their handiwork. The abbot called out and the beating of the tambours recommenced.

Ibn Amram barely saw the tumult of people entering the square, seeking prime locations to watch the event. His mind's eye looked inward, shunning the spectacle in the square for a moment of inner calm. It was difficult to focus on a coherent image. Glimpses of *Koheleth* flashed before him: "Man knows not his time, like the fish caught in an evil net and like the birds caught in the snare. Like these are the sons of men ensnared at an evil time, when it falls upon them suddenly."

Images flickered before him, some blurred, others distinct. His mind flitted to Naomi and his son, to Yerucham Halevi, even to Yissaschar Rikuv and Joshua ben Judah.

It was the conclusion he sought. The conclusion which would bring him the inner peace of *Koheleth*: "The end of the matter . . ." He disciplined his jumbled brain to remember. "The end of the matter is, let us hear the whole. Fear the Lord and keep His commandments, for this is the whole duty of man. For every deed will the Lord bring into the judgment concerning everything that had been hidden, whether it be good or it be bad."

Ibn Amram felt strangely uplifted and strained to see another vision. Dim at first, then slowly gaining clarity, his inward sight perceived a page of the holy Torah. The letters seemed to rise off the page with inky gravity, displaying their contours against a suffused light. As he concentrated, the blurred edges came closer together, bunching into words which spread their edges into whole phrases. And then the crownlets! A deep satisfaction swayed his very being. Ibn Amram could see not just a crown of majesty on the letters, but a series of crownlets, soaring like the bejewelled diadem of the sun. Perfect in their symmetry, the words seemed to wave and balance in distant celestial winds. Unfathomed by those around him, he marvelled at the secret. The words of *Shema* were now clearly visible to his inner sight and waiting to be read.

He would savor this moment. If he must die *al Kiddush Hashem*, he would say the *Shema* in his best and purest voice. The very letters of the *Shema* would ascend heavenward with him. But he must prepare for the moment in purity and holiness.

The noise of the thronging multitude in the square faded from his ears. Ibn Amram did not hear the chants of the monks, nor the sermon of Peter. Nor did he notice the jangle of armor and the heavy tramp of King Alfonso's palace guards as they suddenly appeared in the plaza.

"Halt the execution!" the sergeant-at-arms commanded. "This proceeding has not been sanctioned by the authority of the King of Castile!"

"Do not impede the holy work of the Church to root out heresy and black magic from the realm," the Abbot of Cluny warned, rising suddenly from his chair.

"There will be no execution!" the sergeant declared, striking the butt of his battle ax upon the paving stones of the plaza for further authority. "The accused will come with me. It is the command of His Majesty, King Alfonso of Castile!"

A nervous tic caught the corner of the abbot's eye. "The execution has been postponed," he said, making the best of a difficult situation. "And I will personally accompany the accused to the royal court."

Ibn Amram's mind was reeling from the fast-paced turn of events. He and the swooning Muslim were rapidly untied and placed under the protection of King Alfonso's guards. The crowd parted in confusion as the phalanx of guards led the way across the plaza to the royal palace.

Yet another phrase from *Koheleth* passed through Ibn Amram's mind: "Cast your bread upon the face of the waters; for after many days you will find it again."

Alfonso looked up with barely concealed agitation as the door of the throne room opened. He nodded to the sergeant but raised a hand when the prior attempted to follow the procession into the room.

"Just the abbot and the Jew," the king declared. "The rest must leave."

The king waited until the door closed before he spoke.

"You are quick to incinerate whoever opposes you, Peter," he said bluntly. "Did you forget to consult me?"

Peter the Venerable stared down his cold gaze. "I overlook nothing in matters that concern the health of the Church. When a threat to the very heart of the Spanish Church is perceived, we must act with haste and courage."

"You will do nothing of the sort," King Alfonso retorted. "Do not think you can abridge my authority and do not dare mince words with me when your authority is enfeebled. I know your ways, Peter! While we talk, your prior hastens to the palace of Archishop Bernard. But times have changed and the influence of the bishop is not what it was."

"The Jew is an astromancer, as is the smarmy Muslim," Peter shot back. "They must both die!"

A fit of coughing stopped further words in the abbot's outburst. Standing alone beside the abbot, Ibn Amram paused a moment, then steadied his enemy with a hand to the elbow.

"Perhaps in Cluny your words would go unchecked," Don Garcia suggested, watching the gaze of the abbot fall on the king's astrolabe where it lay on the table. "If stargazing were indeed an abhorrent form of divination, then your anger would be valid."

"You dare rebuke my anger? Do you permit stargazing and its evils to propagate like weeds in our garden?" the abbot wheezed in surprise.

"I dare to follow true knowledge for the good of my realm," the king affirmed. "Facts and science, Peter, not superstition and rumor, shall reign in Burgos. Tell me, Peter, have you an explanation for the curious rumor I heard among the townsfolk that the Karaites must be brought back and the Jews expelled to expiate the darkness?"

A veiled look was drawn across the features of the abbot. His face was expressionless. "I know nothing of what you speak, King Alfonso."

The young king shrugged and raised his astrolabe thoughtfully.

"You may as well know that for a long time I struggled with my own calculations, never coming closer to the ultimate truths hidden within the stars. Now a Jew of the Realm has pierced the cloak of mystery, if only for a moment, and shared that precious knowledge with me. It was his wisdom and the quick action of his student in warning me of the onset of the eclipse that assured my realm of peace. His message put me in control of the dark afternoon. I was able to explain to my citizens that neither Karaites nor Jews played any part in this natural occurrence. There was no terror in Burgos, only wonderment and awe."

"You lie! It cannot be!" The abbot interrupted.

The king contained his anger with difficulty, then resumed his seat again.

"Yes, while you chased phantoms in the countryside, I assured my people of the sustained love of the Almighty. They understood that the darkness was not a punishment, only a natural event which would soon pass. They understand now that their king truly loves them and protects them from ignorance and superstition. They are prepared to work all the harder of the good of Castile. From darkness has come a hidden light. Not panic in the face of the unknown, but a renewed confidence that each day will dawn in peace."

"I am appalled to think you would believe this astromancer," Peter said in a fluster of words and coughing. "His

Holiness the Pope shall hear of this."

"Let him hear. And let him weigh my Christian piety. You're right that there has been far too much heresy of late, but our own true faith is beset by dangerous enemies from within. I ask you on your long trip to the Holy See to consider the justice of your actions. Do you think you must strengthen Christianity at the expense of the Jews? What would the Karaites do if they discovered they were used as a foolish cat's paw in a court intrigue? Can you tell me that?"

The king stared intently at the embarrassed expression on Peter's face, then dismissed him with a wave of the hand.

"Carry the message to the Holy See that King Alfonso of Castile will yet begin the charting of the heavens. The greatest astronomers of the Mediterranean will soon be assembled in Burgos under the able hand of the Astronomer of the Realm. Carry that message, Peter!"

The guard opened the door for the abbot who dragged his heels with despondent dignity.

"I thank Heaven that Joseph reached you in time," Ibn Amram sighed once the door had closed. "Many were the moments when I despaired of his reaching you in time. As for your plans, they are ambitious and most worthy of a noble ruler."

"They will not be complete without your involvement," King Alfonso said. "Great powers of insight and organization are needed to make sense of the myriad calculations that will comprise the tables. That is why the Astronomer of the Realm must be appointed to oversee the enterprise. That is why I must appoint you to that position."

Ibn Amram sucked in his breath, still shocked at the news which he had suspected would follow the plans for the tables.

"Your Grace," he said simply. "I am deeply honored by your confidence in my abilities. It is a project that will require many decades to complete and I am sadly lacking in time. My life is like the ebb tide that pounds the shore with muted vigor. With each approach, the retreat is more and more pronounced. Those who know me well realize I have taken a vow of poverty and feel compelled to wander, always seeking a distant goal. I must soon leave to distant lands."

"You would dare reject my offer at a time when I saved you from the flames?" the king asked wryly. "Why did I bother, then? For every favor, there should be a payment in kind. Do you not owe me your service as Astronomer of the Realm?"

"I owe you my life," Ibn Amram agreed. "If I were a great astronomer of the Muslim world, I would jump at the chance to join in your ambitious plans. In truth, the Muslim who was to burn with me has been taught by an expert in the art. Perhaps he and his family could serve as the core of your royal astronomers. But I am a simple rabbi, schooled in the values of my faith and only desirous of fulfilling those duties which the Compassionate One has given me powers to pursue. What need do I have for more?"

King Alfonso sighed and reached forward to pick up his astrolabe. There was a gentleness in the motions of his fingers which told clearly of his love for the magnificent instrument. His index finger ran lightly along the gold engravings of the outer ring. He twisted it until the light from the window danced on the carved numerals.

"For such an astrolabe, the caliph of an eastern dynasty would pay a pretty ransom. But it is not for sale! Yet I feel in my heart a longing to share its rare beauty with someone who truly appreciates our science. Take it, Rabban Ibn Amram. My astrolabe is yours!"

His hand reached out with the precious gift. His eyes were bright with mixed emotions. Ibn Amram stumbled in his thoughts. He knew he could not accept such a remarkable gift, crafted for a monarch, not a rabbi; it expressed in finest metalwork the nobility of a king. No, he could not accept it, yet he could not chance to hurt the feelings of the young ruler.

Standing before him was the king of a powerful domain, holding daily matters of life and death in his hands. He stole a furtive glance at Don Garcia, wondering how the master tutor of the realm would handle such a delicate problem. Don Garcia gazed back impassively, revealing little of his own thoughts, save for an index finger poised at the tip of his greying hair. A hidden sign!

Ibn Amram took heart with that time-honored skill that he had exercised for years in teaching the sons and grandsons of great scholars. He realized that Alfonso, though more advanced in years, was much like his other students. He felt his mouth crease into an easy smile.

"You honor me, Your Grace, with such a gift," he said, accepting the astrolabe in his hand with quiet awe. "I recognize the value of this instrument as few can measure its worth. I could travel far and learn much from its sighting planes. But I am old and growing older with each day. Even now my hand quivers to excess in the morning. There is potential in this astrolabe which would be lost in my hands. But in yours . . ." He strode forward as a teacher approaching a favorite student and reached for Alfonso's hand. "In your strong right hand, this worthy astrolabe will record its future for generations to come!"

"You will not take it?" Alfonso asked, wavering between astonishment and pride at Ibn Amram's encouragement of his skills.

"I will not take the astrolabe for you will accomplish more with it than I," he answered. "Now there are two great achievements of your reign already. You have begun to teach your subjects the value of science and reason. Such enlightened rule can only enhance your future. What is more, with your new understanding of the way of the desert, you will be able to deal constructively with the Caliph Al-Kumi as befits a knowledgeable monarch. Do not weaken when that time comes! You now understand him as does no man in Iberia. You will use that wisdom to great advantage. With peace at last procured, the hidden workings of the stars will reveal a sense of the Divine plan. You see, I am more a rabbi than an astronomer."

"You should be exactly what the Almighty has ordained. No more and no less. If that does not include the title of Astronomer of the Realm, then so be it. My heart is heavy at the thought of losing you, but perhaps it will be as well. You mentioned distant lands. Where will you go?"

"If it please Your Grace, I wish to travel north to the County of Champagne. I have scholarly friends there with whom I can exercise my mind on matters of the holy Torah. And I would travel with my student, if that favor can be granted."

The king twirled the astrolabe absent-mindedly, catching and releasing the latch. He looked up and caught the gaze of his guard.

"Summon the young Jew who brought me word of the darkness," he commanded. "He and the sage shall journey to Champagne under my royal protection. See to it that they are well provided for a journey of many days. May all your days be happy ones, rabbi. And even when you walk in the shadow of the sun, may you always find the hidden light."